I0831378

The Loyal Nine

Book One
The Boston Brahmin Series

A novel by

Bobby Akart

Copyright Information

Other Works by Amazon Top 50 Author, Bobby Akart

The Doomsday Series

Apocalypse

Haven

Anarchy

Minutemen

Civil War

The Yellowstone Series

Hellfire

Inferno

Fallout

Survival

The Lone Star Series

Axis of Evil

Beyond Borders

Lines in the Sand

Texas Strong

Fifth Column

Suicide Six

The Pandemic Series

Beginnings

The Innocents

Level 6

Quietus

The Blackout Series

36 Hours

Zero Hour

Turning Point

Shiloh Ranch

Hornet's Nest

Devil's Homecoming

The Boston Brahmin Series

The Loyal Nine

Cyber Attack

Martial Law

False Flag

The Mechanics

Choose Freedom

Patriot's Farewell

Seeds of Liberty (Companion Guide)

The Prepping for Tomorrow Series

Cyber Warfare

EMP: Electromagnetic Pulse

Economic Collapse

Dedications

To the love of my life, you saved me from madness and continue to do so daily. Thank you for loving me.

To the Princesses of the Palace, my little marauders in training, you have no idea how much happiness you bring to your mommy and me. Seeing your wiggly butts at the end of a long day behind the keyboard makes it all worthwhile.

To my friends and readers, please heed the warning of this series. A cyber attack can strike in an instant. No bombs, no bullets, no swordfights. Just a few keystrokes on a computer, and we're done. I write this book to entertain you, but also to get you ready for the coming cyber war.

To the Founding Fathers, whose vision and bravery built America. My apologies for what we've become.

Acknowledgements

Writing a book that is both informative and entertaining requires a tremendous team effort. Writing is the easy part. For their efforts in making The Boston Brahmin series a reality, I would like to thank Hristo Argirov Kovatliev for his incredible cover art, Pauline Nolet for her editorial prowess, Stef Mcdaid for making this manuscript decipherable on so many formats, Joseph Morton for bringing my words to life in audio format, and the Team—whose advice, friendship and attention to detail is priceless.

Thank you!

Choose Freedom!

ABOUT THE AUTHOR

Bobby Akart

Author Bobby Akart has been ranked by Amazon as #55 in its Top 100 list of most popular, bestselling authors. He has achieved recognition as the #1 bestselling Horror Author, #2 bestselling Science Fiction Author, #3 bestselling Religion & Spirituality Author, #6 bestselling Action & Adventure Author, and #7 bestselling Historical Author.

He has written over twenty-six international bestsellers, in nearly fifty fiction and nonfiction genres, including the chart-busting Yellowstone series, the reader-favorite Lone Star series, the critically acclaimed Boston Brahmin series, the bestselling Blackout series, the frighteningly realistic Pandemic series, his highly cited nonfiction Prepping for Tomorrow series, and his latest project—the Doomsday series, seen by many as the horrifying future of our nation if we can't find a way to come together.

His novel *Yellowstone: Fallout* reached the Top 50 on the Amazon bestsellers list and earned him two Kindle All-Star awards for most pages read in a month and most pages read as an author. The Yellowstone series vaulted him to the #1 best selling horror author on Amazon, and the #2 best selling science fiction author.

Bobby has provided his readers a diverse range of topics that are both informative and entertaining. His attention to detail and impeccable research have allowed him to capture the imaginations of his readers through his fictional works and bring them valuable knowledge through his nonfiction books.

SIGN UP for Bobby Akart's mailing list to receive special offers, bonus content, and you'll be the first to receive news about new releases in the Doomsday series:

eepurl.com/bYqq3L

VISIT Amazon.com/BobbyAkart, a dedicated feature page created by Amazon for his work, to view more information on his thriller fiction novels and post-apocalyptic book series, as well as his nonfiction Prepping for Tomorrow series.

Visit Bobby Akart's website for informative blog entries on preparedness, writing, and a behind-the-scenes look into his novels.

BobbyAkart.com

And this is good old Boston,
The home of the bean and the cod,
Where the Lowells talk only to Cabots,
And the Cabots talk only to God.

Author's Introduction to the Boston Brahmin Series

Works of fiction are often based upon a historical premise, and the Boston Brahmin series is no exception. The Loyal Nine takes its name from nine patriotic Bostonians who took a stand against the tyrannical rule of Great Britain. As the British exerted more control over the colonists, especially in the form of taxes — anger and resentment rose to a crescendo, resulting in the War for Independence. You can read about the history of the original Loyal Nine at the end of the story.

Similar to the events leading up to the Revolutionary War, a string of disastrous social, economic and institutional crises will conspire in *The Boston Brahmin* series to land the newly minted Loyal Nine at the same critical decision point reached in 1765 by their ancestors—choose tyranny or freedom. Of course, nothing is exactly what it seems in the Boston Brahmin series, which will make the Loyal Nine's choice even more important for the survival of an independent United States.

Writing a series of this magnitude takes a considerable amount of planning and research. It also asks the reader to become vested in the journey of the characters. Read with us. Learn with us. Get involved in the backstory and details of the novels by visiting our frequently updated, fan dedicated website TheBostonBrahmin.com . We encourage you to interact with us on social media. We truly enjoy conversing with our fans — all of whom we consider friends.

I hope you enjoy this epic, history-rich thriller series. Torn from the headlines, The Boston Brahmin Series presents a nation plunged into chaos by enemies "foreign and domestic". Only The Loyal Nine, a patriotic group of descendants of our Founding Fathers can stop the collapse and restore the American republic.

Join The Loyal Nine in their quest to save our country from collapse. Thanks for reading!

Epigraph

We hold these truths to be self-evident, that all men are created equal, that they are endowed by their Creator with certain unalienable Rights, that among these are Life, Liberty and the pursuit of Happiness.

~ Declaration of Independence, July 4, 1776

*****

The secret of freedom lies in educating people, whereas the secret of tyranny is in keeping them ignorant.

~ Maximilien Robespierre, French Politician (1758 – 1794)

*****

Those who cannot remember the past are condemned to repeat it.

~ George Santayana, philosopher and novelist

*****

America will never be destroyed from the outside. If we falter and lose our freedoms, it will be because we destroyed ourselves.

~ Abraham Lincoln

*****

The following five attributes marked Rome at its end: first, a mounting love of show and luxury; second, a widening gap between the very rich and the very poor; third, an obsession with sex; fourth, freakishness in the arts, masquerading as originality, and enthusiasms pretending to be creativity; fifth, an increased desire to live off the state.

~ Edward Gibbon (1737-1794) in his Decline and Fall of the Roman Empire

*****

The real rulers, you'll never see.

~ Anonymous

The Loyal Nine

Book One

The Boston Brahmin Series

PROLOGUE

Thanksgiving
Hanover Square
Boston, Massachusetts

One by one, nine men entered through the front door of one of Boston's many taverns. The blowing snow on this early winter blast followed behind them but quickly melted under the heat of the large fire warming the patrons.

Benjamin Edes, the first to arrive, sat quietly in the corner, nursed his drink, and imperceptibly nodded to them as they entered. Each man was powerful in his own way. He had his own invaluable contribution to the cause they passionately shared. For Edes, his role was that he wielded the power of the press and with it, the ability to shape public opinion. With his words, he was able to whip the people into a frenzy and draw the ire of the government he so vehemently opposed.

After the last of them entered, crossing quietly through the tavern, and disappearing through a nondescript wooden door toward the rear of the building, Edes finished his libation and lifted his hefty frame off the oak chair to join them. He caught the attention of the barkeep who knew his role—*warn them if their meeting was discovered.*

Then, he motioned to the evening's special guest who sat quietly on the other end of the tavern. The man joined Edes and followed him into a room filled with tobacco smoke, muffled voices, and the occasional sound of laughter—although this was far from a social occasion.

The group's meetings had been shrouded in secrecy for if their location was known, they would be arrested, or killed. Their professions were diverse. Two were in the liquor business while two more were in manufacturing. One was a ship's captain and another was a jeweler. They were ordinary men pursuing an extraordinary cause.

Edes and Henry Bass, a cousin of a future President, had collaborated on various insurgent activities in protest of the government's overbearing tariffs and laws. Over time, they'd grown to respect one another even though they had political differences of their own.

During the prior six months, they'd conferred with likeminded neighbors and business associates. The group became close knit and found they shared a common love of country and freedom. At this meeting, agreements impacting the future of a nation would be reached and a revolution would be born.

"Welcome my friends," announced Edes as he entered the candlelit room. "Thank you for braving this early taste of winter."

Edes was greeted heartily and offered a pouch of tobacco for his pipe. He politely declined and took his seat at the head of the long, carved wood table. His guest, a young attorney of thirty years old, sat to his right. The man was Harvard educated and known for his taking up legal cases against the government. He had written several opinion pieces for Edes' newspaper and was considered an *up-and-comer* within the group's movement.

"Of course, Ben," said John Avery, the group's secretary. He kept notes of their meetings and established the agenda for future activities of the group. "My wife was not particularly fond of a Thanksgiving meeting, but she understood the need."

Several members of the group nodded their agreement and toasted their mugs of ale. The goals of the nine men were lofty and could not be achieved without the support, as well as discretion, of their families.

"Good," started Edes. "Until now, we've operated as a group of nine. Tonight, that is about to change. I think all of you are acquainted with our guest this evening—John Adams."

"Welcome, John!"

"Cheers, my friend."

"Thank you for coming, Humphrey Ploughjogger!"

John Adams led the chorus of laughter as the men raised their mugs and toasted their guest. As Adams had become more notorious in his opposition to the tyrannical government's activity, he was increasingly harassed by those in power. He reprised his pen name, Humphrey Ploughjogger, to write four scathing articles about the government's heavy handed approach in dealing with taxation and control of its citizens.

"Well, thank you for the hearty welcome and it's my honor to join the nine of you this evening," said Adams. "I applaud all of you for your efforts in leading the opposition to tyranny. Like Ben Edes, I am a man of words—both written and spoken. Until now, they have served me well. But times have changed."

"How so, John?" asked George Trott, a jeweler.

Adams took a deep breath and responded. "George, there comes a time in history when words aren't enough. In order to effectuate change, our numbers must grow. Real change, whether in the form of a revolution or a declaration of independence, must necessarily require more active participants than the loyal nine men in this room. It requires groups like this one, but one-hundred fold, from the Province of New Hampshire to Savannah in the south."

"What do you propose, John?"

"We must take our cause to the people and recruit likeminded individuals to assist us. Sacrifices must be made and risks will be taken, but they are necessary to make us truly free, independent men."

Edes stood and walked to a table which held a plate of cigars. He chewed off the end and spit it on the floor. With the rolled tobacco extending out of his mouth, he leaned into a candle and lit it, allowing the smoke to billow to the ceiling before he rejoined his brethren.

"John, I sense you have more on your mind than recruiting men to start a revolution, am I right?"

"Yes, Ben. As freedom-loving patriots, we have big dreams of a country free of tyranny. I look at your faces and I know what's in your hearts. It's the same as the people who live throughout Boston and across this great land. But, fighting for freedom is only the first part of the battle."

"What are you saying, John?"

"Liberty once lost, is lost forever. It is incumbent upon us, and our ancestors, to maintain the freedoms we earn out of our actions, which will necessarily require losses of life and property to obtain."

"We are all committed servants," said Edes. Several of the attendees toasted mugs and said *hear, hear.*

"Then, you must commit to an eternity of service, binding your families now, and your ancestors forever to the cause of opposing tyranny and maintaining the freedoms we desire. And gentlemen, you must pledge to take whatever actions necessary to live up to this commitment."

The group began to speak amongst themselves and their words grew louder within the room to the point where Edes had to bring them to order.

"Gentlemen, please," he said as they began to quieten down. Edes turned his attention back to Adams, the future second President of the United States. "John, please continue."

"Ben, tonight, we must submit our lives to politics and war, so that our families and all Americans will have the liberty to teach their children mathematics, philosophy, the arts, and the religion of their choosing. They should be able to speak their mind without fear of retribution. They should be able to read the opinions of others in the press without a tyrannical government stopping them.

"More importantly, we must maintain the virtue and spirit of our soon to be fledgling nation. Without the American spirit, the republic will be lost although it may still exist in its form."

Again, the nine men began to voice their opinions to one another. Avery, always intent on keeping notes for the group's meetings, tapped his mug on the table to bring the group to order. He turned his attention to Adams.

"John, you have stated that we should form a government of laws, and not of men. We all agree with you. What is the guiding principle that you are asking us to follow, so that we may impart the same upon our ancestors for generations?"

John Adams rose from his seat, tugged on the lapels of his coat, and looked at each of the nine men, one at a time. "It is quite simple. When faced with the choice between compromising our principles or choosing freedom—we should always choose freedom."

The year was 1765. The seeds of liberty were sown by The Loyal Nine, and a man who'd become known as one of the greatest orators for the cause of freedom the world had ever known.

PART ONE

Two hundred and fifty years later…

CHAPTER 1

December 15, 2015
Shirokino, Ukraine

No warning preceded the artillery barrage. A sharp detonation shook the BTR-7 Defender, knocking the American halfway off the troop compartment bench, as fragments thunked against the armored personnel carrier's thin protective plate. Personal equipment and gear attached to the inside of the starboard-side hull popped loose, tumbling into the tight aisle.

He traded knowing looks with the Ukrainian Special Operations team assigned to escort him. There was nothing they could do to improve the situation. Combat was defined by probability and statistics, and they all knew what to expect next. The second round in the barrage would either land closer or farther from the vehicle, deciding their fate—and there was no way to hide from it.

The next explosion straddled the road, violently rocking the vehicle on its eight-wheel chassis. Fragments punctured the port-side hull, hissing and ricocheting through the armored coffin. The soldier seated to his right snapped backward against the vehicle's hard interior and slid motionlessly off the bench. Screams of pain pierced the compartment, quickly muted by successive high-explosive blasts. He tucked his knees into the metal bench, making room for the team's medic, who sprang into action from the back of the vehicle.

"This one is gone," the American said in broken Russian, lifting the dead soldier's black watch cap.

A jagged, charred hole appeared above his left eyebrow, evidence that a small red-hot fragment had passed through the wool hat and penetrated his skull. The Special Operations medic directed a flashlight beam at the grisly sight and nodded, pushing through the cramped compartment to reach the source of the screaming near the vehicle's turret. By the sound of the soldier's cries, the wound had to be severe. Special Operations soldiers had a predilection for suffering in silence, and this one was kicking and screaming.

The barrage lifted as quickly as it arrived, leaving them alone for the rest of the short ride to the Shirokino front. A few minutes later, after they had calmed the wounded soldier, the vehicle commander's voice echoed through the vehicle, spurring the soldiers into action. A pair of soldiers lifted the hatches above the troop compartment, squeezing their equipment-laden torsos through the openings. Shirokino was a fluid battlefront against pro-Russian separatist forces, and the vehicle commander wanted three hundred and sixty degree situational awareness as they approached their destination. Freezing rain sprayed through the hatches, driven by a brutal wind that had accompanied a rare Crimean weather front.

The vehicle slowed, and his escort team slid toward the starboard-side exit hatch. When the vehicle stopped, the soldiers opened the two-piece door, disappearing through the hull. The mercenary followed them into the driving rain, sprinting toward a series of drab, pockmarked Soviet-era buildings surrounded by barren trees. He stole a glance at the BTR-7 behind them, seeing two shredded tires. He'd always thought four tires on each side was overkill, but maybe the Soviets had been onto something with their original BTR design.

He kept pace with the commandos, stopping at a low-profile, earthen bunker just inside the tree line. Two serious-looking, heavily armed men wearing dark green camouflage uniforms and ballistic helmets greeted them at the sunken, heavy-wooden-beam-framed entrance to a reinforced defensive checkpoint. Splintered tree trunks and mangled branches gave him reason to believe the area was frequently targeted by separatist artillery. The cold rain was bad enough.

The gruff-looking soldiers fired a string of questions at the Ukrainian commandos, who rapidly answered and stepped aside. All he understood from the exchange was the word *Amerykans'kyy.* The

Ukrainian and Russian languages didn't share enough in common to assure mutual intelligibility.

One of the soldiers asked another round of questions, clearly frustrating the Ukrainian commandos. The second soldier stared at him intensely, almost pathologically, as the rain streamed down his helmet.

"Is there a problem?" he said in Russian, hoping to break this little stalemate.

"Big problem. Our commander doesn't want to meet with you today," said the psychotic-looking soldier.

"That's not what I was told an hour ago," he replied. "Good men have died bringing me here."

The man scoffed at the statement, causing a visible scowl from one of the Ukrainian commandos.

"You got a problem?" asked the soldier, nodding at the commando.

The Ukrainian Special Operations officer shook his head and muttered in Russian, loud enough for them to hear, "Militia scum." Instead of the lethal knife fight or point-blank gun battle he expected, the unstable-looking soldier took a step back and laughed.

"Well, this militia scum has liberated more territory in a month than the Ukrainian military has recaptured in a year," he said, motioning for him to step forward. "We'll return this guy after the meeting. Go on—before the separatists drop more shells on your head."

He nodded at the commando leader, who had been assigned to deliver him, unarmed and unharmed, to the Azov Battalion's forward headquarters in Shirokino. Andriy Biletsky, the ultranationalist founder and leader of the Azov Battalion, promised to meet with him during an inspection of the battalion's front-line positions. He would have much preferred to catch up with Biletsky in a quiet bar or swank restaurant in Kyiv, but the enigmatic leader had proven elusive and especially distrustful of foreign interests. His benefactors' research indicated that Biletsky's battalion was bankrolled exclusively by Ukrainian oligarchs, a sign of his ultranationalist loyalty.

His mission was to change that. The former Navy SEAL officer turned mercenary had been sent to make an offer his benefactors hoped Biletsky wouldn't refuse. It wouldn't be an easy sell. Azov Battalion had fought hard to recapture Mariupol from the pro-Russian rebels, pushing the separatists to the outskirts of Shirokino, where the battle had stalemated for months. His benefactors' offer of guaranteed, continued arms shipments and financial support came with a high price tag. A price tag he was afraid to mention.

"Follow me," said the soldier, motioning toward the building directly ahead of them. "He has a bunker beneath the building. You speak Russian, huh? *Amerykans'kyy* still study Russian?"

"Some enemies never change," said Nomad.

The man laughed, slapping him on the shoulder before heading toward the abandoned apartment block. As the two men drew closer to the structure, he could tell that the buildings had been subjected to sustained bombardment. The sturdy, four-story concrete testaments to Soviet construction stood unfazed despite extensive superficial damage to an otherwise featureless façade. Sturdy construction was about all these buildings had going for them, and in the end, it was all they needed. He seriously doubted any similarly sized building designed in the United States could have withstood this kind of high-explosive facelift.

He detected a sniper on the third floor, four windows from the corner; the faintest glare from the shooter's scope contrasted with the darkness of the room beyond the missing window pane. He guessed the sniper was relatively inexperienced, possibly assuming that the rain and overcast skies would be enough to conceal him. Maybe to the untrained eye, but certainly not his. He'd started scanning for possible sniper hides as soon as his feet hit the frozen mud next to the armored vehicle.

"Inside that door," said the soldier, pointing to the blasted frame of a double-sized doorway in the middle of the ground floor. "Another group will escort you to the colonel. They're watching us."

He nodded and jogged toward the opening, detecting movement inside the darkened entryway. He hated gigs like this. Multiple handoffs, different personalities—the perpetual feeling that you're one twitchy finger away from being shot in the face. Staring into the shadowy entrance, he had no doubt that more than one set of stone-cold killer eyes had already lined him up through the iron sights of an AK-74.

"Hello?" he yelled, cautiously approaching the abyss.

The distinctive whistle of a passing artillery shell replaced the silence, spurring one of the hidden militiamen to lurch out of the darkness and grab him by the jacket.

"Get inside, you idiot," the man grumbled, tossing him through the opening as he yelled, "Incoming!"

He stumbled over broken glass, striking a cinderblock wall several feet into the building. A pair of hands seized his shoulders from behind, steering him through a maze of dark hallways to a set of stairs lit by a hanging kerosene lantern. A soldier appeared inside the door leading into the hidden bunker, partially illuminated by the soft glow of the lantern.

"*Amerykans'kyy*," said his unseen escort.

"*Spasybi*, Vika, I'll take him from here," said the soldier, instantly switching to classroom-taught English. "You're late. He's been waiting."

"We had to take a detour outside of Mariupol. The roads don't appear to be secure in this sector," said Nomad, sensing that he was finally talking to someone in charge.

"No kidding. We're anticipating a Russian-backed assault on Mariupol any day now. Russian Spetsnaz are roaming the countryside, creating havoc. The front line here is more or less a sham at this point. Whatever you have to say to the colonel better be quick. We're pulling the battalion back within the hour. Anton Teresenko, Colonel Biletsky's deputy subcommander," said the soldier, extending a hand.

"Nomad. I'll keep my proposal short and to the point," he said, accepting the man's solid grip.

"Good. He doesn't like foreigners, just in case you hadn't heard," said Teresenko.

"I don't blame him. They tend to get in the way of a nation's affairs," said Nomad.

"Follow me, and don't speak unless spoken to. The colonel's not in a good mood," he said, rapidly descending the stairs.

The corridor extending beyond the bottom of the stairwell was lit by randomly hung kerosene lamps, leaving shadowy gaps in the long, sterile hallway.

"Fallout shelter?" asked Nomad.

Teresenko chuckled as he responded. "Actually, it's a relic from the Cold War. The central building in every housing block was equipped with one of these. Local Communist Party officials received preferential placement in these coveted buildings. Even the adjacent buildings were considered upgrades. Can you imagine? The Soviets were geniuses in that respect."

A soldier in full-body-armor kit stepped out of a doorway several feet away, his rifle held in the low-ready position. He snapped to attention at the sight of Teresenko.

"At ease," said the deputy commander, releasing the soldier to his hiding spot.

"The colonel is fanatical about security. He's been attacked more times than any of us care to count," said Teresenko.

"I was a bit surprised to be X-rayed in Mariupol. Seemed a bit excessive," said Nomad.

"I would have thought the same thing four weeks ago, but Russian SVR agents in Donetsk forced a plastic surgeon to swap Semtex for silicon in an unsuspecting stripper's breast implants. The surgeon tipped off local authorities after somehow ducking SVR surveillance. The scumbags blew her up in her apartment, with the police right outside the door. We're not taking any chances," he said, pointing to the next doorway on the left. "That's our door."

He led Nomad inside a well-lit room occupied by several men in camouflage uniforms. He immediately recognized Biletsky standing in front of a large, wall-mounted map. Standing average height, he wore a black ball cap pulled tightly over his head. A scruffy, half-grown beard extended from the sides of his cap, ending in a goatee.

He looked more like a millennial in a camouflage jacket than the leader of the Ukraine's fiercest, pro-nationalist militia group. The man's icy blue eyes portrayed a different story. As Teresenko suggested, he waited to be addressed.

"This better be good. I have more important things to do than play CIA games," said Biletsky, turning his attention back to the map.

"I'm not with the CIA," said Nomad.

"Everyone is working for the CIA, or the SVR, in one capacity or another," said Biletsky.

"I assume you received the money?" asked Nomad.

"You wouldn't be standing here if I hadn't. You can thank the CIA for their kind donation to our cause," said Biletsky.

Kind donation? Two million dollars in an untraceable account was considered "kind" by Biletsky. This might be harder than he originally thought. What if his benefactors had been wrong in their assessment? The oligarchs had made generous donations to the Azov Battalion, but two million was supposed to be in line with current levels of private-sector support. If money didn't get Biletsky's attention, he'd have to change tactics.

"Can you hold Mariupol?" Nomad asked, deciding to take a more direct approach.

"Excuse me?" asked Biletsky, turning to face him.

"It's no secret that the Russians have stepped up activity around Mariupol. Can you hold the city?" he asked.

"I liberated that city from the separatists. I have no intention of losing it again," said Biletsky. "Is that all you have?"

"No. I have a dozen T-80 main battle tanks to donate to the Azov Battalion," said Nomad.

Biletsky cocked his head and walked around the map-strewn table, approaching him with a cold stare.

"Tanks?" he said.

"And a comprehensive training package, along with the necessary support vehicles to keep them running," said Nomad.

"I'm listening," said Biletsky, stopping a few feet in front of him.

"You're not going to like what I say next," said Nomad.

"No?"

"No. In order to get the tanks, you have to abandon Mariupol—"

Biletsky's eyes bored through him; the man's previously uncommitted gaze suddenly turned murderous.

"Temporarily," added Nomad. "And there's far more to this deal than tanks."

"Like what?" asked Azov Battalion's commander.

"The opportunity to destroy a Russian motorized infantry battalion, en masse, on Ukrainian soil, in front of the world," said Nomad.

"Now I'm really listening," said Biletsky.

CHAPTER 2

December 15, 2015
Harvard Kennedy School of Government
Cambridge, Massachusetts

His students shuffled into their seats and unpacked the tools of their trade—computer tablets, voice recorders, various and sundry electronic gadgets—all designed to let them pay attention to their professor without fear of distraction or falling behind on the lecture.

"So we find ourselves at the end. Last class of the semester," said the professor to a chorus of uplifting murmurs. "And finals will be on Tuesday." His patented kill shot transformed the positive mood as students throated their distaste for the reminder.

"Oh, I see how it is. Happy to see the last of me, but the thought of finals is the end of the world as we know it."

Laughter filled the classroom as the moods lifted. Professor Henry Winthrop Sargent IV, affectionately known as Sarge, once again wondered if the students' collective response meant they truly enjoyed his lectures—or the pleasure of his academic company paled in comparison to the terror of his final exam. He'd probably never know for sure, he thought, as the title of his final lecture appeared on the screen.

CYBER WARFARE
IS IT AN ACT OF WAR?

The words had a sobering effect on the muffled conversations in the room. While they absorbed the question of the day, Sarge looked at the faces and placards containing their names. Some of these people would be rich and powerful someday. The Harvard Kennedy School—John F. Kennedy School of Government—deserved the respect that its prestigious name implied. The school's history dated back to the late 1930s, but its rise to prominence came in 1966 when it was renamed for the late president John F. Kennedy.

The school's alumni list was a who's who collection of government leaders, journalism headliners and business aristocracy. Names like Ban Ki-moon, United Nations Secretary General; Paul Volcker, former chairman of the Federal Reserve; and outspoken talk show host Bill O'Reilly of Fox News fame. Even the president of Harvard, Lawrence Summers, a former professor at the Kennedy School, had been an economic advisor to the World Bank and United States presidents.

When Sarge was offered an academic position at the school, he had big shoes to fill—not exactly a problem for a direct descendant of Daniel Sargent, a wealthy merchant during the time of the Revolutionary War and a notable member of the memorable Sons of Liberty. This historical and financial lineage provided Sarge the necessary status to be considered for Harvard, where he received a bachelor of arts, combined with master's and doctorate degrees in public policy and government. It also didn't hurt that Sarge had important *friends*, most of whom he had never met. From an early age, Sarge understood that he had been groomed for his position as professor, on top of "other duties."

"The world has come a long way since the Minutemen fired the first shots at the Battles of Lexington and Concord in 1775. Today, cyber warfare is used by the military to attack less traditional battlefield prizes—command and control technology, critical national infrastructure systems and air defense networks, each of which require computer automation to operate."

"Prior to the Russian invasion of Ukraine," said Sarge with a facetious cough, eliciting some quiet laughter from the class. "I mean the *separatist uprising*, Russia followed a template that worked successfully during its invasion of Georgia in 2008. Ukraine experienced the same cyber chaos that wreaked havoc in Georgia before Russia rolled in with its tanks. The writing on the wall was literally written in the malicious computer code propagated throughout Ukraine.

"Before Crimea seceded to Russian control in early 2014, Kyiv was overwhelmed by a series of sophisticated and coordinated cyberattacks, crippling communications networks and shutting down government websites with denial-of-service attacks," Sarge continued, with the room's rapt attention.

"By the way, if you think that couldn't happen in the U.S., think again. Early this year in northern Arizona, *vandals* cut a critically sensitive fiber-optic cable, disrupting police and state government databases, banks, hospitals and businesses for several hours. No ATMs. No credit card transactions," he said, pausing. "And no Internet—heaven forbid."

The class laughed at this lighthearted jab at their generation.

"What I found interesting about all of these reports was that investigators used the terms *vandals or vandalism* repeatedly, implying a bunch of bored high school kids might be responsible; plausible? I don't think so. The fiber-optic cable was encased in a two-inch-thick steel pipe. Breaching this pipe would have required more than a simple hacksaw as reported. Even a battery-powered reciprocating saw might not do the trick. And yes, I did some research. These hands don't see the use of hacksaws very often," said Sarge, drawing more laughter.

"The question has to be asked: *Was the Arizona event a trial run for something bigger?* Is there a rogue nation or terrorist group contemplating an attack on the United States using the Russian template so successful in Georgia and Ukraine? Probably not, unless this starts happening more frequently. Time will tell. Fortunately for you, the new face of warfare might be a little clearer."

Sarge looked out into the classroom. When teaching, Sarge enjoyed having instructive dialogue with his students. He employed the Socratic Method, named for the Greek philosopher Socrates. Universally feared by law students, he employed a more productive version of Socrates' contribution to academia, asking question after question until the entire class came to a collective conclusion—no small feat when so many cultures and political points of view were represented in one room.

"Mr. Feltzer," said Sarge, bringing the young man to attention in his seat, "are you familiar with the cyberattack on Sony Pictures in 2014, which cost them nearly a billion dollars?"

"Yes, sir," replied Feltzer.

"Was this an act of war?" asked Sarge.

"No, sir," replied Feltzer.

"Well, I agree, although I believe if Sony Pictures had real cannons, they would have found somebody to shoot," said Sarge, to a room of laughter. "In fact, the President made a point in a CNN interview to call the attack *cyber-vandalism.*"

He strolled along the front of the room, studying the young minds soaking in his words.

"Ahhh," continued Sarge, "there's that word again—vandalism. An attack upon the private sector that results in economic loss does not give rise to an act of war. Would everyone agree with that statement as our first premise?" Sarge observed heads nodding all around.

"Thank you, Mr. Feltzer. Miss Crepeau, you're up," said Sarge.

The young woman who sat in the front row was eager to jump into the discussion, as always, thought Sarge. Sarge recognized from day one he had to be careful with *that one.*

"Let's continue with the *Russian Template*, as we'll call it. I have a hypothetical for you, Miss Crepeau. We have already discussed the vandals who cut the fiber-optic cable in Arizona. What if these *vandals* simultaneously, via a cyber attack, took down Tucson Electric and the Salt River Project that services Phoenix? Now do we have an act of war?" asked Sarge.

"Not yet," she replied. "Although these acts are coordinated by these vandals, there has not been sufficient corresponding death and destruction to warrant military action."

"How many deaths?" asked Sarge.

"Excuse me?" she replied.

"For all of you," said Sarge, addressing the entire class, "how many deaths from this type of coordinated attack would warrant a military response?" As Sarge looked around the class, he heard responses of *hundreds, thousands* and *just one is enough.*

"Thank you, Miss Crepeau. Therein lies the rub," said Sarge, quoting *Hamlet.*

"I heard answers ranging from one to several thousand. The challenge for any government is to identify a standard—a breaking point—that requires a nation to go to war," said Sarge.

"For most governments, the standard is vague and leaves a lot of wiggle room. By the way, that is a global governance term of art—*wiggle room,*" said Sarge to a few stifled laughs.

"Officially, both the White House and the Pentagon consider a cyberattack emanating from a foreign country an act of war. But they do not spell out when a cyberattack is serious enough to constitute an act of war. As Miss Crepeau suggests, I suspect a cyberattack that produces death, damage and destruction similar to a traditional military attack might merit retaliation through the use of force," concluded Sarge.

Sarge had set them up, just as Socrates would have in the fifth century B.C. The class now seemed to agree death and destruction was a prerequisite to military retribution. *Let's twist them around a little, starting with the law student.*

"Mr. Robbins, let me begin with you," said Sarge. "Did you agree with the consensus of the class that the cyberattack on Sony Pictures was not an act of war?"

"Yes, sir, I did," responded Robbins authoritatively.

"Mr. Robbins, do you believe that a coordinated cyberattack could devastate the U.S. economy?" asked Sarge.

"It would depend on the severity and what systems were affected. Professor, would you consider it an act of war if the Sony Pictures attack was made in conjunction with a shutdown of the stock market?" asked Robbins, Socratically.

Well done, lawyer-to-be. You answered a question with *it depends* and threw it back at me with another question of clarification.

"Let's look at a real-world example, shall we?" asked Sarge.

"In 2007, once again, our friends the Russians," said Sarge with his voice trailing off. "After today, I'm sure to have my travel privileges to Russia suspended. He continued.

"In 2007, the tiny country of Estonia mistakenly poked the Russian bear by moving a controversial Soviet-era memorial from the town square in Tallin to a remote location. The large Russian minority in Estonia protested, as did the Russian government. For weeks thereafter, Estonia businesses and utilities suffered a barrage of cyber attacks that brought the private sector to a screeching halt.

"While the Estonia attacks were not the largest on record, they were sufficient to bring a country considered to be especially *wired* to its knees. The resulting recession was considered a direct result of the cyberattacks," said Sarge.

"The Gross Domestic Product of the United States economy is eighty percent services. In economic terms, a service is an intangible commodity. Any event that disrupts the ability of those services to be rendered will necessarily result in a downturn of the economy. For example, according to a Department of Commerce report, the economic losses caused by Superstorm Sandy, a storm event lasting twenty-four hours, totaled one hundred billion dollars."

"Mr. Robbins, if a rogue nation, via a cyberattack, caused economic losses in this country totaling one hundred billion dollars, would that be an act of war?" asked Sarge.

"No, sir. If I were president, and one day I will be, only significant loss of life warrants a war response," said Robbins.

"Mr. President-to-be, I will submit there have been many wars fought over a lesser economic impact than the hypothetical we have described, and I suspect we will see this scenario play out in our lifetimes," said Sarge.

"I'm going to conclude this semester with a teaser for the companion course that will start in January." Sarge changed the screen.

GLOBAL GOVERNANCE
+
ECONOMIC POLICY

"For years, U.S. officials have dismissed the need for international negotiations and cooperation on cyberspace, but now appears to be in the process of collaborating with our allies to develop rules for the virtual world. The trend appears to be headed toward the creation of cyber policy, including establishing a threshold where a cyber attack constitutes an act of war. This trend reflects the growing sentiment that our domestic efforts to secure cyberspace are inadequate. We will study whether the impact on the U.S. economy is driving this change in the government's approach," said Sarge, bringing up the final slide for the day.

FINAL TUESDAY
12/18/15

The collective grumbles in the background were lost on Sarge as he gathered his notes from the lectern. Sarge replaced the cap on his Mont Blanc pen and tucked it away in his shirt. An uneasy feeling of dread and foreboding hit him, casting his mind adrift.

CHAPTER 3

December 15, 2015
73 Tremont Street

Donald Quinn waited patiently at the traffic light, preparing to turn left onto Tremont Street. Before him, he observed the northeast corner of Boston Common—all but deserted in the winter. Joggers, tourists and leaves had all gone into hibernation, taking the vitality of this historic city space with them. In the summer, the pedestrian circle was filled with passersby swarming the locally famous Donut Cart or Giuseppe's Italian Ice. There weren't many patrons for Italian Ice in mid-December. Despite his new training regimen, Donald might have splurged on a bag full of arepas, which was a corn pocket stuffed with a variety of savory fillings, a staple in South America. But, alas, even the warm offerings had flown south for the winter.

After parking the *jalopy*, as Mrs. Quinn teasingly called his 1972 Jeep CJ5 Renegade, Donald began his trek up the hill toward 73 Tremont. Now painted flat black, Donald chose this vehicle as his *company car*. Sure, he had his pick of the litter. As the *Director of Procurement*, any flashy vehicle was an option, but the only flash that concerned him was an electromagnetic pulse bomb detonated over the good ole U.S. of A.

When he showed Susan his choice, she understood the reasoning. However, *for appearances,* she said, her choice would be something more conventional—a Cadillac Escalade. Donald thought his choice was a wise one, despite her misgivings. The Renegade was obscure and undistinguished, blending into society unnoticed—as did Donald.

Donald was new to the preparedness lifestyle, having only

embraced the concept in the last six or seven years. It started with an unsolicited novel by William Forstchen, followed by a series of books in the genre sent to him by Susan. The concepts in the books struck a chord, and he began to perceive world events differently. He became a student of prepping, and devoured every book and preparedness guide available on the subject.

He and Susan married in 2005 with a well-attended wedding. Susan had just completed her military career in the Air Force, and Donald was firmly ensconced at the accounting firm of Vitale Caturano—VC. Although they were not Big Four, VC was one of the most prestigious firms in Boston, boasting an international clientele. Donald, the consummate accountant, was of average height, stocky and relatively nondescript. Susan, a devout Christian and the daughter of a wealthy Bostonian with roots dating back to the Lowells, loved him dearly. Soon after marriage, life took an interesting and unexpected turn.

Upon taking their wedding vows, Donald and Susan envisioned a simple life. Good jobs, a two-car garage, two kids and the requisite Labrador retriever. Instead, Donald *took one for the team*. In 2009, with a three-year-old wreaking havoc on the Quinn household and another child on the way, Donald plead guilty to seven counts of a federal indictment, to include charges of money laundering and conspiracy to commit income tax evasion.

VC's client list consisted of many wealthy, connected Bostonians, all requiring complex tax, estate and retirement planning. Donald was tasked with assisting a friend of his father-in-law with his estate plan, despite his relative inexperience with estate plans of this magnitude. His new client was adamantly opposed to the concept of federal estate taxes, particularly the newly proposed changes to the inheritance tax. Further, he was concerned with protecting his assets from an ex-wife, who had openly voiced that she was entitled to his estate—because she had "paid her dues."

Unknown to Donald, the client had already made several ill-advised attempts at financial planning, which included large transfers of money to exotic locales like the Turks and Caicos Islands, Tortola, and Nevis. How the client was able to transfer several million dollars to the banks in these countries was never fully disclosed to Donald.

One evening, Donald returned to their home in Waltham to a welcoming committee that would alter the course of his life. Present were his visibly shaken and very pregnant wife, his father-in-law Charles Lowell, the client, and a mystery guest—an older gentleman who was never formally introduced and remained silent during the entire meeting.

Within an hour, Donald agreed to plead guilty to the federal charges, taking full responsibility for the client's ill-advised scheme. Despite the magnitude of the crime, Donald was assured that he would receive no more than a twenty-four-month sentence. The plea agreement had already been negotiated. With good time, he would return home within twenty-one months—to a new house in Brae Burn Country Club in West Newton, a guaranteed high six-figure income, and a position dealing in large part with the *Mystery Man.* Susan kept her composure throughout the meeting, smiling reassuringly with the occasional tear. She was a real soldier.

Donald reported directly to the Federal Medical Center on the grounds of Fort Devens, just forty-five minutes west of Boston, where he was immediately assigned a serious medical condition—despite being in perfect health. All part of the complex illusion of his incarceration, he would discover.

What immediately struck Donald was the fact there were no fences or guard towers surrounding FMC. It looked like any other group of buildings. Over time he realized why they called this type of facility a *country club.* It wasn't the Brae Burn lifestyle that awaited him, but it certainly beat a federal penitentiary. Mystery Man couldn't buy Donald's way out of prison, but he could apparently purchase a medical condition—the next best thing in the Federal Bureau of Prisons. His condition came with perks.

Ordinarily, any other inmate would miss many of the life-changing events on the outside like the birth of a child. Not Donald. He was whisked away on a "medical emergency," requiring outside medical treatment, for the birth of their second daughter, and was allowed to stay with Susan for a couple of nights.

Despite being away from Susan and the girls most of the time, Donald changed for the better during his stay at FMC Fort Devens. He started to exercise regularly, replacing thirty pounds of fat with lean muscle in the facility's weight room. Donald also became a prepper, reading every book sent to him and taking detailed notes.

Donald's final wake-up inside FMC was little more than a physical formality. His mind had already been awakened and conditioned with a different view of the world. The memories of his time away from Susan were a constant reminder of how his life had changed, and the opportunities which opened up as a result of the sacrifice he made. With a renewed sense of purpose, Donald confidently walked up Tremont Street for a meeting with his *benefactor*, curious as to what the day might bring.

CHAPTER 4

December 15, 2015
Boston, Massachusetts

Sarge bounded down the front steps of the Belfer Center like a kid released for summer break—only to be greeted with a brisk winter breeze and an MBTA bus roaring down Eliot Street. The temperatures were already far milder than the previous year, spurring hope they might avoid a repeat of the one hundred plus inches of snowfall that wreaked havoc in the eastern United States. A cold breath of air, supplemented with the exhaust of the MBTA bus, was a welcome relief from hundred-car pileups on the highways and scenes of downed power grids in Tennessee.

He resisted the urge to run into Dunkin' Donuts, opting instead for a quick cash withdrawal at the Bank of America ATM. Long lines inside the branch caught his attention. *Odd for closing time on a Tuesday; maybe everybody is going Christmas shopping.*

Part of Sarge's *duties and responsibilities*, in addition to his profession, was to keep up with world events, especially related to global economics. As he shoved the twenties into his pocket, he thought about how worthless these paper notes might become someday. Today's modern banking system manufactured money out of thin air. Like a magician's sleight of hand, global bankers had the power to create money and control credit markets. With the stroke of a pen or the punch of a keyboard, they could deliver wealth to whomever they chose.

Ironic, Sarge thought to himself as he pressed the key fob on his new Mercedes-Benz G63 AMG. *Am I hypocritical to condemn the activities of the global elite, the same powerful people who provided this G-Wagen to me as a company car?* As he settled in, the earthy smell of the Nappa leather refocused him on the task at hand—Christmas shopping.

Sitting behind the heated steering wheel of the G63 was like entering the cockpit of an airplane. Having taken delivery just a few days ago, Sarge hadn't taken the proper time to familiarize himself with the interior. Starting the engine was the easy part. Then he adjusted all of the comfort features, which fortunately included lots of heating elements. Finally, of course, the ultimate in driver distraction was the G63's COMAND system with an 80 GB hard drive navigation system, Bluetooth, HDTV and Sirius radio. No wonder Apple and Google developed self-driving cars. Sarge would never use all of these gadgets. His rare 1968 Toyota OJ40, Bandeirante model, was more his speed. No frills, no thrills. The only thing these two vehicles had in common was a Mercedes-Benz engine. No fancy electronics in the Bandeirante, he thought. *That might be a good thing someday.*

Pulling out of the garage onto Eliot, he fumbled with the COMAND system and nearly struck the back tire of a bicycle—the backpack and winter coat laden student long gone by the time Sarge took a deep breath and exhaled. *See! This is what I'm talking about.* Finally getting his mind straight, Sarge managed to navigate south onto JFK without taking out any of the Kennedy School of Government's student body. An adjustment of the COMAND volume brought the voice of his friend Neil Cavuto to life.

"*Markets closed flat today amid continued uncertainty about whether Greece, Italy and Spain would reach bailout agreements with Eurozone officials. After the markets closed, a rumor swirled that a tentative agreement had been reached, which sent DOW futures higher. However, conflicting reports out of Frankfurt made by Deutsche Bank officials said otherwise, driving futures back to a negative position.*

"*To discuss all of this, I have as my guest Jon Wellington with Barclays UK in London, how are you, sir?*" asked Cavuto.

"*I am chipper as usual, Neil, and glad to be on with you this evening,*" said Wellington.

"*What do you make of this news, and how does it affect the markets?*" asked Cavuto.

"*All day long it was like watching a classic Wimbledon tennis match of troubles, with investors volleying between radio silence from a closed-door meeting amongst Eurozone leaders on the Mediterranean members and the brightening outlook of a cease-fire agreement in Ukraine. Markets would push higher on the positive reports out of Ukraine and then fall lower on the uncertainty surrounding the Eurozone trio of trouble—Spain, Greece and Italy. Add to that a late-day press conference from the President regarding his use of executive powers and you had one bloody day of jittery stock trading,*" said Wellington.

"*So what should investors consider as a plan of action?*" asked Cavuto.

"*Neil, markets like stability. As we have seen over the last five to six years, despite relatively sluggish growth worldwide, markets have risen to tremendous heights. Unfortunately, we are one bad news story away from deflating this incredible run for stocks,*" said Wellington.

"*I'm a 'glass half full' kinda guy, Jon. What would you suggest for those of us who espouse to the 'glass half empty' outlook on investing?*" asked Cavuto.

"*In my experience, a 'glass half empty' investor is typically cautious and is likely to sell at the slightest hint of a market downturn. Then there are those few daredevil opportunists who fearlessly attack a potential downturn to turn a healthy profit. They short sell,*" said Wellington.

Sarge was travelling south on Soldiers Field Road along the River Charles, enthralled by this conversation. His job duties did not require managing investments. Those responsibilities fell on the shoulders of others. But it was important for him to understand the mechanisms of the markets and how it affected the geopolitical landscape. He passed Boston University, home of Rhett the Wet Noodle Terrier. *Lame-ass mascot.* He turned his attention back to the conversation.

"*Short selling,*" continued Wellington, "*is the sale of a stock the seller does not own, but has merely borrowed. It may sound like an odd practice, but it is actually done often by seasoned investors. Short selling is typically prompted by speculation or by a desire to hedge downside risk. It is a risky proposition for the average investor and is only recommended it be used by experienced traders who are familiar with the great financial risks.*"

"Is now a good time to short sell?" asked Cavuto.

"*Neil, no investor has a crystal ball. For the last several years, financial pundits have warned that the financial markets are overvalued and the central banks of the world, like the Federal Reserve, are out of bullets to deal with a financial crisis. Yet the markets keep rising. This meteoric rise is probably a function of all-time-low interest rates. Investors are willing to gamble their money in stocks rather than receive little or no interest in banking-related investments. But, to answer your question, in the absence of a 'bad news story' I referenced earlier, equities are still the way to go!*" said Wellington.

Sarge thought to himself—investing like a bunch of drunks. *They have no idea.*

CHAPTER 5

December 15, 2015
73 Tremont Street
Boston, Massachusetts

Donald crossed Tremont Street and walked purposefully up the sidewalk toward the Park Street intersection. Parking was available at 73 Tremont, but Donald made it a habit to park off-site on his rare visits to the *Penthouse*. Donald believed in maintaining some semblance of a gray-man strategy, especially when meeting with his benefactors. Better to blend in with other visitors to the building.

Waiting on the traffic to clear the crosswalk, he admired the historic Park Street Church across the boulevard. Despite his lack of historic bloodline, which flowed through the veins of his *benefactors*, Donald was an avid Revolutionary-era historian. He and Susan had long ago graduated from the touristy Freedom Trail, which included well-known attractions like the Old North Church, the USS *Constitution* and the site of the Boston Massacre. They now explored a lesser known, but equally important layer of history that blanketed Boston.

Crossing the street, Donald checked his watch, noting that he was early. *I insist on punctuality*—the words rang in Donald's head. He *insisted* on a lot of things. Beyond the curb, a tour guide dressed in the cold-weather version of traditional eighteenth-century garb began his presentation. Donald took a moment to listen. Despite its distinction as one of the Freedom Trail's most prominent features, the Park Street Church was a historic gem that never grew old.

"Welcome, everyone, and thank you for daring the brisk weather to continue on the Freedom Trail tour. I see most of you stretching to look skyward at the magnificent steeple, which sits atop the historic Park Street Church here on Tremont Street. By the way, did you know Tremont is always pronounced *trem-mont* in Boston, not *tree-mont*?" asked the guide.

Heads nodded affirmatively, although Donald suspected none of them knew this until now.

"Rising toward the heavens, the two-hundred-seventeen-foot steeple, designed by architect Peter Banner, was once the first landmark travelers saw when approaching Boston. Today, the first landmark a traveler sees is a series of illuminated road signs reading 'forty-five-minute delay on the Mass Turnpike.' Things have changed, have they not, my friends?" asked the guide, to hearty laughter.

"Built in 1809, the church took a prominent role in the abolishment of slavery. Speakers came from all over New England to advance their mission of human rights. On July 4th, 1831, the patriotic song 'My Country, 'Tis of Thee,' written by Samuel Francis Smith, was sung a capella during a children's Independence Day celebration," said the guide.

Passing the tourists' parked carriage—a red Hop-On, Hop-Off Trolley Bus—Donald continued up *trem-mont,* humming the words of the famous song.

"My country, 'tis of thee, Sweet land of liberty, Of thee I sing; Land where my fathers died, Land of the pilgrims' pride, From every mountainside, Let freedom ring."

If only that were still true. He somehow doubted the Founding Fathers would recognize the state of the republic they had left behind for the American people. Donald pushed his way through the impeccably polished, brass revolving door, pausing to wonder what would happen if he did a 360 and drove home. Nothing good.

Entering the lobby, Donald was struck by the magnificence of *la grande entrée* of 73 Tremont. After a major renovation in 1988 added several stories to the existing neoclassical granite structure, the building took on a character of its own. From the Carrara marble inlay floors to the forty-foot-tall vaulted ceilings, the lobby was gracefully appointed with polished brass, mahogany wood and elegant soft lighting. Despite a level of grace and style that would rival the finest five-star hotel, the lobby was sparsely decorated to minimize the chance of an impromptu street gathering. Everything in 73 Tremont had been designed with a purpose.

Replacing the historical bellhops of the former Tremont House were subtle reminders of the buildings twenty-four-hour armed security team. A careful look revealed numerous security cameras shrewdly incorporated into the architectural finishes—an odd feature for a building owned by a trust set up to benefit Suffolk University. Of course, Donald knew all too well that the building had little to do with the university.

"Good morning, sir, how may we help you?" asked a well-dressed concierge behind the reception desk.

Donald could feel the eyes studying him from above. *I am not paranoid, just aware.*

"Yes, I have an appointment on the thirteenth floor," said Donald.

Two members of the building's security team emerged from a shallow alcove to Donald's right. *Men in Black* types. Definitely not your typical campus security arrangement.

"Your name, please?" asked the concierge, picking up a phone receiver.

Donald provided his name and waited several seconds. He wasn't sure why they put him through this drill. They'd probably identified him a block away. The concierge listened to the phone and nodded, replacing the receiver. Two more men emerged from the alcove, bringing the total to five.

"Before these gentlemen escort you upstairs, sir, we must ask if you are carrying any weapons—including sharp objects. If you have any weapons, please allow us to check them for you," said the concierge.

Donald had received his concealed-carry weapons permit shortly after his release from prison. He had never owned a gun prior to "going away," but it soon became clear his new job duties would require personal protection. Within weeks of returning, he received correspondence from the Office of the Pardon Attorney in Washington, D.C., granting him a full Article II pardon and restoration of his civil rights, permitting gun ownership. An application to the Massachusetts Parole Board, marked *APPROVED,* arrived a few weeks later, completing the process. Everything had been prearranged on his behalf. He'd never seen the applications.

"Yes, I do have a weapon to *check,*" said Donald.

The concierge motioned for him to follow the men through a door, where he voluntarily surrendered his Springfield XD-S 9mm to the solemn gentlemen who hadn't smiled—much less spoken. One of the security team members released the magazine and cleared the chamber before locking it away in a wall safe. After a brief search of his Hartmann signature tweed briefcase, they motioned for him to follow. Although Donald had been through this procedure a few times before, it never failed to reinforce the importance of the man he had come to see.

Three members of the security crew entered the elevator; one of them inserting a key into an unnumbered slot on the brass elevator keypad. They rode to the thirteenth floor in awkward silence. When the elevator opened, Donald strode confidently to the reception desk, which was hosted by two attractive, professionally dressed women. On closer inspection, Donald could see how they trained their eyes on him—no doubt performing a threat assessment. He suspected their security training equaled, if not exceeded the men escorting him. Though it had been several months since Donald's last visit to the top floor of 73 Tremont, he felt an increased security presence. One of the women broke eye contact to glance at one of his escorts, who simply nodded. *Do they have mental telepathy too?*

"Just one moment, Mr. Quinn," she said, never taking her eyes off him again.

Pushing a button on her desk, she spoke softly into a wireless microphone attached to her jacket collar. "Mr. Quinn is here to see you, sir."

The male escorts stepped back to flank the elevator while one of the women circled the desk. She pointed to an intricately carved set of mahogany doors at the end of the reception hallway. *This is new.* He took in the details of the woodwork. Sheep and sheepdog on a hillside. Donald searched for the meaning, knowing these functional works of art had been purposely commissioned. The security guard opened the right door before he could form a theory.

"This way, please," she instructed, leading him past a wide bank of windows.

Of the many incredible views of Boston from the city's high-rise buildings, none matched the view west across Boston Common from the top floor of 73 Tremont. From the thirteenth floor's unique vantage point, one could also observe the Charles River, Commonwealth Avenue and the Massachusetts State House on Beacon Hill. The State House was particularly spectacular in the late afternoon, with the setting sun reflecting off the State House's twenty-three-karat gilded gold-leaf dome. The dull winter scene blazed to life, drawing the viewer's attention away from the bare trees and naked sidewalks directly below.

Opening another mahogany door, she motioned for him to enter his host's office—the inner sanctum. With slight trepidation, Donald stepped into a world out of reach for most. Measuring more than forty feet wide, the office was bigger than most Americans' homes. Gas fireplaces flanked both ends, rising through the two-story ceiling. The furnishings consisted of oriental carpets, dark chestnut furniture and overstuffed chairs, more resembling a gentlemen's lounge than an office. On the broad leather inlay desk centered in the middle of the room, two crystal glasses sat beside an opened bottle of Perrier.

Donald stood silently, waiting for the man standing in front of a set of velvet-clad French doors to acknowledge him. Appearing deep in thought, his benefactor finally spoke.

"Hello, Mr. Quinn, thank you for coming," he said, in the New England accent associated with people of aristocracy.

"Yes, sir, it is a pleasure to see you again," said Donald. *Not that I had a choice.*

He didn't expect the pleasantries to last for too long. The meeting had been hastily arranged. Something was brewing.

"I trust you have everything you need for your various projects," he said.

"Yes, sir, and I hope my reports are satisfactory," said Donald.

Donald always remembered to choose his words deliberately and concisely.

"Of course. Mr. Quinn, you will need to take care of something for me—immediately following the close of the markets today," he said. "There are a number of transactions to be made, and you must use the highest levels of discretion."

I knew it; this couldn't be trusted to a phone call. Donald retrieved a small Louis Vuitton notebook from his suit jacket pocket.

"Immediately following this meeting, you are to execute the following transactions," said Donald's benefactor.

Listening intently, Donald took meticulous notes. The instructions represented the largest series of transactions he had executed to date. Donald had established a complex network of international brokerage accounts, which enabled him to effect secretive transactions—but never anything of this magnitude. *He knows something.* Donald jotted down country names in the left margin—Cook Islands, Dominica, St. Kitts, Turks and Caicos Islands.

The intricacy of the trades was significant, but not nearly as noteworthy as the sums of money involved—over one billion dollars. *This would take days.*

"Mr. Quinn, this must be completed before the opening of the Asian markets," he said, jarring Donald's attention from the notebook.

"Sir, I believe it is roughly five in the morning in Tokyo. Their markets open in about four hours. The New Zealand and Australian markets open an hour sooner, in roughly three hours," said Donald.

"Mr. Quinn," he said sternly, "you are prepared for this, are you not?"

Donald felt flush, taking a moment to respond carefully.

"Yes, sir, I have the systems and procedures in place. It's the scale of the transactions that concerns me," said Donald. "Currency trades of this magnitude will have repercussions throughout the global financial system. Although I have total confidence in the structure I have established for you, there is also the possibility of enhanced scrutiny from the Commodity Futures Trading Commission. Taking a six-hundred-million-dollar short position in the euro, coupled with a six-hundred-million-dollar long position in the dollar, will wreak havoc in the equities markets as well." *And I'd rather not return to jail, regardless of how comfortable you can make my stay.*

His concerns rose above the scrutiny of the CFTC. The FOREX market was the largest foreign exchange market in the world, with currency changing hands continuously—but the size of these trades would rival the currency manipulations of George Soros. The potential upside was beyond contemplation—*more than a billion dollars.*

"Mr. Quinn, I have thought through this request thoroughly, and I am fully aware of the potential for international examination. Nevertheless, you will move forward. In addition, you are to short sell all of my positions in the following equities," he said, listing nearly a dozen U.S. and European companies. He said *all.* Donald quickly did the math—another four hundred million.

"Yes, sir," was all Donald could muster.

"I will have you escorted to an office, where you can execute my directives. A secure line is available, and you will have the complete assistance of a member of my staff if needed. Do you have any questions, Mr. Quinn?"

Yeah, what the hell do you know that nobody else does?

"No, sir," replied Donald.

Donald rose to leave. He took one more glance at his surroundings. *So this is how you pay for this stuff?*

As if reading Donald's thoughts, his benefactor added, "I hope your wife and children are doing well."

Oh yes, very well, thanks to you, sir.

"They are, sir. I thank you for the very generous gift on the birth of our daughter. She will benefit from a Harvard education," said Donald.

"You're welcome, Mr. Quinn. There is no substitute," he said, turning his attention to the view of Boston Common.

That was it. He was dismissed. Donald let himself out without another word and was escorted by a young man to a conference room on the other side of the thirteenth floor. The room was well appointed, featuring a full bar and six wall-mounted televisions.

"May I offer you anything to drink?" asked the young man.

Donald smiled and nodded. With the delivery of the Evian, the young man closed the door and left him alone. He took a quick inventory of the tools at his disposal. Telephones. Old school, but no doubt filtered by the securest encryption technology available. He pulled a chair in front of the phones and thought about Susan and the girls for a moment. They were extremely happy together as a family. Did their happiness come with a heavy price tag? Currency trading was practiced every day, right? *Not $1.2 billion at once, followed by another $400 million in stock manipulations. What did it matter? Forget the dollar amounts, make the trades and go home to your family.*

He pulled off his jacket and flung it into an empty chair. Unbuttoning and rolling up his sleeves, Donald executed the first in a series of steps that would make front-page news tomorrow morning.

CHAPTER 6

December 15, 2015
Newbury Street
Boston, Massachusetts

After turning right on Clarendon Street, Sarge crossed Commonwealth Avenue and started looking for a parking space. He considered parking at home and walking—Newbury Street would no doubt bustle with Christmas shoppers. He passed the First Baptist Church and admired its architecture. The congregation's history dated back to the mid-1600s and was commonly considered one of the oldest Baptist Churches in America. The current church, built in the late 1800s, was on the National Register of Historic Places. The Sargent families had been prominent members of this church since the Boston Baptists congregated in the North End. His grandfather, former Governor Francis Sargent—of "Put Sarge in Charge" fame—attended services regularly. The current-day "Sarge in Charge" had not attended since he was a boy.

Easing his Mercedes SUV onto Newbury Street reminded him of the maze of one-way streets created in Back Bay. Tourists must think the street layout was designed as a sadistic game to keep them out. Clearly, the city's nineteenth-century planners didn't anticipate the population boom. The Newbury Street shopping district had an interesting history. Until the mid-nineteenth century, this area of Boston was under water—part of the Boston Harbor.

A massive public works project was undertaken in 1857 to remove dirt fill from neighboring communities and their once substantially higher hilltops. Boston Harbor was slowly landfilled to create the affluent Back Bay section of the city. Completed in 1882, a majority of the original European-designed buildings were still standing today. By 1900, the prestige and exclusivity of Back Bay surpassed the renowned Beacon Hill. Today, Newbury Street was commonly known as the "Rodeo Drive of the East" and was home to a unique mix of shops, high-end fashion stores and stylish restaurants.

Sarge, like most men, was not a *shopper.* He was a *buyer.* He ventured onto Newbury Street with a singular mission—buy a Christmas gift for a Harvard colleague who loved Tommy Bahama products. Sarge noticed the sidewalks were not bustling with happy shoppers. In fact, the bulk of the inhabitants were not carrying any packages. *Is December 15th too early for Christmas shopping?*

Sarge spotted a parking space in front of Steve Madden shoes. He wondered if the customers of Steve Madden would care that Madden was a former bunkmate of my friend Donald Quinn at Fort Devens. Probably not, he surmised. *What's a little income tax evasion among friends, right?* He maneuvered the G63 into the space, hitting the pavement with a mission as he strode towards Tommy Bahama. *Hello, ladies,* he thought as a group of female boutique shoppers marched up the sidewalk toward him. *Give them plenty of room; you're on their turf now.* They looked expensive in a "how much would it cost to keep them satisfied" sort of way. Plenty of casual smiles were exchanged except for the one toting the most bags. *I need to introduce her to my brother.*

His smartphone buzzed, stopping him long enough to avoid a speeding SUV in the Dartmouth Street crosswalk. Looking at the display, he grimaced.

"Well, if it isn't Julia of the Jungle," answered Sarge.

"Screw you, Sarge!" was the caller's retort.

"You don't scare me, lady," he replied.

"Well, you should be scared. Is your phone broken? Did you not pay the bill? Lose my number, perhaps?" interrogated the caller. *He was doomed.*

"No, no, no and no. I've been winding up the semester," replied Sarge, knowing the lame-ass excuse would not be a sufficient justification for his lack of a call.

He really didn't know why he hadn't called her.

"Fine. I'm hungry and you should feed me proper. What's your status?" she asked.

"Lucky for you, I'm down by Tommy Bahama's on Newbury Street, picking up a Christmas present. When can you meet me at Stephanie's?" asked Sarge.

"Are you buying something for your sailor-boy brother?" she asked as her innate seventh sense of shopping kicked in.

"No, are you kidding? He'd tie me to a line and drop anchor if I bought him something from there. Besides, he's working this month. This is for a Harvard buddy. So, are you on your way yet?" asked Sarge, trying to deflect attention from the previous interrogatory.

"Yes, sir," she stretched out her response. "Private Julia Hawthorne will report to Stephanie's at eighteen hundred hours!"

"Well done, Private—first class, out!" added Sarge with emphasis.

This worked out well, thought Sarge. He had been meaning to call Julia and, in fact, missed her company. Sarge—the buyer—hopped up the stairs through the cast-iron rails with a new sense of purpose—besides the acquisition of a Tommy Bahama XXL Jungle Jingle camp shirt.

CHAPTER 7

December 15, 2015
Newbury Street
Boston, Massachusetts

Stepping out of Tommy Bahama's, Sarge caught a last glimpse of the setting sun, watching as the gas lanterns took over the responsibility of illuminating Newbury Street. Ambling down the wide sidewalk, under a canopy of leafless trees, he safely stored Jungle Jingle and its signature marlin-emblazoned Tommy Bahama bag into the car.

Briskly walking to Stephanie's, his thoughts returned to Julia. Their relationship was complicated. Convoluted may be more descriptive. The two were close—in a *friends with benefits* sort of way—yet there had never been the slightest hint of taking it to the level of dating, much less marriage. In a sense, their side work cast a cloud of doubt over the possibility of a long-term relationship. *The Quinns do it,* Julia had whispered into his ear on more than one intimate occasion. That was true, but their roles were different, insulating their family from certain risks.

It pained Sarge to keep her at a distance. Julia was an incredible woman. She'd attended the prestigious Boston University School of Journalism, which would have made their ancestors proud. The families of George Peabody and Nathaniel Hawthorne shared an ancestral background dating back to the Founding Fathers—a particular badge of honor in Boston. They also shared a sense that their destinies were predetermined. This unease didn't prevent them from being intimate or working together, but it did give them reason to hold back from a more permanent union.

Approaching Stephanie's, he saw Julia's town car pull up to the valet stand in front of the restaurant. Not waiting for the driver, Julia emerged from the car—one long leg after another. Julia was incredibly beautiful and impeccably appointed. Christian Louboutin shoes, Hermes Birkin JPG bag designed by Jean Paul Gaultier, Stella McCartney trench coat, and a variety of glistening baubles. She drew the instant attention of men and women alike wherever she appeared.

"Yo, Adrian," bellowed Sarge, in his best Rocky Balboa voice.

"You are so full of it, Rocky, or Bullwinkle, whichever you choose," said Julia laughingly, presenting her cheek to Sarge for a proper kiss.

Sarge observed the driver, who seemed to enjoy the playful banter between the couple, smiling at them as he dutifully shut the back door. Maybe they should give *it*—the couple thing—a try.

"C'mon, I'm powerful hungry," said Sarge, befitting Stephanie's reputation for offering sophisticated comfort food.

During milder weather, the wrought-iron enclosed outdoor dining café was packed with locals and tourists alike. Located at the corner of Exeter and Newbury, Stephanie's outdoor dining provided an idyllic setting to watch the hustle and bustle of the world go by. Once inside, you were surrounded by dark walnut, a fireplace in the bar, soft golden lighting and casual conversation over what Chef Stephanie Sidell called "love food."

"I have big news," started Julia as they waited to be seated. "We earned a Marconi."

The *Boston Herald* was one of the oldest daily newspapers in the United States. Founded in 1846, it had been the proud recipient of eight Pulitzer Prizes. Julia's rise at the *Herald* was meteoric. Following her graduation from Boston University, she was immediately assigned to cover Senator John Kerry's 2004 campaign. Through some remarkable investigative reporting, she uncovered voting irregularities in Florida and Ohio, which stemmed from dual state registrations. Julia earned a Payne Award for ethics in journalism.

Later, Julia was named the first political editor in the paper's history, consistently delivering a libertarian viewpoint. The journalist community panned the move as risky, warning the shift would reduce the *Herald* to "tabloid status." Their analysis couldn't have been further off the mark. The *Herald* was rewarded with a tremendous surge in its circulation. By 2012, its readership increased at a time when most print media outlets had declined. Even *The Old Gray Lady*, as the *New York Times* was often referred to, had reduced its staff. Once again, the *Herald* was rewarded for its efforts by being named one of the *10 Newspapers That 'Do It Right'* by the newspaper industry magazine—*Editor & Publisher*.

Unfortunately, Julia's stewardship of the *Herald*'s editorial content was not given the proper credit by her counterparts, since the *Herald* often contradicted the mainstream media's left-leaning bias. Scorned by the establishment, she dug deeper into the numbers, motivated to prove them wrong. When the marketing department reported a surge in online readership of the *Herald*'s political content, she found what she needed. In 2013, Julia launched the Boston Herald Radio network, which broadcast locally on the AM band, but more importantly reached an audience of millions worldwide via their website. The overnight success of the venture sent the media pundits scurrying. Eighteen months later, Julia was ready to share more big news about her career.

"Sargent, party of two?" asked the perky hostess.

Sarge smiled and nodded affirmative.

"Right this way," she added.

The wait staff at Stephanie's was crisply attired with starched white button-down shirts, burgundy ties and waist-high aprons. Sarge always admired a professionally run restaurant operation, especially one with well-trained staff. A restauranteur may have found the best location, perfectly designed, with a fabulous chef, but if a guest was not greeted by a smiling face and the proper level of attentiveness, the restaurant was doomed to failure. Sarge and Julia were seated at a cozy table next to the window.

"Angie and John will be your servers this evening. Enjoy," said their hostess, handing a menu to each of them and a wine list to Sarge.

Sarge settled in and admired Julia. He could get used to *this*.

"Tell me more about your Macaroni," said Sarge, knowing he was about to be abused for his intentional mistaken reference.

The swift kick in the shin from her red-soled heels was his answer.

"Ouch," exclaimed Sarge.

"Shut up or I'll do it again," said Julia. Sarge knew she meant it.

"Good evening, I'm John," said John the server.

"And I'm Angie," said Angie the server.

"We'll be happy to serve you this evening," said *John-Angie* in unison. *Shtick, I like it.*

"This evening we are featuring two of Stephanie's favorite comfort foods—a pumpkin cider-brined pork chop served with a maple bourbon squash and a stuffed twice-baked potato, or you might prefer our fabulous Irish beef stew, served with mixed root vegetables," said Angie.

Sarge and Julia were noncommittal as they examined the menu. Sensing their need for additional time, John suggested an appetizer.

"Perhaps we could start you out with the pan-sautéed crab cakes, or everyone's favorite—baked macaroni and cheese balls."

"I think we've had enough talk about macaroni tonight," said Sarge, trying to keep his composure.

He made eye contact with Julia, and they both started laughing at the Marconi reference.

"Sorry, guys, inside joke. We'll both have a couple of single malts, make it Glenlivet, with a splash," said Sarge, putting on his best "I'm sober, really I am" demeanor.

"Yes, sir," said John. "I take it no appetizers this evening?"

"No, thank you. We'll take a moment to look at the menu," said Sarge, still avoiding eye contact with Julia.

As *John-Angie* tucked tail and hustled off, Sarge thought it safe to look at Julia and found this to be in error. She had both cheeks puffed out like she just swallowed a mouthful of baked macaroni and cheese balls. *Dammit.* It was on again, he thought as the both of them burst out in simultaneous laughter.

"Now listen," said Sarge, leaning back in his chair. "You are causing a disruption in this establishment, and we may get kicked out."

"Me," defended Julia. "You started this whole *macaroni* thing. Are you going to let me tell you about the Marconi or not?"

Angie delivered the eighteen-year-old Scotch whisky to the table.

"Give us a little time before we order, Angie," said Sarge, sharing a clink of the tumblers with Julia.

His first sip of full-bodied Scotch went down smoothly, not that he expected any different from the Glenlivet distillery.

"This is a *big deal*, Sarge," began Julia.

"I know, Julia. I'm well aware of the prestige associated with a Marconi. Congratulations."

The National Association of Broadcasters established this award in honor of Nobel Prize winner Guglielmo Marconi over twenty-five years ago. The Marconi Award recognized radio stations and broadcasters for their excellence in a variety of categories. The award had never been given to a predominantly Internet broadcasting medium, until now. In yet another first for Julia, and the *Herald*, the Marconi Award for News/Talk Station was granted to the Boston Herald Radio. It was a *big deal*.

"We received the call today from the NAB announcing the decision. When we were included in the call for entries back in May, I didn't think we had a chance," said Julia, lifting her glass for a toast. "They've never granted a Marconi to an Internet broadcast. We're the first."

"I am so proud of you," said Sarge, clinking her glass and taking a sip.

He could see his words warmed Julia, further recognizing the deep-seated effect on her. Her talents and accomplishments amazed him.

"As you know, the concept of taking Internet radio to this level had less to do with winning awards and more to do with the dissemination of information worldwide. Our *friends*," said Julia, with a nod of her head toward downtown Boston, "were very supportive of the project when we approached them in 2012."

There it was, the reminder—the *aide-memoire*. Their lives were dependent upon an association, known only to a few, that prevented a normal relationship. Sarge leaned forward to speak.

"You and I have discussed this many times. I am proud of what we have accomplished with our *side work*," said Sarge with a hushed voice. "But I get the sense our participation is going to escalate in a big way."

"What do you mean?" asked Julia, her inquisition interrupted by their servers.

"So, what may we serve you for dinner tonight?" asked John.

They both scrambled to take a last minute look at the menu.

"I will have the Asian yellowfin tuna salad, please, and another cocktail," said Julia, noticing Sarge's smirk.

Sarge ordered the Irish stew.

"What?" asked Julia, after the servers disappeared.

"Asian, imagine that. I could have taken you to Panda Express," said Sarge, spreading his legs apart to avoid the expected kick—which he did.

"Ha!" exclaimed Sarge proudly.

"You're adapting," said Julia, bringing her heel down on his toes.

"Hey!" squalled Sarge.

"Do you think I only have one cannon to fire, Monsieur? Do you want a war? I will give you a war!" said Julia, switching to a French accent.

"*Je me rends*," said Sarge in French, raising his white cloth napkin in surrender.

The two had a good heartfelt laugh. He really missed her and vowed to do something about that.

"Speaking of the French," said Julia, changing the subject slightly. "They seem to have brokered a peace in Ukraine."

"Maybe," said Sarge. "It seems to me they gave the Russians everything Putin wanted, including the two French-built Mistral-class warships bought and paid for by Moscow. The price tag on those two battleships was one point six billion, but closing the deal was more symbolic than anything. The administration used words like *ill-advised* when criticizing the sale, but it came down to economics for the French. They need the euro.

"The Eurozone's finances are in shambles," continued Sarge. "Spain, Italy and Greece are technically bankrupt. Their national debt to GDP ratio is approaching two hundred percent. It's unsustainable, yet these three countries refuse to implement any form of austerity measures. Germany and France have coddled them for too long. They no longer fear any repercussions for their fiscal mismanagement."

"So the sale of the ships to the Russians was about economics?" asked Julia.

"I think so," replied Sarge. "Also, appeasement. The French are tired of fighting our battles, not that they do much anyway. As for the *brokered peace* you referenced, it's a farce just like all of the other cease-fire accords reached the last few years. Every time a peace agreement is reached, Putin reloads and advances. This time is no different. Apparently, a deal has been reached allowing the Russians to bring 'aid supplies' along the northern coast of the Sea of Azov, effectively creating a much sought-after land bridge from Russia to the Crimean Peninsula.

"Putin is a nationalist and he's wildly popular in Russia right now. In fact, his popularity is widespread around the globe, except in Kiev and Washington, of course. And there's good reason for this. Putin is principled. Everyone knows what his goals are, namely the restoration of the Soviet Union."

"I get that," said Julia. "Standing on your principles is a rare trait these days. Why is this land bridge to Crimea so critical?"

"Strategic geopolitical decisions are rarely made based on a single factor. Putin is an incredible strategist on the world stage, unlike our present leadership. The United States has been outmaneuvered at every turn, and Putin's conquest of Crimea and eastern Ukraine is no exception. I believe initially, Putin thought he was *losing* Ukraine to NATO and the West. Perhaps Crimea, with its huge ethnic Russian population, was an easy and likely target to gain a foothold.

"Think about it. The actual acquisition was rapid, bloodless and highly effective because Russia already had boots on the ground, and the pro-Russian populace welcomed them with open arms. Geographically, Crimea is easy to defend. At first, Putin may have underestimated the effect of the Western-imposed sanctions, especially the Saudi's complicity in driving the price of oil way down. But in the end, it's all about money, and the price of oil returned to one hundred dollars a barrel."

"That didn't take long, did it?" added Julia.

"No, which brings us back to the original premise," said Sarge. "The premise that there is a peace accord in Ukraine is a joke. The pause in the conflict allowed Putin to regroup and advance his goals. In this case, he receives a land bridge to Crimea, which was one of his early military strategies. But more importantly, he now has direct access to the Black Sea via the port of Sevastopol, the traditional home of Russia's Black Sea fleet. Russian naval power in the Mediterranean will grow exponentially."

John-Angie politely interrupted to deliver their meals. They were attentive but unobtrusive, like any upscale servers should be. Sarge surveyed his Irish stew. Stephanie's self-described comfort food was very comfortable indeed. Julia seemed to be pleased as well because she dug into her salad. With food on their minds, they changed the subject, exchanging less serious talk about the world. Sarge melted into his surroundings, wishing with every smile and comment that he could have a real relationship with Julia. Before he realized it, John the server had deftly slipped the check onto their table in the customary American Express leather check presenter. Sarge stuffed it with twenties and sat back in his chair, noticing a group approach their table. He stood up to greet one of his students, Michelle Crepeau.

"Hi, Professor Sargent," said Crepeau. "I would like you to meet my parents. This is my daddy, Kenneth Crepeau, and my mom, Lou."

"Pleasure to meet you both," said Sarge, returning Mr. Crepeau's firm grip with a handshake.

He introduced Julia, and handshakes were exchanged. "Did you folks enjoy your dinner?"

"We did," said Kenneth Crepeau. "My Michelle has spoken very highly of you, Professor. It appears you have a real fan."

"Well, let's see how she feels after finals," said Sarge to a round of smiles and giggles from Miss Crepeau.

Sarge noticed Julia studying him.

"It was very nice to meet you both. I'm sure your daughter will do fine," said Sarge reassuringly.

Sarge settled back in his chair as the Crepeau family left, turning his attention back to Julia. *Death stare.*

"Is she one of yours?" asked Julia casually.

"One of my what? Students?" replied Sarge.

"You know," pressed Julia. *Oh boy.*

"No, I don't know," said Sarge. *Buy time. Hide the legs.*

"A groupie student chick. I saw how she looked at you—*Professor*," said Julia with her best schoolgirl voice.

Every fiber of his being screamed, *Run, Sarge, while you still can, before she breaks your legs.*

"Wait, what? No way. You don't get your nookie where you get your cookies," protested Sarge. *She isn't serious, right?*

"I'm just kidding you, Professor. Jeez, touchy. You can put your legs back in front of you now," said Julia, laughing. *It was over, fortunately.*

Pushing his chair back, Sarge helped Julia with her coat, and they walked toward the front door. Stephanie's had a long wait list at this point. The entry and the bar overflowed with groups waiting to be seated.

"Would you like to come up for a nightcap?" asked Sarge, as politely as he could muster.

Julia locked her arm in his and leaned against him, reminding Sarge of what he had been missing.

"I'll take that as a yes," said Sarge, as the couple strode out into the cold night air.

CHAPTER 8

December 16, 2015
Mariupol, Ukraine

Nomad lay shivering on the rusted steel decking of the northernmost blast furnace tower in the thirteen-hundred-acre Azovstal Iron and Steel Works facility. Rising more than one hundred feet over the industrial site, the multileveled access tower gave him a commanding view of the bridge over the Kalmius River, along with the span of Highway M14 running parallel to the steelworks. He felt exposed and trapped in the tower, but the terrain south of the river didn't give him many choices for a less conspicuous observation post. He was getting paid a lot of money to ensure this operation met Colonel Biletsky's expectations, and the view from the furnace stack gave him the situational awareness required to pull off a two-pronged attack.

"Here they come," said Nomad, tapping Anton Teresenko, Biletsky's subcommander, on the arm.

"Right on time for once," said Teresenko in broken English, raising his binoculars to examine the approaching armor column.

The two of them, along with three snipers from Azov Battalion, had climbed the towers in the middle of the night, concealing themselves in various locations among the steel girders before dawn. Nomad and Teresenko occupied the highest platform while the snipers nested one level below—scanning three hundred and sixty degrees for Russian or loyalist patrols. So far, all of the civilian ground activity in and around Mariupol had been restricted to the far side of the bridge, closest to the city's central square. Few traveled outside of the heavily populated areas, for good reason.

The loyalist-backed government in Mariupol was still leery of the cease-fire, which resulted in the unconditional withdrawal of Colonel Biletsky's ultranationalist Azov Battalion. Despite multiple confirmed media reports and sightings of the battalion driving in Odessa, more than three hundred miles away, memories of Biletsky's brutal siege of the city remained fresh in pro-Russian memories. The smart citizens stayed close to the seat of loyalist power near the city center. The wisest had left long ago. After today, anyone with a speck of common sense would abandon the strategically located city.

"Can you estimate the lead vehicle's speed?" asked Nomad.

"Thirty kilometers per hour—very rough estimate. They're moving at a normal road speed for armored vehicles," said Teresenko.

"Any heavies?" asked

"Not yet. I'm seeing a long line of BTR-82s. No tracked vehicles," said Teresenko.

"They'd tear these crappy roads to pieces. Tracks and asphalt don't mix. The T-90s and BMP-3s are probably sitting on railway cars inside Russia, waiting for the green light. This is a publicity run, just like my intelligence sources predicted," said Nomad.

"Let's hope your sources are right. The unexpected arrival of a tank platoon would spell disaster for the battalion," said Teresenko, lowering his binoculars.

"Don't worry, my friend. These sources have never been wrong," said Nomad, grabbing his encrypted satellite phone. "I'm going to start the sequence. There's no going back from here."

"There was no going back for any of us once the battalion abandoned Mariupol," said Teresenko, moving one of his hands to activate his headset.

"Biletsky will get exactly what I promised, and Mariupol will be back in Ukrainian hands by nightfall," said Nomad.

Teresenko stared at him for moment, absorbing his words before issuing several orders through his headset. Nomad pressed one of the saved numbers on his satellite phone, immediately connecting with a drone operator located somewhere in western Ukraine. High above, in the partially cloudy sky, a "company" co-opted MQ-9 Reaper watched over the bridge, ready to execute a highly unconventional mission.

"Skyfall, this is Nomad. We're launching the barge. The show is yours," said the mercenary, nodding enthusiastically at Teresenko.

"Copy that. Waiting for cast off," said the voice on his phone.

Teresenko gave him a thumbs-up and whispered, "The barge is clear of the dock."

"The barge is underway, Skyfall. Once your mission is complete, request a five-minute surveillance run east of Mariupol. I'd like to know what the Russians have in reserve," said Nomad.

"Understood. Skyfall will proceed accordingly before returning to base. Preliminary electronic intercepts and predawn thermals support original intelligence estimates. First Battalion, 35th Separate Motorized Rifle Brigade is travelling ahead of the brigade to secure Mariupol. The closest ground response will come from 2nd battalion—fifty plus kilometers away at the Ukrainian-Russian border," said the drone operator.

"Air assets?" asked Nomad.

"Nothing detected. The land bridge deal didn't include airspace concessions, but the Russians are free to operate in the Black Sea. We'll let you know if the situation changes."

"Fair enough. I'll let you concentrate on driving the barge. Looks like she's responding," said Nomad.

"We have positive control of the barge. You'll get your fireworks," said the operator, disconnecting the call.

"Everything is on track," said Nomad, pointing toward the two lane concrete span.

Teresenko crawled behind him to get a better view.

"Keep an eye on the Russians for me."

"There's nowhere to go on that road," said Nomad.

"Until there's somewhere else to go," said Teresenko.

"Point taken," replied Nomad, shifting his binoculars to the approaching vehicles.

Russian soldiers protruded from the top and side hatches of the

BTR-82s lining the M14 highway, preparing for a warm reception from the pro-loyalist factions lining the downtown streets on the other side of the Kalmius River. Instead of AK-74s, they carried short poles featuring the white, blue and red striped Russian Federation flag, ready to wave in celebration of the historic event. Ukraine's withdrawal from the areas surrounding Mariupol tacitly approved the formation of a "land bridge" between the Russian-Ukrainian border and the pro-Russian Crimean Peninsula.

"How are we doing over there?" asked Nomad.

"The barge is moving swiftly upriver. Are you sure it can fit under the smaller bridge?" asked Teresenko.

"People a lot smarter than either of us did the math. The flat-deck barge will clear the smaller bridge by three feet at high tide. They should have five feet of clearance right now," said Nomad.

"I'm more concerned with side-to-side clearance. The bridge supports are tightly spaced," said Teresenko.

"The drone will be directly overhead for this. They have it under control," said Nomad.

"I hope so," said Teresenko.

Nomad mentally added *for your sake* to Teresenko's comment. He held no illusions about the price of failure on this mission. Teresenko and the three snipers stood one radio command away from trying to kill him. For all Nomad knew, the order had already been issued. He was ready at a moment's notice to fight his way out of here. Separate transportation had been arranged in the event of a double cross, and Skyfall carried two Hellfire missiles as an insurance policy.

His satellite radio LED screen displayed a text message. *30 seconds TOT.*

"Thirty seconds until the lead Russian vehicle reaches the bridge. Get your people set," said Nomad.

Teresenko warned the various commanders scattered among the buildings lining the northern and eastern edges of the Azovstal facility. From their concealed positions in the structures, they would launch a coordinated attack against the Russians travelling the M14 highway. Most importantly, a small team of Azov Battalion commandos would detonate an explosives-packed train car positioned underneath the M14 overpass at the very northeast corner of the industrial compound. The destruction of the overpass would effectively trap the vehicles traversing the three-kilometer stretch of highway running parallel to the steelworks factory and prevent reinforcements from directly supporting their beleaguered comrades.

"Fifteen seconds," said Nomad, watching the lead vehicle pass due north of their tower.

The sound of automatic small-arms fire broke Nomad's concentration on the barge passing under the smaller of the two side-by-side bridges crossing the Kalmius River. On the far side of the bridge, men dressed in loyalist paramilitary garb fired at the barge as it vanished under the bridge. They quickly scrambled to the other side, emptying their magazines into the metal beast lumbering through the water. The bullets had no effect on the steel contraption, sparking and ricocheting into the water and concrete bridge struts. A nearby rifle report competed with the automatic fire, one of the snipers attempting a fifteen-hundred-foot shot from the platform below him. Nomad focused on the group of loyalists, catching the bullet's impact. One of the militia dropped into the river, disappearing behind the unmovable barge. Nomad held his breath as the rest of the barge emerged, headed straight for the second bridge less than a hundred feet upriver.

They needed the smaller, local-traffic bridge to remain intact for Biletsky's triumphant return to Mariupol. Reports of the battalion's withdrawal to Odessa had been accurate in all aspects but one. Soon after the battalion's arrival in the port city, a dozen Ukrainian-built BTR-94 armored vehicles had been secretly loaded onto a merchant vessel destined to return to Mariupol. Offloaded under the cover of darkness at the Azovstal Iron and Steel Works shipping terminal, they joined Billetsky's recently arrived shock troops.

Four hundred ultranationalist militia soldiers, backed by armored personnel carriers, stood poised to retake Mariupol. Only one thing stood in their way—an unsuspecting Russian battalion. Another militia soldier dropped from sniper fire as the top of the lead Russian vehicle came into view at the bottom of his binoculars' field of vision.

"Lead vehicle has crossed the eastern edge of the bridge," said Nomad, squinting in anticipation of the blast.

The first BTR-82, a long, eight-wheeled armored vehicle, continued one-third of the way across a flat bridge before stopping, the vehicle commander's attention obviously drawn to the loyalist militia running toward his column from the western side. The barge passed under the center span as a military-style jeep screeched to a stop along the riverbank between the two bridges, its gunner firing a roof-mounted heavy machine gun toward the water.

"Blow the bridge already," whispered Nomad, watching the vehicle commander duck into the vehicle and close the hatch next to the driver's station.

"What's happening?" asked Teresenko, his voice rising. "Why isn't that bridge gone?"

Before he could answer, the view through his binoculars disappeared, followed by a shockwave that rattled the platform.

"Stay down," said Nomad, pressing his body flat against the grated steel under him.

A few seconds later, projectiles peppered the tower, sounding a cacophony of dissimilar metallic impacts. When the last of the zinging sounds whipped past them, Nomad risked a look at the bridge. Large pieces of metal and concrete rained down on both banks of the river, shredding trees and light fixtures lining the roads connected to the bridge. A geyser of water came down with it, obscuring most of his view of the span, but there was little doubt that the bridge was gone—along with four BTR-82s. A quick glance confirmed that the second bridge remained intact, though he had no intention of testing its structural integrity himself.

A series of smaller explosions drew his attention north, toward the rest of the Russian armor column. Without the help of binoculars, he saw at least three vehicles tumbling through the air, victims of powerful improvised explosive devices (IEDs) planted last night by Biletsky's soldiers. To the distant north, a rising column of smoke signified the likely destruction of the railway overpass. The bulk of 1st Battalion, 35th Separate Motorized Rifle Brigade was trapped on an exposed section of the M14 highway, sandwiched between Biletsky's forces and the Kalmius River.

A fierce gun battle erupted on the near side of the destroyed bridge as Azov Battalion vehicles engaged the confused Russians with their BTR-94s' twin 23mm cannons, ripping through the thin turret and hull armor. A volley of smoke trails left the buildings below, thrusting rocket-propelled grenades toward the surviving BTR-80s, punching holes through the scrambling vehicles. Another series of explosions rocked the main stretch of highway beyond them, catapulting more vehicles into the air.

"The ground attack is underway," said Teresenko.

Now for the moment of truth, Nomad thought to himself as he contemplated whether the mission was a success in the eyes of his employers.

"Time for me to say goodbye," said Nomad. "I have a plane to catch out of Volgograd International."

"I don't think you're going to have any luck crossing the Russian border, my friend. Not after this," said Teresenko.

"Who said anything about a road?" asked Nomad, nodding at the wide channel next to the mouth of the Kalmius River.

The white plume of a fast-moving boat entered the channel, which abutted a series of massive piers used to supply the blast furnaces with raw materials directly from shipping vessels.

"Sneaky devil. Good luck to you, *Amerykans'kyy*," said Teresenko.

"*Amerykans'kyy?* I didn't see any Americans here," said Nomad, as the tempo of fighting rose to a crescendo along the highway.

CHAPTER 9

December 16, 2015
Mariupol, Ukraine

A sharp pain creased Lieutenant Miroslav Lazarev's right arm, causing him to reflexively drop the wooden flagpole he'd held propped against the vehicle's hull. The blood-spackled flag momentarily draped across the open hatch in front of him before it slipped down the side of the BTR-82's armor, pulled to the pavement by the weight of the pole. The sound of distant small-arms fire reached him, jerking his attention to the bridge. A snap passed in front of his face, barely drawing his attention away from the mayhem unfolding more than a kilometer away.

A massive concussion rippled through the vehicles in front of him, immediately knocking him against the BTR's remote-controlled turret. The armored personnel carrier screeched to a halt on the road, flinging him forward against the lip of the metal hatch. The lieutenant's body-armor kit absorbed most of the impact against his chest, dropping him into the vehicle as metallic chunks pinged off the frontal armor.

"You're hit, sir," said the driver, leaning over to pull the lieutenant's hatch shut.

Lazarev touched the bloodied rip in his camouflage-patterned, heavy-weather jacket.

"I'm fine," he muttered, listening to the discordance of panicked voices squawking on the company command frequency.

"None of this makes any sense," said Lazarev, straightening his helmet before peering through the small ballistic-glass windshield.

Pieces of the bridge fell in the river, chasing a wall of water that raced up the Kalmius, swamping the tree-lined field between the riverbank and the highway. *That was a big blast.* Ukrainian attack aircraft? The battalion's arrival in Mariupol was supposed to be unopposed.

"Shut your blast screen, sir," said the driver, pulling a latch that slammed a heavy metal shutter down over the ballistic glass in front of the driver's seat.

Without thinking, Lazarev did the same, catapulting the front compartment into darkness. He pulled the rotating viewport down and leaned into the binocular-style eyepiece, hoping to make some sense of the bridge's destruction. With the cold metal pressed against his cheekbones, he searched for signs of the bridge, finding nothing but jagged concrete and twisted metal where M14 once crossed the river.

"I hope we didn't have any vehicles on the bridge. It's gone," said Lazarev, not sure if the battalion commander had reached the first span when the explosion occurred.

"What's gone?" asked the driver, hunched forward to peer through the semicircle of fixed viewports.

"The bridge!" said Lazarev, twisting in his seat to switch the radio to the battalion command frequency.

Confusion reigned on the battalion net, with multiple stations trying to contact the battalion commander. Lazarev raised his handset and gave it a try.

"Liberator, this is Liberator Three One. Over." *No response.*

He wasn't sure if his request had transmitted over the net. Too many voices competed over the single frequency.

"Everyone has lost it—and we have zero situational awareness," said Lazarev, kneeling on his seat and raising the commander's hatch.

"That's not a good idea, sir!" protested the driver.

Lazarev raised his helmet-protected head far enough to see beyond the lip of the hatch.

"There's nothing going on out—"

The BTR-80 directly ahead of them disappeared in a blast of dirt, smoke and asphalt—emerging moments later in a midair spiral toward the riverbank. Dust and fragments pelted the front of Lazarev's vehicle as the young lieutenant dropped into his seat.

"Get us out of here!" screamed Lazarev.

The vehicle lurched forward and turned left, stopping a few seconds later.

"We don't have anywhere to go!" yelled his driver.

"Hold on!" said Lazarev, poking his head through the hatch against his better judgment.

Bullets ricocheted off the turret and hull of his vehicle while he scanned the road ahead. Several vehicles lay shattered on both sides of the road, their hulls pouring thick black smoke. To his left, Lazarev spotted muzzle flashes in the upper floors of the rusty, four-story industrial buildings.

"Gunner!" he screamed into the hatch. "Targets bearing left. Upper levels of the buildings. Engage!"

As the turret traversed to find the targets in the buildings, two smoke trails launched from the ground floor of the building closest to the bridge, arcing skyward after clearing the windows. For a brief moment, the lieutenant didn't understand what he'd witnessed, until the missiles reached the zenith of their flight paths a few hundred feet above the buildings—and dove into the vehicles on the highway. Only one type of guided antitank missile on the world market conducted a top-down attack—the FGM-148 Javelin, an American missile.

Consecutive explosions gutted two BTRs a quarter of a kilometer down the road, showering the highway with smoking metal debris and burning fuel. Several smoke trails appeared simultaneously from the buildings running parallel to M14, leaping skyward to gain altitude. Any one of the missiles could be targeting his vehicle's infrared signature. Once again, his training kicked in. He pressed the transmit button for the intravehicle communications net linked to his helmet.

"Smoke screen! Smoke screen! Missiles inbound," he said, keeping his eyes fixed on the arcing Javelins.

Just above his head, the turret's three starboard-side 81mm smoke grenade launchers fired a spread of grenades that exploded in midair twenty meters from the vehicle. Combined with the three grenades fired from the other side of the turret, they created an instantaneous, infrared-opaque smoke screen that rapidly drifted over the vehicle. As the noxious cloud enveloped him, the Javelins reached their targets—Liberator Three One was not one of them.

The turret's 30mm gun fired a short salvo through the thinning smoke, its high-explosive rounds tearing chunks out of the concrete next to one of the windows used to launch the missiles. Lazarev wasn't sure what to do next. The grenades fired by the "Tucha" 902V system generated a chemical cloud capable of obscuring the infrared seeker used by the Javelin missile—but the smoke would clear his vehicle in several seconds.

"Turn hard right and get us into the trees next to the river. We're going back the way we came," he said, feeling the fifteen-ton vehicle respond.

"We're too heavy for the riverbank!" said the driver.

"This thing is amphibious! Just get me into the trees. We'll run parallel to the highway with a little natural cover," said Lazarev, bracing himself as the vehicle trampled the guardrail.

Tracers and rocket-propelled grenades followed them into the sparse row of trees, exploding branches and kicking up the grayish-brown river water beyond the eastern bank. The 30mm turret continued to fire during the maneuver, the remote gunner seated behind him doing his best to keep the gun engaged against targets of opportunity. When they reached the trees, the vehicle turned sharply northeast, putting the thinly spaced tree trunks between the incoming fire and their half-inch-thick armor.

Smoke screens floated off the highway, passing through the trees ahead of them, as more of the battalion's vehicle commanders came to their senses. A quick glance at the road revealed five burning vehicles in his company of twelve, including the company commander's vehicle, which had been flung into the air like a toy right in front of him. Before he finished the mental count, a retreating BTR exploded in flames; its rear wheels lifted several feet off the ground before bouncing against the frozen dirt next to the highway.

"Enemy vehicles crossing the rail yard, bearing two o'clock. Engaging," said the gunner through his headset.

"How many vehicles?" asked Lazarev, peering through the smoke.

"Two Ukrainian 94s. Where the did they come from?" asked the gunner.

Lazarev didn't have an answer for the sergeant. They had been assured safe passage by the Ukrainian government and the psychotic ultranationalists operating in the region. Obviously the cease-fire was a load of crap.

The 30mm automatic cannon fired as they navigated the trees, its outbound projectiles shredding the barren trunks in a desperate attempt to reach the approaching BTR-94s first. Despite the fact that the 30mm cannon packed a more effective punch than the BTR-94s' twin 23mm cannons, caliber effectiveness played little role at this range. Both calibers would tear right through each other's thin armor, and the twin 23mm cannons could fire twice as many projectiles in the same time as Lazarev's gun. Sergeant Bilikov's skill as a gunner would decide their immediate fate.

Lazarev spotted the first Ukrainian vehicle as one of Bilikov's salvos connected with its turret. Sparks and metal pieces erupted, followed by a premature detonation of a turret-mounted smoke grenade. *Mission kill. One more to go.*

Multiple supersonic cracks passed overhead, forcing Lazarev to duck inside the vehicle. He turned in his seat to address the gunner when jagged holes punctured the far right side of the vehicle's hull—shearing limbs and exploding body-armor-encased torsos. Blood sprayed the tight compartment, covering the hull with a thick layer of crimson gore. A second burst of 23mm projectiles struck just behind the gunner's station, dismembering a young soldier firing his AK-74 through the forwardmost gun port. A few explosive rounds struck the turret's hydraulic mechanism, adding a fine mist of hydraulic fluid to the panicked interior.

Lazarev pulled the shell-shocked gunner forward, anticipating another burst of 23mm cannon fire from the Ukrainians. The vehicle jolted and swerved for a few seconds, without taking more hits. Frantic moans filled the armored personnel carrier as the wounded survivors recovered from the initial shock of the attack. There was nothing he could do for them right now, besides get Liberator Three One to safety. He pushed the gunner back into his seat and squeezed next to him.

"Is the turret down?" asked Lazarev.

The gunner gripped the controls and checked the digital targeting display, which appeared undamaged. When he tried to move the turret with the thumb switch, the hydraulic spray intensified, and the turret gears failed to turn.

"Down hard, sir!" said the gunner.

"Crap!" said Lazarev, returning to the commander's seat. *They were out of the fight.*

He stuck his head out of the hatch and scanned for the Ukrainian BTR, finding it in flames on the highway between two of the battalion's burning vehicles. Someone had saved them. *But who?* He didn't see many surviving Russian BTRs. A quick count through the trees accounted for ten of his company's vehicles; all destroyed. He needed to get them out of here. They were easy targets, even in the trees. He quickly assessed his options, coming to a grim realization. They had one option left, and it wasn't a good one.

"Hard left. We're crossing the river," said Lazarev, pulling his hatch shut.

"What? We're full of holes, sir?" asked the driver.

Lazarev twisted the small wheel above his head, tightening the hatch's seal.

"Just do it," said Lazarev, pressing the transmit switch. "Button up! We're going into the water!"

Bodies scrambled behind him, preparing the BTR for an unsure venture into the freezing waters of the Kalmius River. Lazarev examined the compartment, noting the location of the holes. Most of them would take water since the BTR rode extremely low in the water. All he could do was hope they didn't take on enough water to capsize.

"Submerging!" said the driver, moments before Lazarev was thrown against the metal dashboard.

He felt a sudden drop when the BTR sank below the surface of the Kalmius. A bobbing motion quickly replaced the sensation as the vehicle settled on the surface and the rear-mounted propellers pushed them forward through the water. He said a small prayer for the engine, hoping that it didn't choke on the backflow of water entering the topside exhaust vents.

"We're leaking!" screamed one of the soldiers behind him.

Lazarev took a quick look, grimly noting several steady streams of water shooting across the compartment.

"Sergeant, get back there and help them jam something in the holes. Anything!" he said, turning to the driver. "How fast are we going?"

"Eight kilometers per hour. I think we're fighting the current," said the driver.

The soldier was probably right. In addition to the bobbing motion, he felt the vehicle yaw left and right as the water rushed by. He didn't remember if the river was ebbing or flowing, but he hoped it was flooding. He didn't want to be pushed anywhere near the demolished bridge.

Lazarev opened his hatch and checked on their progress. The vehicle drifted upriver, which meant it was a flood tide. Good news, even though it could take them more than a minute to ford the two-hundred-foot distance between riverbanks. Assuming they didn't sink.

He lifted himself out of the vehicle, taking a seat on the hatch's lip. From his vantage point, he searched the trees for surviving BTRs. A smoke trail caught his attention, flying erratically over the barren trees and slamming into the water less than five meters from the left side of the vehicle. A cold spray blanketed the front of the BTR, dousing him with freezing water. Someone had fired one of the Javelins in direct-attack mode, which meant they couldn't lock onto the vehicle's mostly submerged infrared signature.

Unguided rocket munitions poured out of the tree line, skipping off the water or detonating harmlessly under the surface. Lazarev checked again for Russian vehicles before shutting the hatch and sealing it. The river's waterline had risen significantly against the BTR's armor in the short period of time he'd been topside. He pushed the latch to open the front windshield's blast screen, noting that a thin line of water covered the very bottom of the window. His driver glanced through the window, sharing a doubtful look.

"It's going to be close," said Lazarev.

"And wet," added the driver. "Very wet."

"Let's hope not," said the lieutenant.

They looked into the rear compartment at the same time, and Lazarev grimaced. Six inches of water sloshed around on the metal deck.

"Get us to the other side. I don't care if we lodge into the side like a torpedo. Tell me when the water is over the windshield," said Lazarev.

"Yes, sir," said his driver.

Lazarev planned to open at least one of the top hatches when the water climbed over the window, hoping to expedite the full flooding of the compartment. The concept went against all conventional logic, but the BTR's hull was airtight when it wasn't full of 23mm holes. Submerged with the hatches sealed, they wouldn't be able to force the hatches open until water from the holes filled the compartment, equalizing the pressure. By that time, they'd be at the bottom of the Kalmius. He needed to get them as close as possible to the opposite side of the river before abandoning the BTR.

He spent the next thirty seconds helping his soldiers plug the holes with wooden plugs supplied from the vehicle's flooding kit. They sliced their hands on the jagged holes, struggling futilely to block the relentless flow of frigid water. Crouching in the rising bloodstained pool, Lazarev floated a headless body toward the front of the vehicle.

"Lieutenant, the water's over the window!" said his driver.

He nodded at the driver before turning to the infantry sergeant next to him.

"Tell your men to remove their body armor and helmets. We might have to swim ashore," said Lazarev.

The sergeant stared at him for a second before barking orders. Within moments, the five surviving soldiers started to rip the Velcro latches securing their body armor. Lazarev opened the centermost hatch, peering outside. They were less than sixty feet from the western bank, drifting rapidly upriver. He felt hopeful until he saw a thin film of water break over the top of the hull. *We aren't going to make it.* They'd submerge too far from the river's edge.

"Sergeant, get your men topside! We'll ride this thing as far as it takes us, then swim the rest of the way," he said, wading through the water to get to his driver.

"Dmitry," said Lazarev, "open your hatch and gun the engine for the western shore. We're going topside. I'll pull you up when it's time to jump."

"No. I can't swim," said the driver.

"Dmitry, I'll two you to shore. Point this tub west and gun it. I'll be right back," said Lazarev, returning to the rear compartment area.

After he pushed the last soldier through the hatch, he scanned the interior for any wounded soldiers that could be moved—finding nothing but partially submerged bodies. Water poured over his head, warning him that it was time to go. Lazarev squeezed through the hatch as a one-foot wave of water washed over the BTR. The muddy water rushed through the opening, creating a hissing vortex of water over the hatch.

He climbed over the turret, splashing to the deck next to the driver's hatch. Already submerged below the waterline, water poured violently through the oval hole, obscuring the driver's head. Lazarev dropped to his knees and reached both hands into the vehicle, grabbing his driver by his tactical vest. Coughing and spitting, Corporal Dmitry Kaparov surfaced from the whirlpool, squinting in the bright light. The lieutenant quickly removed Kaparov's tactical vest, discarding the heavy body armor over the side of the vehicle. By the time he finished, the water tugged at their thighs, as the driverless vehicle lost its direction and turned with the current. *Time to go.*

When Lazarev hit the water, clutching his driver, the cold knocked his breath away like a gut punch. He submerged two feet below the surface, momentarily wondering if it was worth the effort to kick for the surface. The excruciating cold squeezed his exposed head and hands in a painful embrace, adding to the hesitation. Kaparov's muffled underwater screams brought him back from the dead, and he started frog kicking. He broke the surface seconds later, taking a frozen breath before pulling for the shore. The sinking BTR scraped against them, headed wherever the tidal flow commanded it. Lazarev and his men were at the mercy of the river—and his weakening limbs.

Lazarev's feet scraped the riverbed after a momentous fight to keep Kaparov from drowning. Several times during the thirty-foot swim, he considered releasing him to the Kalmius River. Each time he cursed himself for the thought and pulled harder. When his feet found solid purchase under the water, he lurched toward the brown shoreline, dragging Kaparov until he could stand in the river. A quick count of his men confirmed that everyone had made it ashore. *Six soldiers, including him. Five swallowed by the river.*

On shore, a few of the soldiers gasped for air, shaking uncontrollably from the swim in the icy water.

"Keep moving," uttered Lazarev. "They can still range us."

The soldiers, on the verge of hypothermia, hesitated for a few seconds—until bullets started to kick up dirt and water along the shoreline. The disheveled and exhausted group clumsily shuffled into the nearby tree line, lying flat behind thick tree trunks. Lazarev examined the far side of the river, disgusted by what he saw. A Ukrainian armored personnel carrier, trailed by militia fighters, drove up to a squad of Russians huddled near the riverbank—firing point blank into them with its 23mm cannons. Similar atrocities occurred up and down the eastern shore, as the last of the surviving Russians were corralled and murdered while trying to surrender.

Lieutenant Lazarev's anger grew until he started muttering. He had no idea what he was saying until Kaparov patted him on the shoulder.

"Don't worry, Lieutenant. Division will turn this whole place into a smoldering ruin by tomorrow."

"I hope so, Kaparov. I truly hope so," said Lazarev. "These Ukrainians can't be trusted. I hope Division destroys the whole place."

PART TWO

CHAPTER 10

January 5, 2016
100 Beacon Street
Boston, Massachusetts

Sarge stretched his chest on the way out of the bedroom, leaning into the doorway while grasping the doorframe with both arms. He'd pushed it a little too hard at the gym, but physical conditioning was important to him, and he never felt satisfied without adding more to each workout. He glanced through the spacious windows running the length of his residence, catching a glimpse of the snow-covered Charles River. The sidewalks lining Storrow Drive looked equally blanketed by the latest blizzard's fury. *Running is not an option today. I have enough on my plate anyway.*

Satisfied with his assessment of the outside conditions, Sarge visited his favorite coffee shop, the Keurig K-cup machine, for a freshly brewed Gevalia mocha latte. Sipping the frothy goodness, he turned to survey his loft. The apartment measured nearly 4,000 square feet, divided into two bedrooms, two and a half baths, his study and a 2,400-square-foot great room dubbed "The *Great Hall* Overlooking the River Charles." Sarge's residence on the top floor of the prestigious 100 Beacon address was opulent, one of the perks that came with the position of power and leadership bestowed upon him by his benefactors.

As part of his daily routine, Sarge closely monitored the news. Getting a true picture of world events required monitoring several news networks at once. Each mainstream media source had an agenda, delivering tailored news content to those who patronized their advertisers, leaving bits and pieces of the real story to be reassembled. Sarge picked up his tablet and opened the uRule app. Centered in the room was a two-story, fourteen-foot-wide fireplace surrounded by six wall-mounted televisions—a decorator's nightmare.

One by one, Sarge powered up the fifty-five-inch LG flat-screens, featuring talking heads from CNN, Bloomberg, FoxNews, BBC, CNBC and Al Jazeera. MSNBC used to be included in this group, until its format was changed to all sports following the consistent decline in its news ratings. Sarge was fascinated at what news stories took precedent across the political spectrum of the various networks. FoxNews might spend a considerable amount of time on the latest administration scandal, which was barely mentioned on the other five networks. CNN might cover the latest scandal of a congressman with his hands caught in the cookie jar, but the story was barely given a mention on FoxNews because it involved a Republican. The news Sarge received from BBC and Al Jazeera always piqued his interest, because these networks focused on other parts of the world.

He smiled. In the news business, there was an old saying—*if it bleeds, it leads.* At least they still had one thing in common, he mused. Images from Ukraine continued to dominate the twenty-four-hour news cycle. Sarge unmuted the BBC television to listen to *News at One* anchor Matthew Amroliwala report the latest from the war-torn region.

"*Fighting has intensified today between pro-Russian rebels and Ukrainian government forces in the strategic town of Volnovakha in Donetsk Oblast. This small town of twenty-four thousand is of particular significance because it serves as the capital of the Volnovakha District of Donetsk Oblast, and is a key transportation hub. If the pro-Russian separatists take control of the area, the town of Mariupol to the south will be cut off from Ukrainian reinforcements deploying out of Donetsk. The Russian stronghold in the east of Ukraine will be too much for the Ukrainian government to overcome, and Russian forces will advance unimpeded to their ultimate goal of the Crimean Peninsula.*"

Images of elderly Ukrainian civilians wandering through the streets of Volnovakha flashed across the screen, followed by a

Reuters-supplied video of pro-Russian rebels launching short-range surface-to-air missiles from their 9K35 vehicle launch system. Jane Hill, Amroliwala's co-anchor, broke in with a question.

"Matthew, what prompted the flare-up in Ukraine after a negotiated cease-fire had been reached such a short time ago? It appears hostilities have been taken to a new level," said Hill.

"Jane, eastern Ukraine has returned to a full-scale conflict, and now the façade of Russia's lack of state-sponsored intervention is completely removed. Ukraine and the separatists agreed upon a cease-fire, the latest of many, but it never held entirely. Both sides used the lull to rebuild and resupply their forces.

"During the weeks following the cease-fire agreement, President Putin worked behind the scenes to secure a land route from Russia to Crimea. NATO and its members seemed to acquiesce to the route, allowing humanitarian aid to the Crimean people," said Amroliwala.

The BBC then flashed images of the destroyed bridge crossing the Kalmius River and numerous Russian BTR-82 armored personnel carriers smoldering along Highway M14 leading into Mariupol. Hill reported on the imagery.

"Matthew, for the benefit of our viewers, we are providing images of the destruction wrought upon the Russian battalion on December 16 as they entered Mariupol. This attack caught the Russian Army off guard, to be sure," said Hill.

"It certainly did. The Russian battalion came under an unexpected, seemingly unprovoked attack by Ukrainian ultranationalists, who were clearly well-trained and armed with advanced weaponry. The Russian ambassador to the United Nations immediately cried foul and produced evidence that American-made Javelin missiles were an integral part of the attack. The ambassador further asserted the Ukrainian government conspired with the United States to deceive Russia, allowing for the ambush of their convoy of humanitarian aid to Crimea. As a result of these events in Mariupol, President Putin considers Russia to be formally at war with Ukraine. The question becomes—what will NATO do, if anything?" asked Amroliwala rhetorically.

Indeed. The United States and its NATO allies conceded the land bridge to Putin, as a form of appeasement, obviously under the impression that a permanent cease-fire might result. The surprise attack on the Russian forces in Mariupol made little sense to Sarge. It reeked of CIA, and his *employers*, involvement.

He turned his attention to all of the networks and hit the pause buttons. Al Jazeera proudly displayed another ISIS-related video. BBC conveyed images of the Ukraine war. Bloomberg and CNBC covered the continued sell-offs in the global equity markets—down fifteen percent in the last two weeks. CNN reported on its favorite topic—racial injustice in America and the Black Lives Matter movement. Finally, FoxNews covered, in depth, the trauma suffered by American children resulting from the new low-calorie school lunch programs. *My fellow Americans, do you realize how fragile our way of life really is?* Sarge, staring intently at his six wall-mounted televisions, took another sip of his latte. He pondered this question until the sound of his K-cup machine roaring to life once again snapped him back to reality.

"Good morning, sunshine," said Sarge, turning to the kitchen.

"Best ever!" replied Steven.

His brother, Steven, stood shirtless in front of the coffee maker, with his back to Sarge, waiting on a cup of his patented motor oil. Folger's dark roast, on the strongest setting—times two per cup. Simple, but effective. He couldn't help notice Steven's chiseled figure. The two brothers were similar in many ways, both staying in peak physical shape, but his brother took it to the next level. He didn't really have a choice. His life frequently depended on it. Sarge understood one day his might as well, but there was a difference between understanding and knowing. Steven's body differed from Sarge's in more than one way—it had seen battle. Toned, tanned and covered in scars, Steven had skirted death and endured torture time and time again, always emerging victorious. He once bragged his seven quarts of blood had been recycled several times. Sarge worried about his brother, but knew a life of complacency would be the death of him. The world was a dangerous place, and Steven was the guy Sarge always wanted by his side. Apparently, his brother was the guy everyone wanted by his side, which explained his string of "absences."

"So, I gather you enjoyed your belated Christmas gift?" asked Sarge.

His brother turned his head and smiled.

"Whoa! Be sure to thank Santa for me," exclaimed Steven.

On cue, a leggy blonde emerged from the guest room, wearing nothing but one of Steven's long-sleeve shirts. As she stood on her toes and reached around Steven's waist to give him a kiss, Sarge caught a glimpse of what she revealed underneath the shirt. *Whoa is right.*

"I need coffee," said another woman, a well-endowed brunette strolling out of Steven's lair, wearing nothing but a pair of boxers. The girls giggled as they tried to operate the Keurig.

"Where did you find these two frog hogs?" asked Steven, using the slang terminology for Navy SEAL groupies.

He took a sip of motor oil and admired his conquests.

"They are on retainer by our *friends*," replied Sarge, nodding toward the east and downtown Boston. "After your latest vacation, I thought you needed something to get the blood flowin'."

"No problem there, bro," said Steven proudly. "The blood and all of the other parts checked out just fine, but thank you very much for your concern."

Sarge turned his attention back to the girls—although they never really lost his attention. *I am such a boy.*

"Ladies, Steven and I have a busy day. Would you mind getting your coffee to go?" asked Sarge with a tone of dismissiveness.

Christmas morning was over. The girls whined in protest, offering to hang around quiet as mice, woefully underdressed mice.

"C'mon, Sarge, we'll be good. Let us hang with you guys today," said the leggy one. *Tempting, but no.*

"I'm sorry, ladies, but not today," said Sarge.

Maybe I should be led into temptation, as they say. I'm not married. But something always held Sarge back from partaking of women. *Was it his feelings for Julia?*

"Besides, I want to live to my fortieth birthday and somehow I feel you two could put me six feet under," said Sarge.

As the women returned to Steven's bedroom, he found his brother staring at the paused images on the television. Sarge waited until Steven's Christmas gifts had closed the door.

"So, is this your handiwork?" asked Sarge, pointing toward the media wall with his latte glass.

"Which one?" replied Steven.

"Really? Do you think I'm referring to the fat parents and their equally fat kids complaining about eating healthy foods in school?" asked Sarge.

"You know the drill, bro. I can neither admit nor deny my involvement in the blowing up of Russki military hardware," said Steven with a grin.

Sarge unpaused the televisions and the talking heads came back to life. He liked the still-life versions better. He often wondered what the world would be like if time stood still or, better yet, returned back a couple of hundred years to the nineteenth century. *Would we be better off?*

"Here's the thing," began Steven. "I follow orders. I'm really good at what I do. A soldier does not question his orders, he executes them. I'll leave it to smart guys like you to determine the best course of action on the political side."

Steven mussed Sarge's hair playfully. Sarge was the older brother, but Steven took on the role of protector. They were perfect complements to each other, and the chemistry they enjoyed would prove useful in the coming years. Steven would never question Sarge's plan, and Sarge would never question Steven's execution of it. The women returned a few minutes later and said their goodbyes. Steven escorted them to the elevator with a final round of kisses and butt squeezes. *Lucky hound dog.* He returned to the kitchen and fixed himself another double cup of full-strength coffee upon Sarge's request. They had more to discuss than the Ukraine.

CHAPTER 11

January 5, 2016
Antrim Street
Cambridge, Massachusetts

Professor Andrew Lau navigated his Subaru Forester into a cramped parking space on Antrim Street. As was his custom, he made a point to avoid parking near the house. In America, the residents of quiet neighborhoods seemed to hustle into their garages or front doors, with the sole intent of avoiding eye contact with their neighbors. The discreet community of Mid-Cambridge was no different. Lau had rented the house several months earlier, furnishing it with rudimentary, professorial decor. The house itself was unobtrusive—beige with scalloped lap siding, two story, white trim and a chain-link fence—perfectly suiting Professor Lau's needs.

The neighbors would have described him as quiet, introverted and somewhat of a recluse. They also knew him as a professor at MIT, but Cambridge was full of professors, so the title drew little attention. He drove a Subaru, but what good liberal didn't. Lau even dressed down, frequently seen in jeans, a Red Sox cap and his Koji Uehara Red Sox jersey. Uehara was Japanese and Lau was Korean, but his neighbors didn't know the difference, and that was exactly what Lau wanted.

Lau was a professor of computer science and engineering, and the associate director of the Microsystems Technology Laboratory at MIT. One of 750 students and staff who performed all types of research in electronic circuits and photonic devices, his team effectively created the technology that made corporate giants Xerox and IBM extremely wealthy. Lau was paid a salary commensurate with his position as a professor, but he was not paid for the results of his research, which was "generously" shared with some of the university's wealthiest benefactors—behemoth technology companies.

Pretending to check for mail that was never there, Lau unlocked the chain-link fence gate and nonchalantly strolled up the front steps of the house to the front door. Out of habit, he glanced quickly over his shoulder to scan for nosey neighbors that never appeared. Satisfied, he entered the cramped foyer. *Hi, honey, I'm home.*

The 1,800-square-foot home was typical for the neighborhood. Built in 1905, it was solidly constructed with twelve-inch walls, featuring hardwood floors and vaulted ceilings. To a visitor, the foyer looked like any other home on Antrim Street, as did the sitting room immediately to the left. A beautiful oak staircase wound its way upstairs to a second level, also concealing a cellar door. *Nothing to see here, typical home on a typical street, in a typical neighborhood, in the good old U.S. of A—land of opportunity.*

But if one listened carefully, blocking out all distractions, they might hear the sounds emanating from above—*click, click, click.* Professor Lau of the Massachusetts Institute of Technology was a professional hacker and this was his "hack house"—home of the Zero Day Gamers.

CHAPTER 12

January 5, 2016
100 Beacon Street
Boston, Massachusetts

"So what's the plan for today?" asked Steven. "Are we gonna work out? Go to the range? Chill here?"

"*The plan* is…I have a full schedule in class today, and you are on your own," replied Sarge.

He's such a man-child. Sarge explained today was the first day of classes, and he had after-class interviews with the students new to his lectures. It would be a full day at the school.

"Okay, that's cool. I'll drop you off at Harvard Kennedy, then I want to run up to Marblehead to check on the *Miss Behavin'*," said Steven. "She's been winterized, but I really want to check on her and grab a few things."

Sarge sensed he *really wanted* to drive his new G-Wagen around.

"Don't wreck my new car," scolded Sarge.

"Why would I do that?" asked Steven with faux innocence.

"You have a history of wrecking my cars. This is a *company car.* Don't bust it up. Do you wanna take the FJ instead?" asked Sarge, hoping Steven would take him up on the offer.

"It doesn't have heated seats. The G-Wagen will keep my ass warm," said Steven.

"Listen, in case you haven't noticed, there's a lot of hostility out there," said Sarge, gesturing toward the windows. "I've advised everyone to carry—including you, soldier."

In recent months, racial tensions had exploded across the country. The shooting of an unarmed black man in Ferguson, Missouri, in

2014, ignited protests and riots throughout the country. Almost a year ago, tensions escalated to new levels when two police officers were shot by a black gunman during a Ferguson protest. The undeclared war on law enforcement officers fueled the racial divide. America was on edge. The thin veneer of civilization was being threatened by political agendas and the corresponding frenzy associated with biased media reporting.

"You know that's not a problem for me," said Steven.

Sarge led him down the hallway, where he stopped one-third of the way down and pressed an unobtrusive wainscot panel below the chair rail. The hinged panel popped open, revealing several shelves. A puck light automatically illuminated the treasure inside.

"*There is a great big world out there for you, son,*" their father's words during "the talk" to his sons long ago rolled through Sarge's mind. "*Always wear protection.*"

Sarge doubted his beloved Heckler & Koch HK45C was what Pop had in mind, but his father had lived in a different world. Sarge placed his hand on the biometric safe to reveal its contents. Together with the .45-caliber compact, a well-worn Galcon double time holster and a 5.11 Tactical belt finished out the ensemble. Sarge had been issued a concealed-carry permit in Boston for many years. Massachusetts had been a "may issue" state for a long time, although "may" had become more like "sorry, screw you and your second amendment rights." Over the past few years, Sarge felt more and more comfortable carrying the pistol as his country edged closer to chaos. Carrying a firearm felt as natural as wearing pants in public. His peers at Harvard would probably faint at the thought of a weapon in their hallowed halls, not that he'd ever let them know. Firearms or weapons of any kind were strictly forbidden by university policy. He transferred the pistol to a secret compartment in his briefcase when he entered the campus—a gun-free and "safe" zone. *A new world indeed.*

He removed the 5.11 belt and converted the Galcon to its tuck-in-the-waistband mode. The cold leather shocked his skin, but the feel of the weapon warmed his heart. He stood out of the way to let

Steven make his selection. He chose the Glock G38 together with a paddle-style right-hand holster, tucking the combination in his jeans. No surprise there. Steven was also a .45 kind of guy. The brothers were protected.

"Are you sure you don't mind me crashing here until winter takes a hike?" asked Steven.

He'd stayed on the boat last winter and complained to Sarge incessantly about it. Having him at 100 Beacon would avoid the complaining, and allow them to hang out.

"Absolutely, but keep the wine, women and song to a minimum," said Sarge, knowing full well Steven's shore leave would be a challenge.

Sarge led them into his study to gather his briefcase and lecture notes.

"No prob, bro," replied Steven, likely unmindful of the point Sarge was making.

Sarge's study, the professorial equivalent of a home office, was his pride and joy. Despite being single and not having to succumb to the decorating whims of a significant other, he always felt the need to have his own space. A retreat within a retreat. The two floors below the penthouse, which he also occupied, did not count. They fell under the category *man cave.* The study was a special place. Bookshelves adorned the entirety of the west and north walls. Sarge, embracing his lineage, was compelled to collect old works. The authors dated back to the turn of the eighteenth century and included the names Hawthorne, Peabody, Minot and his namesake, Sargent. *This is history. History must be preserved.*

Sarge gathered the notes located on his pride and joy—a nineteenth-century partner's desk crafted from oak, with tooled leather inserts and decorated with brass appointments. The desk was a gift to Winthrop Sargent Gilman when he opened the banking house of Gilman, Son & Co. in New York City around 1900. It had been passed down through the years to his father, and then to Sarge. He was honored to be a lineal descendant of 250 years of American history. It had its perks and *great responsibilities.*

CHAPTER 13

January 5, 2016
The Hack House
Antrim Street
Cambridge, Massachusetts

Lau dropped his briefcase next to the oak foyer table and tossed his keys by the Tiffany lamp. *Home sweet home.* Pushing up the red sleeves under his jersey, he bounded up the stairs and opened the solid wood, double doors of the home's master bedroom turned hacker's heaven. The entire second floor of the Antrim Street house had been gutted and furnished with modular workstations, each housing a powerful computer and one of MIT's finest student hackers—the Zero Day Gamers.

"Good afternoon, class," said Lau sarcastically.

He was greeted with a few laughs, a couple of *good afternoons* and a paper wad that barely missed his head. The crew was handpicked by Lau and his graduate assistants, Anna Fakhri and Leonid Malvalaha, from the top computer coders and programmers at MIT. Lau was fluent in Korean. Fakhri spoke a variety of Arabic languages, and Malvalaha spoke fluent Russian. The three had unofficially worked together for more than a year, until last fall when they took their hacking enterprise to a new level. As with any business, in order to grow and prosper, you need more employees. There were now a dozen hackers rotating in and out of the Hack House daily.

Lau's *business plan* was relatively simple, unlike the strings of code typed on the screens in front of him. A zero-day threat is an attack on a computer operating system that uncovers a previously unknown vulnerability. Hackers conduct reconnaissance of the systems applications and look for openings known as vulnerability windows.

The Zero Day Gamers, like seasonal hunters, might spend days or weeks searching for their prey, without meeting success. But once a hacker discovered an initial compromise opportunity, the entire team looked for a foothold in the computer network. Once a foothold was established, a hacker team consisting of a coder and a programmer escalated privileges within the network until they reached an administrator's status or higher. Once in place, the hacker could navigate the entire system, making changes. Then the game began—the zero-day game.

The term *zero day* was used because the system programmer had zero days to fix the flaw. A patch for the vulnerability was not readily available. Over the past several years, an underground gray market had arisen, where a hacker contacted the system administrator and made them an offer they couldn't refuse—pay us to leave you alone, or we will sell our information about your vulnerabilities to the highest bidder. Buyers included Fortune 500 firms, foreign intelligence services, terrorists and even the United States government. Payment was non-negotiable, and the consequences of nonpayment were strictly enforced.

Lau looked up at the chalkboard on the back wall of the Hack House. The *end game*, the mission statement of the Zero Day Gamers, was succinct:

One man's gain is another man's loss; who gains and who loses is determined by who pays.

Lau applied the same philosophy to his employees. The Gamers were paid handsomely for their efforts—and to buy their silence. The students came to Zero Day Gamers for a number of reasons. Some needed the money and were trying to monetize the in-class research they conducted for others. Some participated for the thrill and feeling of compromising another's private world. Others simply enjoyed "sticking it to the man." There were similar operations to the Hack House all over the world. Underemployed techies looking for lucrative paydays and a chance to have their talents recognized among their peers. They were located in Russia, Eastern Europe, the Middle East, North Korea and especially China. Hunting for software holes was grueling drudgery, but it was the most lucrative security job available to them. Symantec or McAfee might start a new technology graduate at eighty thousand dollars. At the Hack House, an employee could make that in a day, if they played the right "zero-day game."

"I'm in!" exclaimed one of the Gamers, holding his hands high over his head.

Lau snapped to attention and turned his Red Sox cap backwards. *Game on!*

"Talk to me," said Lau.

"I've been pen testing these guys on and off for days. My gut told me there was an opening, so I kept trying," said Herm Walthaus, an MIT grad student.

Lau had not been particularly impressed with Walthaus thus far. His best hack was entering the Applebee's Restaurant servers. They were unable to secure any funding from Applebee's, and eventually settled for scrambling their computerized register system known as Squirrel. Within an hour of being denied payment, and finding no interested buyer for the vulnerability, Lau settled for changing all of their menu items to some form of nut. Applebee's Burgers became Walnut Burglars. Sizzlin' Fajitas became Spoiled Veruca, paying homage to Willy Wonka. The restaurant chain was forced to close their doors for days. The economic impact to the company was reportedly in the millions and hammered their stock on the NASDAQ. *They should have paid us something.*

Pen testing was just what it sounded like—a test to see whether you could penetrate a network. Pen tests had huge value when done correctly. Even if done incorrectly, pen testers enjoyed the thrill of the hunt. If thwarted, the hackers could disrupt a system using denial-of-service tools—DoS. These tools might simply fire off an attack on the system, causing internal reactions to seal network vulnerabilities, which resulted in the unintended consequence of destabilizing the entire network. At a minimum, a visitor to a website might receive a

"Page Cannot Be Displayed" error message. At worst, the entire network misfired, requiring a reboot and repairs of possible network damage.

"Okay, Walthaus, settle down," reassured Lau.

Walthaus was sweating, and his face was getting red from excitement. The extra weight crowding his waist didn't complement the scene. The last thing Lau needed was a heart attack victim at the Hack House. He calmly placed his hands on the young man's shoulders.

"Tell us what you have going on. Slowly," said Lau.

"Professor, I have breached the firewall of TickStub," said Walthaus.

Lau leaned over and surveyed the screen. It appeared TickStub utilized a Windows-based RRaS server—routing and remote access server. This was not uncommon. Windows servers were the most widely used, a piece of cake for a novice hacker. Walthaus was well beyond the RRaS firewall, having penetrated the TickStub ordering system. Step one, the initial compromise was complete; now Lau needed to evaluate what was exposed. Once he gained a foothold in the system, he could expand his perusal of the network later.

The screen read:

Welcome to the TickStub ordering system.
You must login to start.
Username:
Password:

The room was deathly quiet. All keyboard activity had ceased, and full attention was upon Walthaus and Lau. Lau stood upright and adjusted his cap.

"Listen up, everybody," said Lau. "As you know, we have a limited time frame now. Once we start this process, it's rock-and-roll, got it?"

A few *yes, sirs* were audible over the tension.

"I'm going to let Walthaus take the lead on this one. He's done a good job so far. But everyone will play a role in the next critical steps. I will be giving a lot of direction, and the requests will come to you fast. Pay attention, do your jobs and, above all, learn. This is a classroom, remember," said Lau.

His subtle joke eased the tension, and he could feel himself exhale a little.

"Malvalaha, I want you to coordinate the DDoS attacks on my *go*. Once we're in, we need to confuse the network to think they're receiving heavy volume," said Lau. "Use the Russian handlers, they'll get the blame. Sorry, Malvalaha."

"I don't care, I was born in Brooklyn," said Malvalaha with a shrug.

DDoS, or distributed denial of service attacks, were used to temporarily or indefinitely interrupt a web server's ability to connect to the Internet. The common method of attack saturated the target network with external communications requests to the point it could not respond to legitimate web traffic. The result was server overload and an excellent distraction while Lau conducted the rest of his "business." A DoS, denial of service, attack generally involved one attacker. In order to truly overload a system, the DDoS attack was preferable. Lau had established multiple servers throughout the world to act as *handlers*. The handlers were accessed remotely by the computer systems located in the Hack House. Each computer station controlled multiple handlers, and each handler controlled multiple compromised private computers. On Lau's signal, if necessary, the entire handler system would be activated to attack the targeted web server at TickStub.

"Fakhri, have your group on standby for research," said Lau. "As we begin to elevate our privileges, we may need to implement our password-cracker tools."

"On it," said Fakhri. "I'll have my guys searching the web to learn all we can about their IT people. We always find them on forums and techie blog sites. It doesn't take long to put two and two together."

"Here we go," said Lau. "First, now that we're past the firewall, we're going to bypass the web server and leave the domain alone.

Our first stop will be the database—the SQL server."

"Walthaus, initiate an SQL injection. Let's see how well their coding techniques are. Their DBMS, database management system, may reject the query, but it will return legitimate data in response."

Walthaus immediately began entering keystrokes and sat back in his chair to observe the results. Lau watched intently.

"Now, let's introduce some cross-site scripting to compromise the DBMS server. In the username field, enter *foo' OR 1=1;--* followed by admin in the password field," said Lau. The screen changed and now read:

Welcome to the TickStub ordering system foo' OR 1=1;--

"Excellent!" exclaimed Lau. "Now we can use an injection vulnerability to send commands to their back-end database server in order to elevate our privileges. This will allow the DBMS server to run commands for us. It's time for the next step."

Lau knew the web-based server controlling the domain and its web traffic was fully secure and had its necessary patches in place. Most IT departments placed all of their focus on the web server because it was utilized by the public via the Internet.

"Most likely the web server is secure. Why beat our heads against the wall trying to crack its code, when we can simply give ourselves administrative access by elevating our internal user privileges, right?" asked Lau, playing the role of professor.

"Let's pull out our toolbox and make our job easier, shall we?" asked Lau, clearly in his element. "Walthaus, upload Netcat to the DBMS server."

Walthaus dutifully complied.

"Now enter *Xp_cmdshell* into the command field and we'll see how complex their administrative system is," said Lau. Lau watched as the screen changed, providing him the c-prompt he anticipated.

"Okay, everyone, Netcat has enabled us to attain our first foothold, and we are well on our way to overtaking the network. We are no longer an anonymous user. We are now an insider," said Lau.

A few claps were heard from the team.

"Class, we need a name; who am I?" asked Lau.

"Whoami," said Walthaus. "You know like the old Abbott & Costello routine—'Who's on First?' Our username should be *whoami*."

Lau laughed heartily. It was perfect.

"Absolutely, Walthaus, whoami it is," said Lau. "Okay, Mr. Whoami, run an ipconfig on the system so we can determine the lay of the land. Let's see what our new system is made of."

Lau watched as the server IP addresses scrolled down the screen, including their internal Ethernet connections. He instructed Walthaus to screen-cap everything and print it for reference.

"We now have effectively taken over the web server. From what I can see here, we have complete connectivity between the web server and the SQL server, which gives us total control over the domain—TickStub.com.

"Before we go for the big prize, the database, let's pull another tool out of the toolbox. Dump a Trojan in the web server so we can come back in the front door in the event an administrator busts us and we have to run out the backdoor," said Lau.

The Trojan would install a credential manager, which allowed the creation of usernames and access privileges at the highest levels.

"Final step. Fakhri, how'd you do?" asked Lau.

She approached him with a printout of potential user names and passwords derived from their Internet search. Lau handed the same to Walthaus and gestured to give them a try.

"Bingo. I'm in the back-end data center, which contains all of the usernames, passwords and stored credit card information. I went ahead and tried this combo on the TickStub corporate server and succeeded there as well. We have full access to employee files, W-9s, retirement plans and health care records," said Walthaus.

Lau took a deep breath and looked around the room. He could feel what they were thinking—big potential payday. He studied the wall for a moment, once again reciting the words in his mind:

One man's gain is another man's loss; who gains and who loses is determined by who pays.

"Malvalaha, run this by Bogachev's people in Russia. Fakhri, contact SEA, the Syrian Electronic Army. Discreetly put the word out. This company does nearly half a billion dollars a year in revenue. It's time for Mr. Whoami to make the call."

CHAPTER 14

January 5, 2016
Steps of the Massachusetts State House
Boston, Massachusetts

"*We are coming to you live from the front steps of the Massachusetts State House in Boston, where we are waiting for first-term Senator Abigail Morgan to announce her bid for reelection to the United States Senate. The announcement comes as no surprise to anyone; however, it does come with its share of controversy. Senator Morgan ran as an independent six years ago, but has consistently caucused with the Republican majority since 2014. Some have accused her of hypocrisy, but as we know, in Washington, hypocrisy is in the eyes of the beholder. Massachusetts Democrats have made it clear; should Senator Morgan be tapped as a possible vice presidential nominee on the Republican ticket, which is a good possibility, then she will receive a stern challenge to her senatorial candidacy. Back to you, Chris,*" said the CNN reporter.

Abigail Morgan stood behind a backdrop featuring the United States and Massachusetts state flags, listening to the reporter's introductions to her remarks. She was accustomed to this challenge and didn't give it much thought. She had bigger plans than senate reelection. *Why should she settle for number two on the ticket?* The present occupant of the White House was a freshman senator when he ran for the job. *Why couldn't she do the same?*

Abbie, as she was called by family, friends and constituents, was a rock star within political circles. When she ran for senate six years ago, she chose to run as an independent, touting her libertarian leanings. Getting elected on a statewide ballot as a Republican had been extremely difficult in Massachusetts, even in an anti-incumbent year like 2010. She campaigned hard during her first election cycle, espousing her core beliefs centering on free markets, limited government, peace through strength and individual self-reliance. Her stunning appearance, strong ability to articulate the issues, and the support of a very wealthy donor base made Abbie a Tea Party darling and a viable alternative for the center left.

The stagecraft surrounding her announcement had been calculated for maximum effect. The podium and the backdrop were placed on the second tier of steps entering the State House, above the street level. Commonwealth Avenue had been temporarily closed for the event, allowing a massive gathering of supporters to congregate. All of the media cameras and reporters stood on the brick sidewalk, at street level, allowing for camera angles to catch the gold-leaf dome of the State House as her backdrop. Abbie would look stately, as intended. When she was given the one-minute signal, she glanced down and noticed her friend Julia Hawthorne, who was present on behalf of the *Herald*. Beyond friendship, she and Julia shared common interests—and benefactors.

"...and now I am pleased to present to you the present and future senator from the great state of Massachusetts, Senator Abigail Morgan!" introduced former Massachusetts Governor William Weld.

With perfect timing, the loudspeakers erupted with a rendition of *All Hail to Massachusetts* sung by Boston Pops star and Tony Award winner Marin Mazzie. Abbie approached the microphone and soaked it in. She was born for this job. Like her friends, Abbie knew she would have an important role to play on the world stage. Everything in her life, including this moment, played a part in the intricate and nuanced script. Abbie cleared her throat and stepped forward to deliver one of the most important speeches of her career.

"Thank you, thank you. Thank you so much, everyone—especially for braving this crisp January weather. Thank you as well, Marin Mazzie, for your beautiful rendition of *All Hail to Massachusetts*!" said Abbie with special emphasis at the end, drawing cheers from the crowd.

Chants of *Abbie, Abbie, Abbie* filled Boston Common. She was comfortable speaking in front of sizable crowds, but she did notice the media presence was much larger than normal. She stole a glance up and to her left. *Was he watching?*

"Six years ago, I ran for office, because like most Bay Staters, I was alarmed at the problems facing our great nation. The economy was stagnant and the so-called recovery was uneven. Federal spending was out of control, and our national debt approached nearly unrecoverable levels. A disastrous, unconstitutional nationalized health care plan was enacted. The foreign policy of this administration was naïve and misguided. Above all, our civil rights and liberties as American citizens were under assault!" Abbie soaked in the cheers and made eye contact whenever possible with her supporters.

"I have drawn attention to these problems and others here in Massachusetts. I have sought to work with any and all who are eager to find solutions and promote reforms. As an independent senator, I have united with members of all parties to seek a balance in government, where we have worked together to avoid the gridlock which has plagued Washington for so many years!

"Our country was founded upon principles we all hold true in our hearts today. The Constitution is our only protection against a heavy-handed government. If the Constitution is not followed and honored, then the power of the federal government goes unrestrained. Once the federal government gains a foothold, it is extremely difficult to reverse that trend. Freedom is the bedrock of our society. Freedom is what makes our great nation exceptional—and our freedoms are under attack, both here and abroad!

"Prosperity is not created by rewarding those who do not earn it. Prosperity is achieved by hard work, effort, risk and the implementation of great ideas. Our Constitution guarantees all Americans the right to pursue happiness and achieve the outcome of their dreams. However, our Constitution does not guarantee equality of outcomes. Prosperity can only be achieved through effort. It cannot be achieved by exacting an unfair tax burden on those who are successful—on any level!

"Success at home depends on stability worldwide, and it goes without saying, we have plenty of enemies beyond our borders. It is incumbent upon our government to protect us by securing those borders and gaining peace through strength. Of the limited powers enumerated to the federal government by our Constitution, security is the most important. Our security as a nation and as a people, from threats foreign and domestic, economic and weaponized, should be one of the top priorities of the federal government!

"Finally, and most importantly, our Founding Fathers would be appalled at the state of legislative affairs in Washington. I am a direct descendant of John Adams and John Quincy Adams, and I believe they would call upon our nation to achieve unity as Americans. In 1789, John Adams, the second president of the United States, predicted today's sad state of affairs in Washington. He said, 'There is nothing which I dread so much as a division of the republic into two great parties, each arranged under its leader, and concerting measures in opposition to each other. This, in my humble apprehension, is to be dreaded as the greatest political evil under our Constitution.' Wise words spoken by President Adams over two hundred years ago are frighteningly accurate.

"If we could set aside our political differences and simply talk to each other, we might realize our distinctions aren't as vast as we have been led to believe. I firmly believe our divisiveness comes not from our disagreements about policy, but from our attempts to force those beliefs on those who don't agree. The pundits talk about the *big tent*—a coalition that accommodates people who have a wide range of beliefs. I submit to you, unless all of us find a way to live together under such a *big tent*, our country will continue to suffer.

"I stand with all of you in this fight. I hope to continue together in the task of repairing and revitalizing our great nation. So, with the support of my family, my colleagues and the lovely people of the great state of Massachusetts, I proudly announce my reelection campaign to finish the work I began six years ago in the United States Senate!"

Abbie stood back from the microphone and waved to the crowd, which was now larger than moments ago. The roar of *Abbie, Abbie,*

Abbie intensified below her. She made direct eye contact with both the television cameras and also the press pool photographers. With the help of her staff, her announcement would become one of the most important media events of this twenty-four-hour news cycle. But as Abbie snuck one final glance at the penthouse of 73 Tremont, she knew bigger news could always be in the making.

CHAPTER 15

January 5, 2016
73 Tremont
Boston, Massachusetts

John Morgan stood at one of the windows in his inner sanctum and surveyed the inhospitable winter landscape of the Common and Beacon Hill. As the years stretched on, his tolerance for the cold waned, but he would never join the ranks of those retreating to warmer climates during the winter months. Pink flamingos were not his cup of tea. Despite the bitter temperatures below, the scene was far from barren. Camera crews and media types scurried into position. Police barricades blocked Commonwealth Avenue, allowing onlookers to enjoy a rare opportunity to stand in the middle of a busy Boston thoroughfare and listen to one of *his* rising stars.

Abigail had intended to delay her announcement until March, when the weather would be more tolerable. Morgan insisted the announcement take place early in the year. When she questioned him about the early announcement date, he simply smiled and told her it was for the better. Abigail was not that different from others Morgan controlled, outside of the fact that she was his only child. Not an insignificant fact by any measure. *It is part of the blueprint for your success, my dear. A blueprint we must all follow.*

Morgan had followed the same blueprint, just like his father and his father's father before him. For generations, the Adams and Morgan lineage defined American politics, banking and philanthropy. His great-grandfather was J.P. Morgan, cofounder of Morgan Stanley. His mother was Catherine Adams, a direct descendant of President John Adams. For centuries the two families formed the historic core of the East Coast establishment and the upper class of New England society.

Following his graduation from Harvard Law, Morgan formed the Morgan-Holmes law firm with William Holmes, grandson of Supreme Court Justice Oliver Wendell Holmes Jr. Together, Morgan and Holmes built a practice of international notoriety, expanding their families' sphere of influence well beyond U.S. shores. Morgan was tapped as Secretary of State, during the first two years of the Carter administration, finding himself at odds with the President on most policy issues. He used the time to expand his contacts around the world, remaining mostly a figurehead.

After resigning his post as Secretary of State, Morgan, following in his great-grandfather's footsteps, formed Morgan Global, an international banking and investment concern. With the law practice capably administered by Holmes, Morgan devoted his time to this ambitious project. Morgan Global was destined to be the banking house of choice for the world's super wealthy. Morgan and others like him demanded secrecy, in addition to ample returns on their investment. Morgan Global provided both. By the mid-1980s, Morgan Global boasted over one billion dollars under management.

In 1979, following his return to private life, Morgan had a very public wedding to Eleanor Sargent, the sister of his lifelong friend Henry Winthrop Sargent III. The marriage, while not prearranged, was expected. Families with historic lineage like the Morgans, Adams, Sargents and Holmes were expected to marry each other—*within the family.*

Abigail, named in honor of Abigail Adams, was the only child of John and Eleanor Morgan. Complications during pregnancy prevented Eleanor from having more children. Complications of lineage prevented the Morgans from considering adoption. Now John Morgan stood watching his daughter, a fiercely intelligent, beautiful woman, take the podium to make her announcement. He turned up the volume on the television monitor.

"*…especially for braving this crisp January weather. Thank you as well, Marin Mazzie, for your beautiful rendition of 'All Hail to Massachusetts'!*"

Morgan viewed the crowd cheering. Abigail had a flare for the dramatic and had a tendency to micromanage her campaigns. Thus far, her approach had worked, resulting in her becoming a media magnet. In politics, good exposure was everything. It was all about branding. With her success, Morgan tried not to interfere in her approach to campaigning—unless circumstances dictated modifications.

"The foreign policy of this administration was naïve and misguided. Above all, our civil rights and liberties as American citizens were under assault!" Morgan knew her announcement would be her boilerplate stump speech. Abigail was an astute politician. She knew the political landscape of Massachusetts required her to run as an independent. At times, her libertarian leanings concerned him because they did not mesh with his interests. Thus far, that had not been a problem. Morgan knew the national political scene and how it related to geopolitical interests. If Abigail continued her rise to national prominence, securing a place on the presidential ticket, Morgan would have to "discuss" some of those libertarian policy positions with her.

"So, with the support of my family, my colleagues and the lovely people of the great state of Massachusetts, I proudly announce my reelection campaign to finish the work I began six years ago in the United States Senate!"

Morgan was pleased with the text of her speech. *Well done, young lady. This year will have a profound effect on your political career. I will guide you all the way.*

CHAPTER 16

January 5, 2016
73 Tremont
Boston, Massachusetts

A tap at the door interrupted his thoughts.

"Come in, please," said Morgan.

His longtime assistant Malcolm Lowe entered the room. Lowe was an undersecretary of state during Morgan's tenure. Now in his mid-forties, Lowe could have advanced his career in any number of ways, but he remained loyal to Morgan and was paid handsomely for his loyalty. Morgan muted the television.

"Mr. Morgan," said Lowe, exercising the professional method of addressing his boss when guests were present in the penthouse. "Several of your guests would like to express their congratulations to you, sir, and for the benefit of your daughter."

Morgan had instructed Lowe to put together an impromptu gathering of his close associates for coffee and pastries. They were all astute individuals and were fully aware of Morgan's intentions—kiss the ring of the kingmaker and make a deposit into Abigail's campaign coffers.

"By all means, Malcolm, bring them in one at a time. Please invite them to stick around for a brief private meeting with the senator," said Morgan.

Morgan adjusted his jacket and walked around his desk to greet his loyal friends informally. At six foot four, Morgan was an imposing figure. Standing behind his massive desk, he could be quite intimidating.

"Hello, John," said Lawrence Lowell, son of the former president of Harvard and a direct descendant of John Lowell, a federal judge in the first United States Continental Congress.

"Welcome, Lawrence. Thank you for coming to join us today. This is a momentous occasion for Abigail, and she certainly appreciates your support," said Morgan.

Morgan didn't emphasize the word support, but it should act as a reminder to his dear friend of the task at hand.

"Of course, John, I wouldn't miss Abbie's announcement under any circumstances," said Lowell.

Lowell had known Abbie since she was a child, and referred to her by her nickname, despite Morgan's consistent use of the more formal Abigail. Lowell reached into his jacket and retrieved a check.

"Toward that end, this is for Abbie's political action committee. It's the least I could do," said Lowell.

Morgan accepted the check and continued eye contact with his friend. It would be rude to immediately hold up the check as if to scream *how much support?* Morgan would wait until Lowell turned to leave before glancing at the number.

"Thank you so much, Lawrence, and thank your wife as well. This means a lot to us," said Morgan.

Morgan reached out to shake Lowell's hand both in thanks and as a form of dismissal. There were several others waiting their turn—no time for small talk. "I hope that you can stay for Abigail's appearance here."

"Yes, naturally," said Lowell.

As he turned to open the door, Morgan glanced at the Lowell family contribution—one million dollars. *Good start.* Placing the check in his jacket inner pocket, he turned his attention to the next "friend of the family."

"Good morning, John," said Walter Cabot, heir to the Cabot shipping fortune and direct descendant of Captain John Cabot, founder of America's first cotton mill and a revolutionary war hero. The Cabot name was synonymous with American aristocracy.

"My dear friend Walter, how are you?" asked Morgan.

He sincerely liked Walter Cabot and the two had transacted many successful business deals, including the acquisition of Huntington Ingalls Industries. HII, along with General Dynamics, dominated the shipbuilding contracts for the United States Navy. With Morgan Global securing the necessary financing, Cabot Corporation expanded its shipbuilding capabilities and greatly increased its stature with lucrative military contracts.

"I am well, John, and very proud of your daughter," said Cabot. "However, there is one minor issue of which I must raise objection."

Morgan became uneasy. *What could have upset my longtime friend and business partner?*

"What is it, Walter? How can I help?" asked Morgan.

He watched as Cabot pulled a check out of his jacket and then promptly wadded it up and stuck it in his pants. Morgan was deeply concerned.

"We Cabots are not accustomed to *following* a Lowell. Lawrence was shown in before me and this needs to be rectified," said Cabot.

Morgan began to feel a sense of relief as a big smile crossed Cabot's face. Cabot pulled out his checkbook and with a stroke of a pen, presented Morgan with a check for two million dollars.

"I know Lawrence gave you a check for a million dollars, thinking that would place him *ahead* of the Cabots. He was sadly mistaken. Please accept our check on Abbie's behalf for two million dollars," said Cabot proudly. "Perhaps next campaign, I will be the first to see you with hearty congratulations!"

The two old friends shared a sincere laugh. Morgan extended his hand and as the two men shook, he leaned in to whisper.

"Fret not, old friend, we both know that the Cabots talk only to God," said Morgan.

At this, Walter Cabot roared with laughter.

"Never a truer word spoken, my friend!" exclaimed Cabot, obviously pleased with himself.

Morgan was pleased as well. In fact, he would remember Cabot's reaction and use the talk-to-God phrase *before* it was time to write the next campaign check.

One by one, the old, wealthy families of Boston paid their respects and good wishes to John Morgan. The names were synonymous with New England gentry and would be familiar to anyone who had studied American History in high school—Hancock, Tudor, Warren, Bradlee, Crowninshield, Winthrop, Endicott, Peabody, Sargent, Adams and Morgan. Morgan greeted them all heartily and with genuine respect. They were more than his wealthy, powerful friends. They were members of an exclusive group of patriotic Americans dating back to the War for Independence. The members of these families were lineal descendants of the Sons of Liberty—our Founding Fathers.

They were the Boston Brahmin.

CHAPTER 17

January 5, 2016
Harvard Kennedy School of Government
Cambridge, Massachusetts

Sarge sat in silence as Steven navigated the G-Wagen onto Memorial Drive. He was deep in thought, weighing his personal life, career and "other" responsibilities. He envied Steven's lifestyle, though it was consumed by excessive indulgences. Everyone has a way to relieve stress—blow off steam. Steven's life put him in life-threatening situations. *Why shouldn't he play hard after returning from a mission?*

Sarge didn't have any life-threatening stresses—yet. His instincts told him his talents and services would be called upon sooner rather than later. *So what is preventing me from having a balanced personal life with my careers—both of them? Is that what's holding me back from a relationship with Julia?* Sarge hated deep thinking and turned up FoxNews on the G63's COMAND system.

"*So, with the support of my family, my colleagues and the lovely people of the great state of Massachusetts, I proudly announce my reelection campaign to finish the work I began six years ago in the United States Senate!*"

Gee, thanks, universe. Your timing couldn't have been better. Sarge physically rolled his eyes and shook his head at this thought. *Is Abbie the reason I can't move forward with Julia?* The two had practically grown up together after Sarge's father died. Her dad was Sarge and Steven's godfather. Sarge and Abbie had a serious romantic tryst a little over ten years ago. Abbie was practicing law at her father's firm, and Sarge had just received his offer from Harvard. The two were made for each other in many respects, but Sarge always got the impression that her father disapproved of the relationship. Rising careers pulled them apart, which had made things easier for everyone. In the past few years, their work on the *project* had put them in close contact. Sarge still felt an attraction, but the spark was gone. The spark, however, was there with Julia.

"Here you go, Miss Daisy, your tips are greatly appreciated," said Steven, pulling up to the curb of the Taubman Building. "Have you spoken to Abbie?"

"No, I didn't know she was coming to town," replied Sarge.

He found it odd that she didn't touch base. Maybe this was a quick trip for purposes of the announcement. He really couldn't think of a reason for her not calling.

"We don't have anything to discuss right now, but *we* all need to get together soon," said Sarge, reaching into the backseat and grabbing his briefcase.

"Have a nice day at school, young man. Did you remember to bring your Scooby Doo lunch pail?" teased Steven.

Sarge half turned back to him, holding up his free hand to distinctly show five fingers. "Talk to the hand, my friend," he said. "This also means to be back here at five!"

Sarge jogged towards the entrance of the Taubman Building before Steven could volley another load of crap in Sarge's direction. The tires squealed as Steven presumably took his beloved G-Wagen on a date from hell. He wondered if the living arrangement with his brother would survive until the spring thaw, when Steven would be back on the *Miss Behavin'*—where he belonged.

CHAPTER 18

January 5, 2016
Harvard Kennedy School of Government
Cambridge, Massachusetts

Sarge lived for the sense of excitement ushered in by each new semester, a sure sign that he loved his job. He brought up the first slide on the screen as his new students filed into their assigned seats.

GLOBAL GOVERNANCE
+
ECONOMIC POLICY

The course, similar to his last semester's offering, focused on the interrelationship between global entities: nation states; international organizations such as the United Nations, the World Trade Organization, the International Monetary Fund and the World Bank; along with multinational corporations and civil activist organizations like Anonymous. Students would discuss the international economic impact these entities interplayed, ultimately focusing on their relationship to the United States economy.

"Good morning, everyone, please find your seats," said Sarge, finding a few familiar faces in the crowd—like the ever-present Miss Crepeau.

Everyone settled in their seats, and as was his custom, he surveyed the faces to determine who was serious and who was simply following daddy's orders to be there. *They all look remarkably serious. Maybe they're paying attention to the news.*

"I see many new faces this semester and look forward to meeting you. After class, I would like students new to my lectures to schedule an appointment so we can discuss my expectations, and yours," said Sarge.

"This class is the second in a series of lectures on the topic of global governance. Last semester, we narrowed the topic to the subject *global governance in the context of new modalities of modern warfare.* This semester we will focus on world economic policies. Let's start with a recap of the concept of global governance. I'll pick on some old hands first—Miss Crepeau," said Sarge, already identifying the teacher's favorite.

Miss Crepeau had recorded a near perfect score on last semester's final. Sarge had an inner debate about how to deal with a young female student who was clearly enamored with him. Most professors would push her away to deter any appearance of impropriety. Sarge decided to encourage her through classroom attention and avoid personal contact outside of class. She was a gifted student, and he did not want to discourage her. *Gotta hide this one from my brother.*

"Yes, Professor Sargent," said Miss Crepeau.

"Provide a summary of the global governance movement," said Sarge, adding, "in one hundred forty characters or less."

The Twitter reference brought muffled laughs. *Imagine if all conversations required the speaker to maintain a strict 140-characters-or-less policy. People might engage in real dialogue.*

"Global governance refers to the complex conduct of international affairs. Without a global government, the concept relates to the different ways governments, organizations, institutions and businesses administer their affairs," said Miss Crepeau. "The theory allows for consensus-forming among these various entities, which generate formal and informal guidelines affecting governments and multinational entities."

"Thank you, Miss Crepeau," said Sarge. "We live in an interconnected world. Without a single government to establish the necessary laws governing this interaction, some level of cooperation must be achieved; otherwise every nation would build a wall around their borders, both real and virtual. Of course, politics plays a significant role."

There were a few mumbles exchanged between the members of the class. His students were well tuned to politics. Statistics suggested that half of his students would hold public office sometime in their careers.

"On the left side of the political spectrum, global governance under a one-world government is appealing, because it helps protect the poorest nations, which often fall prey to stronger nations or international organizations.

"Conservative thinkers argue that this neoliberal approach is a direct threat to the independence of the nation state, and thus its sovereignty. Therefore, a balance must be achieved, in our interrelated world, to satisfy the political objectives of nation-states while maintaining the sovereignty of those who wish to remain independent."

Sarge surveyed the room. Everyone looked interested, so he opened the discussion with questions.

"For those of you who are new to my lectures only, who has a question?" asked Sarge, watching as over a dozen hands flew up in near unison.

"Excellent. Let's try it this way. I will point at each of you, and as I do, please provide your question concisely. Remember, one hundred forty characters or less. I know you can do it, tweeps."

Sarge wanted to determine if there was a consensus question, and this also enabled him to determine what each student's political leanings were. The students, one by one, fired off their interrogatories. The issues were anticipated—fairness, wealth transfer, socialism, border protection, level of participation. One young man mentioned nation bullying, piquing Sarge's interest. The issue of alliances and building of global powers across nation-state boundaries intrigued Sarge.

"Mr. Ocampo, you are new to my lectures, right?" asked Sarge.

The young man appeared unsure of himself. Sarge decided to give him some confidence.

"Yes, sir. I am a first year law student and in the dual-degree program. I was approved to take this course as a first year elective," said Ocampo.

Sarge recognized the surname. Marcos Ocampo was the grandson of the former United Nations Under-Secretary of Economic and Social Affairs. At twenty, he was the youngest law student at Harvard, and probably the youngest student in Sarge's tenure. This young man grew up in a household where these topics were regularly discussed. Sarge decided to test his mettle.

"Mr. Ocampo, lawyer-in-training, what do you mean by nation bullying?" asked Sarge.

"Well, Professor Sargent, most people might associate the word bullying with larger, wealthier nations asserting their will upon the smaller countries who don't have the same leverage in international matters. I believe the concept of global governance allows for just the opposite. Smaller nations may band together to force the wealthier, more powerful nations to participate in global governance initiatives against their will," said Ocampo.

"For example," interjected Sarge. *He liked Ocampo already.*

"One example is global shaming," stated Ocampo. "The United States is continuously accused of being the root cause of global environmental issues because of our reliance upon fossil fuels. Our country must react by enacting laws or promulgating regulations restricting the ability of our businesses to operate. Many times, these laws are not reciprocally enacted in other countries—like China, India and Russia—who are just as guilty of environmental abuses, if not more so. The increased regulatory apparatus in the United States places our businesses at an economic disadvantage on the world stage."

"To summarize, those organizations and nations active in global governance have used the *power to shame* the United States to gain an economic advantage," said Sarge. "Any other examples?"

"Yes, sir. Another example is the formation of major trade partners and alliances. For a long time the G20 and G8 dominated the world trade markets. In the last five years, the BRICS alliance has been formed between Brazil, Russia, India, China and South Africa. The first four countries represent nearly half of the world's population and the most lucrative emerging market trade partners," said Ocampo.

Sarge could learn from young Ocampo. He observed the faces of the fellow classmates. Often, the egos of other students would get in the way of their learning from a student. Ocampo had captured their attention. This was why Sarge loved teaching.

"You mentioned the first four countries as being the most lucrative trade partners in the emerging markets. I assume that would exclude the United States, because we are clearly the world leader in trade—therefore not considered an emerging market. Why is South Africa included in the BRICS alliance?" asked Sarge, already knowing the answer.

"Gold," replied Ocampo. "South Africa is the fifth largest producer of gold in the world and is the largest producer of many precious metals, including platinum and palladium. Not to mention the diamond mines. Their natural resources compliment the other four nations nicely. Plus, the acronym BRICS, instead of BRIC, sounds better."

This drew some laughs and you could see Ocampo was gaining confidence on this first day of class. *Time to let him breathe.*

"Thank you, Mr. Ocampo," said Sarge. "The BRICS alliance, as Mr. Ocampo points out, is having a significant impact on the world economy, and the United States in particular. Last semester, we discussed the changes in modern warfare. This semester, our focus on economic policy will also include another form of warfare—economic warfare. The BRICS alliance has the potential to cause substantial damage to the United States economy, if they so choose."

And there was little doubt that the BRICS countries would make that choice.

CHAPTER 19

January 5, 2016
The Hack House
Antrim Street
Cambridge, Massachusetts

Lau sat across the desk from his two trusted lieutenants, Fakhri and Malvalaha. It was time to make the call. Lau had several firewalls of his own in place to avoid detection. Using a program called VyprVPN, Lau established a virtual private network that could extend beyond a public network. Since he had administrative user status within their network, he decided to make a clear and convincing point by contacting the TickStub chief technology officer directly through their Antec internal communications system.

The VyprVPN software would mask his location, and he utilized a Voxal voice changer to alter his voice. Voxal combined and stacked vocal effects like pitch, echo and volume to confound other listeners, like the FBI.

Lau would keep it simple. He'd provide TickStub with verifiable information only an internal administrator with a high level of security and administrative privileges could access. He would demand payment, wired to various bank accounts around the world, followed by a promise to leave them alone. They'd get one hour to provide an answer and another hour to comply. Walthaus and company would monitor TickStub's internal servers, looking for evidence of last minute anti-hacking activity. If TickStub tried to plug the leak during the two-hour window, Malvalaha would unleash a series of DDoS attacks on their server. If TickStub's IT team persisted, the domain would be taken offline, leaving a message that read:

We have your credit card information and it's too late to do anything about it. Thank you for visiting the new TickStub.

"Showtime," said Lau, connecting to TickStub's interoffice communications system. Wilson Bittermint, TickStub's soon-to-be-former chief technology officer, appeared on the screen in front of him.

"Hello, Wilson, we need to have a chat."

"Who…what's the meaning of this?" demanded Bittermint. "Who gave you access to this network? Why are you wearing that bizarre mask?"

Lau had donned the distinctive Guy Fawkes mask worn by members of the Anonymous group, adding a theatrical touch to the interaction. He also thought it might provide some misdirection for TickStub's investigation.

"You may call me Mr. Who-am-I," said Lau. "I do the talking and you take notes. This won't take long. First, you will take no action to notify the FBI or any other alphabet agencies of the oppressive American government. Second, you will take no action to modify, alter or otherwise patch your corporate servers. The system is under our control, and we'll know if your IT minions attempt any damage control."

"This is outrageous. You're out of your mind," screamed Bittermint. "I'm done with this charade."

He attempted to end the call, but his keyboard was unresponsive.

"Wilson, you need to calm down. Your keyboard will not work, and your administrative privileges have been suspended," said Lau. "I suggest you allow me to finish. Now, do I need to repeat items one and two for you?"

"No," replied Bittermint.

"Third, you will be asked to verify the authenticity of my statements. I will allow you the next hour to do so," said Lau.

Lau proceeded to provide Bittermint private information on the

TickStub CEO, including the fact he had stage two cancer invading his lymph nodes. He provided a couple of TickStub usernames and corresponding credit card information. Finally, Lau provided Bittermint's salary information and the social security numbers for several top-level employees.

"What do you want?" asked Bittermint defiantly.

"You're going to convince your superiors to pay us what we ask to make this go away. Be sure to remind them the Super Bowl is less than two weeks away. They don't want to screw this up!"

"How much?" asked Bittermint.

"You see, Wilson, this is a zero-sum game. In this game, one man's gain is another man's loss; who gains and who loses is solely determined by who pays. We have other bidders, but the *Buy It Now* bid for you is fifty million. You will be contacted in one hour. Get to work!" Lau disconnected the transmission.

Now they wait.

CHAPTER 20

January 5, 2016
73 Tremont
Boston, Massachusetts

Abbie walked into the bookshelf-lined conference room, overwhelmed by raucous applause. As a public figure, she was accustomed to this type of reaction from her regular constituents, but this group was different. The faces greeting her inside 73 Tremont evoked long-standing memories. The people crowded into her father's office had known Abbie since she was a child. Their children and grandchildren were neighbors on Beacon Hill. Forming the backbone of Boston's historical elite, they were a tightly knit collection of families. The significance of bringing them together in one place was not lost on Abbie. Her father had orchestrated this event for a reason. John Morgan stepped forward to greet her with a hug.

"Hello, Father, what did you think?" asked Abbie.

Her relationship with her father was loving, but formal. He put on a tough, reserved exterior with everyone, including Abbie. Her mother, now deceased, always reminded Abbie of her father's status, and that it was important to treat him with the utmost respect, in public and private. She scanned the faces again, searching briefly for Sarge. *I should have called him.*

"You were splendid, young lady," said Morgan. *Splendid. Nobody else would describe her announcement as splendid.*

"Thank you, Father. I can't remember the last time I've seen so many of your friends in one place," said Abbie.

"Our friends," he whispered, stepping forward to address the room. "Everyone, may I have your attention?"

Within moments, the cheering and applause ceased.

"Abigail and I certainly appreciate your generosity and support as she embarks on her reelection campaign. I believe we all agree, Abigail has represented the interests of Massachusetts admirably—not to mention *our interests.*"

Abbie winced inside. Opposition research in political campaigns had risen to new heights over the past decade. Restaurant waiters wore recording devices. Tiny cameras were hidden in decorations on dinner tables. Abbie didn't need her campaign overtly associated with the special interests of the nation's rich and powerful.

"Before Abigail says a few words, I would like to add something," said Morgan.

Abbie sensed her father's blueprint for her life was going to take an interesting turn.

"I have this on good authority. My daughter is on every vice presidential short list, for the leading candidates on both sides of the aisle!"

She felt light-headed as the applause crescendoed, forcing herself to smile. Her father wasn't one to boast or make grandiose claims. John Morgan had struck a deal, sealed with promises of wealth and power. Was this part of her father's plan? *Is this what she wanted?*

Part Three

Chapter 21

February 3, 2016
100 Beacon
Boston, Massachusetts

The UDT Chronosport's persistent alarm drew Steven Sargent out of a deep sleep. Rummaging one of his hands over the cluttered nightstand, he located the offending hunk of precision metal and stabbed at the buttons—silencing it. His other hand ran down the sleeping beauty beside him—one Katherine O'Shea. Katie began to stir, which stirred Steven as well. No time for this, he thought, his body begging to differ. He swung his legs out of the sheets and onto the hardwood floor, squinting at the window.

"That watch is pretty rude," complained Katie, pushing herself up in bed. "Hey, you're not taking *that* away from me, are you?"

Steven pulled a pair of sweatpants over *that* and turned around.

"*We*," he said, looking at his sweatpants for emphasis, "have a Jet Blue shuttle to catch to D.C.—and Sarge is on NewsCenter5 this morning with that *hottie,* Emily Riemer."

"I'll show you *hot*," squalled Katie, throwing a pillow at his head.

He ducked the shot and jumped into bed, kissing her through a tangle of fiery red hair before sliding off the bed.

"Seriously, I have to roll. Duty calls, even when I'm stateside."

"You're the one missing out," she replied, gathering the blankets around her.

"Believe me, I'm well aware of that," he said, wishing there was a way to skip out on his trip to D.C.

He'd love nothing more than to spend the rest of the day in the bedroom with Katie. It had been a while since they'd been together—long enough for him to forget how much fun they had together, in and out of the sheets. Steven and Katie met years ago as midshipmen at the United States Naval Academy. They both elected to pursue a bachelor's degree in Cyber Operations, which put them in many of the same classes—and facilitated a steamy relationship that made his restrictive days at Annapolis more than tolerable.

Following their graduation, Steven entered the Naval Special Warfare program, successfully completing Basic Underwater Demolition School (BUD/S) and reporting to SEAL Team 10, based out of Little Creek Naval Amphibious Base near Virginia Beach. During his tenure as a platoon-level officer, he deployed with SEAL Team 10 to Iraq and Afghanistan, developing a solid reputation within the Teams.

Katie put her degree to work as a Naval Intelligence officer, eventually accepting a position with the CIA as a counterintelligence threat analyst within the National Clandestine Service. Steven's and Katie's paths crossed again at Joint Special Operations Command (JSOC), where she had been assigned to brief outgoing Special Operations commanders on the evolving al-Qaeda threat in Iraq. Then Lieutenant Commander Steven Sargent attended one of these briefings prior to assuming command of a platoon headed to Ramadi, Iraq. After the briefing, Katie and Steven found an empty office and got "reacquainted," staying in touch ever since. Katie's career in the CIA skyrocketed soon after, thanks to a well-placed suggestion by Steven's benefactors.

"Sarge is about to go on the show," hollered Steven from the Great Hall.

He'd managed to turn on Sarge's wall of televisions, filling the screens with the show's host, Emily Riemer. Katie emerged from the bedroom wearing a tee shirt which read *Spooks Rock.*

"I see your *hottie* doesn't have the same effect," said Katie, nodding at the deflated front of Steven's sweatpants.

"Nobody has the same effect," he said, grabbing his mug of motor oil from the kitchen counter. She swiped the mug from his hands and took a sip.

"What the hell is this?" she said, grimacing.

"Coffee," said Steven. "For men. The foo-foo stuff is in the cabinet above the machine."

He retrieved his precious coffee from her outstretched hand and turned up the volume. His brother's smiling *I-am-a-published-author* face appeared on the screen, next to the cover and the title of his book.

CHOOSE FREEDOM OR CAPITULATION:
AMERICA'S SOVEREIGNTY CRISIS

The cover featured the American Flag split in half, with the stars and stripes on one side and the flag of the United Nations on the other half.

"Great cover," said Katie. "Do the *bosses* know about this?"

Steven shrugged. All of them had free rein to pursue their careers, trusted to know when their career paths might conflict with other interests. Sarge had received a blessing of sorts.

"*Today we are pleased to have Harvard Professor Henry Winthrop Sargent the fourth, with his new book* Choose Freedom or Capitulation: America's Sovereignty Crisis. *Now, you have pleasantly admonished me to call you 'Sarge,' so I will. Good morning, Sarge, and thank you for joining us,*" said Riemer.

Steven admired his brother and his accomplishments. Both of them wondered how much outside influence was exerted to help them advance their careers. They had spent many a night on the roof of 100 Beacon, in the hot tub, overlooking Stowers Avenue and the Charles River Esplanade. Fueled by Samuel Adams lagers, the two compared notes and wondered if their successes were earned or preordained. By the end of these conversations, the conclusion was always the same—*who cares, it works for me.*

"*Thank you for having me on, Emily, and congratulations on the birth of your new baby,*" said Sarge.

Nice touch, bro. When in the den of the media lions, a little opposition research might give you just the advantage you need to survive.

"Why, thank you, Sarge. I've been blessed," said Riemer. *"Tell us a little about yourself. You are a native Bostonian, correct?"*

Steven listened with disinterest as Sarge fielded his host's introductory questions, waiting for the substance of the interview. That's when things sometimes got interesting.

"*What is the premise of* Choose Freedom?" asked Riemer.

Steven couldn't discern whether Riemer had a particular political leaning. Her questions were open-ended and fair, thus far. Sarge appeared to be in his element.

"*Emily, our Founding Fathers gave us a highly decentralized, republic form of government. Their intentions were to vest the vast majority of the power in the states because state governments were closest to the people. Over time the federal government has shifted this ever so slowly to centralize power at the top. This power grab was anticipated by our Founding Fathers, so they wrote language into the Constitution to guard against this loss of sovereignty of the states,*" said Sarge.

Finally in his element, Sarge relaxed in his chair and looked directly toward the camera.

"*Over the last several decades, arguably against American public opinion, steps have been taken that have eroded our sovereignty globally. Globalization has become a political ideology as well as an economic fact. Technology, corporations and international organizations have become more involved in the level of interaction without historical precedent.*

"*With this increased interaction comes the desire to dissolve national boundaries, blend all cultures and merge all nations into one big socioeconomic system. Years ago, the discussion of a New World Order, a single totalitarian government, would bring cries of conspiracy theories. Today, the conspiracies of several decades ago are part of a barely concealed global governance agenda,*" said Sarge.

"Hit 'em with it, Sarge. Tell them how the world is goin' down the toilet!" yelled Steven at the six televisions.

"*My novel,* Choose Freedom or Capitulation, *is intended to make Americans think about the implications of global governance. Should America act as an independent, sovereign nation—participating in good faith as a citizen of the world? Or should America subjugate the Constitution and the freedoms it provides to the will of global rules and standards that might not necessarily comport with our own?"*

Steven watched Sarge sit back in his chair. This was why Sarge was in charge. *None of us, including Abbie, can spell it out quite like Sarge.*

"*Sarge, my producers tell me you have effectively blown up our Twitter account—@WCVB. We have nearly 130,000 followers and I think they all are weighing in on the subject matter of your book,*" said Riemer. "*Would you mind taking a couple of questions from Twitter?*"

"Of course," said Sarge.

"*This first point comes from @JohnQPublica, who opines that America risks being labeled isolationist if it overreacts in its attempts to protect its sovereignty,*" said Riemer. "*Is protecting America's sovereignty an isolationist policy?*"

"*The policy of the United States doesn't have to be isolationist. Let me use an analogy,*" began Sarge. "*After 9/11, our country became hyperaware of the potential for terrorist acts on our soil. Women pushing baby strollers into Disney World were frisked and asked to empty their child's diaper bag in the name of national security. And they liked it! In the name of safety and security, for a time, Americans were willing to succumb to an arguably excessive intrusion upon their right to privacy. After that period of time, there were no further terrorist acts on American soil, and the public began to decry the continued actions of the government, like excessive airport screenings by the TSA.*

"*My point is this. A balance must be struck between participating on the world stage in matters of security and economics with the intent of our Founding Fathers to protect America's independence as a nation—its sovereignty,*" said Sarge.

"*How do ordinary citizens have a realistic effect on an issue as important as this?*" asked Riemer.

"*My first suggestion is for people to educate themselves on the topic,*" said Sarge, holding up his book for the camera. "*May I suggest my book as a start?*"

"That's my boy," said Steven.

"*Next, contact your elected officials and ask them where they stand on the issue,*" added Sarge.

"Professor Sargent, Sarge, this has been very enlightening for me and provocative for our viewers," said Riemer. *"Please let everyone know where they can find your book, the name of your website and your social media accounts."*

"Thank you for having me on, Emily," said Sarge. *"You may purchase my book in eBook format on Amazon. It is also available in paperback via Amazon and on my website ChooseFreedomBook.com. There you will find excerpts of the book, blog posts and links to my social media pages, including Twitter, which is @Choose__Freedom."*

Steven turned off the televisions and eyed Katie O'Shea. He had some time to kill before his flight.

CHAPTER 22

February 4, 2016
The Hack House
Antrim Street
East Cambridge, Massachusetts

Andrew Lau and his graduate assistants, Fakhri and Malvalaha, sat alone in the downstairs parlor of the Hack House. The Cambridge home was quiet as Lau confirmed their wire transfer for the TickStub payday. In the end, after speaking directly with the CEO of TickStub, Lau accepted $20 million on behalf of the Gamers. Lau kept half while Fakhri and Malvalaha received $2.5 million each. The rest was split between the students, who had been given the night off.

"We're getting better at this," said Lau. "But as the old saying goes, pigs get fat and hogs get slaughtered. Let me give you an analogy."

Lau was about to remind his young associates that they were involved in a criminal enterprise, and their "game" came with very high, freedom-losing stakes. If the high payouts didn't keep them loyal, the threat of going to jail would—Lau hoped.

"In the drug business, a dealer can make a decent, albeit dangerous, living. The dealer can become more successful by becoming a distributor to many dealers. He can become a kingpin by becoming an importer or manufacturer feeding the distributors. In that respect, the drug business is no different than any legitimate multilevel marketing scheme," said Lau.

"The problem with the drug trade is the conspiracy law," said Lau. "Benjamin Franklin once said *three can keep a secret if two of them are dead*."

Fakhri and Malvalaha furtively glanced at each other. Good. The concept of jail was a little too obscure for two Ivy League graduate students, and prison sentences could be avoided—by making a deal with the feds. Lau wouldn't push this any further. Message received.

"I'm not talking about killing anybody, especially you two." Lau laughed, visibly easing their tension. "I'm simply making the point that in any criminal enterprise, the more people who know about it and the longer you do it, the more likely it is that you will be caught."

"We grabbed a nice payday with TickStub, not to mention a lot of street cred within the hacker community," said Lau.

Fakhri and Malvalaha started nodding, anticipating Lau's words as the picture became clearer.

"I don't think it's necessary for us to spend hours on end upstairs looking for vulnerabilities in networks," said Lau. "I propose that the Zero Day Gamers become hackers for hire. We have the track record, now let's build a brand. The Zero Day Gamers—at your service."

"I like it," said Fakhri. "We can post to several open source lists until we land a regular client."

"I'm in," said Malvalaha. "I read about HackersList on the Hackers for Hire Review blog. Companies hire hackers to conduct pen tests, just like we're doing when we search out zero-day vulnerabilities."

Lau was glad the two were on board, though he wasn't interested in doing the "legitimate" kind of work Malvalaha suggested. That's not where they'd find the big money.

"I'm glad to hear you're on board with this change," said Lau. "We stand to make a lot more money, doing a lot less work. Plus, this will reduce our overall exposure. We can hit seven figures just working with Russian oligarchs, don't you think?"

"Absolutely," said Malvalaha. "The Russian hackers are just *hacks* compared to us. With the contacts we've established all over the world, we could build up a nice clientele. We have a nice setup here, but it might be in our best interest to relocate. If one of the kids talked, I don't think any of us want to follow the advice of Ben

Franklin. We could just go underground. I'd be willing to reinvest some of my money to upgrade our equipment and get a more secure location."

Fakhri nodded enthusiastically. "This will work. Count me in."

"Perfect. I suggest we retain a core group of students that we absolutely trust," said Lau. "Walthaus paid his dues, so I would like him to come on board. Pick a couple more for consideration while I secure a new location. I'd like to be out of here sooner than later."

CHAPTER 23

February 5, 2016
73 Tremont
Boston, Massachusetts

John Morgan was surprised that Walter Cabot hadn't asked for this meeting sooner. The Secretary of Defense had recently proposed an enormous reduction in the defense budget, extending well beyond the traditional cuts via troop-level attrition and new program spending. The newest round of budget reductions included a substantial hit to the Department of the Navy, which would slash deeply into the fleet's operational budget—and Cabot's wallet.

"Mr. Cabot is here to see you, sir," announced Lowe.

Morgan chose to receive Cabot in the penthouse rotunda, capped on the outside by a green patina copper dome, and decorated on the inside with a mosaic replica of the United States Capitol rotunda. The irony of meeting Cabot under the rotunda did not escape Morgan.

"Hello, Walter," greeted Morgan. "Malcolm, pour us a glass of the sherry we just received from Luis María Linde, the chairman of the Spanish Central Bank. I believe you know Luis?"

"Indeed. We met years ago when he was with the Inter-American Development Bank. I encouraged him to finance the Panama Canal expansion project, which opens next month, barring any unforeseen circumstances. The third set of locks deepens and widens the Atlantic Ocean entrance, allowing our aircraft carriers to pass. We're finishing up modifications to the USS *Washington* in Newport News now," said Cabot.

"Sounds like a lucrative contract, with noble purposes," said Morgan. "Can I tempt you with a Montecristo #2? I just received them from Cuba."

Morgan was trying to relax his friend so they could have a reasonable conversation. Cabot had a tendency to get worked up when money was involved, despite the fact his family was worth billions.

"Thanks, John, I will have one," said Cabot. "And if you don't mind, I'd like to get right to the point. I have followed your advice and tolerated this administration for close to eight years. Heretofore, they have not affected my interests one way or the other, but the most recent defense cut proposals baffle me. The world is pretty dangerous, John, doesn't he realize that?"

Morgan didn't sense that he was about to stop, which was fine. He'd let Cabot vent before interjecting his thoughts.

"I'm a military man, John. My family, like yours, built this country on military preparedness and action," said Cabot. "I'm having a real hard time sitting idle while our military is weakened."

"Walter, I agree with everything you just said," said Morgan. "I have addressed this issue before, and the President will not budge in his approach. We knew that he would lead the country in this direction, and we have tolerated it to an extent. He is very much aware of how we feel, trust me."

"So what are we going to do about it?" asked Cabot.

Morgan relaxed in a Natuzzi Italian leather chair and sipped his sherry. Taking a draw from his cigar, he watched as Cabot mimicked his actions. *Relax, Walter.*

"Walter, sometimes the direct approach is neither feasible nor effective," said Morgan. "*We* have been very successful in giving this President direction when necessary. Generally, he has been receptive. It requires give and take, does it not, my friend?"

"I am fully aware of what it *costs* us, but most of the time, he seems to *take*," said Cabot.

"That's right, Walter. There are costs when it comes to negotiations. You have always trusted my judgment in these matters, have you not?" asked Morgan.

"Yes, John, without fail," replied Cabot.

"Good, Walter. I need you to trust me again. I have already addressed the issue in a way that will make you proud of your military heritage—not to mention make both of us a lot of money. Now let's enjoy our sherry and these fine cigars. How's your wife?"

Chapter 24

February 8, 2016
Lausanne, Switzerland

Steven Sargent eased the Range Rover right on Avenue des Acacias, watching the dashboard-mounted GPS screen out of the corner of his eye. The orange-yellow-painted four-story building on the corner of Acacias and Mon Loisir matched the destination on the screen.

"We're in this puke-yellow building," said Steven.

"Are you kidding me?" asked Bugs.

Bugs shifted uneasily in the front passenger seat, fingering the lock/unlock button. A former Army Special Forces medic, Bugs, aka Paul Hittle, left the Green Berets for the lucrative overseas contract security field. Quickly building a solid reputation as a discreet and dependable operator, he was taken off the market by Steven's employer and put on a generous retainer. He had a sixth sense they had learned to trust over the years.

"Take it easy, brother. The place has been vetted. Our gear's waiting inside," said Sargent.

"Looks like a hippie youth hostel," muttered Bugs.

"It'll be fine. The place comes with a private garage," said Steven, examining the building's exterior.

He had to admit, it wasn't exactly their usual digs for a job like this, but choices had been limited on short notice. With the peace talks kicking off tonight, the city was booked. A last minute Airbnb opening fit the bill, giving them two bedrooms in a quiet neighborhood. He booked the room and contacted his handlers, who verified the suitability of the location and delivered their gear.

"I don't see a garage," grumbled Slash from the backseat.

Slash, aka Drew Jackson, had been with the group as long as Steven, and was notorious for giving him a hard time when it warranted. He'd left the SEAL Teams around the same time, bouncing around outfits like Blackwater until Steven rescued him from Iraqi convoy-security details and Omani-apartment-complex guard shifts. He was particularly handy in close-quarters combat using a blade, hence the nickname.

"It's around back, where one usually finds a garage," said Steven.

"Screw you," said Slash.

"Hey, guys, sorry this isn't the Ritz-Carlton. We can always dump the detail, and our paychecks."

"Just busting your balls, man," said Bugs. "I'm still a little irritable about ditching the family in Nevis. I'm going to catch endless razzing from Claire when I get back."

"Take her to Tiffany's," mouthed Sharpie. "That'll shut her trap."

"First time he talks since we picked him up, and he's gotta dig on my wife," said Bugs.

"I'm not digging on her, Bugs. The light blue bag has a way of easing the pain of business trips," said Sharpie.

Sharpie was still a bit of an enigma. He'd left Delta Force a few years ago to pursue a private equity fund venture with a few of his Harvard buddies, all business school grads except for Raymond Bower. He consistently showed up for European operations, suggesting that his ties to the equity fund may still be intact. It didn't matter to Steven. They all ran separate lives outside of Aegis Corps. As long as they all reported for duty when requested and performed their jobs flawlessly, he didn't care if they ran a bakery back home.

"Listen to Sharpie get all upscale and *chi-chi*," said Bugs.

"What can I say, I'm the crème brûlée of this team," said Sharpie, slapping Bugs on the shoulder through a gap in the front seats.

"Are you guys done?" asked Steven, pulling into the concrete alley behind the building.

The garage doors lined the back of the building, looking questionably tight for their SUV.

"Are you sure we'll fit?" asked Bugs.

"We'll find out," said Steven, pressing a black remote control.

The third door from the start of the alley lifted on a track, rapidly disappearing. Steven edged the Range Rover forward, cringing as they passed under the top of the garage without scraping the roof.

"Aegis is thorough with their assessments."

"You didn't look so sure," said Bugs, opening his door and hitting the side of the garage. "Good thing I went on a diet."

Steven shook his head and squeezed out of his side, joining the team at a locked door. He unlocked the deadbolt and the doorknob before testing the door—which wouldn't budge.

"Try the code," said Steven, making room for Bugs.

The lanky, fair-skinned operator punched a code into his smartphone and pressed send, shrugging his shoulders. He waited a few seconds before turning the knob and pushing the door inward.

"Open sesame. Aegis added a cell-phone-triggered locking mechanism to this door, which will serve as our only authorized egress-ingress point. The less the neighbors see of us, the better," said Steven, pressing the button to close the garage door.

The foyer beyond the door led to a laundry room equipped with a matching set of stainless steel appliances and an empty closet. A stairwell rose above the closet space, taking them onto the second level, where he found a tasteful, yet inexpensively furnished common area and eat-in kitchen.

Slash swiped a brochure from the kitchen table, thumbing through it, as Steven made sure the sliding door to the balcony was locked.

"You weren't kidding about this being a rental," grumbled Slash, the stocky, Scandinavian-looking operative.

"Air bed and breakfast. People around the world just rent rooms or their places to complete strangers, or in our case, government operatives," said Steven.

"Weird name," said Slash, tossing the brochure onto the table. "Where's our gear?"

"Upstairs. Bedroom on the right."

They proceeded upstairs, taking a right at the top of the staircase. A quick search turned up a suitcase-sized, hardened-metal lockbox stuffed under the bed. Steven's index finger triggered the biometric lock, giving them access to the tools of their trade.

"Not a lot of gear," stated Bugs.

"We're not officially here," said Steven. "Aegis wants us to maintain a low profile. This package reflects that priority."

"Looks like we're low priority. No ballistic vests?" asked Bugs.

"You know the deal," said Steven.

"I know. Wishful thinking," replied Bugs.

They all knew the deal. The team was here to rapidly and discreetly neutralize any previously undiscovered threats to the peace conference. If activated, they would hit the identified target and immediately leave Switzerland by way of a luxury yacht docked in the harbor—leaving nothing behind besides their rental SUV. The kit came with them wherever they traveled in Lausanne, including the container, which is why Aegis had gone light on the gear.

Sharpie reached into the opened case, removing an MP-7 submachine gun.

"These'll work," he said, unstrapping a long cylindrical suppressor from the case.

"They always do," said Bugs.

The MP-7 was their preferred primary weapon for these details. Compact and easily concealed, the MP-7 fired a unique 4.6X30mm hardened-steel bullet capable of penetrating soft body armor and some hardened vests at two hundred meters. In close combat on the streets or inside buildings, the bullets passed through car doors and walls, giving them a considerable edge over other compact weapons typically employed in tighter confines.

"And so do these," said Steven, patting a series of small gray explosive charges used for door or wall breaching.

"Not very discreet," said Sharpie.

"Only to be used as a last resort."

"Second to last resort," replied Sharpie, digging deeper into the case.

He withdrew two plastic-wrapped bricks of orange-colored plastic explosives.

"Semtex? That's a first," said Steven, glancing at Bugs.

Without asking, he knew what Bugs was thinking. It was written all over his face. His *spidey sense* was tingling.

CHAPTER 25

February 8, 2016
Harvard Kennedy School of Government
Cambridge, Massachusetts

Sarge was late for class. A massive pileup on the Mass Turnpike, near the Beacon Park rail yard, forced him to drive the long way, via Beacon Hill and East Cambridge. Ordinarily, he would enjoy the change of scenery, but he had already been running late. He and Julia had a sleepover—devoid of much sleep.

He entered the classroom to a round of throat clearing, followed by sarcastic applause. He gathered his thoughts and brought up the first slide on the screen:

ALL EMPIRES COLLAPSE EVENTUALLY

He turned to the class and took a moment to gauge their reaction. *Let's see what they think about this topic.*

"Okay, guys, what do you think I mean by this?" asked Sarge.

A few hands shot up. Sarge pointed at a meek student in the back of the room. *Time to come out of your shell.*

"Mr. Lin, what say you?"

"Professor Sargent, I believe that in the history of mankind, every civilization ever formed has eventually disappeared or been replaced," said Lin.

"How does this come about, Mr. Lin?" asked Sarge.

"They either go broke or get their asses kicked," said Lin.

This elicited a round of laughter from his classmates. Sarge was also amused. *So much for Mr. Lin's shell.*

"Thank you, Mr. Lin, for that concise, articulate answer," Sarge chuckled. "All empires collapse eventually when they are defeated by a more powerful enemy or when their funding runs out."

"Ladies and Gentlemen, there have been no exceptions in the history of mankind. Empires are not typically the result of conscious thought. Empires form when a group of people is large enough and powerful enough to impose its will on others—or *kick their asses*," said Sarge with a nod and smile to Lin.

"But empires are expensive," continued Sarge. "Throughout history, how did the mighty empires of the world finance themselves?"

Sarge saw the hands pop up. He chose Miss Crepeau.

"To the victor go the spoils," she replied.

"Exactly. Thank you, Miss Crepeau," said Sarge. "In the early 1800s, this phrase was coined by a New York politician, but we have President Andrew Jackson to thank for the modern-day patronage system, which is so prevalent in our government today. President Jackson believed it was healthy to clear out the prior administration's workers and bring in fresh faces. This patronage policy resulted in many *Jacksonian Democrats*, his political supporters, being placed into important government positions."

Sarge allowed the playful banter between warring political factions in the class to settle down before interrupting.

"Before the Republicans point fingers, I will remind you—the Southern Democrats of the early nineteenth century are the political equivalent of today's Southern Republican base," said Sarge.

The class erupted in another round of political posturing.

"So," said Sarge, pausing to bring the class back to attention, "to Miss Crepeau's point, empires have historically financed their governments through force and theft. The great empires conquer their lesser opponents, take everything they have, and extort protection money out of the conquered citizens. This is how all of the great empires of the world were formed.

"Some might argue that the United States is different—and in some respects it is," said Sarge. "America was not formed by conquering another, less powerful opponent, although the Native Americans might disagree. The Founding Fathers sought independence from what they considered oppressive rule from Great Britain. But the formation of the great American empire, if you will, is only part of the equation."

Sarge brought up a new screen.

Who's going to pay for this new empire?

"Part two of the formation of a new empire involves financing its operations," said Sarge. "America didn't conquer another nation and plunder its wealth. The premise of the American Revolutionary War included a revolt against the implementation of taxes on the citizenry. Clearly, there wasn't a stomach for that. What did they do to pay for this new government?"

The young law student, Ocampo, eagerly raised his hand.

"Mr. Ocampo," said Sarge, "what do you think?"

"They fired up the printing presses, sir," said Ocampo.

"That's true to an extent," said Sarge. "The Constitution provided in Article One that the federal government had the sole power *to coin money and regulate the value thereof*. But the Constitution was devoid of reference to paper money. You see, the Founding Fathers had some experience with paper money. The Continental Congress, as Ocampo suggested, fired up the printing presses and financed the American Revolution with a newly minted currency — *continentals*. Unfortunately, although I would argue predictably, the *continentals* became worthless by the end of the war—to the point they were never spoken of again.

"It wasn't until the Civil War when the National Banking Act was passed that the paper dollar became the fully accepted currency of the land," said Sarge. "The United States adopted a gold standard, and its currency value became universally accepted. This leads us to one of the most important acts of participation by our country in global governance in its history—the Bretton Woods Conference."

Sarge changed the slide.

"After the conclusion of World War II, delegates from the forty-four Allied nations participated in the UN Financial and Monetary Conference in Bretton Woods, New Hampshire. This conference produced the International Monetary Fund and the World Bank," said Sarge. "At the time, the United States was the world's greatest economic power and had a lot of influence on the agreements reached. Study the history and background of the Bretton Woods system. This is a prime example of the impact of global governance." Sarge changed the slide again.

The Nixon Shock

"Welcome to the Nixon Shock, the mother of all government economic intervention," said Sarge. "In essence, among other things, President Nixon abandoned the gold standard and the United States dollar became strictly a fiat currency. This is when we fired up the printing presses, Mr. Ocampo, and we haven't stopped since.

"You see, America never grasped the whole concept of being an empire. We conquered, but we did not take anything like our predecessors. In fact, history will show that we lose money on every conquest. Typically, after destroying another country in battle, we then move in and pay to fix it back. We lose money every time," said Sarge, returning to a previous slide.

Who's going to pay for this?

"So how does a nation that conquers without obtaining the spoils of victory sustain itself?" asked Sarge. "They do it with debt. No other empire has ever tried to finance itself by borrowing from others. No other nation has ever tried to borrow its own currency, which it prints any time it chooses. As we have seen in recent years, if the burden of repaying this debt is too high, the Federal Reserve simply prints more dollars to satisfy its creditors. They call this Ponzi scheme *quantitative easing*. The United States government is paying its prior debt obligations by issuance of new debt obligations or the printing of new money out of thin air. There are people sitting in Federal Prison for this exact type of scheme.

"Today, our national debt, the amount we owe our creditors, is twenty trillion dollars. Every year, we add another one point two trillion to this total," said Sarge. "Many argue that this trend is unsustainable, which leads us back to our original premise." Sarge changed the slide back to the beginning. He had come full circle.

ALL EMPIRES COLLAPSE EVENTUALLY

"All empires collapse when they are defeated by a more vigorous empire, such as China, Russia or any of a number of rogue nations who possess nuclear capabilities," said Sarge. "Or empires collapse when their financing runs out. America has built up a tremendous amount of debt that is owed to countries that do not like us very much—like China and Russia.

"I want you to consider this. Should China and Russia elect to devalue our currency, resulting in our allies such as Germany and Japan becoming skittish about purchasing more of our debt, what would be the fate of the almighty dollar?" asked Sarge rhetorically. "If the United States cannot continue to finance itself via debt instruments, then it must tax its citizenry at an unprecedented rate. I submit to you that there isn't enough income or wealth in this country to cover the bill."

Sarge pointed to the screen.

"I will leave you with this. If all empires eventually collapse, does this premise also apply to the United States? If so, is this the beginning of the end?"

CHAPTER 26

February 9, 2016
Lausanne, Switzerland

Steven disconnected the call and scrambled out of the master bedroom, poking his head into the room across the stairwell landing. Slash sat up in one of the beds, reading his Kindle. Steven didn't have to say a word. The look on his face told Slash everything he needed to know.

"How far away?" asked the operative.

"Less than a kilometer. Bring everything with you," said Steven.

"This is all I brought in," said Slash, following him down the stairs.

"We're on the move. Control has identified a recently arrived ISIS-backed terror cell less than a kilometer west of here. Intelligence suggests they will move against the Iranian delegation later tonight," said Steven.

The team rose from their seats without speaking and rapidly descended the stairs to the garage, taking their assigned positions inside the Range Rover. Each operative's MP-7, suppressor and individual gear had been stowed in a dark brown nylon backpack in the passenger compartment, while the metal box rested in the SUV boot. Ammunition magazines for their concealed-carry pistols and the MP-7s were distributed between the backpacks and specially designed cargo pockets sewn into their pants. When they stepped out of the SUV near the target, they'd resemble well-dressed Europeans wearing backpacks. Four identical backpacks.

Steven carefully backed the SUV out of the garage, onto the dark pavement, while the team screwed the suppressors to their submachine guns. If possible, they would make as little noise as possible taking down the terror cell. Once the SUV hit the street outside of the alley, he started to brief the team.

"We're headed to 4 Rue Voltaire. Sharpie, plug that into your phone and land us one block over," said Steven. "Bugs, attach my suppressor before we arrive."

"I'm one step ahead of you," said Bugs. "What are we looking at?"

"Four, possibly five ISIS-trained European-zone-based jihadis holed up in a third-floor flat. Intel suggests they're prepping for an attack later tonight, so we'll either catch them off guard, praying for a good death, or we'll meet them head-on ready to leave," said Steven.

"I'm hoping for the former," said Sharpie. "ROE?"

"Terminate with extreme prejudice. Control doesn't want to deal with smuggling anyone out of Lausanne. Not with the conference underway less than a mile from here," said Steven.

"Jesus, the delegates are still at the hotel?" asked Sharpie.

"Yes. Control wants to keep this as quiet as possible, for as long as possible," said Steven.

"What if that's—not possible?" asked Bugs.

"Highest priority is given to eliminating the threat," said Steven. "Which way am I turning?"

"After the Metro overpass, take a left onto Avenue Floreal and start looking for a parking spot. Voltaire will be the first east-west street after making the turn onto Floreal. We're less than a minute out," said Sharpie.

"Got it," said Steven, keeping the SUV's speed under the posted limit.

As he drove the SUV under the concrete Metro overpass, Steven slowed his breathing, hoping to slow his heart rate and calm his racing mind. Control usually provided a more detailed threat assessment, which added to his anxiety. They had an address and a rough number of targets, leaving a ton of variables unexplored and questions unanswered. Most of the answers lay on the other side of the door to apartment 3B, 4 Rue Voltaire.

"Take a left up here," said Sharpie.

Bugs shifted the MP-7 from his right hand to his left and disengaged the safety, preparing to put the weapon into action covering the passenger side of the SUV. Two more clicks confirmed that the rest of the team was ready for an ambush approaching the target building.

Steven turned the Range Rover onto Avenue Floreal, searching for a parking space on the cramped, one-way street. At 10:12 on a weekday evening, he'd be lucky to find a spot.

"I'm not seeing a lot of parking options," said Bugs.

"Not any legal options. I'll put us halfway on the sidewalk near the intersection," said Steven, slowing down next to the last car on the street.

"If a police car rolls down Voltaire, our illegally parked Range Rover will attract attention," said Bugs.

"Voltaire is a dead end to the left, and a one-way street to the right," said Sharpie. "The chances of a police car passing by are slim to none. Most of the police will be busy with the Beau-Rivage Palace Hotel."

"We should be in and out of the target building quickly. Sharpie, you'll stay street side and provide overwatch. If the police show up, they'll most likely ticket the vehicle and leave," said Steven.

"What if they don't?" asked Sharpie.

"Call a cab and have it meet us a few streets away. Control can deal with the car," said Steven, pulling the SUV onto the curb.

They exited in unison, clipping the MP-7s to custom-stitched anchor points under their mid-waist-length jackets. The weapons' suppressors were partially visible below the jackets, but wouldn't attract attention from a distance. With their weapons and backpacks in place, they strode onto Rue Voltaire, scanning the doorways and windows for anything out of place. Sharpie crossed the street and headed toward a recessed stone porch that would give him a view of the intersection and the street in front of 4 Rue Voltaire.

Steven led the rest of the team down the left sidewalk, passing a small neighborhood store with a red awning featuring "*tabacs*" and "*journaux*" in white letters. Some things are the same everywhere. He left the dark storefront behind, sliding next to a tightly manicured row of thick, leafless bushes. Streetlights suspended by electric lines between the apartment buildings cast an orangish glow on their approach.

He read the building numbers as they passed several walkways cutting through the barren hedge wall, quickly surmising that the next five-story building on the left contained their targets.

"Sharpie, this is Nomad. Radio check," Steven whispered into the microphone hidden in his collar.

"I read you Lima Charlie. Street level is quiet," said Sharpie.

"Copy. We're making our approach to the outer door," said Steven.

"Understood. See you in a few minutes," replied the former Delta Force officer.

Steven turned onto the paver walkway leading to the building, peering into the shuttered windows above. Satisfied that they'd arrived undetected by anyone in the windows, he motioned for Bugs to take care of the door. The entry was a surprisingly unsecure, thick wooden door. Within thirty seconds, Bugs had picked the lock, holding the door open for Steven and Slash.

Once inside, he rapidly paced the long foyer and assessed the building's layout, determining that it consisted of a central hallway on each floor. Based on the number of balconies observed outside, he guessed that each side of the hallway contained four apartments. He had no idea if 3A faced the street or the back of the building. A stairwell entrance and a single elevator door were located in a small lobby in the middle of the foyer.

"We're inside. Everything is clear," he said, getting a quick response from their lookout.

He unclipped the MP-7 from the jacket's interior hitch and extended the telescoping stock before opening the heavy, fireproof stairwell door. Electric wall sconces lighted the marble stairs, adding to the luxurious feel of the well-appointed Lausanne apartment building. Not the kind of place you'd expect to find ISIS extremists,

Earl Edward Grey, I miss you every day.

JACQUI BLEU, BOUNTY HUNTER

ELIZABETH ANNE GREY

Cover Design | Editing | Book Design & Typesetting
Enchanted Ink Publishing

Dark Citrine LLC

First Edition:

ISBN: 978-1-7378365-9-9 (Hardcover)
ISBN: 979-8-9910336-0-2 (E-Book)

Dark Citrine LLC
PO Box 3563
Arlington, WA 98223

www.darkcitrine.net

For information about upcoming books written by Elizabeth Anne Grey, you can follow Elizabeth Anne Grey on Facebook, @darkcitrinewriter on TikTok, and @darkcitrinellc on Instagram.

Printed in the United States of America

JACQUI BLEU, BOUNTY HUNTER

but certainly the last place Swiss authorities would think to look. Fortunately for the Swiss, they weren't the only ones looking.

When they reached the third floor, Steven paused at the door.

"If we can pick the lock quietly and breach, we'll go with that option. If not, we'll make some noise. I'll make that assessment at the door. This is a no-flashbang, dynamic entry. I go first and peel right. Slash goes left. Bugs gets inside and follows whoever has to clear another room. We don't know the layout. Clear?" he said.

The two men nodded, and Steven opened the door, peeking into the warmly lit hallway. All clear. He turned left and walked swiftly to the first door on the street side of the hallway. 3E. He shook his head and pointed toward the other side of the elevator lobby, following Slash and Bugs down the long hallway to the last door on the opposing side. 3A.

Slash crouched to the left of the door, covering the offset entry across the hallway, while Bugs scanned the door with a military-grade, handheld metal detector. He ran the black device up and down the crease of the door, trying to uncover any internal locking mechanisms, like a deadbolt or floor-mounted security jam. He stopped two-thirds of the way up the door, two feet above the deadbolt. Bugs shrugged his shoulders and shook his head. They'd have to make some noise. The question was how much?

Steven leaned in and whispered in Bug's ear. "Small charge on doorknob and slide bolt. We don't have time to get hung up on the door."

Bugs nodded and started preparing small, pre-wired charges while Steven passed the information to Sharpie. The likelihood of a neighbor calling the police was about to climb exponentially. When Bugs finished planting the charges, they double-checked their weapons and edged away from the door before Steven counted down from three with his fingers. When the last finger disappeared, Bugs remote detonated the *door poppers*, initiating their attack.

Steven pushed the scorched door open, immediately scanning for targets in a ninety-degree arc to the right. He was oblivious to anything that didn't resemble a human being, his eyes lining up a head in the MP-7's Zeiss reflex sight. A single trigger squeeze sprayed the wall dark red as he shifted the sight to a man seated at a table in front of a flat-screen computer monitor. His second bullet punctured the next man's forehead, knocking his limp body off the chair. He never heard the two suppressed bullets fired by Slash into the targets he'd seen in his peripheral vision.

"Clear," Steven hissed, after walking past his two targets and searching the gourmet kitchen.

"Bedrooms clear," said Slash from somewhere in the apartment, as Bugs shut the damaged front door.

Steven widened his focus, taking in the room. The two men he had killed had been working at computer stations, which seemed at odds with Control's target details. Had they hit the wrong flat? No. This was obviously not a friendly gathering of Lausanne's citizens. The computer gear was sophisticated, bordering intelligence grade. He counted four stations, plus two mobile servers and an uninterrupted power source. With his foot, he turned the closest man's head to examine his face. Dark skin. Dark hair. Cropped beard. Looked Arab enough.

"Nomad, you need to see this," said Slash, poking his head out of the closest bedroom.

"We don't have time for show and tell. We're out of here in five seconds," said Steven.

"This crew has all kinds of sophisticated surveillance gear. Wireless bugs, cameras, laser microphones, personal bug kits—this wasn't an ISIS hit team," said Slash.

"Our work is done here. Bugs, lead us out," he said, pausing to transmit to Sharpie. "Four targets terminated. The team is on the way out. Keep an eye out for the possible fifth."

Slash stood in front of the couch where his two targets sat, their lifeless eyes staring at the ceiling.

"This guy looks about as ISIS as Bob Hope," said Slash, nodding at a balding, grey-haired man wearing a navy blue suit and wire-rim glasses. "I think you should call this in."

"We don't have time for that right now. For all we know, this guy might have been their contact in the city. Some kind of banker. Let's go," he said, emphasizing the last part.

Slash followed him out without saying a word. When they reached the ground-level foyer, Sharpie called them over the radio.

"Nomad, this is Sharpie. I have one Middle Eastern-looking gentleman holding two take-out bags walking toward the intersection of Floreal and Voltaire from the south. Hold in position."

"Copy that," he said, taking up a hidden position in the foyer with his team.

"He's turning in your direction," whispered Sharpie.

"Can you take him out? I need you in the Range Rover, ready to pick us up at the intersection in ten seconds, or we're going to be running from the police," said Steven.

"You want me to drop him on the street?" asked Sharpie.

Slash started to protest, but Steven held out a finger, silencing him.

"We'll toss him in the bushes on the way out. Mission accomplished," said Steven.

"Don't you want to know who these people are?" asked Slash.

"Not really," said Steven. "I'm not being paid to gather intelligence, and neither are you. Drop him, Sharpie."

After Sharpie reported "target eliminated," they left the building and crossed the road, heaving the body over a waist-high hedge lining the sidewalk. Sirens wailed in the distance as they drove south on Avenue Frederic-Cesar-de-la-Harpe—toward their marina. Slash spoke up for the first time since they left the apartment building.

"Did anyone check the Semtex for a buried detonator?" he said.

"That was the first thing I did when we staged the gear in the SUV," said Bugs.

"Guys, I know this one stinks a little, but it doesn't stink that bad," said Steven.

"This one reeks, brother. You just wait and see. I don't know who we iced back there, but they sure weren't preparing to attack the peace conference. Might have been spying on it, but that's it," said Slash. "One way or the other, Control got their intel wrong—or they purposely gave us the wrong information. Neither scenario works for me."

Bugs stared at Steven with a neutral face.

"What do you think?" asked Steven.

"I think I might have another look at that Semtex before the boat gets too far in the harbor," said Bugs.

CHAPTER 27

February 10, 2016
73 Tremont
Boston, Massachusetts

John Morgan sipped coffee as he glanced at the headlines scrolling across the television monitor in his office. His thoughts were interrupted by an intercom buzz from his assistant, Malcolm Lowe.

"Yes, Malcolm," said Morgan.

"Sir, Miss O'Shea on the line for you," replied Lowe.

Morgan pushed the phone's speaker button without acknowledging Lowe and gruffly took the call.

"Good morning, Miss O'Shea," said Morgan.

"Good morning, Mr. Morgan," said Katie. "As requested, I have a synopsis of the Switzerland matter, which I will be providing to DNI Clapper this morning."

"Go ahead with your summary."

"Yes, sir," said Katie. "Sir, the security team assigned to the Lausanne peace talks was notified of a potential ISIS terror cell. Active intelligence suggested this cell was prepared to initiate an attack on the Iranian delegation to the talks on the opening night of negotiations."

"Continue, Miss O'Shea."

"Sir, Langley notified the team through their customary channels of the imminent attack and the team responded accordingly. However, there was a problem," said Katie.

Morgan was stoic. "Get to the point, Miss O'Shea."

"Mr. Morgan, the information passed on by the CIA was flawed," said Katie. "They did not encounter an ISIS operation, but rather eliminated a deep-cover Mossad surveillance team and a senior Israeli diplomat."

Morgan was not surprised by this revelation. The peace talks needed to fail *with* a resulting escalation of hostilities between the participants. The death of the Israeli diplomat was collateral damage but enhanced the effectiveness of the operation.

"What else will your report reveal?" asked Morgan.

"Swiss officials are incredulous, especially with the Israelis," said Katie. "The entire European Union delegation has condemned the attack but has also sternly objected to the espionage activities of Mossad during a peace conference such as this one. Likewise, the Iranian delegation has rebuked the Mossad operation and returned to Tehran. Tensions have intensified after the Israelis formally accused Tehran of sponsoring the attack. I have just received word that a Sa'ar 5-class corvette has fired upon and destroyed a coastal radar site near Chabahar on the coast of the Gulf of Oman."

You see, Walter Cabot, this is why you should trust my judgment. The Sa'ar 5 fleet was built for the Israeli navy by Huntington Ingalls Industries, which Morgan helped Cabot purchase. Morgan would be sure to inform Walter Cabot of this ancillary benefit to the Lausanne operation. War had always been a lucrative business for the United States. Keeping the weapons factories and high-tech plants fully operational not only created jobs but generated valuable exports for the economy. War had little to do with one adversary versus another. War had everything to do with who got the biggest part of the Defense Department's lucrative pie.

CHAPTER 28

February 10, 2016
The Hack House
Binney Street
East Cambridge, Massachusetts

Lau orchestrated the systematic and inconspicuous transfer of the Antrim Street Hack House to the Lofts at Kendall Square, a location far better suited to their needs. Situated within convenient walking distance to MIT, the Zero Day Gamers traffic would attract little attention. Besides location, the Lofts had been designed to serve as residences and workspaces. Open floor plans, private balconies and sound-insulated walls were just a few of the key amenities intended to attract engineering and technology professionals. Lau especially appreciated the lack of on-site security. The last thing he needed was a documented log of arrivals and departures. He designated one of the bedrooms as his crash pad and the other as his office. The open spaces had been optimized for the Gamers and their new business venture, which got off to a rocky start.

Lau and company had received numerous offers via HackersList and two other prominent online services—NeighborhoodHacker.com and HackerForHire.com. Most of the requests were mundane privacy intrusions, with fees ranging from a few hundred to several thousand dollars. Lau and his coconspirators had started to lose hope, when an interesting request hit all of the boards at once.

We need a raise.
We need leverage.

We need justice.
We need your help.

Lau stared at the post for hours, trying to decipher its meaning. The words held a particular significance to Lau, because they were his impetus for creating the Zero Day Gamers—*raise, leverage, justice, and help.* After careful consideration and a long meeting with his partners, Lau reached out to the anonymous poster. The specifics of the request required a meeting. *There are criminals, and then there are criminals.* The ethical implications of their new business had to be discussed.

He leaned across the kitchen island, one of the few horizontal surfaces not occupied by electronics equipment, and nodded at his trusted associates.

"We have a serious offer on the table—mid six figures most likely," said Lau. "But the offer brings up an issue we haven't discussed."

Lau had their attention. Malvalaha, a Red Bull addict, cracked another can and perked up in his chair.

"We've been contacted by the Culinary Union in Las Vegas," said Lau. "The CU Local 226 represents nearly sixty thousand casino and hotel workers in Vegas. They also have very strong political ties. For our purposes, they have extremely deep pockets, and I get the sense they will spare no expense to maintain their power over the industries they serve."

"Why don't they just call on their politician friends?" asked Fakhri. "Lining pockets is their job."

"True, but in some states, their influence has been significantly diminished. Think Scott Walker in Wisconsin and Brian Sandoval in Nevada," said Lau.

"What do they propose?" asked Malvalaha.

"Contract negotiations with the major casinos of Las Vegas are at a standstill," said Lau. "Rank-and-file members are living paycheck to paycheck, so they don't have the stomach for a prolonged strike. The casinos, bolstered by Governor Sandoval, have refused to come to the table. They need our help to gain some leverage over the negotiations, but first they want to send a message," said Lau.

"How big of a message?" asked Fakhri.

"They want us to shut down the casinos," replied Lau.

"Shutting down a casino won't be a problem," said Malvalaha.

Lau interlocked his fingers and cracked his knuckles before responding.

"They want us to shut them *all* down."

CHAPTER 29

February 12, 2016
The Hack House
Binney Street
East Cambridge, Massachusetts

Lau was deep in thought driving down Cambridge Street. The Zero Day Gamers' first deadline rapidly approached, and they hadn't identified a foolproof way to achieve the Culinary Union's desired result—a coordinated takedown of the Las Vegas Strip's power grid.

Lau took a right on Fulkerson Street toward their new location on Binney. As he passed the Kennedy-Longfellow School for Children, he read their signage. *Real-life curriculum through field experiences.* Lau laughed out loud in the car, realizing that his role at the Hack House was similar to the teachers at Kennedy-Longfellow. He was leading his Gamers through some very real-life experiences—*for a profit, of course. You better step up today and teach them something, Professor Lau.*

As he waited to turn left onto Binney, Metallica's "Enter Sandman" blared through the Forester's speakers. Before the light turned, he pounded the steering wheel with both hands. "That's it, of course!"

Lau squeezed his car into a tight parking space a block away, not wanting to waste the time searching for a rare spot closer to the Lofts. He jumped out of the car and jogged down the street, forgetting to take the keys out of the ignition. He composed himself near the lobby entrance to avoid attracting attention. *Why didn't I think of this before?*

When Lau entered the Hack House, he found everyone clicking away at the tools of their trade.

"Listen up, everybody. Let's recap what we know so far. Starting with the obvious. The big prize—the Hoover Dam—is out of reach, because it hasn't presented us with any internet-connected vulnerabilities," he started.

"Our best option is to create a series of cascading failures. By taking down one major power plant, we can create cascading failures throughout the grid. The hell with the Hoover Dam, right?" Lau stopped to take another deep breath as the Gamers nodded their heads in agreement. *This is a teachable moment.*

"Fakhri, we have a primary cascade target, right?" asked Lau.

"Yes, the Clark Generating Station on the east side of the valley," said Fakhri. "This is Nevada Energy's primary power plant, generating one thousand one hundred megawatts from several sources. Electric, natural gas and solar. It's the valley's largest energy supplier."

"What happens when we take Clark Station offline?" asked Lau.

"All of Nevada Energy is interconnected," said Fakhri. "When Clark goes down, nearby grids take up the slack, including the generating stations like Chuck Lenzie in the northern part of Clark County. Our research shows that Lenzie can't handle the entire load transfer from Clark Station. At a minimum, Las Vegas would experience temporary rolling blackouts. The worst-case scenario, or best case in our view, would be a total blackout—especially if we hit Clark Station at night."

"In a perfect world, we would be doing this in the middle of summer, to allow for the added power requirements of air-conditioning units in the one hundred ten degree desert heat," said Malvalaha.

"Walthaus, why haven't you attempted a pen test on the Chuck Lenzie system?" asked Lau.

"Lenzie has newer technology, and its firewall has proven to be impenetrable," said Walthaus. "We believe the Lenzie Station primarily services the residential power grid of North Las Vegas. This is just a theory, but we don't believe Nevada Energy will have the balls to create rolling blackouts along the Strip, on a Saturday night, in order to keep the lights on for North Las Vegas. They'll drop the suburbs before they drop the Strip."

Lau was proud of his class—*they have done their homework.*

"Malvalaha, what do we know about the Clark Station operating system?" asked Lau.

"It appears they have a Trend Micro built system running Windows-based Server 2008 or newer," said Malvalaha. "Our pen tests have allowed us to sneak a peek, but we didn't want to prematurely alert them to vulnerability. Getting in is one thing, having fun is another."

"There's an important issue regarding the Clark Station that we haven't discussed," said Lau. The room stared at him, not sure if he was asking them a question or if he'd answer it himself. "Didn't we learn through a press release that Nevada Energy hired OSI Technology for its infrastructure communications network—the SCADA software?"

"Yes," replied Malvalaha. "OSI created SCADA, which is an acronym for supervisory control and data acquisition. SCADA is used by industrial utilities to provide interconnectivity across various platforms and networks throughout the utilities' network. In '09, Nevada Energy announced an upgrade to its system by incorporating the SCADA network."

"How does SCADA work?" asked Lau.

"The entire network is interconnected," said Malvalaha. "For example, in the case of a water utility, SCADA interacts with multiple remote terminal units, or RTUs. These RTUs have programmable logic controllers, which process data via sensor signals and communicate the information back to SCADA. If there were a major 10-75 alarm fire, significant water resources would be required and a heavy demand would be placed upon the water provider in the region. The RTU in that sector would detect the increased flow requirement and communicate the information back to SCADA, which in turn would control pump speeds at other RTUs in the utilities' system to accommodate the increased need."

"Exactly!" exclaimed Lau. The room listened in silence, awaiting the basis for their professor's excitement. "It came to me on the way over here. I heard *Enter Sandman* by Metallica."

"*Sandman*, I'm not familiar with that. Is it a virus?" asked Fakhri.

"No, no, no!" interrupted Walthaus.

Lau watched as Walthaus searched furiously through his jacket pockets until he revealed a small spiral notebook that was barely held together. Walthaus frantically thumbed through the book, stopping on one of the stained, crumpled pages. "Yes, yes. Here it is—*Sandworm*!"

"Congratulations, Walthaus, you go to the head of the class," said Lau.

The kid has potential. Lau turned his Red Sox cap backward and approached his computer station. *Game on!*

CHAPTER 30

February 12, 2016
Hotel del Coronado
San Diego, California

Julia and Sarge stepped out of the limousine onto the brick sidewalk of the Hotel del Coronado. Julia's eyes immediately sought out the pristine white sands of Coronado Beach. The San Diego weather never failed to disappoint. The high temperatures rarely exceed the upper seventies, and the lows were usually above fifty. Mild temperatures coupled with less than a foot of rainfall each year earned San Diego the well-deserved slogan — *365 days of ahhh.*

"I could get used to this," said Sarge as he reached for Julia's hand to assist her out of the car.

"We ain't in Massachusetts anymore Toto," laughed Julia. She hugged him as they admired the view. One could easily mistake them for being on their honeymoon, but this was a working trip for Sarge — with some pleasure mixed in. Two snazzy dressed bellmen in their khaki pants and signature red vests scurried to assist them with the luggage.

"Good afternoon fine lady and sir, welcome to the Hotel del Coronado," said the elder bellman with pride. "May we help you with your bags?" Sarge smiled at them approvingly and stepped back as the driver provided the bellmen access. Sarge quickly reached for his briefcase and a hard plastic case. This caught the bellman's eye, but he shrugged it off.

"Are you folks here for business or pleasure?" asked the bellman. The bellman was sizing up the couple, another friendly salesman trying to enhance his gratuity.

"We're only here for the night as part of the conference," said Julia. Julia wasn't planning on attending the Republican Governor's Conference, allowing The Herald to pick up the high points from the Associated Press news wires. Like most daily newspapers, budget constraints did not lend themselves to flying reporters all over the country to cover purely political events. But when Sarge told her about his scheduled final day address to Governors, together with a two night stop in Las Vegas over Valentine's Day, she invited herself and got busy booking their flights.

Sarge's new book was a rousing success. He quickly reached number one best seller status on Amazon for his genre, as well as the bestseller lists for the New York Times and USA Today. His publisher was already pushing him to sign up for another book, but Sarge was too busy enjoying the notoriety. She knew he was not fond of traveling but book promotion was a big part of the business, and at least he was scheduled for fabulous destinations. More than anything, the trip allowed the two of them time away from their normal duties — together.

She was thrilled to learn that the conference was being held at The Del. The beautiful Victorian resort is one of the last surviving examples of the wooden beach resorts left in America. For 130 years, The Del hosted over a dozen United States Presidents, numerous Hollywood stars and even the incomparable former New York Yankee — Babe Ruth. Its lobby was a mind blowing combination of classic Victorian architecture and crystal chandeliers. Julia loved the romantic feel.

After they had checked in, the bellmen promised to deliver their luggage upstairs for them. Julia noticed a small crowd in the lobby piano bar and tugged Sarge in that direction. Portly Governor Chris Christie of New Jersey was holding court with an audience that included fellow Republican Charlie Baker from Massachusetts. As Julia and Sarge approached, Governor Baker immediately pulled away from the group to greet Julia.

"What a wonderful surprise Julia. Elizabeth didn't tell me you would be here this weekend," said Governor Baker. Julia knew the

Governor's press secretary Elizabeth Guyton fairly well from her days as an aide to former Senator Scott Brown. She hadn't contacted Guyton because she had no intention of writing a story for the paper regarding the conference.

"Hello Governor, it's nice to see you," said Julia. "This is strictly an off the record visit for me. I am here with my friend whom I would like you to meet. This is Professor Henry Sargent. He has just published his new book, Choose Freedom or Capitulation: America's Sovereignty Crisis." Julia stood back to allow the two men to greet each other.

"Of course, I've met Sarge before," said Governor Baker. "Our mutual friend, Governor Weld, introduced us when I explored running for Governor after Mitt decided not to seek re-election. I admired your grandfather when he was Governor of our fine state."

"Hi Governor, you're correct and thank you," said Sarge. "We met nearly ten years ago. Congratulations on what you have accomplished thus far in office." Julia knew that Governor Baker was stymied in many of his initiatives by a Democrat-controlled state house. He chose to take on a bloated state budget immediately after his inauguration dragging members of both parties kicking and screaming into the world of government fiscal responsibility. With his budget passed, the era of cooperation was over. It was back to politics as usual.

"I truly enjoyed your book, Sarge, as did many of my colleagues," said Governor Baker motioning to some of the members of the conference standing behind them. Governor Mike Pence strolled over to them with a bottle of Perrier in hand. Governor Pence flirted with a presidential run but with a large field on the Republican side, his campaign never garnered sufficient traction to compete with the campaigns of Donald Trump, Senators Rand Paul, Marco Rubio and former Florida Governor Jeb Bush. Governor Baker paused as Governor Pence approached.

"Mike, I'd like you to meet some folks," said Governor Baker as he extended his hand to offer the Governor of Indiana to join the conversation. After some pleasantries, he turned and introduced Julia and Sarge to Governor Pence. "Professor Sargent is tomorrow's first speaker. His new book is a New York Times bestseller."

"I saw your presentation on the program for tomorrow Professor. I look forward to hearing more on your examination of state sovereignty," said Governor Pence. Julia saw this as an excellent opportunity for Sarge to discuss his book and meet some influential politicians on the national stage. She had forgotten that Sarge's black plastic case contained two handguns. California was a zero tolerance state regarding the possession of weapons in a bar, and here they stood chatting with two of the most well-known Governors in America. However, it didn't seem to adversely affect Sarge's passion for the subject matter of his book.

As Sarge spoke about the interrelationship between sovereign nations and the global institutions transcending their boundaries, Julia took turns admiring Sarge in his element and the casual interaction among the governors in the lobby. What would it take to reach this level of cordial cooperation across political boundaries?

The conversation turned to the subject of cyber warfare as Governor Christie brought up the issue from the previous night's televised debate.

"The Chinese don't take us seriously under this President," Governor Christie said. "They have pushed us around economically, and now they perpetrate cyber attacks upon our government with impunity. If it were up to me, the next time they pull this crap, they'd see cyber warfare like they have never seen before."

"What are you suggesting Chris?" asked Governor Baker.

"What I'm suggesting, Charlie, is sending them a clear message. Don't screw with us!"

"What do you do? Cyber attack them back?" asked Governor Pence.

"Maybe, or more," said Governor Christie. "What do you think Sarge? What's an appropriate response to the constant barrage of cyber intrusions into our government, military, and the private sector?"

A small crowd gathered at the bar around the group. Sarge had lectured on this subject before.

"For many years, Washington has dismissed the need for international negotiations and cooperation on the issue, but now there is a push to develop rules for the virtual world," replied Sarge. "The trend appears to be headed toward the creation of a cyber policy based upon the realization that our domestic efforts to secure America's borders from cyber attacks are inadequate."

"If this administration is finally waking up to this reality, is it because of the impact on the economy, or the threat to our military secrets?" asked Governor Pence.

"Both Governor," replied Sarge. "For example, the Chinese use cyber warfare to obtain military and technological secrets. This enables them to keep up with us militarily, and surpass our private sector economically."

"What is the administration doing to combat this?" asked Governor Baker.

"The interests of China and the United States are often fundamentally opposed when it comes to issues of cyber activity and its governance. The U.S. plan calls for transparency and freedom of information while China relies upon state control over information in cyberspace. So far, China and the U.S. have restricted their cyber activities to military and economic espionage, rather than other forms of cyber attacks that might give rise to an act of war."

"What about the Russians then?" asked Governor Christie. "They're just as bad as the Chinese."

"The Russians are notorious for using criminal groups and other hackers with no clear links to the Russian Government," replied Sarge, taking in a deep breath. "Russia is well known for its military mentality. Remember the cold war? It has taken nearly a decade for nations to realize the true threat of cyber warfare. Today we're dependent on computers. Russia opened the eyes of the world to the looming threat of cyber warfare after their attacks on Estonia in'07. Now, Russia's state-sponsored cyber forces have opened up a new front in cyber warfare. Cyber attacks and cyber weapons are now recognized as strategic arms and useful offensive weapons."

"Do you believe the Russians could use a cyber attack as a preemptive strike against us?" asked Governor Christie.

"It wouldn't be the first time the Russians used cyber warfare as a precursor to war."

CHAPTER 31

February 13, 2016
The Hack House
Binney Street
East Cambridge, Massachusetts

The Zero Day Gamers had spent all night studying the technical aspects of the Sandworm malware. Sandworm had been utilized in a Russian cyber-espionage campaign against the European Union, NATO and a broad variety of utilities. Ironically, Sandworm wasn't a true worm virus. A malware program by nature, it exploited a true zero-day vulnerability, instead of mindlessly copying itself and infecting multiple systems in the same network. Essentially, it was a targeted virus. Sandworm was especially effective in a Windows-based environment, often inserted via PowerPoint files—INF files in particular. INF files were text files that contained components used to install software updates and drivers on PC systems.

Microsoft developed a patch that blocked applications like PowerPoint from sucking in and launching external files like an INF. The Sandworm malware circumvented the patch.

"I think we're ready, Professor," said Malvalaha.

Lau walked over to Malvalaha's desk and motioned for the other Gamers to gather around.

"Windows will block an attempt by a typical INF file to enter the operating system," said Malvalaha. "So what we have done is create two files with innocent-looking names, in this case—*slides.inf* and *slide1.gif*. I say innocent-looking, because they are typical names and extensions used as part of the PowerPoint program itself."

Lau stood back to allow the students to inch closer to Malvalaha's screen.

"Slide1.gif has been created as an executable program file and slides.inf is designed as an installer file that will rename slide1.gif to *slide1.gif.exe*," said Malvalaha. "Once inserted into the Clark Station server, slide1.gif.exe will create a registry entry that will allow activation of the Sandworm program. In this particular case, we will not be able to run the program directly, but the SCADA software will have ingested a yummy PowerPoint GIF-and-INF cocktail."

Malvalaha leaned back in his chair to catch his breath.

"The malware itself is not embedded in our PowerPoint file. Rather, it is retrieved by a drive-by install—the download of updates to Java, Windows, ActiveX or Adobe will trigger the activation. We have obfuscated the malicious code in Sandworm to avoid detection by their antivirus software. When SCADA is used in any capacity today, the malware will activate, and the Clark Station will go offline."

"Were you able to use Sandworm to affect the outlying generation plants?" asked Lau.

"We added an interesting twist to the GIF-and-INF cocktail," said Fakhri. "We wrote the code to reject requests from the Chuck Lenzie Station as a potential DDoS attack. The normal operating functions of SCADA are compromised to the extent that Clark Station will deny SCADA access from the outlying stations."

"There's one more thing," interrupted Malvalaha. "All of the major casinos have standby power systems. I've done some research on the standby system at Caesars Palace and found it to be typical of the major hotels that have a backup in place."

"What is the standby system's capability?" asked Lau.

"Most of the buildings have the typical battery-powered security lights that will remain on for an hour or so," said Malvalaha. "But the batteries will eventually lose their charge. The major casinos claim to be cognizant of guest safety, but they are really more interested in keeping the slots running. They employ a more sophisticated backup system called a *paralleling system*."

It figures.

"How long will the paralleling system maintain power?" asked Lau, his voice showing obvious concern about this new twist.

"Fear not, good sir," said Malvalaha. "We've got this."

Lau relaxed—a little.

"The consulting engineers who provided the Cummins Power paralleling system to Caesars Palace were very proud of their work," said Malvalaha. "The engineers were so proud they detailed the entire project on their website. Here's what I learned from their dot-com."

Malvalaha went on to detail how the paralleling system at Caesars consisted of nine sections of switchgear and two sections of low-voltage controls, including a digital master control.

"Here is where they failed," said Malvalaha. "The entire apparatus includes a DMC 300 digital master control, which employs a simple-to-use icon-based touchscreen interface. This simplifies their diagnostics and operation."

"So," started Lau, motioning for him to get to the point.

"Sooo," interrupted Malvalaha, "they wired the DMC 300 control panel to the Nevada Energy SCADA system in order to receive instantaneous notice of an outage. Their client insisted that those slot machines never miss a beat."

"Hell yes!" exclaimed Lau. "Let me guess, you stirred in a little something for the DMC 300 in the cocktail. When the grid goes down, the backup system will fail as well."

"Yes, we did," said Malvalaha proudly. "We've done the same for the rest of the hotels with similar systems."

"Let's get started," said Lau. "The program will execute at what time?"

"I have it set for 8:00 p.m. Pacific Time," said Malvalaha. "It will release the system in exactly forty-eight hours, as requested by the client. This should be an interesting Valentine's Day weekend for Sin City."

"Walthaus, are you ready?" asked Lau.

Walthaus had gained the respect of his peers and was allowed the honor of generating the keystrokes. He brought up his screen and was inside the Clark Station servers within moments.

"We have identified the optimal zero-day vulnerability in Windows as the *packager.dll* file, which is part of OLE, a Windows *Object—Linking—Embedding* property. Our GIF-and-INF cocktail will be embedded in an OLE object and installed into SCADA. Kudos to Trend Micro for creating a solution to the INF intrusion. Unfortunately, they didn't consider our workaround. Just like that, SCADA drank up our cocktail and is ready to belch one hot mess tonight at eight."

The group briefly exchanged high fives and settled back in their seats—like professionals ready to work on the next task. The Zero Day Gamers were becoming more proficient and expert at cyber espionage. *How far can this take them? More importantly, how high, or how low, will they go?* All important questions for later.

CHAPTER 32

February 13, 2016
Brae Burn Country Club
West Newton, Massachusetts

"Come on, girls, hurry up!" Susan Quinn hollered up the stairs for her daughters to pick up the pace. "Dr. Warren and his guest will be here shortly, and I don't want you running around like wild Indians!"

"Suze, it'll be all right," said Donald. "J.J. won't care. He loves the girls like a grandfather would."

"He's hardly old enough to be their grandfather," replied Susan. She pulled a platter of meats and cheeses out of the Thermador refrigerator and placed them on the kitchen island. "I want the girls to learn some responsibility when it comes to being on time—especially when guests come over."

"Honey, they're ten and seven. They've barely mastered the concept of cleaning their rooms," said Donald. As if on cue, however, the girls hopped down the stairs in perfect bunny-rabbit unison until, with one final slap, they reached the marble floor with their feet. "Come here, my gorgeous girls, and let me hold you."

"No way, Daddy, we're dressed and we've put our faces on," said Penny, the Quinns' oldest child.

"You have?" asked Susan. "Just where did you get these fabulous *faces* to put on?" She reached out for both of their mushes and gave them a squeeze, causing the girls to squeal with delight.

"Remember, Mommy, Uncle J.J. gave us each a make-up set for Christmas," scolded Rebecca, age seven going on thirty.

Donald was amazed at how fast they grew up. He knew there

would be a time in the not-so-distant future when he would have to scare the bejesus out of their potential suitors. He would be ready for them when the time came.

"Listen up, girls. We're going to have some snacks for dinner tonight—meats, cheeses, shrimp and some raw veggies. Would you like to have some of that, or shall I fix you something else to eat?" asked Susan.

Donald admired his wife as she treated the girls like young ladies. Susan was excellent at providing the kids real-world choices. The girls might prefer a plate of hors d'oeuvres tonight rather than shoving mac and cheese down their throats just because it came in the shape of some creep named SpongeBob. Donald watched as the girls pondered their options. They whispered back and forth. This was a high-level decision.

"We'll take mac and cheese, please," they announced in unison. *So much for your theory, Daddy-O.* The girls ran off singing, "Easy peasy, mac and cheesy. Easy peasy, mac and cheesy."

"I'll grab some wine," said Donald. He made his way down the marble hallway to a built-in, climate-controlled, wine-storage nook. The McMansions of 2006 became the foreclosures of 2008. Nobody needed a 5,800-square-foot house with a built-in wine nook. But the Quinns were rewarded with this palatial home as a result of Donald's agreement to spend a couple of years *away*. His *vacation* was now a distant memory. Their new life was filled with wine nooks, singing children and new friends, such as Dr. John Joseph Warren—J.J. to his friends.

He and J.J. became close friends after they met during Donald's stay at FMC Devens. J.J. was an accomplished Army Battalion Surgeon who was deployed to Joint Base Balad as part of the 310th Sustainment Command—located on the former Al-Bakr Air Force base north of Baghdad. J.J. rose to the rank of major during his decorated career with the Army. He spent time at FMC Devens monthly to visit with the handful of former military personnel who had run afoul of the law. J.J. offered them support and encouragement. Donald, who held the job of office custodian at the time, struck up a conversation with J.J. and the two became better acquainted.

Upon his release from FMC Devens, Donald watched an interview J.J. gave to Boston's Fox 25 about his service. The reporter asked him about his time at JBB and what were some of the highlights. J.J. was borderline incredulous. *That's a tough one to answer. It was either working on our brave men and women who lost parts of their bodies or Carrie Underwood visiting in '06. What do you think? Highlights, there were no highlights.* The interview was over.

J.J. carried a lot of anger with him following his retirement. He was disappointed in the lack of appreciation the veterans of the wars in Iraq and Afghanistan received in the media and by politicians. J.J. was particularly irate over the political football the war had become. Donald became his friend, confidant and sounding board. In a way, Donald was J.J.'s PTSD shrink.

As so many of the Army Medical Corps do, J.J. took a job with Veterans Affairs at the VA hospital in Jamaica Plain. The VA New England Healthcare System was headquartered in Bedford and the Jamaica Plain campus was where J.J. was assigned. Unlike many of his fellow members of the Medical Corps, J.J. wanted to make a real difference in the lives of the returning vets who were *damaged*. In addition to providing primary care for vets, VA Jamaica Plain was home to the National Center for Post-Traumatic Stress Disorder. He was having trouble coping with what he experienced in Iraq, so he wanted to help others with PTSD as well.

Once again, J.J. became disillusioned and the anger set in. When the Veterans Health Administration scandal surfaced in 2014, J.J.'s response was simple: *Where the hell have you media people been?* J.J. had observed how hospital administrators manipulated records in order to receive their coveted bonuses. He heard the complaints of the soldiers who were ferried from one waiting list to another, but never received treatment. J.J. realized the practice was systemic throughout the VA. When the reports surfaced in '14 identifying thirty-five veterans who had died while waiting for care in the Phoenix VA system alone, he submitted his resignation.

Donald recognized that his friend needed an outlet—a purpose in life. Donald and Susan introduced J.J. to prepping. The couple appreciated the importance of having a trained physician as part of their group. Just as important, J.J. was a real patriot. He proved that during his service as well as afterwards with his commitment to helping his fellow veterans. In addition, as if fate had waved her wand over the entire relationship, J.J. was a direct descendant of Dr. Joseph Warren, an original member of the Sons of Liberty who played an early, leading role in the War for Independence. J.J.'s bloodline was directly linked to our Founding Fathers. Members of his family were field surgeons at Bunker Hill. John, the younger brother of Dr. Joseph Warren, founded Harvard Medical School. J.J.'s familial roots ran deep into the soul of the United States.

Donald and Susan discussed bringing J.J. into the group at length. They broached the subject with the other members. A consensus was reached after a little background research and the Quinns were tasked with approaching J.J. about the matter.

Donald remembered the initial conversation well. It was a night in early August of 2012, soon after J.J.'s resignation from the VA. The Quinns invited him over for an afternoon of swimming and relaxation. Donald knew that J.J. enjoyed coming over to their home. He never married and did not have any children in his life. He simply adored the girls. Like any good uncle, J.J. would spoil the young ladies with age-appropriate gifts. On that day, the girls received mermaid swim fins. As the adults sat around the pool and talked, the little mermaids practiced their whale-tail splashes with their pink fins. J.J. had quipped, *Maybe they'll let women become Navy SEALs by the time these two grow up.* Donald laughed to himself as Susan's eyes got real big at the thought of her two precious pups becoming full-blown SEALs. Donald knew better. *Not on her watch.*

Donald broached the subject carefully, tying the concept into the current state of world affairs. At the time, the media was covering events in India. On July 31, 2012, India had experienced the largest power outage in world history. Generally, India's power grid was deemed unreliable at best. On the 30th, a circuit breaker tripped at one of its outlying power stations. Subsequently, this tripped the breakers of another transmission station nearby, and power failures cascaded down the grid until twenty-five percent of India's population was in the dark—three hundred million people. India was in a drought due to the late arrival of their monsoon season. Extreme heat prevailed throughout the country, including in New Delhi. The twenty-three million residents of Delhi, packed in at a density of nearly thirteen thousand people per square mile, were without power for days. Bedlam emerged as the city remained in the throngs of a heat wave, and in the dark.

Donald brought up the hypothetical to Susan and J.J. about the possibility of a similar occurrence in the United States and the ramifications of a widespread power outage. This conversation led to the threats of cyberattacks and electromagnetic pulse weapons. The Mayan Apocalypse was even thrown into the mix. By the time the trio had finished discussing the various threats we face as humans, J.J. was the one suggesting the need for a preparedness plan. Donald remembered thinking to himself: *That's how you introduce someone to prepping. You show them the real world threats and let them draw their own conclusions about the need to get prepared.*

By the end of the long day of swimming and conversations, the three agreed to meet again to discuss the concept in more detail. Donald provided J.J. with some homework consisting of the two preparedness books delivered to him by Susan while he was at FMC Devens. Donald and Susan agreed to discuss J.J.'s interest one more time with the group. They also wanted to put together a plan for J.J. as it related to the big picture.

The Quinns knew survival medicine was one of the most important elements of a preparedness plan. After a catastrophic event, people would not have access to a doctor, much less a hospital. Available treatment would be scarce and required medications even scarcer. If someone became injured or sick, help would not be on the way. Today, injuries could vary from minor, such as a scratch, to major, like head or chest traumas. In a collapse scenario, a minor scratch could kill you. Drinking contaminated water could cause dysentery, dehydrate you and result in your death. Finally, safe disposal of the inevitable dead bodies was an important medical and hygiene issue.

Tonight, the Quinns hosted this get-together not only as a social gathering, but as one of the many preparedness meetings the three had held since 2012. Dr. J.J. Warren was their *Armageddon Medicine Man.*

CHAPTER 33

February 13, 2016
Brae Burn Country Club
West Newton, Massachusetts

Susan Lowell Quinn instructed the girls to give Uncle J.J. and his lady friend a hug together with a good night kiss before she led them upstairs to bed. Susan knew how impressionable girls were at this age and she worked tirelessly to instill manners in them as well as feelings of self-worth and confidence. Penny, who was ten, was at an age where she would learn to make positive choices about her own life and for others. Susan and Donald both strived to raise their daughters as young adults while avoiding the external social ills prevalent in today's society. Only a parent could appreciate the fears of their beloved children taking a wrong path.

Susan was raised in a religious family, dedicated to the teachings of the bible. Dating back to the 1700s, the Lowells were practicing Christians and active in their church. The Lowells were notoriously independent throughout their history, hence their active involvement in the War for Independence. This also held true in their religious beliefs. While the Catholic Church dominated the religious landscape of Boston for centuries, Protestant Christian churches were established as early as 1592. Known as separatists or independents, the Congregationalists distinguished themselves from the more *in vogue* Presbyterians and were considered more progressive in many social reform movements, including abolitionism, suffrage and temperance.

By the time Susan's great-great-grandfather Charles Russell Lowell became a Unitarian minister of the West Congregational Church in

Boston, the Congregationalists were widely viewed as pioneers in allowing a laissez-faire approach to societal values in relation to the worship of God. Susan, while holding to these same Christian precepts, still feared that her children might be exposed to the unintended consequences of letting societal norms take their own course without interference or moral compass.

Determined to raise the girls as Christians, yet providing them a well-rounded childhood, Susan chose to expose them to adults as much as possible within their home. This evening was an important opportunity to introduce them to the horrors of war without the shocking images, online or in the media, that have jaded so many young people.

J.J.'s guest tonight was former Marine Second Lieutenant Sabina del Toro, who served in Iraq at the same time J.J. was stationed there. Sabs, as she preferred to be called, met J.J. at Joint Base Balad. She had been deployed to Iraq, and the thirty-two-member Marine platoon she commanded was assigned to the 6th Marine Regiment under the 2nd Marine Division based in Camp Lejeune. The 6th was primarily a peacekeeping force deployed throughout the Sunni Anbar province, which included Fallujah, just west of Baghdad.

Political pressures in the United States had converted our soldiers to a neutered police force. The rules of engagement should have been renamed *rules of disengagement.* Yet Sabs and her platoon followed their orders and performed admirably. Sabs described Iraq and Fallujah in particular as a world where unidentified enemies lurked around every corner. It was impossible to determine a friendly from a hostile. After coalition forces advanced into Fallujah in '04, insurgents were either extinguished, fled or went into hiding in plain sight. It was important for the coalition forces to receive the assistance of the Iraqi people in flushing out hostiles. One of the methods employed was for the soldiers to endear themselves to the children by handing out candy, personal hygiene items and toys during their patrols. More and more, the children of Fallujah would walk away with smiles and pockets full of goodies, and their parents became more open to the United States-backed security forces. As the Sunni people turned against al Qaeda, the insurgents became few and far between. Eventually, a more relaxed atmosphere prevailed in Fallujah. This proved to have deadly consequences.

Sabs was on a routine patrol with her platoon through an open-air market near sundown. A young girl and boy were standing near a fruit and vegetable stand. Sabs approached them and reached into her pockets, providing the two adorable kids some Tootsie Pops. All of the kids preferred the chocolate-flavored ones.

Sabs noticed a man park a car next to the produce stands and quickly walk across the street, looking nervously behind him. When he reached the other side, he ducked down behind a car and Sabs instantly knew the car was rigged with explosives. She shouted *BOMB* and hugged both children, falling to the dusty road on top of them.

The explosion ripped through the market, killing a dozen people and wounding another twenty-three—including Sabs. Half of the market was destroyed, and Anbar province was shaken to its core by the senseless act of violence.

Two days later, Sabs awoke in the level one trauma center at Joint Base Balad to the face of Dr. J.J. Warren, who had just amputated her left leg and left arm. J.J. leaned down to hear Sabs whisper *the kids.* J.J. was pleased to report her heroics saved the children's lives.

Susan gave each of her daughters a proper tuck in their respective beds. They no longer shared the same room, but leaning against the banister, she could see them both through their doorways. *We live in perilous times. How can I protect our children from the evil that exists? Can't I lock them in a room or wrap them in a bubble for the rest of their lives?*

Susan prayed for her safety and thanked God for brave soldiers like Sabina del Toro.

CHAPTER 34

February 13, 2016
Undisclosed Location, Commerce Street
Las Vegas, Nevada

The banner hanging over the empty conference room read *Changing Fifty Thousand Lives.* Alberto DePetri remembered the early days of labor organization in Las Vegas—riddled with stories of organized crime. He studied the banner and contemplated its meaning. DePetri did not believe all of the sensationalist stories of the union's rise to power here. He only cared about the results. If a union's activities resulted in higher pay for its members, *so be it.*

DePetri had just issued orders to members of the Culinary Union 226 and volunteers from the Progressive Leadership Alliance. DePetri was a longtime official from the Teamsters Union in Chicago. He understood brass-knuckles politics. He had participated many times in *persuasive techniques* to convince a politician to see things the Teamsters' way. He was also an expert in work slowdowns and stoppages.

DePetri received the call early that morning to fly to Las Vegas the same afternoon. He was instructed to take a jet chartered by their friends at the UAW, where he would be provided a package of materials explaining the nature of his trip. His job was simple—to coordinate chaos when the city lost power. In his forty-three years as a loyal member of the Teamsters, he had undertaken many tasks to advance the cause of their members. He rarely questioned his directives. This job was different. *Exactly how did they plan to turn off the lights?*

A little over an hour ago, DePetri sent teams of trusted members of the CU 226 and handpicked partners from the other area community organizations throughout the city to high-profile hotels and casinos. Earlier in the day, with the assistance of CU 226 officials, all of the union reps in each of the major hotels were contacted and told to report to their on-site offices. They were told to watch for a signal—signs of trouble—and observe the activity within their location. If they determined that the business was maintaining an unsafe work environment, the union reps were instructed to notify all members on site to leave the premises immediately. Also, in the name of safety, the union members should encourage their fellow employees to immediately do the same. If any member of management attempted to intervene or protest, the union rep was to provide the business card of CU 226 president Ted Pappageorge.

DePetri was tasked with this assignment because of his exceptional organizational skills, background in disruptive labor practices, and utter disregard for the consequences of his actions. With just twenty-four hours' notice, DePetri orchestrated the largest work stoppage in the history of American labor.

CHAPTER 35

February 13, 2016
Brae Burn Country Club
West Newton, Massachusetts

"I was volunteering during a military job fair last month at Gillette Stadium, sponsored by the Wounded Warrior Project. The folks at MassVetsAdvisor wanted someone to advise our vets about medical benefits and services available to them outside the VA system," said J.J. "They have an excellent newsletter—*At Ease!*—which provides the latest information for vets who may need additional medical and mental services."

Susan returned from tucking the girls into bed and joined the conversation. She gave Donald's shoulders a squeeze. He reached up to her hand and they held each other for a moment. J.J. noticed the brief show of affection between the two and realized his life was empty without a *Susan.*

J.J. was nearing fifty years old and found himself contemplating life and his future. The anger over the atrocities of war and the lack of respect for the soldiers who did their duty had subsided. The Quinns helped him find his way through their mutual dedication to preparedness planning and subsequent introduction to this new family. The Wounded Warrior Project provided him an outlet to help his fellow soldiers cope with a difficult return home. Now, Sabs had come into his life and he was beginning to feel again. He continued.

"As Donald and Susan know, I have been pretty disheartened with the way our vets are treated both within the system and without," said J.J. "I first became involved on a local level with the MassVets because I liked a one stop shopping outlet for soldiers who needed counseling and sought direction for resources to fill their needs.

"We all have a bumper sticker. You know, my kid is smarter than your kid in math." This drew laughs from the two parents in the room. J.J. teased Susan about this because she drove a car with the peel-off stick figures in the back window and a similar bumper sticker about honor students.

"There's nothing wrong with that; it's human nature. My bumper sticker is helping my fellow vets," said J.J.

Sabs smiled at him, and then turned her attention to the Quinns. "I hadn't seen J.J. since the brief moment I opened my eyes at JBB. But I could never forget his face and his comforting words," said Sabs. "I have worked with Wounded Warriors for years because of my situation. MassVets contacted me a year or so ago about counseling wounded vets in the Boston area. I was glad to help." She turned towards J.J. "We have become friends—close friends—since the Gillette event."

J.J. blushed slightly, recognizing that Sabs felt an emotional tie to him as well. They were having a moment. Being around a loving family like the Quinns could produce those same emotions in others around them. J.J. felt it, and apparently Sabs did as well.

"Are you guys dating?" asked Susan.

J.J. squirmed and Sabs began to laugh.

"Susan, men can't handle questions like that," said Sabs. "Just look at him. Maybe I'll give him a great big kiss right now!"

Donald and Susan were laughing at him now. This was not supposed to be a coming-out party. Donald intervened on J.J.'s behalf.

"Listen up, ladies, this is not *The Dating Game*," came the buzzkill from Donald with the added effect of rescuing J.J. Turning to Sabs, Donald said, "J.J. tells me that you two have discussed his preparedness plans. He probably also told you we get together every month or so to get up to date."

"He did, Donald, and I appreciate the fact that you guys trust me, or him, enough to let me participate in all of this," said Sabs. "I have obvious limitations. My prosthetic left leg is limiting in terms of running, but it carries my weight easily. My left arm was removed just above the elbow. It is mobile, to an extent, but it certainly does not make me the bionic woman."

J.J. admired how Sabs could discuss her limitations so frankly.

"I do have serious concerns about our country and the state of society in general," said Sabs. "I would be remiss if I didn't consider my shortcomings in the event of some type of collapse. Being prepared for what life might throw your way is one thing. Living in a post-collapse world with only one arm and leg raises a whole new set of concerns."

J.J. understood her concerns, especially from a medical perspective. A post-collapse America would be extremely difficult for the elderly, children, and people with special needs—both physical and mental. There is no such thing as a one-size-fits-all preparedness plan.

"But I will say this," added Sabs. "I will always be a Marine. When it comes to defending America and her principles, I'll fight side by side with you, albeit with one arm and one leg."

That's the spirit. I really like this lady.

"Well said, Sabs," said Donald. "Being part of a preparedness group involves more than physical capability. Some might disagree with me, but prepping is ninety percent planning—which includes mental preparation. You can't survive on being able to run a marathon alone. It takes a comprehensive set of protocols framed in an organized fashion that makes sense for you."

It was words like these from Donald after that summer evening in 2012 that convinced J.J. to become prepared. He was honored to become a part of the Quinns' group, and as he became more involved, he marveled at the importance of their purpose.

"Honey, where's the remote?" asked Susan. "I think we need to turn this up."

Everyone's attention was drawn to the FoxNews channel on the television. Arthel Neville filled the screen. Next to the FoxNews logo, the words *LAS VEGAS IN THE DARK* were prominent.

"*As we have been reporting in the last several moments—and the information is still coming in to us, as this is a fluid situation—it appears that the entire metro Las Vegas area is without power at this time. Fox News correspondent Dan Springer is in Seattle and is bringing us the latest—Dan*," said Neville. The screen switched to Springer standing in front of a background of the Seattle skyline, including the Space Needle.

"*Thank you, Arthel. As you mentioned moments ago, information on this event is increasingly difficult to obtain. Here is what we know so far. Around eight p.m. local time in Las Vegas, the entire valley comprising the city of Las Vegas began to go dark. I spoke with a friend by cell phone before he lost his signal. My friend lives in a high-rise condominium project overlooking the famous Las Vegas Strip, also known as Las Vegas Boulevard. The outage apparently happened suddenly, in less than a minute. At first, the lights dimmed and then they brightened. My friend described a wave of darkness sweeping across the valley from the north to the south towards Henderson. After the call dropped, I attempted to call my friend back, but I received an 'all circuits are busy' message.*"

The Quinns and their guests continued to watch the events as they unfolded for the next several hours. Despite the late hour, J.J. and Sabs stayed there and took in the reports. Susan provided ample coffee for the weary guests. By three a.m., midnight in Las Vegas, J.J. and Sabs agreed to bunk in a guest room. Reports were coming in to the twenty-four-hour news channels about out-of-control fires and gunshots being heard throughout the city.

"This is one heck of a train wreck," said Donald. "While I feel bad for anyone who is in the middle of this, I can't seem to take my eyes off the screen. I can only imagine what we'll learn when the lights come back on. The cell phone calls getting through to the news stations are eerie enough."

"I'm amazed at how quickly things fell apart," said Sabs. "The power has been off for maybe four hours or so. There are now reports of buildings burning and shots fired. How could this situation deteriorate so quickly?"

"I've always read in preparedness manuals the time frame for societal breakdown is at least seventy-two hours," said J.J. "What could trigger this type of reaction?"

"Opportunists," replied Susan. "In a collapse, the bad people survive and take advantage of the chaos."

"This is why we take prepping seriously," said Donald.

CHAPTER 36

February 13, 2016
Caesars Palace Hotel
Las Vegas, Nevada

"Are we going out after dinner?" asked Sarge. Sarge was beat and would have settled for room service.

"I don't think so," said Julia. "Let's get plenty of rest. Tomorrow is Valentine's Day and a full day of shopping at the Forum Shops."

Julia paused, trying to gauge his reaction, but he just smiled. *This is what married life would be like.* He watched her *touch-up* through the wide door separating the opulent marble bathroom from the spacious high-rollers' suite. She was stunningly beautiful and exceptionally smart. Sexy, with a wicked sense of humor. They were meant for each other—compatible in so many ways. Extending his business trip to include a getaway for the two of them had been a stroke of genius.

Sarge had insisted she come along to cover his keynote address and join him for a two-day stopover in Las Vegas—including Valentine's Day. He knew it was the right call when Julia immediately cleared her schedule, accepting his offer. Sarge had spent the better part of February travelling to promote his new book, which kept the two of them apart far more than either of them liked. The trip gave them a chance to reconnect, in more ways than one, before his next long series of appearances. In fact, he was beginning to wonder if they'd ever leave the hotel room. He could get used to this on a more permanent basis.

Sarge's mind wandered to the Little White Chapel on the Strip. *Wouldn't that be something? Hey, we got hitched on Valentine's Day in Vegas!*

Over eighty thousand people got married in Clark County every year—five percent of the weddings nationwide. Valentine's Day was the busiest day of the year in the *get hitched* business. *Am I ready to pop the question? Would Julia say yes?*

Julia caught him staring off in deep thought.

"Hey, buddy, how're you doin' over there?" asked Julia. "If you're tired, we can just order in."

Sarge considered this tempting offer but decided against it. She'd dropped everything to travel out west with him, and he wasn't going to deny her a night on the town. Besides, she was incredibly gorgeous tonight, as always.

"No way, Bobby Flay awaits," said Sarge. "This city is wide open for business twenty-four seven. It never sleeps, nor shall I, my goddess."

Julia looked at him through the mirror as she put the final touches on her lipstick. She was studying him.

Maybe she is a mind reader. Women are scary creatures.

Sarge looked out the window of the twenty-eighth floor of the Palace Tower and wondered at the magnificence of Las Vegas. Whether you called it Sin City or the City of Lights, it was truly a wonder to behold. Sarge recalled an image taken by the International Space Station, which revealed Las Vegas as the brightest city in the world as seen from space. The accompanying article concluded if all the lights along the Las Vegas Strip were lined up, it would create a train of lights over fifteen thousand miles long. The lights had dimmed to honor Frank Sinatra and Dean Martin, performers comprising the acclaimed Rat Pack with Sammy Davis Jr. They were also dimmed in memory of the 9/11 terrorist attack and the death of Ronald Reagan. Las Vegas was incomparable.

Julia joined his side. "What an unbelievable view. Could you live here?"

Sarge thought about it for a brief moment.

"Believe it or not, I would consider it because of the weather," said Sarge. "Boston winters are getting old."

Sarge stared down at the magnificent Fountains of the Bellagio

Hotel. The show was in progress and the lights flashed as seventeen thousand gallons of water shot into the air to a brilliantly choreographed light display. The water of the Bellagio's manmade lake could fill two thousand swimming pools. This brought back the visual of Lake Mead and Hoover Dam.

"You know what concerns me, though?" asked Sarge.

"What?"

"When we flew in this afternoon, did you notice the levels of Lake Mead upriver from the Hoover Dam?" asked Sarge.

"Yeah, you could see how the banks of the river were a sandy brown color compared to the rest of the red clay walls of the canyon," said Julia. "What are you thinking?"

"I think they're running out of water," he said bluntly. "I guess time will tell."

Ten minutes later, they were waiting for the elevator. It was almost 8:00 p.m.

"This is taking forever," remarked Julia.

"Yeah, it's probably a busy weekend," said Sarge. "The airport and the casino were packed today. I suppose between Valentine's Day and the President's Day weekend, Vegas is getting slammed with the *turistas.* Or, everyone heard *I* was in town."

"Then there's that," said Julia dryly as she began to pull on Sarge's ear. *Ding! Saved by the bell.*

The elevator started out empty, since Sarge and Julia were located on a floor requiring special card access. Systematically, the car descended to the lobby, picking up new passengers.

Ding! Floor twenty-six—happy family of four, including a whiny six-year-old who should be in bed.

Ding! Floor twenty-three—two little old ladies from Pasadena, wearing their finest Lilly Pulitzer spring fashion.

Ding! Floor nineteen—presenting the young couple in love, because they have matching nose rings.

Ding! Floor seventeen—introducing the high roller, clicking his leftover chips in his pockets.

Sarge and Julia pressed against each other as Sarge assumed the role of elevator-car operator. He held the doors open as the new passengers, now numbering eleven, entered and squeezed into the brass and mirror compartment. He looked up and read the safety notice to determine the car's rated capacity—sixteen, five to go.

Ding! Floor fifteen—a smelly, intoxicated man entered and teetered in the remaining space.

"Mommy, I have to pee," squalled the six-year-old.

"Johnny, why didn't you pee before we left the room?" barked his father.

"I didn't have to go then," replied Little Johnny.

Ding! Floor fourteen—an elderly couple in their Sunday best joins the party.

The head count stood at fourteen. As the elevator doors started to close, Sarge heard a shout from the hallway.

"Hold the elevator, please," said a young woman.

The high roller, anxious to win big, barked in Sarge's direction, "Hell no, we're full. Shut that door, pal."

Julia squeezed Sarge's hand, flashing him a quick look that told him to take it easy.

"Mommy, I still have to pee," cried Little Johnny.

"I'll never get to that Monopoly slot machine," whined one of the Lilly Pulitzer twins.

"C'mon, let's go," slurred the drunk.

Sarge was determined to hold the doors for the woman now, especially in light of the protesters' attitudes. The young woman smiled at Sarge and mouthed *thank you*. With the last passenger of the trip safely onboard, Sarge released the button holding the door open. Halfway closed, the lights inside the elevator flickered, and the door stopped. Sarge glanced at Julia, registering a look of concern before she disappeared. She quickly reappeared, bathed in the eerie glow of the hallway's emergency lights, the look of concern replaced by sheer terror. The elevator car sat quiet for a moment, its passengers frozen in place. When the elevator mechanism rumbled, everyone gasped at once. When it shook again, the passengers screamed and surged toward the two-foot-wide exit.

The drunk and the high roller hit the door first, thrashing at the rest of them with panicked limbs.

"Calm down!" shouted Sarge. "We can all get out if we wait our turn."

High Roller ignored him and squeezed through the door, catching his toe in the space between the elevator and floor fourteen. He hit the carpet-covered concrete face first, bellowing a profanity-laced tirade at the empty hallway. The drunk tried to follow him into the hallway, but misgauged the distance between the doors, striking his left shoulder on the solid steel obstruction. He overcompensated for the sudden, unexpected lack of forward motion and careened backward into the elevator, tripping over his own feet. Before Sarge could react, the drunk tried to use Little Johnny as a crutch to lift himself up, pulling the kid on top of him in the process. Julia instinctively scooped the child into her arms, removing him from danger.

With his child suddenly clear of the impact area, the enraged dad landed several hard kicks to the man's stomach, causing him to projectile vomit on the elevator floor. Shrieks filled the elevator, along with the caustic smell of vomit and peach schnapps. With the elevator in pandemonium, the lights reenergized and the elevator door began to close. Sarge reacted by placing a hand in the door, preventing its closure and triggering the inner doors. The gap widened several inches before the power cycled, leaving the elevator car and the hallway illuminated by emergency lights.

Screams and crying promptly filled the small space, joined by voices from the hallway as hotel guests streamed out of their rooms in search of answers. *Put Sarge in charge.* The motto from his father's gubernatorial campaign rang true, giving him the clarity he needed to resolve their immediate problem.

Ignoring the chaos behind him, he placed himself between the elevator doors to prevent them from closing if the power cycled again. Placing his back against one side and pushing with both hands on the other, Sarge opened the door another foot. He was rewarded with a stampede of selfish, unruly passengers, led by Little Johnny's parents. Julia emerged last, covering her nose and muttering obscenities. He pulled her aside, away from the dispersing crowd of panicked passengers.

"You okay?" he asked, hugging her tightly.

"I'm fine. What about him?" Julia motioned toward the elevator.

"I'll take care of it," he said, giving High Roller a wide berth.

The self-important gambler hadn't moved from where he fell, reaching out frantically to grab anyone that staggered into range.

"I need help!" he said.

"Then get off your butt and look for it," said Sarge.

"Screw you, buddy! I'm hurt here," he groaned, grabbing at one of the older women's legs before he passed out.

The people from the elevator scrambled like bugs, eluding his grasp. Satisfied that High Roller wasn't going to pull anyone into his clutches, Sarge entered the car and grabbed the unconscious drunk by the legs. He dragged the guy through his own vomit and deposited him on top of High Roller.

He whispered to Julia as he took her hand and guided her down the hallway. "We need to get out of here."

"I think the stairs are in the middle of the floor, next to the ice machines," she said.

"I knew there was a reason I kept you around," he said, squeezing her hand and kissing her forehead. "I wonder why the backup generators haven't kicked in."

"EMP?"

"Don't say that word, Julia. Please don't say that word. Do you know how much trouble we'd be in if that were the case?"

"Based on what I just saw in the elevator? We'd be screwed," she replied.

"And stuck in a city dependent on electricity to run everything. Screwed might be a kinder-than-warranted assessment," he said, spotting the stairwell door.

A few feet in front of them, a male guest dressed in a white terrycloth bathrobe started kicking his door.

"Dammit, I'm locked out of my room!" screamed the man.

"Try your key," said a female voice from behind Sarge and Julia.

"Power's out, key won't work, you idiot," said the man. *Oh boy, here we go.*

"Don't call my wife an idiot!" exclaimed a second voice.

He pulled Julia past the robed door-kicker, barely escaping the inevitable fray. Sarge glanced over his shoulder in time to see a goateed man in jeans and a green Celtic T-shirt body-slam the guy against the door he was kicking, knocking it wide open. The man slid to the floor in a heap, half in and half out of the doorway. The Celtics fan cocked his foot back to deliver a kick, but stopped when the man's terrycloth robe parted, exposing his private parts.

"What happened?" hissed Julia, trying to look beyond Sarge.

"Trust me, you don't want to see. Keep going," he said.

They reached the fire exit door and opened it, staring into the darkness. Screams and the sound of trampling feet filled the stairwell.

"No lights," said Sarge as he squinted his eyes to make out any signs of activity.

"Not a problem," said Julia, illuminating the stairwell with her smartphone.

"Clever lady."

"Another reason to keep me around?"

"I can think of others, but this will do for now," he said, kissing her neck. "Hey, do you have a signal?"

She pulled the phone closer to their faces. *Full reception.*

"The good news is that this wasn't the result of an EMP," he said.

"What's the bad news?"

"We still have thirteen floors to go, followed by the lobby. If it's like this on the guest floors, imagine what it will be like out there," said Sarge.

CHAPTER 37

February 13, 2016
Caesars Palace Casino
Las Vegas, Nevada

Johnny Bagwell, aka *J-Bags*, checked the time—7:59 p.m. *Almost showtime*. He took one more glance around the casino to get his bearings. The plan was to allow the initial shock to settle, and then create a panic. Every union member had a different role throughout the casino floor. If the desired goal wasn't reached, he had the authority to escalate the situation. J-Bags hoped this option wasn't necessary. *The place is filled with innocent people.*

J-Bags had compared notes earlier with the new guy, DePetri. Several of the rank-and-file members of the union provided input on what happened during power outages in the casinos.

All of the major Las Vegas Strip hotels had massive diesel backup generators. A year ago, the Mirage, Stratosphere Casino and Circus Circus lost power when squirrels hit a Nevada Energy transformer, knocking out the substation. The power outage only lasted about an hour, but it exposed the procedures to be followed in the event of a power outage: Nevada Gaming Regulations require all gaming tables to stop operating, although the hand in play may be completed. Casino pit personnel immediately move into place to preserve the status quo and monitor the chips on the tables. Hotel security takes up positions near the exits in order to intercept anyone attempting to steal from the casino.

For the first several minutes following the Circus Circus outage in 2015, gamblers held their positions and remained calm. Circus Circus did not have a backup generator system like the other major hotels

For planning purposes, the Circus Circus scenario was most illustrative of what to expect, because J-Bags and his associates were told the backup generator systems would fail. He had no idea how the union would pull that off, and he didn't want to know. A strict "*do as you're told and don't ask questions*" policy had kept his career in the union on a steady, lucrative track. He had no intention of screwing that up tonight of all nights.

A sudden darkness overcame the casino floor, resulting in a collective gasp from everyone in the building. Despite knowing the exact moment the power outage would occur, J-Bags felt the same way. Frightened. The battery-powered emergency lights lining the vast casino cast a feeble, shadowing illumination throughout the room. Once his eyes adjusted to the new lighting scheme, he observed the patrons and the employees. *What will be their reaction? Will some type of primal instinct take over, causing the gamblers to make a desperate grab for the chips on the tables and run for the exits? Will opportunists take advantage of the weak by stealing their purses or wallets?*

A few screams penetrated the general chatter, but overall, the crowd remained surprisingly calm. The bulk of the noise came from casino managers and pit bosses passing sharp instructions to the table operators. Their crisp, staccato orders probably contributed to the illusion of control, delaying the inevitable panic. Unexpectedly, the lights brightened, producing a round of nervous applause. Several seconds into the jubilee, the lights went out again—this time to the sounds of annoyed gamblers.

J-Bags leaned against a nearby slot machine and listened to the growing signs of chaos. It started with the slot machine players, their concerns revolving around the credits stored in the machine they were playing. Did the power outage wipe out the machines' memories? Would they get their money back? The tide of irritation spread, resulting in raised voices and a few tense standoffs between angry, intoxicated gamblers and the casino staff.

J-Bags glanced at his illuminated Casio watch again. He and the boys had agreed they would wait five minutes after the lights went out. It had been four minutes. Close enough. Maybe it was time to start the fireworks. He made eye contact with one of his associates and nodded.

A few seconds later, shouts of *stop, thief* echoed through the darkened blackjack pits as a man ran through the casino, clutching a bag. Casino personnel ran after the man in vain.

"I want my money!" screamed a man from the slot machines.

A crashing sound accompanied his protest as security personnel rushed to the scene. J-Bags detected a noticeable shift in the general mood. In the dim light, from his vantage point next to a raised bank of slot machines, J-Bags could tell that the casino staff was nervous. They had expected the backup generators to kick in at this point. *Time to escalate this party.*

He moved to a bank of unoccupied slot machines near a plate-glass window overlooking the massive circular entrance to the hotel and lit a pack of Black Cat firecrackers. Incredibly, the exploding fireworks didn't have the intended effect on the gamblers. Most chose to stay with their money. *Are you kidding me?* Before J-Bags could put his *nuclear option* into action, he heard feedback noise from a bullhorn, followed by a familiar voice.

"All members of the Culinary Union and the Service Employees International Union, please listen up," shouted the man, silencing the room.

"Pursuant to our contract, we have declared this facility to be an unsafe work environment. It is our opinion that you are in danger of serious injury or even death as a result of these present conditions. Accordingly, under the Occupational Safety and Health Act, we are declaring a work stoppage and ask that you leave the premises immediately."

J-Bags watched as hundreds of employees simultaneously walked through the darkness toward the exits. Management personnel looked back and forth between each other, then upward out of habit—toward the inoperable cameras. Despite the bizarre exodus, casino patrons held steady, waiting for the lights to come on or the casino to refund their money. *For pete's sake. Time for the nuclear option.*

J-Bags systematically walked through the casino floor, placing eight RIS Mark 4 electric smoke grenades (ESG) in concealed locations. Thumbing the wireless firing system in his coat pocket, he walked to the nearest exit and activated the grenades. *This should do it.* Smoke billowed from the devices, immediately grabbing the nearest casino guests' attention. Shouts of "FIRE!" quickly followed, giving J-Bags an excuse to pull a fire alarm on the way out.

"Nuclear, plus," he muttered—unaware he had just killed or injured several dozen people with his unnecessary finale.

CHAPTER 38

February 13, 2016
Fourteenth Floor, Caesars Palace Hotel
Las Vegas, Nevada

Sarge and Julia stayed pressed against the wall inside the stairwell. Sarge needed to gather his thoughts before they stepped off on the long journey down. He wasn't convinced heading toward the lower levels was the best course of action. The casino and Forum Shops concourse had been jammed with people when they checked into the hotel. They needed to weigh their options. Stay on the guest floors, where it was less crowded, or take their chances down below.

"Something's off. I don't know this for a fact, but I have to assume that Caesars Palace would have a substantial backup generator. Power outages can't be rare in a city that draws this much juice. Why hasn't it kicked on?" asked Sarge.

"Right," said Julia. "But wouldn't the backup system operate independently of the power grid. Do you think the entire grid might be down? Wait, we need a window."

"Good idea," said Sarge, opening the door to assess the hallway situation. "Looks like things have calmed down out here."

Sarge and Julia eased into the hallway, slipping past a group of whispering guests. They headed toward the opposite side of the hotel floor, away from the elevator bank and the naked man sprawled halfway into the hallway, searching for a room with an open door. The sounds of a bickering couple drew them further toward a partially open doorway several rooms away.

"Look inside the room, but keep walking. Never know," said Sarge.

He slowed their pace as they drew even with the door, searching inside for a glimpse of the windows. Total darkness, except for automobile lights in the distance. They stopped a few doors down to discuss what they saw.

"I think we can safely rule out an EMP. I saw a ton of car lights. I've read conflicting opinions on the effect of an electromagnetic pulse on vehicles, but that's too many for even the most liberal EMP assessment," said Sarge.

"Solar flare?" asked Julia.

"I doubt it. I check solar activity forecasts every day. Today was no exception. There has been no significant solar activity and certainly no geomagnetic storm warnings."

"Then it had to be a deliberate attack on the grid," she said.

Sarge thought for a moment, deciding to reveal a secret he had kept from Julia.

"I think you might be right. I find it very odd that the backup generator system didn't take over. Those systems shouldn't be susceptible to general power outages. This could be a cyberattack," said Sarge. "A well-executed cyberattack could be more localized than an EMP. Hackers could have shut down the entire Las Vegas grid and the Caesars Palace network at the same time. Do you remember how the lights suddenly brightened and the elevator began to work again?"

"Sure," she said.

"It's possible the backup system attempted to fire, but was shut down," said Sarge. "This has all of the earmarks of a cyberattack. The question is how long will it take for the power company and the hotel to bring things back online?"

"We need to make a decision. Take our chances here, or take this show on the road?" asked Julia.

"Or try to get back into our room," suggested Sarge.

"Even if we go upstairs, there's no guarantee we can get in our room," said Julia. "That guy was kicking his door pretty hard."

"Wait, I just thought of something. It's not an option. The twenty-eighth floor requires a keycard. I assume that applies to the stairwell too," said Sarge.

"Then I guess we're going down," she said, starting for the stairwell exit.

When Julia opened the door, the sound of a fire alarm filled the hallway.

"Are you kidding me?" asked Sarge. "This changes everything."

Sarge took Julia by the hand and pulled her back into the hallway of the fourteenth floor.

"Let's wait here for a moment," said Sarge. "I suspect there will be a mass migration of crazed hotel guests descending those stairs in the next few minutes."

"Do you really think there's a fire?" asked Julia.

"It wouldn't surprise me," said Sarge, nodding down the hallway.

Soft, flickering light adorned a few of the doorframes, the rooms' occupants likely using their cigarette lighters to see in the dark.

"It's only a matter of time before some fool catches the place on fire."

"This is miserable," said Julia, shaking her head.

He held her tight and gently stroked her hair. Julia had a tough exterior, but everybody had a breaking point. She needed a moment, and so did he. They'd wait until the stampede died down before descending into the unknown.

CHAPTER 39

February 13, 2016
Roman Plaza Grounds, Caesars Palace Hotel
Las Vegas, Nevada

Sarge and Julia escaped the building unharmed. Despite a few hotel guests pushing their way down the stairwell in sheer panic, the majority of guests calmly arrived in the lobby, which had been cleared by hotel staff by that point. Sarge looked for an open area to let Julia sit and rest. Her feet were raw from walking down the thirteen flights of concrete stairs without shoes. She'd wisely abandoned her Versace high heels on the fourteenth floor, or they might be dealing with a sprained ankle. Her feet didn't require medical attention, but she needed to stay off them for now. He pulled off his jacket and wrapped her in it. High desert temperatures dipped significantly in the evening, especially in the winter. A comfortable seventy-degree day could rapidly turn into a cold, low-forties evening. They hobbled toward a display nestled between two boxed planters of flowers. No one had found this area, except for a few elderly people huddled on a bench next to the flowers.

"Here's a bench, darling," said Sarge.

She looked up at him and smiled.

"Much better," said Julia.

Sarge took off his shoes and removed his socks, slipping them on her feet.

"This is going to be a long, cold night," said Sarge.

"Chivalry is alive, even in the form of smelly socks," she teased.

He was glad to see she still had her patented sense of humor. Any different, and he'd be worried about the night ahead of them.

"If we can stand the cold, it would be best to stay in one place. Hopefully, the fire department will check out the hotel and find there's nothing wrong. If we get the all clear, at least we can go back inside until they let us back in our room."

Julia squeezed Sarge's hand as they heard gunshots in the distance. The sounds of car horns honking permeated the darkness.

"I'd like to stay right here for now," she said.

"Sounds like a plan," he said, sitting on the bench next to her. "This is exactly how I pictured it, you know."

"Our Valentine's weekend?" she said.

"Ha! I knew I might see some action in Vegas," he said, winking at her. "But this wasn't what I had in mind."

"I wish we had stayed in our room for more of that action," she said, taking his hand. "So, what did you picture?"

"Societal collapse. From the moment the power went out, until right now, the reaction of people has been astonishing. There was no cooperation, much less any courtesy. There was a visceral reaction ranging from fear to panic. Every man and woman for his or herself. The level of selfishness was astounding."

"It's like we've discussed before," said Julia. "People appear to be agitated, on edge. It seems to be getting worse."

Julia kissed Sarge on the cheek, hugging him tightly. He glanced over their shoulders and gestured toward the statue behind them.

"Besides, he'll have our back." Sarge laughed.

"Who will?" asked Julia.

"Him," he said, standing to examine the display.

"And who might that be," she said.

"I think I know, but let me read the placard," said Sarge, squinting to read the words.

He started laughing.

"Come on, tell me," insisted Julia.

"Well, my dear, our protector is sitting in the middle of a replica of the Hindu Erawan Shrine," said Sarge, shaking his head. "It appears that the original Erawan Shrine, located in Thailand, houses a similar gold statue."

"Who is it?" asked Julia.

"Our protector here," said Sarge, "is Phra Phrom, the four-faced representation of the Hindu God *Brahma*."

"No way, really?" Julia laughed.

"It's a small world, my darling," said Sarge. "This is the original Brahmin."

PART FOUR

CHAPTER 40

March 14, 2016
The Boston Herald Editorial Conference Room
Boston, Massachusetts

Julia reviewed her notes, waiting to address the editorial board. Her eyes darted up when Joe Sciacca, the *Herald*'s chief editor, activated the room's large-screen television. Images of Massachusetts Governor Charlie Baker filled the screen.

"The budget I have submitted is fair and comprehensive. It will require sacrifices on the part of many state agencies. I believe Bay Staters have no appetite for new taxes in this current economic environment. They also agree that a two-billion-dollar shortfall in the state budget is unacceptable. We don't have a revenue problem in Massachusetts, we have a spending problem."

Governor Baker stepped back from the podium while his Chief of Staff Elizabeth Guyton whispered something to him. He returned to the microphone.

"I'm advised there's time for a few questions. Bob Salsberg, Associated Press," said Governor Baker.

"Governor, thank you. For the fiscal 2015 budget, you implemented a twenty percent increase in the funding for the Massachusetts Bay Transportation Authority. Now, you aim to reduce their 2016 fiscal budget by the same amount, on the heels of a string of brutal winters," said Salsberg.

"Bob, is there a question on the horizon?" the governor interrupted, eliciting muffled laughter.

"Governor, is this budget cut retaliation for the criticism you have received from union leaders representing MBTA workers over the new commission convened to examine MBTA operations?" asked Salsberg.

Julia knew Bob Salsberg well and considered him to be a fair journalist. She also knew Elizabeth Guyton to be a very shrewd political operative. Governor Baker *wanted* this question, without appearing to welcome it.

"First of all, the entire Massachusetts government will see some belt-tightening. In the context of the situation we face and the circumstances we're dealing with, these are reasonable appropriations.

"Second, I stood up for the MBTA in last year's budget, by providing them a sixty-five million dollar increase in state subsidies. No other Massachusetts agency received such a generous increase. However, this additional funding was not used for its intended purpose—an upgrade of the T's infrastructure to prevent the types of breakdowns and interruptions in service we have seen this winter," said Governor Baker. *"When the people's money is mismanaged, there needs to be an accounting. As the highest elected official in this state, I'm willing to take ownership of the problems facing the T. But towards that end, I did empanel a committee of experts to examine the operations, which necessarily includes all of its contracts—including those with its unions."*

Governor Baker called on another reporter.

"Mac Daniel, Boston Globe,*"* said Governor Baker.

"Thank you, Governor," said Daniel. *"James O'Brien, president of the Boston Carmen's Union said, and I quote, 'He's no Scott Walker.' He's obviously referencing the Wisconsin governor's success against the teachers' union. Are you trying to break the unions at the MBTA?"*

"The Carmen's Union is one of the oldest and largest in the city," said Governor Baker. *"But the T's financial situation and past union contracts are more than problematic—they have made the T nearly insolvent. This cannot continue, and Mr. O'Brien knows this."*

Sciacca muted the television. Julia looked at her notes and then immediately towards her editor.

"Julia, what do you have on this?" asked Sciacca.

"Joe, my sources tell me the governor has swatted a hornet's nest," said Julia. "Union leaders around the country are concerned about the campaign rhetoric of certain Republican presidential candidates. Governor Walker's victories over the teachers' union in Wisconsin had a devastating effect on union influence and power across the nation. I'm told by contacts within the union that

Governor Baker's action will have serious, potentially ugly repercussions."

"Did they expand on the meaning of *repercussions*?" asked Sciacca.

"I asked the same question and the response I received was *Vegas*," said Julia.

Julia had been at ground zero during the Las Vegas incident. She and Sarge survived Saturday night unharmed, but the rest of the city didn't fare so well. By the time power was restored on Monday evening, one hundred and eight citizens of Las Vegas had been killed by the power outage, with more than two thousand injured. Property damage from fires and vandalism was conservatively estimated to top five hundred million dollars.

"Your source obviously alludes to the walkout of the CU 226 and the SEIU during the power outage," said Sciacca. "Has there been any connection between the power outage and the work stoppage?"

"Official statements from the FBI and Homeland are noncommittal. Based on anonymous statements by hotel management, the FBI believes an orchestrated walkout occurred. There has been no official word on the root cause of the blackout…" she said, trailing off.

"But?" asked Sciacca.

"You didn't hear this from me, but hotel IT personnel suspect a cyberattack," she said.

"I don't like the sound of this. Your union source knows more than he or she will admit—and they're playing with fire," said Sciacca.

"Frankly, I'm surprised they would cite Vegas as a model for repercussions. It's tantamount to murder," she said.

"Please don't repeat that outside of this room," said Sciacca. "All right, let's hear from Sandra on the interest rate story."

Ordinarily, Julia would tune out at this point, but the Federal Reserve had just increased the rates by another half point—a move that had repercussions across all departments.

"The fed funds rate—the rate at which one bank lends to another bank—has risen substantially over the last six months," said Gottlieb.

"It now stands at three percent. This is news, because the Federal Reserve chairman stated earlier that no additional rate hikes would be necessary in the near future. The Friday announcement came as a surprise, magnified by the size of the increase. This represents a three hundred percent increase over the last six months."

"Have your contacts at the Boston Fed weighed in on this?" asked Sciacca.

"Unofficially, yes," said Gottlieb. "The Fed appears to be concerned with inflation."

"We've experienced inflation in this country before," said Sciacca. "What's different?"

"My sources tell me that Yellin waited too long to begin raising rates," said Gottlieb. "In addition, economic growth is stagnant, hovering around two-tenths of one percent annualized. Of course, the velocity of money is increasing."

"Velocity of money?" asked Sciacca.

"We are dangerously close to a hyperinflationary scenario," said Gottlieb. "Despite a stagnant economy, inflation has increased dramatically. High velocity means banks, foreign governments and large institutional investors are dumping dollars and buying up hard assets like real estate. If this continues, coupled with the continued devaluation of the dollar, there could be a major meltdown in global financial markets."

And that was why Julia tended to listen when Sandra Gottlieb spoke about interest rates.

CHAPTER 41

March 17, 2016
St. Patrick's Day
South Boston, Massachusetts

Marion La Rue had the perfect vantage point from his hotel room at the Renaissance Boston Waterfront Hotel. His unobstructed view of South Boston, across the Seaport District, allowed him to take in the afternoon festivities, without getting close. The St. Patrick's Parade held in South Boston was the second largest parade in the country, viewed by nearly one million people and countless more on live television. The parade took a year of planning. La Rue's plan comprised eight hours of phone calls. He reviewed the notes taken during the calls.

MBTA South Station, the closest transit station to South Boston, was the largest railroad and intercity bus terminal in Boston. On this day, it typically moved a half-million passengers. The Red Line route was the busiest north-south transportation line, and the Gray Line serviced all of the downtown area before heading east to Logan International Airport. The two lines intersected at South Station, where hundreds of dedicated MBTA buses stood by to transport partygoers to Southie for the festivities.

Like clockwork, the parade kicked off at 1:00 p.m. at the Broadway T Stop. The parade route meandered easterly along Broadway, which would be packed with green-clad revelers—regardless of the weather conditions. For the next two and a half hours, floats, bands and local dignitaries would brave the damp, chilly Boston afternoon, steadily heading east on Broadway, toward the end of the parade route at Marine Park.

By 2:00, parade planners would instruct a parade of T buses to depart Gillette Park and take a northerly route to the back of Marine Park, to pick up parade-goers and return them to designated parking areas near South Station. *Not today.*

At 1:55 p.m., transit police received an anonymous call reporting a suspicious package at the corner of East First Street and Summer Street. Within moments, a second suspicious package was reported at the intersection of A Street and Summer Street. While the Massachusetts Bay Transit Authority dispatch center descended into chaos, a third report surfaced, identifying an unattended backpack package on Summer Street—at the entrance to Marine Park. Transit police quickly determined that the suspicious packages were located along the return MBTA bus route and requested Boston PD's Special Operations Unit. SWAT and EOD teams quickly descended on the packages. Before the specialized units arrived to assess the situation, Captain Richard Kavanaugh, South Boston district commander, ordered an evacuation of the route.

A few minutes after Captain Kavanaugh issued his order, an MBTA Transit police officer reported smoke billowing out of the red line tunnels—at both entrances to the South Boston station. Amidst blaring fire alarms, MBTA personnel and transit police struggled to evacuate the complex, multilevel station, emptying buses and hustling passengers onto Atlantic Avenue.

Within minutes of the ordered evacuations, the Boston Carmen's Union ordered their employees to leave their jobs and seek safety at home, stranding several hundred thousand rowdy parade-goers—as snow began to fall.

La Rue turned on the television and found WHDH, the local NBC affiliate. Adam Williams, one of WHDH's evening anchors, stood next to an unruly crowd of young men gathered near the abandoned reviewing stand. Thick snowflakes pelted Williams as he nodded at the camera, waiting for the intoxicated group behind him to finish their drunken cheer.

"I want to repeat this for our viewers. There have been multiple reports of suspicious packages left along the MBTA route between Gillette Stadium and the

pickup point for parade participants and attendees. We've also received reports of an evacuation at the South Boston station due to a possible fire. At this time, we don't know if the two events are connected. As you can see, the snow is falling heavily now, which is certain to complicate matters," said Williams.

La Rue's cell phone rang. He answered and listened intently for a moment.

"Thank you sir. Yes, sir, anytime you need me," said La Rue.

CHAPTER 42

March 17, 2016 (St. Patrick's Day)
Gillette Stadium Parking
South Boston, Massachusetts

Elijah "Pumpsie" Jones had spent his entire life in Boston. His mom and dad were longtime Red Sox fans, naming their youngest son after the first black Red Sox player, Elijah "Pumpsie" Green. Few were surprised when he took a job as an MBTA bus driver, spending the next thirty plus years driving around the city he loved. Naturally, he joined the Boston Carmen's Union when he was hired in 1982. Like today, union membership was the only way to "stay competitive" in the rank-and-file MBTA organization. Nonmembers tended to quit or get fired at two to three times the rate of union members. The decision was a no-brainer for Pumpsie, and despite the tense work strikes, he had few complaints about the organization that had kept his pay competitive year after year. He put two children through college and had a nice pension to show for his career—an uncommon accomplishment in the recent era of vanishing corporate pensions and annual downsizings.

A year ago, he retired and accepted a part-time position as the transportation coordinator for the St. Patrick's Day Parade—a perk that helped pay for two season tickets to Fenway Park. One for him and one for his grandson Levon. Pumpsie could barely afford the grandstand seats, but stretching his budget was worth it to spend time with Levon. Since Pumpsie's wife, Leticia, had died from a stroke, Levon had become his life. Family had always meant everything to him. Levon and his grandpa sat in the outfield grandstand for fifty-six of eighty-one home games in 2015—school was the only thing that kept Levon from making every game.

With thoughts of family on his mind, he pulled a well-worn Little League baseball card of his grandson out of his shirt pocket—*Levon Jones, Little League All Star.* He replaced the card and scanned the cold families. He couldn't let them stand around fighting for the few taxicabs that might straggle by South Station in all of the confusion. Especially given the circumstances.

When Pumpsie received reports of suspicious packages along the St. Patrick's Day pickup route and smoke billowing out of South Station, he prayed that the city hadn't been targeted again. A terrorist attack against the overpacked station would be devastating. The illusion of an attack rapidly cleared when the drivers poured out of the terminal en masse. The "suspicious package" thing had been orchestrated to justify a union walkout. For the first time in thirty years, he felt ashamed to be an honorary member of the Boston Carmen's Union. Playing on Boston's fears of another terrorist attack was unforgiveable.

Pumpsie surveyed the endless rows of MBTA Transit buses and patted his pocket.

"C'mon, Levon, let's go help some kids and their folks get home," he mumbled.

He reached the first bus in line pointing towards Summer Street and shook his head. The driver hadn't bothered to shut the door. Out of habit, Pumpsie walked the seats, searching for unauthorized riders. Every now and then, a vagrant would slip inside a bus and try to ride all day. Anything to get out of the cold. If they didn't smell too bad and looked generally presentable, he might turn a blind eye to the unpaid fare. Finding the bus empty, he slid his stout frame around the safety bar and settled into the ample driver's seat. Pumpsie caressed the oversized steering wheel like a prized relic. *Just like old times.*

He started the bus and let it run for a few minutes, pulling the lever to close the double doors when he was ready to roll. With his hands wrapped around the wheel, he eased forward and drove to the gated bus entry. Pumpsie activated the windshield wipers to combat the heavy snow melting against the massive front windows. It was going to be nasty out there!

Pumpsie passed Drydock Avenue, the bus rumbling over the Reserve Channel Bridge as it approached the FedEx shipping center. The road was empty, still blocked off for the fleet of buses that would never arrive.

Pumpsie wheeled the bus left onto East First Street, immediately slowing when he spotted a swarm of people headed in his direction. By the time he reached the first MBTA-designated St. Patrick's Day pickup, less than a block away, his bus was swarmed by a sea of green-covered Bostonians. Pumpsie brought the bus to a halt, the air brakes squeaking, then exhaling air. He decided to offer seats to the elderly, children and one of their parents first. *It was a start.*

He opened the door, expecting to be greeted by a relieved crowd of Bostonians, but was instead treated to angry accusations of MBTA incompetence, unspeakable vulgarities and racial-charged slurs. Instead of boarding the bus in an orderly manner, the green mob jammed into the doors. The women, kids and elderly he imagined would board first were nowhere to be seen; long ago discarded by the unruly jackals squeezing onto his bus. Within a minute, the bus had swallowed far more passengers than it was authorized to carry. Pumpsie shouted at the crowd trying to enter.

"Please everyone, this is the only bus running. I can't leave with this many people onboard!" pleaded Pumpsie.

"That's a bunch of bull!" yelled one man.

"Why don't you people do your job?" shouted another.

Pumpsie stood to block the entrance, but was immediately pressed against the handrail as more people shoved their way into the bus. Shrieks filled the air as the people in the back of the bus were squeezed together in the aisle.

"That's it! No more! No more!" yelled Pumpsie, reaching for the door lever.

"I'll drive this thing myself," screamed a man, who grabbed his arm and slung him into the people trying to push up the bus steps.

The crowd ripped at him, pulling him through the tangled mass of people until he was out of the bus. Once on the sidewalk, he was shoved and punched by the drunken horde, his body bouncing back and forth like a pinball between angry, faceless hooligans. When the smell of stale beer and cigarette smoke mixed with the scent of blood, Pumpsie's survival instinct kicked into high gear. He started swinging his arms wildly, punching in every direction. The mob reacted by grabbing all of his limbs and tossed him head first into the side of the red brick building.

Barely able to move from the jarring impact, he painfully rose up on his hands and knees—only to be kicked in the stomach by a man passing by. Flattened on his stomach, he lowered his head into a widening pool of blood and stared blankly toward the Little League fields caddy-corner to the MBTA stop. Beyond the chain-link fence separating the street from the fields, he caught a glimpse of a little boy holding a green leprechaun balloon. Pumpsie's hand dug between his chest and the cold cement, finding the Little League All Star card. He slid his hand next to his face and smiled at his beloved Levon as his vision faded.

CHAPTER 43

March 18, 2016
100 Beacon
Boston, Massachusetts

Steven stood and watched the continued coverage of the St. Patrick's Day disaster on the televisions in Sarge's living room.

"Sarge, did you want to see this?" asked Steven.

Governor Charlie Baker was about to make his first statement concerning the events from his press room at the State House.

"Yeah, hold on," replied Sarge.

"Don't tell me to hold on; it's your boy Baker who's about to speak," said Steven.

Steven left politics to Sarge and the others. He turned up the volume as Governor Baker spoke.

"My fellow Bay Staters and Bostonians, I am speaking to you as more than just the governor of the great state of Massachusetts, but as a dejected, sorrowful human being. The senseless acts of violence in South Boston sadden me to my core. Nineteen people have died in the past twenty-four hours. Victims of the cold. Victims of violence. Victims of the Boston Carmen's Union.

"I have spoken to many of the families who lost loved ones, to express my condolences. To express our city's condolences.

"In particular, I spoke with young Levon Jones, the grandson of Elijah Jones, and assured him that his grandfather was a hero, and that the people responsible for his grandfather's death would be brought to justice."

"It's a shame what happened to that old man," said Steven. "One good guy in a sea of cowards."

"After what we saw in Las Vegas, I'm convinced that the cowards far outnumber the good guys," said Sarge.

"I have patiently waited nearly twenty-four hours to make this statement because I wanted to have full reports from the Boston Police Department, the Massachusetts Bay Transit Authority Police—and from the special commission appointed to review the operations of the MBTA. While I recognize this investigation is still ongoing, certain facts have become abundantly clear."

Governor Baker leaned forward onto the podium and looked directly into the single State House-provided television camera.

"I believe the walkout by the members of the Boston Carmen's Union was orchestrated by their union representatives. Their subversive acts directly caused the events of yesterday, from the pointless death of Elijah Jones, to the resulting damage to property, and the ancillary deaths in the Roxbury and Dorchester riots."

As Governor Baker paused for effect, Sarge reacted to this bold statement.

"Julia called it," said Sarge. "Her source in the union said one word to her *before* this happened—Vegas."

The governor continued. *"Today I have executed Massachusetts Executive Order Number 596, which provides in part that all members of the Boston Carmen's Union and the Service Employees International Union members who abandoned their shifts operating the MBTA transportation buses for yesterday's parade are terminated for cause. Further, the executive order bars any union officers directly under investigation from government property. Like the nearly identical walkout in Las Vegas, which killed more than a hundred people, yesterday's walkout was taken straight out of the new union playbook. I will not tolerate it in our state, and I write the rules."*

"Can he do that?" asked Steven.

"I doubt it," said Sarge. "The state and federal laws are very pro-union. He'll have a fight, but it does send a message about his intentions."

Governor Baker continued. *"I know this executive action will be unpopular with the government employee unions. But I ask all Bay Staters to keep an open mind as we go through this difficult time. Lives were lost yesterday because of a knee-jerk reaction to an ongoing and publicly supported look into MBTA operations.*

"I leave you with this thought. Organized labor has played an important role

in the development of our nation. History has shown that organized labor was instrumental in protecting the rights of workers in private business. I want to emphasize the term private *here. With respect to union activity in the operation of government, the public sector, I choose to follow the words of President Franklin Roosevelt, the patron saint of the American labor movement. FDR cautioned about the growing presence of public sector labor unions in 1937. He recognized the special relationship and obligations of public servants to the public itself and the government for which they work.*

"FDR *explicitly issued this warning, and I quote, 'Militant tactics have no place in the functions of any organization of governmental employees. A strike of public employees manifests nothing less than the intent to prevent or obstruct government.' I believe that the actions undertaken yesterday by the public service unions who owe their service to you, the taxpayers of Massachusetts, was intolerable and beyond belief. I will work diligently to assure you no public employee will ever paralyze our government's services again. Thank you.*"

"Wow," said Sarge. "He just laid down the gauntlet. He effectively created a class war between the unions and the taxpayers. Also, he deflected blame for the deaths of the bus driver and the people during the riots squarely on the shoulders of the union management who ordered the walkout."

"Where it should be. Sounds like we just got thrown back to the days of baseball bats and busted kneecaps," added Steven. "I think we need to get out of Boston for a few days."

"Why does it sound like I'd rather take my chances here?" asked Sarge.

"Because you know me too well," said Steven.

CHAPTER 44

March 19, 2016
The Mall at Chestnut Hill
Newton, Massachusetts

"Look at all of the beautiful coral, Mommy," exclaimed her daughter Rebecca.

She is definitely going to be a beach girl. Susan steered the seven-year-old girl toward the entrance to Vineyard Vines. The pink whale awaited. She watched Donald's reaction, fully expecting him to protest. He was not a fan of the mega shopping malls or going out in public at all. Donald preferred online shopping and spending time at home. Today he appeared indifferent to the "forced" experience, almost nervous.

"Yes, Becca, the coral is exquisite," said Susan.

"Ex-quit?" repeated Rebecca.

"No, it's exquisite, dopey," chimed in Penny, her older sister. "C'mon, guys. I see lots of pink!"

While Rebecca might grow up to be a seafarer like many of her Lowell ancestors, Penny would be the lady of the ship, awaiting another summer cocktail.

"Don't call me dopey, whale breath," replied Rebecca. The girls scurried ahead with the wind at their sails.

"Honey, are you okay?" she asked her husband. "We might find a few things in here for you as well. I'll show the girls around. Why don't you check out the golf stuff?" Susan picked up a dozen Titleist golf balls, which sold for sixty-two dollars. *Isn't five dollars per golf ball a little much?*

"Yes, I'm fine. Just thinking about *stuff*," said Donald. "You girls shop 'til you drop, and I'll see if I can force myself to buy a polo shirt with a pink whale on it."

The two shared a laugh, but Susan wasn't convinced Donald was in a joking mood.

"Okay, I love you. I need to catch up with the girls," said Susan.

Donald gave her a squeeze and said I love you back, but she could sense he was troubled.

Susan caught up with the girls while she watched Donald wander over to the men's side of the store. He stood staring at a large mural of a yacht making a sharp turn in choppy seas. Susan found the image ironic. *We are sailing choppy seas, are we not?*

"Look at this gorgeous wave print on this dress, girls," said Susan.

She held up a pleated dress with blue waves rolling across it in all directions.

"It doesn't have any pink, Mom," protested Penny. *Of course it doesn't.*

"I like it!" squealed Rebecca. *Of course you do.*

"How about this one?" asked Susan.

She held up a tunic-style dress covered in pink sailboats. Both girls squealed with delight. *Compromise.*

"Good work, Mom," said Penny. *How old are you?*

"Now, girls, we need to find you something appropriate for Easter," said Susan. "We can't wear a sailboat dress to church."

"Why not, Mommy?" asked Rebecca. *Legitimate question.*

"Well, honey," started Susan, "you know how we like to put on our Sunday best for church?"

"Yes," replied Rebecca.

"Okay. The sailboat dress is beautiful, but it's really a little too casual. What do you think?" asked Susan.

"She's right, Becca. Let's keep looking," said Penny.

The girls thumbed through the racks while Susan searched for Donald. He was still wandering through the men's section—empty handed.

"Mommy?" asked Penny, holding up a long white seersucker dress complete with a pink ribbon belt.

"That's much better, girls," said Susan.

"This is our *Sunday much better* dress," said Rebecca.

Susan heard a loud commotion from the mall concourse outside of the Vineyard Vines store and turned in Donald's direction. She spotted him walking swiftly toward the front doors of the store. Her husband stopped next to the wide opening and peered into the mall concourse. As the voices grew louder, Donald gestured for her to stay back while the rest of the store's customers walked toward the front of the store.

"Black lives matter! Black lives matter!" she distinguished from the angry discordance of yelling.

The girls dropped their dresses and grabbed Susan around the waist.

"Mommy, what's happening?" asked Penny.

"I don't know, my baby, but your daddy will find out."

The chanting seemed to get louder. She wrapped her arms around the girls and ushered them toward the front of the store, where they could be together as a family.

"What's going on, Donald?" Susan asked.

"Protesters," he replied, never taking his eye off the approaching mob. "I was afraid something like this might happen. I could feel it somehow."

Susan followed his gaze until she found the source of the noise. The lower level of the Chestnut Hill Mall was filled with black protestors wearing white tee shirts that featured a picture of Pumpsie Jones, the victim of the St. Patrick's Day Parade killing. The protestors were rapidly climbing the escalators stairs, spilling onto the upper level—headed in their direction.

"What do we do?" asked Susan, her voice trembling.

"This has been happening all over the country," said Donald. "The last two days have been volatile everywhere."

"Where are the mall police?"

Donald laughed. "Moving quickly in the opposite direction, I would presume. They're not equipped for something like this."

"Somebody has to do something," said Susan.

She craned her neck to look further into the mall. Protestors now outnumbered shoppers twenty to one on the concourse.

"Do you remember a year or so ago when the Black Lives Matter protestors invaded the first floor of the Mall of America in Minneapolis?" asked Donald.

Susan nodded.

"They staged a similar demonstration, but the Minneapolis police were ready. They anticipated trouble and uniformed officers closed off the upper floors for the benefit of the mall shoppers. The protestors were confined to the lower floors. Eventually they left without incident. Let's just wait it out and let the police get things under control."

"But look, they're all running up the escalators now," said Susan, pointing to the right of them. "I don't see any security or police."

As soon as she finished her sentence, the mall's public address system squawked.

"*Attention! Attention, please! This demonstration is not authorized and is in clear violation of the Mall at Chestnut Hill policy. We expect all participants to disperse at this time. Those who continue to demonstrate will be subject to arrest. I repeat, you are ordered to disperse. The mall is now closed.*"

Shouts immediately echoed off the walls and the ceiling of the mall.

"This is our freedom of speech."

"We have a right to be here!"

"Black lives matter!"

"You will not silence us!"

The panicked order to disperse repeated itself, now barely audible over the growing crowd of chanting protesters. A man holding two shopping bags slid into view in front of Vineyard Vines and started shouting at the protestors.

"You people need to shut up!" he shouted. "We are sick and tired of this crap. Go back to Roxbury."

This brought a roar of profanities from the mob.

"What do you mean by *you people*?" one protestor shouted.

"You heard me! Shut up! This is getting old and we're done with it," the man shouted back.

He looked around him as if to seek support or comrades-in-arms. There were no takers.

"This isn't helping," said Donald, easing back from the edge of the opening.

Susan looked beyond the man to the other side of the upper level. Three teenagers dumped their soda cups on the crowd below, igniting a fury of shouts. The protestors sprinted in their direction, tackling them to the ground. The protest had taken one of its final steps toward spiraling into a full-scale riot.

"We need to shut these doors," said Donald. He turned to look into the store. "Where are the employees?"

"I don't know," said Susan.

Earlier, Susan didn't bother to look for any store employees. She and the girls could help themselves. Besides, on a Saturday night, the employees were probably young girls who wouldn't understand the needs of a seven- and ten-year-old anyway. They sure wouldn't be of any help in a situation like this.

"You are hereby ordered to disperse," announced a voice from a megaphone below. "This is unauthorized and you must disperse immediately!"

"The cops must be here," said Donald.

Susan felt a sense of relief. *I just want to get my babies home.*

"Hands up, don't shoot! Hands up, don't shoot!" shouted the protestors in unison.

Susan saw Donald searching the faces in the store for its staff. She could not find any Vineyard Vines personnel either. The idiot in front of the store began shouting towards the police.

"Hey, these savages are attacking three young boys up here! You have to help them," shouted the man.

Susan watched as mayhem erupted in front of her. The man was immediately swarmed by at least a dozen people.

"Who are you callin' savages?" shouted one woman.

"Screw you, honky racist!" screamed another.

Donald pulled Susan and the girls with him to the side.

"I'm going to close the storefront grille gate," said Donald. "Here's the button. When I give you the signal, you push it here where it reads *close*. Okay?"

Susan shook uncontrollably when she reached for the control mechanism. Both girls cried loudly, clinging to her.

"Are you leaving us?" asked Susan. "Where are you going?"

"It's okay," said Donald. "I have to make sure no one gets caught under the gate when it closes. I also want to make sure nobody gets in either."

When Donald started to walk away, the girls screamed.

"Listen up, my big girls," said Donald. "Daddy is going to work with Mommy to close the store's gate. After everything calms down and the angry people go home, we'll go home too. Okay?"

The girls' crying turned into wet sniffles, and they nodded their heads. Donald wiped away their tears and gave Susan a smile before heading toward the entrance. She watched as Donald advised the customers to either step in or step out. All of them chose the former. When everyone was clear, he gave her a thumbs-up. Susan pressed the close button, and the steel-reinforced security gate descended with a loud clanking noise. Susan watched for a reaction outside of the store, but the mob ignored the gate. When the door reached the halfway point, she heard Donald shout.

"You can stay out there, buddy!"

"Let me in. They'll kill me! Please," yelled the man who had challenged the crowd earlier.

The other customers stood back as the bloodied man tried to slide under the rolling gate. Two protestors grabbed the man by his feet and tried to pull him back into the concourse. The man desperately pleaded with Donald.

"Please! These savages will tear me apart!"

Donald shook his head in disgust and grabbed the man's wrists. Arms straining, he yanked the guy's body out of the mob's grasp and into the store, moments before the gate clanged to a stop against the tile floor. The crowd immediately slammed against the steel gate, ramming it with their shoulders and pounding it with their fists. The bloodied man pulled his wrists free from Donald and rose to his feet, pointing at the protesters through the steel grating.

"Ha ha, you idiots," said the man.

Donald hit the man in the face, knocking him unconscious with a single punch. "Shut up."

CHAPTER 45

March 24, 2016
Harvard Kennedy School of Government
Cambridge, Massachusetts

"Good morning, everyone, let's get started on our last lecture before spring break," said Sarge.

GLOBAL GOVERNANCE
and
ASYMMETRIC WARFARE

Sarge had enjoyed the first half of the new semester with his students. The more unstable the world became geopolitically, the more interested his students became in the subject matter of his lectures, and it didn't hurt that his book, *Choose Freedom or Capitulation,* remained a *New York Times* best seller. Demand for Sarge to speak on the subject of America's sovereignty grew to the point his publisher thought he should start charging a fee. A candidate in the presidential campaign even referenced his book during a Republican debate at the University of South Florida in Tampa. Sarge had a hunger for knowledge and he thought it was incumbent to share what he knew with others. His position at Harvard Kennedy, coupled with his book, gave him a forum and—to an extent—a captive audience. *Why shouldn't I give people the ability to formulate their own opinions?*

"How many of you agree with this statement?" asked Sarge. "Wars can be both economic and militaristic."

Sarge planned on counting the hands, but the class was unanimous in its agreement.

"How about this one?" asked Sarge. "A militaristic war can be fought over economic issues."

The show of hands reflected unanimity. *Let's get them involved.*

"Mr. Ocampo, what is a currency war?" asked Sarge.

This young man continued to shine. He had also become *friendly* with Miss Crepeau. *Now that would be a formidable duo someday.*

"A currency war is the battle between countries as they attempt to destroy the value of their own currency," said Ocampo.

"Are you telling the class that a country might deliberately try to devalue their own currency?" asked Sarge. "Why would they do that?"

"Let me use the United States dollar as an example," said Ocampo. "As the dollar goes down in value, the price of our exported goods follows suit. Other countries will increase their purchases of American goods, which in turn stimulate our economy. The net result is American business increases its production and hires more employees."

"Sounds like a good plan if you live in the United States, does it not, Miss Crepeau?" asked Sarge.

"That's true, but it also hurts our ability to purchase imported products when the dollar is weak," said Crepeau. "For example, the bulk of the household goods purchased by Americans come from China. If our dollar is weak, the price of those goods can skyrocket, resulting in inflation."

"That's a very good point, Miss Crepeau," said Sarge. "During a currency war, a nation may take affirmative steps to reduce the value of its currency in order to stimulate its own lagging economy. But in the process, its citizens pay a price in the form of inflation."

Sarge observed the room. *Let's call on Mr. Mantega.* Mantega's grandfather was the former Brazilian Finance Minister.

"Mr. Mantega, how does a nation devalue its own currency?" asked Sarge.

"There are three ways to devalue your own currency," said Mantega. "Using the U.S. dollar as an example, the Federal Reserve can sell dollars and purchase other currencies, like the Chinese renminbi. Technically, that wouldn't happen, because the two countries no longer have an exchange rate cooperation agreement, but it's just an example. Second, the Fed could print money. The term they like to use is *quantitative easing.* Really, it means they're flooding the world economy with newly minted dollars. By creating a large supply of USD, the demand for the dollar goes down and so does the value. Third, a central bank can lower its interest rate to near zero. Finally, our government officials can discourage currency manipulators from speculating on the dollar by trash-talking our own dollar."

"Very good, Mantega," said Sarge. "A government will purposefully devalue its currency in order to stimulate economic growth within its borders. It does so at the expense of other nations' productivity and the risk of increased inflation, which places a burden on its own citizens. How does that make you feel?"

"Sounds pretty sketchy to me," said Mr. Lin. Sarge and the class laughed with Lin.

"I agree with Mr. Lin; this activity sounds *sketchy* to me as well," said Sarge. "Yet it happens every day on the world stage as governments compete with each other for that almighty dollar, or the renminbi, as the case may be." Sarge switched the slide.

BEGGAR THY NEIGHBOR

"This phrase was coined by the famous political scientist and economist Adam Smith, whose classic treatise *The Wealth of Nations* earned him the title as the father of modern economics," said Sarge. "Smith stood for free trade and laissez-faire economics—transactions should be between private parties thus free from government interference, such as regulations and taxes. Smith coined the phrase *beggar thy neighbor* as a policy through which one country attempts to remedy its economic problems, without regard to the economic problems created in another country.

"In the context of global governance, can you see how the interaction between nations can be complicated by a currency war?"

asked Sarge rhetorically.

The students nodded their heads affirmatively.

"Smith's *beggar thy neighbor* theory can also be applied to international trade," said Sarge. "In this presidential campaign, a significant amount of dialogue has centered around the trade deficit the United States has with China. One candidate in particular wants to levy an import tax on Chinese goods. His theory is that American goods would become more competitive, because the price of Chinese goods would be too expensive with the added import tax."

"Mr. Lin, does that sound *sketchy* to you?" asked Sarge.

"If I were his boss, I would say *you're fired*!" replied Lin to a round of laughter. "An import tax on Chinese goods would raise the price to Americans and result in inflation. Plus, the Chinese would not sit still and take it. I expect they would retaliate in kind."

"You're right, Mr. Lin," said Sarge. "In such a scenario, the United States would make the first move in a trade war and enjoy a modicum of success initially. But China would eventually react, leveling the playing field to protect the domestic and economic welfare of its country."

"What started as a run-of-the-mill currency war has now escalated into a trade war as well," said Sarge. "What could happen next?"

There were no volunteers to answer this question.

"I will submit to you in this geopolitical climate, currency wars can lead to trade wars. Trade wars often lead to hot wars," said Sarge. "When two opposing global powerhouses—bulls, if you will—butt heads repeatedly over currency manipulation and trade embargoes, the next step could be asymmetric warfare, which might include military action."

Sarge changed the slide.

GEOPOLITICAL FOES

"In the 2012 election, Mitt Romney famously said that America's biggest geopolitical foe was Russia," said Sarge. "He was widely criticized by the President and the media for making such a statement. I believe the President's words were 'the 1980s are now calling to ask for their foreign policy back because, you know, the Cold War's been over for twenty years.' How many of you believe we have entered a new cold war with the Russians?"

Most of the class raised their hands.

"Mr. Mann, tell me why you think a cold war exists with Putin," said Sarge.

"Once the Russians took control of Crimea and extended its military reach into Ukraine, the relationship between our two countries hit rock bottom," said Mann. "The Russians have now threatened the Baltic States militarily, and even alluded to the use of nuclear weapons if another country interfered with their attempts to reunify the former Soviet Union."

"Mann has touched on just a few of the most noteworthy events," said Sarge. "There have been sightings of Russian nuclear submarines throughout the waters surrounding Europe. Recently, Russian intelligence ships have docked in Havana, Cuba. Their long-range bombers are routinely observed in the Caribbean and within international waters of the Gulf of Mexico. Sounds a lot like the Cold War to me.

"How many of you believe the Russian economy has been badly damaged by United States-led sanctions and the falling price of oil?" asked Sarge.

The class was unanimous in agreement.

"Should the economic conflicts between the United States and Russia continue to inflict damage on the Russian people, I believe tremendous political pressure will be placed on Putin to react," said Sarge. "If Russia doesn't have any economic bullets to fire at us, they will either enlist the assistance of their new ally—China—or they will consider other, more serious forms of retaliation.

"This is how economic wars based upon currency and trade can escalate into a military conflict. Typically, belligerent nations will exercise restraint. However, the current geopolitical conflict between Russia and the United States could become an asymmetric war of epic proportions."

CHAPTER 46

March 25, 2016
Senate Intelligence Briefing
Washington, D.C.

Abbie patiently awaited James Clapper, director of National Intelligence, and Admiral Mike Rogers, director of the National Security Agency, to appear in the secure briefing room on the lower level of the Capitol Visitor Center. It was almost 4:00 p.m. and nearly two-thirds of the chairs in the room were empty. Most of her colleagues on the Intelligence Committee had opted to catch flights home for the two-week Easter recess, instead of attending what they assumed was a routine briefing.

"Hi, Senator," whispered Katie O'Shea. "It's so nice of you to join the other nine senators who care about what I've got to say. Nice bag, is that a Gucci Aviatrix?"

The women laughed together. Abbie and Katie had become close friends since Abbie's arrival in Washington. Although the two couldn't socialize publicly, they shared many evenings in Abbie's Georgetown townhouse, watching movies and sharing bottles of wine. Abbie loved Katie for her bluntness—and the stories of her sexual escapades. Abbie called her life *The Fifty Shades of Katie O'Shea.*

"I expected you to skip this today," said Katie. "Shouldn't you be campaigning? I would have brought you up to speed."

"My campaign manager says I need to attend all Intelligence Committee meetings and functions," said Abbie. "She doesn't want me to get Kay Hagan'ed"

Abbie was referring to former senator Kay Hagan of North Carolina, who was criticized during her failed senate reelection bid because she missed numerous Armed Services Committee hearings.

"Yeah, makes sense," said Katie.

"What are you doing here?" asked Abbie.

Katie was a rising star in the national intelligence community. Through some assistance, she was elevated to a high-level security clearance within the recently formed National Insider Threat Task Force. The NITTF was formed as a rapid-response agency to address high-profile incidents, such as the Fort Hood shooting, the Wikileaks debacle and the explosive Edward Snowden revelations. After years of focusing on outside threats to the nation's security, the federal government had finally turned inward, utilizing a broad range of technologies and counterintelligence strategies to root out spies, terrorists or leakers. The NITTF was despised within the intelligence community, having dropped the *see something, say something* directive in every department's lap.

"Well, you get to watch me in action today," said Katie. "Director Clapper wants me to brief the Senate Intelligence Committee on a matter that has come to our attention. This information was verified earlier in the day. Director Clapper and Admiral Rogers will declare this meeting classified, and the press will be removed so the senators may ask questions without fear of media spin or intrusion."

"About time," said Abbie. "It should always be that way. Why did they delay the briefing until four?"

"This is going to be a fairly big news story, which is why they waited until late Friday afternoon before the Easter recess, when most of D.C. has left town," said Katie. "Plus, they wanted all major markets to be closed for the announcement."

"What's going on?" asked Abbie.

Director Clapper approached the microphone, and everyone scrambled to take their seats. Katie pulled away to take her seat at the front of the room, but leaned back quickly to whisper something to Abbie.

"Your dad's not going to be happy."

CHAPTER 47

March 25, 2016
73 Tremont
Boston, Massachusetts

John Morgan carefully reviewed the last of the reports provided to him by Donald Quinn. He made notations on the reports, which focused on the European financial situation. Political tensions had begun to boil over in the Eurozone, signaled by several new breaking points identified by direct sources and painstaking analysis. There were new rifts in an already broken alliance.

Germany had reached a critical decision point. The nation had carried the Eurozone economically and politically since its inception. The anticipated European Central Bank (ECB) announcement of yet another round of quantitative easing could cause the euro to spiral downward and push Germany back to the deutsche mark.

Germany's strongly articulated position against QE put them at odds with the French. France's left-leaning politicians had been extremely vocal in their support of more quantitative easing by the ECB. They considered a weak euro to be critical to their economic survival. The far-right Front National party, which made a resurgence in the wake of renewed French nationalism, vowed to take action to restore France's independence from the Eurozone if the ECB devalued the currency to the point of an inflation nightmare. A break from the Eurozone was a long shot, but just the talk of it made the rest of Europe nervous. *The more anxiety, the better.*

On the opposite side of the spectrum, Europe had its leeches, as Morgan liked to call them—Greece, Spain and Italy. Unwilling to adopt austerity measures, they were doomed to economic failure. It was only a matter of time. No level of International Monetary Fund intervention could prevent the inevitable. The IMF was a speed bump on the road to financial ruin for the leeches. An environment of low growth and high unemployment had bred support for radical political alternatives, few with any basis in rational, constructive nation building. Societal unrest in these three countries made the headlines daily, and would only get worse.

Morgan contemplated the practical aspects of the Eurozone's collapse. The demise of the euro would not resolve the problems associated with the U.S. government's excessive national debt. The Eurozone was a major trading partner of the United States, so the implosion of the euro would undoubtedly produce a period of economic pain and instability. He projected five years—long enough for companies and governments to pick up the pieces. It was a small price to pay to liberate the European markets from the old-world European oligarchs whose fortunes and interests currently held Europe hostage. *Serves them right.*

He recalled a statement Winston Churchill made prior to the start of the Second World War. *The era of procrastination, half measures and delays is coming to a close. In its place we are entering a period of consequences.* A collapsed Eurozone would have particular consequences for United States financial institutions that had financed European banks through low-interest money. Morgan scribbled a note on his pad, which read *turn off the spigot.* The intercom buzzed on John Morgan's desk.

"Yes, Malcolm."

"Mr. Morgan, Secretary Lew on the line for you," said Malcom Lowe.

Morgan pushed the button to activate the speakerphone. *This is unexpected.*

"Hello, Jack, you're on speakerphone, but we are alone," said Morgan. "How are you?"

"Very well, Mr. Morgan," said Jack Lew, the Secretary of the Treasury. "I will get right to the point. I have some disturbing news for you."

Morgan sat back in his chair and rubbed his temples. "Go ahead, Jack."

"I'm sure you are familiar with the National Insider Threat Task Force—the NITTF," said Lew without waiting for a response. "They just completed a briefing of the Senate Intelligence Committee. There's a leak in the Treasury Department, affecting the Federal Reserve."

"Jack, what is it?" asked Morgan abruptly.

"We believe someone within the Treasury is going to leak the details of the Federal Reserve System's balance sheet," said Lew. "It's all going to come out, but we just don't know how yet. There have been cryptic messages from the hacker group Anonymous. They claim to be acting on behalf of the *audit the fed* crowd."

"Is the good senator from Kentucky behind this?" asked Morgan.

"We don't know anything for sure at this point, Mr. Morgan. He stands to benefit the most, because he made this a major platform issue in his presidential campaign," said Lew.

"The balance sheet, huh? Break it down for me, Jack," said Morgan.

"The liabilities of the Federal Reserve are eight point seven trillion dollars," said Lew. "This is nearly double the figure the public normally hears."

"That doesn't surprise me," said Morgan. "I assume you have worse news?"

"The assets of the Fed are an even bigger issue," said Lew. "Over half of the Fed's assets are mortgage-backed securities acquired after the 2008 crisis. These securities are backed by distressed home loans, car loans and near worthless derivatives."

"What are the total assets?" asked Morgan.

"Approximately forty-nine billion," said Lew. "That's about half of the commonly assumed estimates."

"Of course. So, the Federal Reserve is currently leveraged at a ratio of two hundred to one?" asked Morgan. "Half of those assets are worthless? Is that correct?"

"Yes, sir," said Lew.

Morgan remained silent as he contemplated the revelation. The only way to increase the assets of the Fed was to print an inordinate amount of dollars and hold them on their balance sheet. They wouldn't become Fed liabilities until they were put into circulation. If the Fed were to pump that much money into the money supply, inflation would skyrocket.

"Are you going to issue more currency?" asked Morgan.

"It's our only option at this point," said Lew. "There is one additional problem."

"I can't wait to hear about it," said Morgan with a tone of incredulity. *How can these people be so incompetent?*

"It's the gold number sir," said Lew. "It is commonly assumed the Federal Reserve has slightly over two hundred billion dollars in gold reserves."

"What's the real number," asked Morgan.

"Twenty-three billion," said Lew.

"Goodbye, Jack." Morgan disconnected the call.

"Malcolm," he barked into the intercom, "get me Katie O'Shea immediately!"

Morgan gripped the arms of his chair like a patient at the dentist's office with no anesthesia. Disclosure of the truth regarding the Federal Reserve would devastate the markets worldwide, bringing an end to the secrecy enjoyed by the shadow bankers in this country—like Morgan and his associates. The buzz of the intercom interrupted his angst.

"Sir, Miss O'Shea on the line as requested," said Lowe.

Morgan slapped the phone to accept the call.

"Miss O'Shea, why did I have to hear about this from that do-nothing Lew?" asked Morgan brusquely.

"I am sorry, sir, but I was in Director Clapper's office during the entire briefing, and was unable to make any calls," apologized Katie.

"Tell me everything you know," said Morgan.

"First, let me summarize the facts," said Katie.

She explained the discovery of the leak and the details of the data obtained. She also assured him all law enforcement and intelligence agencies were working on this investigation around the clock.

"Do you have a working theory, Miss O'Shea?" asked Morgan.

"Sir, Director Clapper is of the opinion—" started Katie, before Morgan interrupted her.

"No, Miss O'Shea, if I wanted Clapper's opinion, I'd call him myself," said Morgan. "Tell me what *you* think."

"Yes, sir," said Katie. "I have not discussed my premise with anyone."

Morgan had been impressed with Katie's astute analysis in the past. She had the ability to see situations differently than her counterparts, and was truly a valuable asset.

"Although my primary responsibilities with the National Insider Threat Task Force deal with internal investigations of intelligence personnel, I have access to information gathered by other agencies within the intelligence apparatus," said Katie. "This week, while coordinating on a matter with the Cyber Threat Intelligence Integration Center, I stumbled onto something that might be related. Certainly you are familiar with the hacker group Anonymous?"

"Yes, of course," said Morgan.

"Recently, another group has emerged that appears equally skilled in cyber tactics," said Katie. "They call themselves the Zero Day Gamers. The analysts at CTIIC believe this group was responsible for the cyberattack on the Nevada Energy power grid, resulting in the Las Vegas blackout last month."

"Has the Nevada incident been officially labeled a cyberattack?" asked Morgan.

"No, sir, the official explanation is a group of squirrels infiltrated the transformers at their primary power generating station," said Katie.

"Why would anyone believe that?" asked Morgan.

"Because the media told them so," replied Katie dryly. "The White House and our office played an active role in controlling the narrative on that one. The White House does not want the world to know about the vulnerabilities of our power grid to a cyberattack.

The United States is wholly unprepared for a coordinated attack on the grid."

"What is the relationship between Anonymous and this new group, the Zero Day Gamers?" asked Morgan.

"Based upon my investigation and the information received by Cyber Threat Intelligence, the two groups operate independently of each other," said Katie. "But that is about to change."

"How so?" asked Morgan.

"A message was posted by Anonymous onto Internet websites frequented by hackers and cyber-security experts this week," said Katie.

"What does it say?"

"It came in the form of a picture sir," said Katie. "With a poem superimposed over the image of the Guy Fawkes mask. It will be easier if I email it to you."

"Aren't your activities scrutinized?" asked Morgan.

"No, sir. Ironic, isn't it? This department was formed to monitor the movements of every government employee, yet nobody is assigned to watch us," said Katie. "I'll send you the image now."

Morgan checked his emails and the image finally came through. The text read

Ode to the Zero Day Gamers,
'tis a game you want to play.
Our name comes with no disclaimer,
we've no need to gameplay.
Our countermove has been made,
of this, the world will soon know.
For us, our legion is on a crusade,
for you, your name is apropos.

WE ARE ANONYMOUS.

"They're taunting the other group, it seems," said Morgan.

"I believe so," said Katie. "The Zero Day Gamers responded with an image of a white skull superimposed over a black and blue computer-generated image. I am sending it to you now."

Morgan received the email and examined the image. It read:

ZERO DAY GAMERS

One man's gain is another man's loss; who gains and who loses is determined by who pays.

"Their name is a play on words," said Morgan. "A zero-sum game is a situation in which one person's gain is equivalent to another person's loss. The net change is zero."

"That's correct, sir," said Katie. "The substitution of the word *day* in the place of *sum* reflects this group's expertise in exploiting zero-day vulnerabilities in a computer network."

"If they took down the Las Vegas power grid, they're playing a dangerous game," said Morgan.

"Yes, sir," said Katie. "It was the act of shutting down the grid, coupled with the walkout of the unions immediately after the outage, which leads me to believe the hackers worked in concert with the unions. This puts them in a class by themselves—as cyber mercenaries."

Katie continued. "You asked for my working theory, so here it is. I believe the Zero Day Gamers have achieved some notoriety in the hacker world through their accomplishments. I believe the Anonymous group has become jealous or envious. As a result, Anonymous has issued a challenge to the Zero Day Gamers—a challenge in the form of hacking the Treasury Department's network. They are now challenging the Zero Day Gamers, in a not-so-friendly game of one-upmanship, in the form of a virtual cyber war."

"When will you know more about this Zero Day group?" asked Morgan.

"Technically, I am not involved in that investigation. The CTIIC will continue to maintain jurisdictional control over both Anonymous and the Zero Day Gamers."

Morgan thought for a moment.

"Miss O'Shea," started Morgan, "I am going to arrange a promotion for you. I am going to contact the President's Chief of Staff immediately. David McDill, or one of his associates, will be in contact with you. You will become the liaison between the two agencies and will report directly to the President's Intelligence Advisory Board. But Miss O'Shea—you will always report to me first, understood?"

"Yes, sir," said Katie.

Morgan thanked her and hung up. If this situation could not be contained, then it must be profited from—now *and* in the future.

CHAPTER 48

March 27, 2016
100 Beacon
Boston, Massachusetts

Sarge sat with his legs propped up on the coffee table in the Great Hall, watching the news networks with Julia. He held her head against his chest and stroked her hair, absorbed in the digital chaos. Neither had said a word in the last half hour. Riots continued throughout the United States. European economies continued to teeter on the edge of collapse, tanking the markets. Tensions were escalating in the Middle East. The collapse Sarge had always feared loomed closer than ever.

"It's happening, isn't it?" asked Julia, breaking the silence.

"I think so," said Sarge. "Sometimes I wonder if my choice of reading material or news networks would provide me a different outlook on life."

"How so?" asked Julia. "Are you telling me you're no longer going to read my column? Did you block me on Twitter?" They laughed.

He took another sip of his Tanqueray and tonic.

"Here's what I mean," said Sarge, pausing all six screens and setting down his drink. "Let's examine the screens one at a time."

The first screen was the FoxNews channel, which showed a picture of retired General Bob Scales—military analyst. In the split screen was a map of Eastern Europe, showing the significant advances of pro-Russian forces into Europe.

"Russia has advanced into Eastern Europe, virtually unchecked," said Sarge. "They were deterred for a time in Mariupol, but all the Mariupol operation did was delay the inevitable. Putin's been quoted as saying his forces could reach any western European city in a matter of a few days. Meanwhile, NATO is scrambling to bolster the land forces they've gutted over the past decade. It won't be enough, and that's only one front.

"Putin sent a small taskforce of warships and troop carriers to occupy an abandoned NATO facility in the Arctic. The polar route for the Russian Navy to our Atlantic Seaboard is closer than most people realize. Combine that with the recently arrived intelligence vessels in Cuba, and I'd say he's testing our mettle."

"The Russians are preparing for war," said Julie.

"Either that, or they're positioning themselves for the power grab that will result from a Eurozone collapse. The current geopolitical climate doesn't exactly favor a strong, coordinated response to Russian aggression."

"We've alienated most of the European countries," replied Julia.

"Exactly," said Sarge. "I doubt the Germans or the French would join in the fray unless they were directly threatened. The English and Canadians will support us, but to what extent? The political climate in both countries won't support a proactive, sustained military posture against Russian expansion. And let's be honest, neither country has the military resources to make a significant difference. Their support will be symbolic at best. Russia, on the other hand, has maintained or bolstered their relationships with key agitator-states around the world. China, North Korea, Iran, Syria. And now, through the BRICS alliance—Russia has gained a foothold in South America and in South Africa. They've assembled a gang of psychotic ruffians while we're losing our grip on key, historic allies. The balance will tip in their favor if this continues."

Sarge pointed to the television providing coverage by the BBC of the Eurozone debt crisis.

"And even if Russia and the United States stop their chest-beating, the Ukrainian conflict has already devastated the euro," said Sarge. "The European- and U.S.-sponsored sanctions against Russia have harmed the Europeans more than the Russians. Russia simply established new trade partners, like the Chinese and Iranians."

"For over a year, the Europeans stood steadfast in refusing to negotiate with the Russians on the trade and energy sanctions," said Julia. "When Russia completely cut off the supply of gas to Ukraine late last year, they called Europe's bluff."

"It didn't help that our administration blocked shipments of gas from the United States due to *environmental concerns*," said Sarge.

Sarge shook his head. He hated to say these things out loud—the threats became more real.

"Ukraine was in a desperate situation regarding its natural gas supplies. They began to tap the pipelines dedicated for European consumption, creating a shortage in Europe that further damaged the Eurozone economy. Between the energy war and the trade war, Europe is on the brink of collapse," said Sarge. "It's just a matter of time before Greece, Italy and Spain fold under the weight of their respective governments' debt. When France and Germany decline to bail them out, guess where they'll turn? The only solvent country still making friends in the world—the new USSR."

"That's a scary thought," said Julia.

"Even scarier for the people of those countries. The old USSR patented the concept of austerity measures. Which brings us full circle to another organization that could benefit from the concept of austerity —The Federal Reserve."

"I was amazed that the information leaked didn't have a bigger impact on markets," said Julia.

"The White House expertly blamed the leak on a disgruntled Edward Snowden type of employee, and the administration-controlled media did the rest. The timing of the announcement didn't hurt, either. Late Friday before the start of Easter weekend? Well played. The story didn't get the airtime it deserved. Momentum is the key to any news story, as you well know. This one will sputter along until it fades into obscurity."

"The Federal Reserve System lives to fight another day," said Julia.

"Maybe. Maybe not. They still have another opportunity to hang themselves. Interest rates have risen dramatically in the last several months. A year ago, the Congressional Budget Office projected interest rates would reach four percent by 2020. According to the CBO, every one percent increase in interest rates would raise our annual deficit by over two hundred billion."

"Two weeks ago, during an editorial meeting, we discussed the volatility of rates. At the time, rates had just been raised a half percent to three points," said Julia. "Rates have risen in the last two weeks by another half point. Is four percent just wishful thinking?"

"I hope not. The rapid interest rate increase has not reached the point of hyperinflation, but if the Fed continues to artificially inflate the money supply by printing it, we're in for a rough ride," said Sarge. "I think we already owe enough money to China."

"What would happen if China stopped buying our debt?" asked Julia.

Sarge wanted to believe China had nothing to gain by collapsing the United States economy. They held large amounts of our debt, and we were the largest importer of their goods.

"The Chinese have chastised us for our runaway deficits and overspending," said Sarge. "And they've already begun to diversify their holdings—away from U.S.-dollar-dominated debt. My bet is that China has plans for a new world currency."

"I saw an image come across the AP wire the other day," said Julia. "It was a picture of a billboard in Bangkok, purchased by the Bank of China. It read *RMC: The Right Choice for the New World Currency*. The Bank of China is owned by the PRC."

"That is significant," said Sarge. "This means China is advertising the renminbi overseas at one of the busiest airports in the world."

"Why haven't the Chinese dumped our dollar?" asked Julia.

Sarge reached forward to finish his drink.

"The U.S. would experience a tremendous amount of short-term pain," said Sarge. "But the world markets would stabilize, and we would call on our allies in the emerging markets to pick up the slack. Simply put, we would replace the Chinese with new creditors. Believe it or not, there are many who believe that would be a good thing. It could certainly give the U.S. more leverage during trade negotiations.

It's difficult to negotiate with your bank when you owe them money—with no repayment in sight."

"Do you think we're facing an imminent collapse?" asked Julia.

"I don't know. We live in a dangerous and complicated world," said Sarge. "There have been times when I felt our preparations were unnecessary. This isn't one of them."

PART FIVE

CHAPTER 49

April 8, 2016
Equinox Sports Club
Boston, Massachusetts

"So then I knocked him out," said Donald.

Sarge stared at him, smiling and shaking his head.

"Well, aren't you the badass?"

His friend impressed him sometimes. Donald had relayed his experience at the Chestnut Hill Mall, with Susan and the girls. They had locked themselves in the store for hours, waiting for police to escort them to their car. The man Donald hit was arrested, leaving Sarge to wonder if any of the thousands of protestors who invaded the mall that night had been arrested.

"Last set, buddy," said Donald.

"Let me do some negatives while I have you spotting me," said Sarge. "Add a plate on each side and I'll drop it down slow."

Sarge and Donald Quinn were finishing up a workout at the Equinox Sports Club downtown. The Equinox was an upscale exercise club featuring a basketball court, an indoor swimming pool, a boxing studio and an internationally renowned squash program. The location was convenient for Sarge, who lived less than a mile away, across Boston Common. For Donald, who had become a more frequent guest at 73 Tremont Street, the Equinox represented a chance to decompress after meeting with their benefactor, and spend time with other friends caught in 73 Tremont's gravity.

Sarge and Donald worked out together frequently. They tried to stay in good shape, although their aging bodies objected more often than not. In addition to the weight-lifting regimen favored by Sarge,

Donald stressed the importance of cardiovascular health. *You never know when you might have to bug out—on foot.* The two friends complemented each other, pushing their limits and keeping them in shape for the inevitable.

"Let's walk the track and cool down," said Sarge. "I need to run some things by you."

For the next thirty minutes, Sarge and Donald discussed the impact of current events on their work and lives. Donald brought Sarge up to speed on a few preparedness ideas he had recently implemented, and Sarge talked about his book and the surprising impact that it had on the presidential campaign. America's sovereignty had become a hot-button issue for many, and attack ads against both the Republican and Democrat front-runners frequently featured a variation of the words or theme—*Choose Freedom.*

"Let's get everyone together soon," said Sarge. "We'll make it a social gathering of sorts. I was thinking about having a get-together on the eighteenth."

"The Boston Marathon is on that Monday. Are we all going to run around the Great Hall until we hit twenty-six point two miles?" asked Donald.

"You'd like that, wouldn't you? I thought it would be a nice day to enjoy some good food and drink while watching the marathon on TV," said Sarge. "That Monday is Patriots' Day, so nobody should be tied up with business. I'll coordinate with anyone out of town right now. You and Susan should come over with the girls the night before. It'll be difficult to get around the city that morning. There's plenty of room."

"I'll talk to Susan about it," said Donald. "She might like the idea of walking the Common early with the girls."

"Perfect," said Sarge. "Let me make some calls and I'll let you know. I have a feeling we may be getting together more frequently."

Sarge hoped he was wrong, but his gut instincts were usually dead-on. Donald checked his watch.

"Hey, I better get a shower," said Donald. "The boss *insists upon punctuality.*"

"Indeed he does," said Sarge.

They shared a laugh as they made their way to the locker room. Sarge enjoyed the relationship he had developed with Donald. Sometimes unusual circumstances resulted in lifelong friendships.

CHAPTER 50

April 8, 2016
Boston Common
Boston, Massachusetts

Sarge stepped into the crisp spring air with Donald. Office dwellers and business types scrambled in all directions on Avery Street. *Too many people.* With the domestic situation deteriorating, he'd started to give more and more thought to the high population density of his beloved city. Logically, putting a little space between him and the masses made a lot of sense, but he simply hadn't reached the point where he could envision living in the country. Rural areas didn't offer him the amenities of the city. Amenities he had grown accustomed to. *But there is security in the country and clean air.* Almost on cue, an MBTA bus roared past, leaving behind an invisible cloud of noxious fumes. Hadn't they replaced all of the diesels with natural gas? Of course not. The money for the upgrades had been siphoned off somehow. He took a shallow breath and shook his head, meeting Donald's glance.

"Good luck up there," said Sarge.

He genuinely meant it. Accountants have been routinely referred to as *pencil pushers.* Donald's duties fell more in line with the position of *envelope pusher.* He didn't seem stressed about it. Maybe he held a *Get Out of Jail Free Card.*

"Thanks, Sarge," said Donald. "Are you walking home? Do we need to work out a little harder next time?"

"Always on my case about the cardio," said Sarge, grinning.

"I consider keeping you healthy part of my job," replied Donald, patting him on the shoulder.

"It's a nice day, and I could use a walk," said Sarge. "I need to clear my head anyway."

"We can add a run along the river to our regimen if our Equinox routine isn't hard enough," pressed Donald.

"You're brutal."

"Catch you later, Sarge. Business awaits—impatiently."

"I don't want to hold you up," said Sarge, nodding as Donald turned away.

The two men went in opposite directions. Sarge started down Avery and crossed Tremont Street onto Boston Common. He continued his casual walk deeper into the park. Boston Common, known as the Common by many Bostonians, was the oldest city park in the country. Dating back to the early 1600s, the Common was part of a series of parks that stretched through Jamaica Plain and ended in Roxbury. Originally, the land was used by the locals to graze their cattle. Over the years, its uses changed, but the city planners maintained the boundaries of all the parks. They became known as the Emerald Necklace and were a destination for people to escape the ever-expanding Boston skyline.

Sarge walked past the tennis courts, eyeing a pair of spiffily dressed retirees volleying back and forth. As he passed the baseball field, the thought of Pumpsie Jones crossed his mind. Images of baseball would always remind him of Pumpsie's pointless death. He carefully navigated the crosswalk at Charles Street, avoiding the traffic turning off Boylston Street. Toward the northwest, the top of his building at 100 Beacon appeared above the brown apartments on the corner of Arlington Street.

At the statue of Wendell Phillips, he took a right on a sidewalk that weaved through the more heavily wooded side of the swan lake. Phillips, a native Bostonian and Harvard graduate, became known for his work in the early 1800s as a staunch abolitionist. He was so committed to the anti-slavery cause that he took great pains to avoid cane sugar and wore no cotton clothing—both having been produced primarily by Southern slaves. Phillips maintained that racial injustice was the source of the perceived social problems plaguing

America at the time. *Phillips had no idea how bad it could get.*

Sarge wound his way through the tree-covered sidewalks and crossed the walkway leading to the lagoon bridge. His peaceful stroll was interrupted by a sudden scream, followed by pleading. He glanced around to look for the source, finding no one else nearby. A female voice yelled, "*Please, not my baby*!" Sarge ran towards the lake, nearly tripping on a portion of broken asphalt in the sidewalk.

An overturned red baby stroller lay beneath a large tree with twisted, exposed roots. Tiny hands waved from the stroller as a man rifled through the back pouches—throwing diapers, bottles and baby clothing onto the ground. Another man straddled a young woman, who thrashed desperately underneath him as he ripped at her clothing. Sarge stood momentarily paralyzed. *Save the baby or the woman?* No time to analyze the decision.

Sarge rushed the man digging through the stroller, tackling him to the ground. They rolled over a bed of twisted, exposed tree roots and landed on the moist dirt near the pond. The man quickly recovered, rising to his feet in front of Sarge. As the man charged forward, Sarge pulled both knees towards his chest and mule-kicked the man in the ribs—knocking him several feet into the lake. A paddling of ducks flapped their wings when the man splashed into the water, skimming the surface and hiding under weeping willow branches along the water's edge.

The other man abandoned his prey and jumped on Sarge's back, putting him in a chokehold. Sarge pulled desperately at his assailant's arm, knowing he didn't have much time before he blacked out. Realizing the futility of the move, his mind instinctively recalled a Krav Maga technique. Sarge quickly turned his chin towards the attacker's hands—away from his elbow. This created a little space between the man's muscular arms and Sarge's windpipe. Before he could take advantage of the space, the man slammed Sarge's head against a tree root, spilling blood down his face. Out of the corner of his right eye, he saw the other assailant crawling out of the lake. If he didn't get loose in the next second or two, the situation would turn lethal for him. The man breathed into Sarge's ear.

"I'm gonna kill you!"

I need a weapon. He felt around for a rock or a twig, but came up with nothing. Sarge was getting weaker—his breathing labored. He'd lose consciousness soon and would be lucky to wake up. The man shifted his weight, jamming Sarge's chest harder against the ground—grinding against the weapon he had forgotten.

Sarge reached into his shirt pocket and removed his Mont Blanc fountain pen, popping the cap with his thumb. Gripping the barrel and sharp nib tightly, he rammed the pen into the attacker's forearm. The man screamed and released the pressure on his arm, giving Sarge the opportunity to escape the grip. With a primal scream Sarge rolled the man onto his side and stabbed him near the collarbone, just missing his target—the carotid artery. He retracted the pen and kicked the man in the solar plexus, crashing him against the tree trunk and dropping him to the ground.

Through his blood-obscured vision, Sarge caught a glimpse of the other man charging toward him. Sarge stepped between the soaking assailant and the baby carriage, assuming a forward fighting stance. The man stopped momentarily before grabbing the other attacker and escaping south along the lake. Sarge stumbled backward, falling to one knee—still holding the bloodied broken pen like a knife. As his breathing slowed and eyes came into focus, the young mother approached him with her now calm baby on her hips. With her free hand she wiped the blood off Sarge's face with a cloth diaper.

"My God, thank you," said the young woman. "You saved our lives, mister. Thank God you came to help us."

She gave him a kiss on the cheek and let her baby touch Sarge's face. *All lives matter.*

CHAPTER 51

April 11, 2016
1st Battalion , 25th Marines HQ
Fort Devens, Massachusetts

"Colonel Bradlee, your visitors are here," announced the headquarters sergeant. "May I show them in?"

Lieutenant Colonel Francis Crowninshield Bradlee, *Brad* to his friends, was the consummate military man. In the early, pre-revolutionary war days, the Crowninshields were known for their seafaring adventures. But as the war for independence came to full fruition, as close friends of Thomas Jefferson, the prominent family became the backbone of the United States Military for years to come. A member of the Crowninshield family held the positions of Secretary of the Navy and Secretary of War under several presidential administrations.

Like so many of the Founding Fathers, the Crowninshield lineage included the surnames Adams, Endicott, Hawthorne, DuPont and Bradlee. Brad's father was the editor of the Washington Post before his death and his mother was a highly respected, influential journalist. While the Bradlee branch of the Crowninshield family tree generally abhorred the military, Brad lived for it. He attended the Naval Academy and during his second class year he chose Leatherneck for his summer training. He received praise from his mentors and surpassed all of the academic and physical standards required to graduate as one of a few dozen Marine Selects.

His career was stellar and after three years as a major, he earned the rank of Lieutenant Colonel. Under his command were 750 infantry designated service members comprising the 25th Marine

Regiment of 1st Battalion. At age forty, he had fast tracked his career to battalion commander.

Brad met Steven Sargent at the Naval Academy and the two became good friends despite their several year age differences. Brad encouraged Steven to become a Marine but he was hell bent on becoming a SEAL via the Navy rather than through the BUDS training option offered by the Marines. Either way, Brad admired Steven for becoming one heck of a soldier and the two stayed close friends over the years. They also realized they have *common interests*, which they immediately pursued.

He was in his fatigues and did not see the need to dress up for his uninvited guests from Homeland Security. Brad wouldn't want to meet with them under normal circumstances, but he received a heads-up from Division Headquarters. These two were *making the rounds*, and it was best to play nice. He knew why they were there, but Brad had no intention of making their visit an easy one. Brad stood up from his chair to greet them.

"Good afternoon, Colonel Bradlee," said one of the gentlemen from Homeland Security. "My name is Joe Pearson and this is fellow agent David Nemechek. We are with the Federal Protective Services—a division of the Department of Homeland Security." *They say it so proudly.*

"Nice to meet you, gentlemen," said Brad. "How can I help you fellows today?"

Brad accepted their business cards, placing them on his desk without examining them.

"Colonel, we have been dispatched by FPS to discuss your role in the event of an attack on our nation's infrastructure or a related insurrection," said Pearson. *How do you define insurrection*?

"Have a seat, gentlemen," said Brad. "I am more familiar with the customs and border protection arm of the DHS law enforcement function. Tell me a little bit about FPS." *These people love to talk about how important they are.*

Brad's friends at the 4th Marine Division gave him the impression the FPS agents were interviewing base commanders to assess their *attitude.* When Brad pressed his friends about this, he was told they wanted to insure commanders would take orders *when necessary.* Brad knew what that meant.

"The FPS provides security and law enforcement functions at federal government facilities," said Nemechek. "There are ten thousand federal facilities nationwide, providing the backbone to our nation's critical infrastructure. It is our job to ensure a safe and secure working environment for our federal workers who conduct the important business of the country." *Just fire half of them and your workload will be cut dramatically.*

"Of course," said Brad.

"At FPS, we conduct comprehensive security assessments of vulnerabilities at governmental facilities," said Pearson. "This includes monitoring systems at all federal facilities for proper performance and security breaches. That is part of the reason David and I are here." *Snoops.*

Brad, like any other paid government employee, didn't like another government employee looking over his shoulder.

"The military has its own set of systems and procedures. We take great pride in maintaining compliance with our military's standards," said Brad. "Is DHS saying the military standards are inadequate?"

Brad was warned not to challenge these two. He was advised to *go along to get along,* but he couldn't help himself.

"No, Colonel, not in the least," said Nemechek. "DHS admires the role of our military and certainly respects the fact that all base commanders such as you run a tight ship. DHS is constantly developing and implementing new protective countermeasures based upon the latest risk assessments. As new threats emerge, both foreign and domestic, DHS will be there to assist all reserve units in the new roles assigned them."

Certain words rang alarm bells—*threats, domestic, new roles.* Brad sat up in his chair. He was not ready to play the game.

"I see," said Brad. "Well, that certainly makes sense. How can I help?"

"Sometime in the next several months, either David or myself will bring an assessment and training team to Fort Devens," said Pearson. "The purpose will be to provide you and key base personnel with orientation materials. Then we will work with you to conduct a facilities-wide assessment of any security vulnerabilities. As part of this assessment, we will determine your capabilities in the event of a crisis and to assess your readiness. Lastly, we will establish a joint monitoring system to ensure proper performance—pursuant to guidelines specifically tailored to Fort Devens."

Brad had heard enough. *Screw this.*

"What happens if I say no?" asked Brad stoically.

Pearson started to stammer a reply, when Brad laughed heartily.

"I'm just kidding," interjected Brad. "Of course, we will welcome you and your team to Fort Devens. We're all in this together."

The two men hesitantly joined in the laughter.

"We were told you were a kidder," said Nemechek. *You were?*

"There is one more thing," said Pearson. "As DHS and various bases around the country become more enmeshed regarding security matters, we envision greater coordination between reserve units such as yours and typical FPS responsibilities."

"I have to admit I'm still a little in the dark about your division's responsibilities," said Brad.

"We're primarily tasked to coordinate a uniformed response to catastrophic events, providing critical security services and logistical support at high-profile public events, and coordinating a timely emergency response following any unforeseen national crisis."

"Isn't that typically the function of local law enforcement or FEMA?" asked Brad.

"In some cases, a coordinated response at all levels of government might be required," said Pearson. "In those events, we will ensure that Fort Devens will be prepared to answer the call of duty." *I've had enough of these jackasses.*

"Of course," said Brad, as he stood up to signal the meeting was over. "Well, gentlemen, speaking for New England and Niagara's Own, we'll be ready when that call comes." *What that call entails will dictate what we will do.*

Pearson and Nemechek shook his hand and exchanged goodbyes, forcing smiles as they left. When they closed the door to his office, Brad shook his head. *Nothing good could come of FPS.* He unconsciously reached out to touch the American flag, which flanked the credenza behind his desk, along with the Standard—the flag of the United States Marine Corps. Brad would never forget the oath he took when he accepted his commission.

I will support and defend the Constitution of the United States against all enemies, foreign and domestic.

He'd long ago recognized that a time might come when his oath would conflict with the orders he received from his superiors. Brad and a loyal group of Marines had created a new oath, which didn't conflict with his duties as an American.

I will not obey orders to disarm Americans.

I will not obey orders to conduct warrantless searches.

I will not obey orders to detain Americans wrongfully labeled as enemy combatants.

I will not obey orders to invade a state that asserts its sovereignty.

I will not obey orders to force law-abiding American citizens into detention camps.

I will not obey orders to assist foreign troops on United States soil to assert control over our citizens.

I will not obey orders to confiscate the property of our citizens, including their food and belongings.

I will not obey orders to impose martial law.

I will not obey orders to infringe upon the freedoms afforded all Americans in the Bill of Rights.

Brad was an Oathkeeper and one of the III%.

CHAPTER 52

April 11, 2016
The White House Situation Room
Washington, D.C.

Katie thumbed through the Morning Book as she waited for the White House Chief of Staff and National Security Advisor to join the rest of the briefing team in the Situation Room. Today marked Katie's first day in her new role on the President's Intelligence Advisory Board.

The Morning Book was prepared through the cooperative effort of several intelligence agencies, which provided representatives to the Situation Room's Watch Team. The Watch Team prepared the Morning Book by compiling the State Department's National Morning Summary, the National Intelligence Daily report and various diplomatic cables. Prepared in the dark hours of the morning, the book accompanied the driver to pick up the National Security Advisor every morning, and was provided to the President, the Vice President and various senior members of the White House staff for their earliest perusal. The fact that she was likely reading it before the President didn't escape her. Neither did the task that lay immediately ahead—an uphill battle for sure.

She was warned she may be asked to explain her findings related to the Nevada Energy cyber attack—which squarely sat at odds with the administration's politically slanted assessment. Her first foray into the highest levels of government was likely to be a rocky one. The National Security Advisor could be rude and overly blunt when provoked. Katie's suspicions were confirmed when Susan Giles, the

National Security Advisor, shot her a poisonous glare upon entering the room with David McDill, the White House Chief of Staff.

"Let's talk about the President's schedule first," said McDill. "At 9:30 a.m., the President and First Lady will depart the White House for Joint Base Andrews. From Andrews they will travel to Newark, where they will be greeted by the governor of New Jersey. After a noon luncheon, the President will participate in a roundtable discussion with the governor and members of the labor community. This roundtable will wind up at approximately 3:00 p.m., when the President and the First Lady will depart for Orlando, Florida. They will appear at a campaign event for Hillary Clinton at 7:00 p.m. There are no scheduled events for tomorrow. After a round of golf with Tiger Woods in the morning, the President will return to the White House. Questions?"

McDill looked over his black-framed reading glasses to see if there were any takers. With none evident, he propped the glasses on his premature gray head and nodded at Susan Giles.

"Who is this?" asked Giles, pointing to Katie. *Not the start she had expected, but she'd roll with it.*

"My name is Katie O'Shea, ma'am. I am part of the executive staff. This is my first morning briefing."

"Miss O'Shea, have you been informed of my rules for the conduct of the President's business during these briefings?" asked Giles.

"Yes, ma'am. Nothing leaves these four walls. Not ever," said Katie. *The President's business? Don't you mean the business of the nation's security?*

"Good," said Giles. "Let's get started."

Giles touched on the high points of the Morning Book, rarely engaging in more than a few minutes on any given topic. McDill was mostly silent, taking notes from time to time. Just as Katie thought the meeting was coming to a close, and that she might escape the National Security Advisor's wrath, Giles thumbed back through the book—opening and flattening it on the table.

"Finally, let's address the matter of the Nevada Energy blackout," said Giles. "Who is responsible for this report?"

"I am, ma'am," said Katie, scrambling to organize her meticulously prepared notes on the subject.

With her head turned down toward the Morning Book, Giles looked over her glasses at Katie, staring at her for several excruciating seconds. *She's sizing me up.* Katie didn't break eye contact.

"I have read your summation and glanced briefly at your analysis," said Giles. "You have characterized the Las Vegas attack as terrorism. Further, you have tied this *terrorism* to a group of cyber hackers working on behalf of one of the oldest and most well-respected unions in America. How long have you been in this position?"

"Two weeks today, ma'am," said Katie. "I have been working on this investigation since it occurred."

"These are your conclusions?" asked Giles.

"Yes, ma'am."

"Does anyone else have an opinion on O'Shea's analysis?" asked Giles.

The room remained silent, everyone finding important documents or pencils to examine. Katie watched Giles survey the room before continuing.

"Miss O'Shea, the conclusions you have reached are inconsistent with the initial reports and statements released by Nevada Energy," said Giles. "A cyberattack is quite a leap from the findings reached by the engineers at Nevada Energy, who determined their power generation system was infiltrated by animals."

Katie remained silent, letting her continue.

"You have defined this incident as terrorism," said Giles. "That's not a word we use around here unless absolutely necessary. It certainly is not a word the President would feel comfortable using in association with the Culinary Workers Union. I think you may have mischaracterized the nature of the event."

"Ma'am, I have conducted a detailed analysis of the events surrounding the blackout," said Katie. "I feel my job is to provide a detailed, accurate analysis of a threat for your consideration, ma'am. My analysis of the facts accurately leads to the conclusion that the

CU 226 acted in concert with a mercenary hacker group called the Zero Day Gamers. Whether the Zero Day Gamers acted as political activists, in the vein of Anonymous, or for hire as a form of cyber mercenary is still unknown," she said, pausing to catch her breath before continuing.

"The facts in my report are clear. Surveillance footage from the major casinos revealed numerous union personnel, some with ties to the Teamsters in Chicago, enter the building just prior to the blackout. At Caesars Palace, cell phone footage obtained from the Las Vegas Review Journal followed one of these men as he planted exploding smoke devices throughout the casino. The man has been identified as Johnny Bagwell of Chicago, a longtime *enforcer* of the Teamsters Union.

"Not to mention the fact that Culinary Union management representatives appeared simultaneously on the floors of more than a dozen major casinos, advising their personnel to leave the premises. Surveillance footage shows that the work interruptions occurred between 8:05 and 8:10 p.m. at every location. I was unable to find a single example of union workers initiating a work stoppage during past power failures," added Katie.

Giles finally spoke. "Even if these allegations prove to be true," said Giles. "How is this terrorism?"

"CU 226 has been in heated contract negotiations with the major casinos in Nevada," said Katie. "The negotiations are going poorly for the union. Governor Sandoval is running for the vacant senate seat this fall and he's actively siding with the casinos in those negotiations."

"So?" asked Giles. *She's trying to throw me off.*

"There is both a political component and a social component," said Katie, noticing that she had near complete command of the room—on *day one.*

"The accepted definition of terrorism includes the use of force against persons or property with the intent to coerce another in furtherance of political or social objectives. The political and social objectives component of the definition has been used repeatedly in defining militia and so-called sovereign citizens in this country as threats to the internal security of the United States—as terrorists. I'm sure you are familiar with the report by DHS entitled National Threat Assessment for Domestic Extremism."

"I'm familiar with the report," snapped Giles. "And I don't disagree with its premise. What direct, substantiated evidence do you have that this hacker group was hired by any of the unions?"

"The investigation is ongoing," said Katie.

Giles immediately exploited the only weakness in Katie's analysis.

"Until you do, this report stays out of the morning briefing, is that clear?" stated Giles.

"Yes, ma'am," said Katie.

She felt defeated. The Las Vegas incident was an important topic for this briefing, because it revealed the vulnerability of the nation's power grid to cyberattack—political factors aside. Katie gathered her notes and filtered out of the room with the other members of the briefing staff. A member of the secret service approached her just outside of the conference room, pulling her aside.

"NSA Giles has requested to speak with you. Please come with me," said the agent.

Day one—and done.

Katie walked next to the agent and turned into a small conference room, where Giles stood with her assistant. The agent backed out of the space and closed the door.

"I know how you were appointed to this position," said Giles. "I have known John Morgan since my days in the Clinton administration."

The National Security Advisor let the words sink in before continuing.

"There is nothing wrong with your analysis—but the report could seriously damage the people who support the President."

"I understand that, ma'am, but—" Katie started.

Giles held up her hand to stop her.

"Katie, you can have a very bright future within this administration and others in the future," said Giles. "But you must be cognizant of the political ramifications of your conclusions. Do you understand?"

"Yes, ma'am, but I thought the contents of my report, as contained in the Morning Book and discussed within the morning briefings, would stay within the confines of the Situation Room."

"Are you kidding me?" laughed Giles, producing a business card from her suit jacket pocket. "More than half the people in that room dislike the President, and they loathe me even more, including McDill. Carol Stannard is my assistant, and this is her card. Contacting her is like contacting me. As this particular investigation progresses, you keep me abreast directly—via Carol."

Stannard, the tall, pixie-cut brown-haired woman standing behind Giles, nodded at her with a severe smile.

"Katie, do you understand what the term *plausible deniability* means?" asked Giles.

"What you don't know can't hurt you—or be tied to you," said Katie O'Shea, Irishwoman.

Giles and her assistant began laughing.

"You are going to do very well in Washington, Katie O'Shea," said Giles, lightly patting her on the shoulder. "Welcome to the team."

CHAPTER 53

April 18, 2016
100 Beacon
Boston, Massachusetts

Sarge and Julia huddled around the coffee bar, fixing a pair of mocha lattes. Patriots' Day gave both of them a rare day off from their careers, and an opportunity to focus on their "other life." A life shared by a close circle of friends. He suspected they would be called into action soon. The signs were obvious. America was on the edge of a dangerous cliff. Like all of the great civilizations before her, the United States was at risk of a sudden, rapid collapse.

"Bringing everyone together was long overdue," said Julia. "Besides, the Great Hall feels more like a home today."

"Julia, Julia," shouted Penny Quinn, running up to her and giving her a hug. "You have on pink jammers with puppies all over!"

After the attack inside the Boston Common, he vowed to gather the group as he'd discussed with Donald Quinn. While it represented an opportunity for everyone to review the state of world affairs and give an update on their preparations, it was first and foremost a social occasion. The group did not come together often enough, which seemed at odds with their common purpose. They were closely linked by powerful forces, entrusted with a greater purpose.

Sarge turned his attention to the elevator doors, which had opened to discharge Donald and Susan Quinn and their daughters. They carried brown-paper-covered packages concealing artwork.

"What are we looking at here?" asked Sarge, taking two of the parcels.

"We felt the need to upgrade your décor, Sarge," said Susan. "This room is in dire need of some artwork." *Great, the obligatory fox and hunt images.*

"When everyone arrives, you can open your gift," said Donald.

"What time do you expect Steven?" asked Donald.

Before Sarge could answer, Steven and Katie appeared, appropriately dressed for once. Having Donald and Susan's children present put them all on their best behavior.

"Right here DQ—reporting for duty," said Steven. "After coffee, of course."

Steven made his way to the Keurig machine, glancing at the brown packages. "What are those?"

"We got Sarge a gift for the loft," said Donald. "We'll give it to him when the others get here. How's the *Miss Behavin'?*"

"I took her out two weeks ago," said Steven. "Did Sarge tell you what I saw?"

"Only the highlights," said Donald. "Have you guys seen any news reports or other confirmations of the Russians' activity?"

"This sort of thing doesn't find its way across the AP wires," said Julia. "My contact at the Washington Free Beacon emailed me his piece on what he was able to learn from his contacts at the Pentagon. According to his sources, two intelligence-gathering vessels have entered the area. One, the *Viktor Leonov*, continued to Havana and has been detected in the Gulf of Mexico. The other ship, the *Nikolay Chiker*, has been seen on numerous occasions off the coast of Georgia and the Carolinas."

"The Beacon's sources are correct," said Katie. "The *Leonov*—one of eight Vishnya-class intelligence ships—is outfitted with a lot of high-tech electronics. It is the ultimate long-range spy ship. Based in Cuba, the *Leonov* can easily patrol the Gulf and snoop on CENTCOM in Tampa or intercept phone calls from soldiers in the Fort Hood area. The *Chiker* is a glorified tugboat that accompanies the *Leonov* in a support role. It has the capability to lift submarines out of the water for repair."

"Are the Russians attempting to reignite the Cold War?" asked Donald.

"It could be a way of throwing their military capabilities in our face, similar to their repeated testing of our air defenses on the West Coast," said Katie. "There is something interesting about the *Leonov* deployment. The CIA is convinced that the *Vasiliy Tatishchev* intelligence vessel was part of the Russian flotilla observed sailing south along the boundary of our coastal waters recently. The *Tatishchev* was recently retrofitted to be Russia's most advanced electronic intercept ship. Based upon intelligence reports, the *Tatishchev* circles the waters from D.C. to our Naval Submarine Base at Kings Bay, Georgia."

"What's your hunch?" asked Sarge.

"The *Tatishchev* is stalking our nuclear subs," said Katie.

"Because they don't want us to know their own subs are right in our backyard," said Steven. "This explains the presence of the *Chiker*. There are some serious Russki sharks circling our waters."

"Mommy," squealed the girls in unison. "It's Steeeeeven."

They ran to Steven, who put his coffee down to absorb the full-on assault of little girl hugs.

"He has this effect on women, big and small," said Sarge.

Katie nodded in agreement.

"Ladies, today is Patriots' Day. Why are you wearing pink and not the good old red, white and blue?" asked Steven, holding each of their arms over their heads as they pirouetted.

"Because we are pretty in pink," said Rebecca.

"Hello, Suzie Q," said Steven, releasing Susan's daughters.

"Good morning, Steven," said Susan. "Nice to see that you dressed appropriately. Sarge was worried."

"For good reason," said Steven.

The digital keypad next to the elevator doors flashed. Only eight other people had the necessary security code to access the three upper floors of 100 Beacon, and six of them were inside his residence. He waited for his final two guests to step out of the elevator.

"Look at this homeless guy I found on the sidewalk." Brad laughed. "I think he might be working undercover for Homeland."

Brad hugged J.J. around the shoulders as the two men entered the Great Hall.

"Hi, guys," said Julia as she greeted them both with a hug. "J.J., have you lost some weight? You look great."

"He's got a new girlfriend," said Susan. "Right, J.J.?"

J.J. turned noticeably red from embarrassment. Sarge knew it was hard for him to be the center of attention when it came to personal matters.

"We're just good friends," said J.J. "Her name is Sabina. I first met her in the hospital at JBB. We ran into each other recently and hit it off."

Brad slapped J.J. on the back and grinned. "Another one bites the dust, which leaves just me and Steven in the single category."

On cue, Steven and Katie stepped into the open.

"You spoke too soon, my friend," said J.J. "It appears your counterpart has met his match."

"Do I need to find Brad a *special friend*?" asked Katie. "Maybe a nice girl out of the counterintelligence corps."

"Forget it, I hear Brad has trust issues," said Sarge. "Right, Brad? You wanna tell everyone about your visit from DHS?"

"First things first," started Brad. "My love life is fine, thank you very much. Second, no spies, please. My motto is question everything; trust no one—but you guys, of course. I don't need a spy in my bed or my head."

"Okay," said Susan. "No more coffee for Brad. It's good to see you."

"Are we all here?" asked J.J.

He glanced around the room and waved at Penny and Rebecca, who were stationed in front of the televisions.

"Not yet," replied Susan. "Abbie had a campaign appearance at the annual Patriots' Day breakfast in Lexington. After her speech, she was going to head this way ahead of the marathon traffic."

"How did her campaign staff clear her schedule for the day?" asked Julia.

"Abbie told her staff she would be holding an all-day private fundraiser," said Sarge. "I forgot to mention it to everyone. Let's break out the checkbooks and bribe her campaign manager to leave us alone for the day."

"I knew it," said Steven. "Subterfuge."

"C'mon, you cheap bum," said Katie, smacking Steven hard in the chest. "You never spend any money on me. At least help Abbie get reelected."

"I spend money on you when we go out," said Steven.

"No, you don't, because we never go out," replied Katie. "You just sweet-talk me into the sack."

"Katie!" exclaimed Susan, pointing in the direction of the girls.

"No more diversions," said Sarge. "Checks, please, but keep them below twenty seven hundred."

Sarge gathered up the checks. The contributions were largely symbolic as both a show of loyalty and an excuse to commandeer Abbie for the day. Sarge's phone buzzed, notifying him of a text message.

"I just received a text from Abbie," said Sarge. "She'll be here shortly. Her security team insists on escorting her up the elevator, but then they'll ride down and wait outside. Unavoidable at her level. Why don't we all gather in the study until I can send them back downstairs? How does that sound?"

"Okay by us," said Penny.

Everyone laughed at the unhampered audacity of a child.

"No, girls," said Donald. "You guys stay here. We have some adult things to discuss. Sound good?"

"Okay, Daddy," said their daughters.

Sarge politely herded everyone towards the study, watching curiously as the Quinns gathered up the brown-wrapped packages. Julia stayed with Sarge to greet Abbie. *Was she playing hostess or guarding her turf?*

The elevator opened, and one of the dark-suited members of her security team entered, followed by Abbie and the female member of the detachment. While in Washington, Abbie was provided around-the clock security. When members returned to their home districts, they were on their own. Her father had arranged twenty-four-hour security—most likely the best in the business from Aegis.

"Hey, guys," said Abbie. She reached out to hug Julia before embracing Sarge. "Where is everybody?"

"We locked them in a closet with Steven," said Julia. "May the strongest survive."

"Abbie," Rebecca squealed.

"It's Senator Abbie, goofy," corrected Penny. "Hi, Senator Abbie. Becca doesn't understand politics like I do."

"Well, Penny, you probably understand politics better than most people," whispered Abbie, kneeling down to hug Penny.

She stood up and politely dismissed the security team. Sarge showed them to the elevator and sent them to the ground floor.

"Abbie, would you like coffee or juice?" asked Sarge.

"I'm fine, thank you," said Abbie. "I'm excited about catching up with everyone. I imagine we have a lot to cover."

Sarge knew their meetings would have to become more frequent. The world had changed significantly since their last gathering. In another five or six months, it might be unrecognizable. As the day progressed, he would explain the dire necessity for making serious changes to their lives. A heightened sense of awareness was required moving forward. He motioned them towards the study, eavesdropping on the ladies. *I hope they don't compare notes.* His brother shook his head as Sarge closed the door behind the women.

"You're screwed, dude," said Steven. "There will be no place to hide when those two are finished with you."

"No doubt," said Sarge.

Julia gave him a wink.

"Greetings, Senator," said Donald. "Polls seem to be strong."

"Thank you, Donald," said Abbie. "When I ran six years ago, the campaign was very intense at this point. There was a lot of hostility among the electorate, especially against the rising voices of the Tea Party. We're not seeing that yet. Everything seems to be on track for November."

"What are your chances of being selected by one of the

presidential candidates as a running mate?" asked Susan.

The question was bold, but they were a family and a team. Everyone spoke freely and honestly, without fear that their words might surface in public.

"It's difficult to predict this early," said Abbie. "The big government Republicans are starting to ease up on us, but we may still be a few election cycles away from an alliance outside of the traditional Republican mold."

"I suspect you're closer than you think," said Julia. "I don't see the Republican Party pulling off a presidential victory without a shakeup. Grabbing the libertarian base might be their only hope."

"I can tell you guys this, if my father wants me on either ticket as Vice President, it would happen. I honestly don't know if I want that yet. Hyper-partisanship is still out of control. The Founding Fathers tried to warn us against the creation of a two-party system. One of my ancestors, John Adams, said he dreaded the division of the republic into strong parties. He predicted it would become the greatest political evil under our Constitution. He was right, and the polls show that a majority of Americans agree. The constant bickering and gridlock has poisoned the country."

"The two-party system has fostered an environment of division between Americans," said Sarge. "I have never seen people so polarized."

"I agree," said Donald. "Lincoln said America would never be destroyed from the outside. If we lose our freedom, it will be because we destroyed ourselves."

Donald reached for one of the parcels labeled number one. He handed it to Sarge. "For you, my friend — a gift honoring the great success of your new book."

Sarge removed the brown-paper wrap, taking in the first of the marvelous paintings. He remained speechless while Donald explained their significance.

"You're looking at hand-painted reproductions of a five-part series of paintings created by Thomas Cole, an English artist that reached his pinnacle in the 1830s. The series is called *The Course of*

Empire. They depict the rise and fall of an imaginary city."

Donald and Susan quickly unwrapped the rest of the paintings and gave them to the others to hold for viewing.

"Imagine an ideal world in its natural state, untouched by mankind," said Donald. "This first canvas is called *The Savage State*. It's symbolic of our planet in its pristine, unblemished condition. It features a beautiful valley, wildlife, a pristine river and only primitive people.

"The second painting is called *Arcadian*," continued Donald. "This painting reveals the development of the land, but with a slow, controlled approach. Notice the structures are very primitive, and the scene is sparsely populated."

He took the third painting from Steven.

"Next in the series is the *Consummation of Empire*. Obviously, ancient Rome is the subject of this work. This painting exudes luxurious self-indulgence, much like the Roman Empire at its peak in around 100 A.D. Notice the ornate architecture and the elaborately dressed inhabitants. The harbor is bustling with ships and the marketplace is full of activity.

"The fourth painting is called *Destruction*. Art historians believe this painting suggests the fall of the Roman Empire around 400 A.D., at the hands of the Vandals. The dark storm clouds envelop the city as the seas rage, rocking the ships back and forth. The towers have fallen, and the city is generally war ravaged. Notice the dead and injured who have fallen as a result of the destruction."

Donald handed this painting to Julia and then lifted up the last canvas—turning it for everyone to see its detail.

"Finally, the artist referred to this painting as *Desolation,* which represents the empire years after its destruction. The city is in ruins, and natural vegetation has taken over the majestic structures. The imaginary city depicted in Cole's artistic works has come full circle."

Sarge surveyed the room as everyone hung on Donald's last words.

"I prefer to call it TEOTWAWKI—The End of the World as We Know It."

"All empires collapse eventually—there have been no exceptions," said Sarge.

"That's why we are all here," added Donald.

CHAPTER 54

April 18, 2016
Top of the Hub Restaurant
Boston, Massachusetts

"Welcome to the Top of the Hub Restaurant, gentlemen, and may I wish you a splendid Patriots' Day," said the tuxedo-clad maître d'.

Morgan nodded as he entered the restaurant with Walter Cabot. The Top of the Hub occupied the upper floors of the Prudential Tower and offered breathtaking views of Boston's skyline and beyond. On clear days, the Atlantic Ocean glistened in the distance beyond the inner harbor. Closer below, the Charles River dominated the cityscape, giving upscale diners unobstructed lines of sight to many of Boston's iconic landmarks. Foremost among them, the ornately constructed Longfellow Bridge stared up at the most connected or lucky patrons seated near a window in the northeast corner. Inspired by European design, the bridge opened in 1906, featuring eleven steel arch spans supported by ten concrete piers. Four ornamental stone towers flanked the central span, providing the bridge's most notable feature. Today, the splendor of the Boston landmarks would take a backseat to the Boston Marathon, which was unfolding just below them along Boylston Street.

Morgan was in good spirits. His choice of the Skywalk Observatory for this private meeting was a change of pace from the usual venue at 73 Tremont. *Lofty goals require a lofty locale.* Without exaggeration, he knew that today's discussions would shape world events. The maître d' led Morgan and Cabot into a private room with seating for nine. A long rectangular table had been positioned next to the window—elegantly adorned with white tablecloths, candles, crystal glassware and fine china. In addition to sparing no expense for their endeavor, he had insisted on total privacy for the meeting. The restaurant's management understood that once lunch was served, they were to remain outside the private dining room until summoned.

They were greeted upon entry by Lawrence Lowell, who was seated closest to the door. He set his cocktail on the table—after finishing it with a long swallow. *Never too early for a cocktail, right, Lawrence?*

"John, it's good to see you," said Lowell. "Cabot old man, you are looking well."

Lowell was heartily shaking Cabot's hand. The Lowells and Cabots were the epitome of New England aristocracy—New England First Families.

"Thank you, Lawrence, and you look well also—for an old man," said Cabot with a deep-throated chuckle.

Morgan surveyed the room over the two men, each of whom stood several inches shorter. He was pleased to see that everyone was present. Tardiness was a sign of personal weakness, a trait that could not be tolerated in this circle. Especially today. The attendees, in addition to Morgan, included the eight members of the executive council—all descendants of America's Founding Fathers. Endicott, Tudor, Winthrop, Bradlee, Peabody, Adams, Cabot and Lowell. Morgan wanted to have a brief chat with each of them before delving into official business.

"Hello, Henry," Morgan said to the great grandson of former Secretary of War William Crowninshield Endicott. "I hope all is well."

"Yes, John, of course it is," said Endicott.

He leaned in to whisper in Morgan's ear. "Thank you for arranging the meeting with the Saudi prince. We have formed an excellent working relationship. They have quite an appetite for our advanced weaponry. Perhaps they will use it on the Iranians since our commander-in-chief won't."

The Endicott family name was synonymous with warfare throughout the world.

"I was glad to help you, Henry," said Morgan. "Please give my regards to your blushing bride."

The men laughed at Morgan's reference. Endicott was on his third wife. The new Mrs. Endicott was younger than most of his children. He approached Samuel Bradlee, who had just retrieved another cocktail from one of the waiters.

"Samuel, you old codger, how's your golf game," greeted Morgan.

Samuel Bradlee was a former Secretary of Defense and a direct descendant of Nathaniel Bradlee—one of the key participants in the Boston Tea Party. He was very well regarded among the group and had taken on the unofficial role of social coordinator.

"Still hittin' 'em straight, John," said Bradlee. "I nearly got a hole in one the other day. I guess if one plays enough golf, he'll get lucky. Even a blind squirrel will find an acorn once in a while, right, old friend?"

"And a broken clock is right twice a day, Samuel. Glad to hear all is well," said Morgan.

"Listen, John, I want to thank you for everything you've done for my nephew," said Samuel. "He's thoroughly enjoyed his tour as 1st Battalion, 25th Marine Regiment's commander, but the Marine Corps has a tendency to move its personnel around—and Brad is due for a reassignment. My brother likes having him close by, and I think you will agree his position could be advantageous at some point." *I know, Samuel, who do you think put him there in the first place?*

"Do not concern yourself with this, Samuel," said Morgan, patting his friend on the shoulder. "I'm sure he'd make a fine commanding officer for the 25th Marine Regiment, located right at Fort Devens. Brad will have a long tenure there."

"John, it goes without saying, but I'll say it anyway. Thank you," said Bradlee.

The catering manager approached and stood inconspicuously to the side, waiting courteously for them to finish their conversation.

"Give me a moment, Samuel," said Morgan, acknowledging the

manager's presence.

"Sir, is there a particular time you would like lunch to be served?" asked the manager.

Morgan looked at his watch, noting that it was 11:40.

"Begin your preparations now, and have all courses except dessert delivered before noon," said Morgan.

"Very well, sir. We will commence immediately," said the manager.

Morgan wanted to speak with one more guest before lunch was served. He found Paul Winthrop stuck in a conversation with Lawrence Lowell.

"Lawrence, may I borrow Paul for just a moment?" asked Morgan. "Lunch will be served shortly."

"Yes, absolutely, John. It is so good to see you again, Paul," said Lowell before he flagged down the waiter for another cocktail.

Morgan turned his attention to the descendant of one of Massachusetts Bay Colony's earliest settlers, and its first acting governor.

"Paul, thank you for coming," said Morgan.

Winthrop's cousin, Henry Winthrop Sargent III, was Morgan's best friend, and father to Morgan's godsons, Sarge and Steven. Morgan felt a special kinship with the Winthrops and Sargents.

"I want to apologize for not keeping you in the loop regarding the matter in Switzerland last month. You do understand why the course of action was necessary?" Morgan examined Winthrop carefully while he answered.

"Of course I do, John," said Winthrop. "I would prefer to keep abreast of these matters, but I understand the need for secrecy."

"The direction of the talks had taken an unexpected turn, and I needed to take immediate action," said Morgan. "This will benefit us all, despite the ruffled feathers."

"Absolutely, John," said Winthrop. "Ah, it appears our lunch is on its way."

In a room full of men accustomed to occupying the power seat in board meetings, diplomatic talks and other high-level functions, John

Morgan strode unopposed to the head of the table as their de facto leader—a title none of them had ever disputed. He waited patiently for everyone to gather around the table.

The business ahead of them was nothing short of monumental. By the time they emerged from the room, the next President of the United States would be decided. These nine men, representing the wealthiest and most powerful families since the country's founding, would once again shape the nation for years to come.

In reality, Morgan knew today's luncheon was a mere formality. Their course of action had already been decided, but tradition demanded the formal meeting, which had taken place since 1860. The group's presidential nominee had won every election for the last 156 years, except for one. 1992. Ross Perot represented the one case in history where no amount of money or promise of power could sway the result. They had briefly considered other, more nefarious, methods, but the group decided that either incumbent would favor their interests. As it turned out, the Clinton years represented one of the group's most prosperous eras—money and power held great sway in that administration.

A small cadre of waiters simultaneously placed their lunches on the table, making final adjustments before withdrawing from the room. Morgan looked to Malcolm Lowe and nodded for him to secure the doors. They were ready to begin.

"Gentlemen, as is customary—a toast," said Morgan.

Everyone stood, raising their glasses.

"To Boston," said Morgan. The room echoed his words—*To Boston.*

"To our forefathers," said Morgan. *To our forefathers.*

"To God and Country," said Morgan. *To God and Country.*

"To the Boston Brahmin," said Morgan, raising his glass high. *To the Boston Brahmin* came the reply.

"Now, let's get down to business," said Morgan.

For the next forty-five minutes, the executive committee of the Boston Brahmin discussed the fate of the presumed nominees for President. Hillary Clinton was the front-runner for the Democratic nomination, and it was widely anticipated Mrs. Clinton would effectively secure the nomination next week during the "winner-takes-all" primaries in her adopted home state of New York, and in Pennsylvania, Connecticut and Rhode Island. Morgan had to reassure them that she could be controlled. She'd focus on domestic issues and allow them to advance their geopolitical goals when the need arose.

On the Republican side, the nomination was undecided based on early opinion polls. Primaries in the northeast favored the underdog, Senator Rand Paul, while most of the contested states favored Jeb Bush. None of the executive committee members favored these two candidates. While their politics favored Jeb Bush, the committee did not see him as a viable candidate against the powerful Clinton campaign. Senator Paul was a candidate the average American could understand, but his position on auditing the Federal Reserve, combined with his dove-like approach to the military, excluded him from consideration—*immediately*.

Donald Trump was discussed at length but it was generally agreed he could not be controlled. Further his populist, nationalist leanings ran contrary to what made the Boston Brahmin the most powerful geopolitical players on the planet. Like Ross Perot over two decades ago, Trump represented a wild card that didn't fit within the confines of their version of a shadow government.

So it was settled, Hillary Clinton was the choice of the Boston Brahmin for President. *Status quo*—effectively a third term for the present occupant. She fit their needs perfectly. She could be manipulated and controlled, just like her husband.

Once they agreed and everyone pushed away from the table, the waiters were allowed back in to refresh drinks. Bradlee pressed his face against the window and recoiled, pointing toward the streets below.

"My God, what's happening down there?" exclaimed Bradlee.

Morgan checked his watch—12:45 p.m.

"It's a riot or something. Look below," said Winthrop.

From the Skywalk Observatory, fifty-two floors above Boylston

Street, they saw throngs of people scattered in all directions in Copley Square.

This is what mayhem looks like.

CHAPTER 55

April 18, 2016
Copley Square
Boston, Massachusetts

"Black lives matter! Black lives matter!" shouted the group marching westbound on Beacon Street.

Jarvis Rockwell—J-Rock to his boys—held his hands high over his head. He knew this was a waste of time, but when the good Reverend Al asked folks to come out and make their voices heard, he felt obligated to stand with his brothers from Mattapan, Roxbury and Dorchester. Protesting was not his thing, but he agreed to lend his support. The time for talk was over.

The crowd marched arm-in-arm past the fancy clothing stores on Boylston Street. More than a thousand men, women and children approached the Clarendon Street interchange, where they collided with the orange and white barriers blocking the entrance to Copley Square. J-Rock's instructions were clear—*march through and do not stop; let your voices be heard.*

J-Rock was the leader of the Academy Homes gang located in Roxbury, one of several Boston gangs heavily invested in drug dealing, gunrunning and human trafficking. The gangs of Boston were divided by ethnicity—Asian, Hispanic and black. The Asian gangs were united by their leader, the White Devil, and ruled the area south of downtown Boston—Chinatown. The Hispanic gangs were controlled by the Central American cartel widely known as Mara Salvatrucha—MS-13. They predominantly operated in the East Boston ghettos, though they had recently started to spread wings and appear all over the city. The black gangs of Boston outnumbered both of these rival ethnicities, but they lacked unity.

They were divided along geographic turf lines. The Academy Homes gang, representing a large territory in central Roxbury near Martin Luther King Boulevard, boasted five hundred members. J-Rock rose up the ranks starting as a runner, and graduated to enforcer by age sixteen, when he committed a double murder against an encroaching gang. At age twenty-three, he was the undisputed leader of the Academy Homes gang. Of course, anyone in Roxbury that disputed his reign didn't last very long.

"Baby, are you ready for this?" asked J-Rock, squeezing his pregnant girlfriend's hand. Monique Perez had been his girl for almost a year and had become known as the *first lady*. With Perez six months pregnant, the two were considered Academy Homes royalty.

"I am, Jarvis," said Perez, holding her stomach. "We need to stand up for ourselves. This is our time."

J-Rock looked back and forth along the front line of the marchers. The gangs of South Boston stood together in solidarity—for the first time ever. He nodded to the two brothers who led the Castlegate Road Gang, grinning when they both flashed their gang sign and nodded back. Turning his head left, J-Rock gave a quick nod to the Franklin Field Boyz. *We may be shooting at each other next week, but today we're brothers.*

"Move those, now!" said J-Rock. Two of his enforcers jogged ahead of the protest line, kicking down the barricades. Other members of the procession followed suit, quickly clearing the road of any obstructions. People within the barricades scattered to make room for the protesters, who picked up speed as they crossed St. James Avenue.

"Black lives matter! Black lives matter!" chanted the crowd.

The bodies pressed forward, and J-Rock started to feel the sheer power the group possessed. *They were getting the attention they deserved. The reverend was right!*

Loud, shrill whistles filled the air, followed by a dozen or so Boston Police officers dressed in full riot gear with shields. They poured out of Copley Park, forming a tight skirmish line that blocked the protestors' access to the Boston Marathon finish line. J-Rock hesitated, slowing just enough to be pushed forward by the crowd surging behind him. The two groups would collide if he didn't slow down the procession, and he hated to think what might happen to Monique in the chaos that would unfold.

"We've got to slow down, baby," said J-Rock. "Everybody slow down!"

J-Rock turned toward the advancing protestors with both hands raised high in the air. The group responded by raising their hands over their heads and shouting, "*Hands up, don't shoot!*"

"No, no, stop! Everybody stop!" screamed J-Rock, his desperate plea cancelled by the frenzy pushing against him.

The incensed mob pushed into the stiff line of police shields, which retreated several feet to give the protesters a chance to slow down. Bullhorns ordered the crowd to stop as dozens of additional police officers joined the newly formed line. J-Rock ran ahead of the group and turned to address the crowd. He was knocked into the advancing mob by one of the riot shields, where he was swallowed by the masses. No longer in control of the protesters, he furiously pushed his way toward Monique, who had been shoved into the police line.

Before J-Rock reached her, he was struck in the face with an expandable baton, which dropped him to his knees. He watched helplessly as a police officer slammed his shield into Perez, knocking her to the pavement, where another officer hit her over the head with his baton. J-Rock tried to crawl to her, but was swept to his feet by the people rushing toward the police.

When the police line broke moments later, several hundred infuriated protesters charged into Copley Park, hell-bent on tearing the finish line apart. In the process, they killed Monique's baby and injured several protesters caught on the ground during the stampede. J-Rock never saw it happen. He was too busy fighting for his life by the time the crowd stopped.

CHAPTER 56

April 18, 2016
100 Beacon
Boston, Massachusetts

"Mommy, the protestors are back," said Penny, poking her head into the room.

Susan left ahead of everyone to see what Penny was talking about. She and Donald had spent days trying to calm their daughters following the incident at the Chestnut Hill Mall. She found the girls standing in front of the bank of television screens, as "breaking news from Boston" filled her vision. Within moments, the rest of the room had joined them. Sarge raised the volume on the CNN-designated monitor.

"Moments ago, we received reports that several dozen people were hurt in a melee near the finish line of this year's Boston Marathon. The information we received from our reporters on the ground in Boston indicate a peaceful protest of the Black Lives Matter group was in the vicinity of Copley Square when fighting broke out with Boston police.

"To provide our viewers some context, the Boston Marathon is a twenty-six-mile race that stretches through Boston to its finish line on Boylston Street in front of the Boston Public Library. Race contestants finish the race throughout the afternoon from noon until 3:00 p.m. Today at approximately 12:45, a large group of activists with the Black Lives Matter movement were raising awareness of the senseless killing of former Boston Transit worker Pumpsie Jones. Reports indicate the march was proceeding peacefully from Boston Commons for several blocks until the group approached Copley Square. We have video provided by our CNN affiliate in Boston—WCVB."

Donald looked to Susan, who nodded her head.

"Girls, why don't you come with me to see the beautiful paintings that Uncle Sarge received today," said Susan.

"Mommy, are those the same protestors from the mall?" asked Penny.

"I don't know, honey. Come with me, girls."

Susan took the girls and hustled them out of the room.

"*At approximately 12:45 p.m. today, all appeared to be normal at this year's Boston Marathon event. Police have maintained a heightened alert level since the 2013 bombing,*" said the reporter.

"*What caused today's disruption?*" asked the CNN newscaster.

"*According to reports, police in full riot gear began to advance upon the Black Lives Matter protestors and pushed them backwards up Boylston Street away from the finish line. We are told the protestors in the front were squeezed between the police skirmish line and the advancing protestors, causing a panic. From what we have been told, police in the skirmish line struck several of the protestors, resulting in an escalation between Boston PD and unarmed protestors. At that point, the situation spiraled out of control.*"

"*Have there been any injuries?*" the newscaster asked.

"*Reports are still coming in to the studio, but it appears there have been several dozen injuries, including a pregnant woman who was part of the protest group. There have been no reports of injuries to law enforcement personnel. Back to you, Don.*"

"This is part of the news every day, isn't it, Julia?" asked J.J. "It's not just in Boston, it's become a national epidemic of sorts."

"These types of clashes are inevitable," said Donald. "We saw it firsthand in the mall. When large mobs of people gather and try to force themselves into a place that is inappropriate, violence is likely to occur. There has to be a better way to get your point across without endangering others."

"We're collapsing from within, just like Lincoln wrote," said Katie. "We are destroying ourselves."

"After World War II, some declared the next one hundred years to be the American Century," said Sarge. "That designation could, in fact, be a bad omen. History has shown that within a century of an empire's peak, or shortly thereafter, things begin to deteriorate.

"Arguably, we are looking at the early stages of collapse. Economically, as a nation, we are declining as a world power. Our credit rating has suffered, and the dollar is systematically being replaced as the world's reserve currency. Militarily, we are being surpassed in technology and strength. A new Cold War was ushered in several years ago, and we have been remiss to react. Rogue nations have the ability to bring us to our knees by cyberattack or EMP without notice."

"Even if none of those events occur, society is coming apart at the seams," said Abbie. "We are more polarized than at any time in our history. Political rhetoric aside, I don't have a clue as to how to bring us together as a nation at this point."

"As a society, politicians and the media have divided us by class and race. Some would argue our societies values and morals have never been lower," added Donald. "I didn't mean for that to include you, Abbie. We all know you're fighting the good fight."

"I know, Donald," said Abbie.

"Well, I don't plan on going down with the ship," said Steven. "We have a good plan to ride out the storm. We may not be able to fight a war against the Russians, but we can make sure we stay alive until things are sorted out. Right?"

"Absolutely," said Donald.

Susan returned from Sarge's study, snapping the group out of its morose mood.

"I've got the girls settled in, if it's okay, Sarge?" asked Susan.

"Whatever makes them comfortable," replied Sarge.

"They'll probably draw for a while and then fall asleep on your sofa. I made some food for everyone. Why don't we grab something to eat before we get started?" asked Susan. "We can't save the world or ourselves on an empty stomach."

CHAPTER 57

April 18, 2016
100 Beacon
Boston, Massachusetts

Donald had long ago earned the unofficial title of *Director of Procurement* for the group. Since returning from prison, he had committed his life to the concept of preparedness. Shortly after his return from FMC Devens, Donald was called to a meeting with John Morgan at 73 Tremont. At the meeting, he met Steven and Sarge. Morgan surprised Donald with his first words: *Gentlemen, we need to be prepared for a collapse event.* Donald recalled looking around the room to measure the reaction of the Sargents, who appeared unfazed. The four men spent several hours discussing the various threats they faced, and the preparedness steps necessary to survive each collapse event.

At the end of the day, Donald was tasked with putting together a comprehensive preparedness plan. He suggested that a like-minded team needed to be assembled—a group of connected, capable and, most importantly, loyal associates.

Over those next few months, Steven introduced Katie and Brad to Donald. In addition to their military training, both of them occupied positions of power and influence within the government. Donald introduced J.J. to the group, where he was warmly welcomed for his medical expertise and military perspective. Sarge suggested Julia join the group because of her international political contacts, and her dedication to unbiased media.

Donald stressed the importance of awareness related to global affairs, and the potential they might have to precipitate a collapse event. The contacts Julia, Brad and Katie had cultivated were invaluable to the assessment of a potential collapse. J.J. was in charge of survival medicine. Donald and Susan took on the roles of gathering information, organizing the basic necessities and planning for the collapse. Steven handled the security and tactics aspect of the group readiness training, while Sarge coordinated the group as their leader.

The final member of the group had been the most obvious, but unexpected addition. During one of Donald's periodic meetings at 73 Tremont, Morgan informed him that Abbie would be the ninth member. Donald immediately recognized the significance of her presence among them. Morgan would spare no expense funding the plans Donald was required to develop—for the nine of them and the Boston Brahmin.

"So we all agree the world is going to hell," said Steven. "Let's see how we're going to survive it."

"Very well. Let's start on the ninth floor, which includes the residences," said Donald.

"Here?" asked Abbie.

"For some of you, this will be new," said Donald. "We've made a few changes in the last six months."

Donald led them to the private stairwell connecting the three floors occupied by the Sargents—the eighth floor and the two penthouse floors above it totaled twelve thousand square feet. When Morgan commented about sparing no expense, 100 Beacon was the first indication that he'd meant it. The top floor, known as Penthouse I, consisted of Sarge's master suite, the guest room suite occupied by Steven, a study and the Great Hall. Penthouse II, located on the ninth floor, had a similar floor plan except there were more bedrooms. A centrally located great room included a media wall similar to Sarge's, next to a series of desks and computer stations.

"The floor plan is similar to upstairs," said Donald. "The master suite is capable of housing Susan and I, with the girls. J.J. and Brad share a bedroom, as do Abbie and Katie. There is also a fourth bedroom which holds eight bunks—*for trusted guests.*

"We've done a lot of work in here since we got together last summer," said Donald. "We have always stressed the importance of having information at our disposal in order to make informed decisions. Katie, this is our situation room."

Katie walked around and turned on some of the computer monitors. Julia activated the televisions, which were tuned to the same news networks as the screens upstairs.

"How are you going to keep it powered in the event of an outage?" asked Brad. "If we get nuked with an EMP, the grid will be fried."

"Even a cyberattack could take us offline for a long time," said Sarge. "Donald has thought about these issues."

"I have," started Donald. "None of the electronics on our three floors are tied to the grid. We have installed standby generators on the roof to service all of our needs. We have disconnected solar panels, which can be easily connected after an EMP, along with shielded and transient protected auxiliary solar equipment. The equipment takes up much of the roof, as you will see later. Most residential users tie their solar array to the electric grid in order to defray costs by selling excess power to the local utility. We have remained independent of the power grid in order to avoid voltage spikes and EMP-induced surges."

"What about solar storms?" asked Katie. "They have the same effect as nukes."

"That's true," said Donald. "The good news is that we'll have advance warning. All of us have space weather apps installed on our computers and smartphones. We will have at least twenty-four to forty-eight hours advanced notice of an incoming coronal mass ejection. The biggest potential disruption to the grid comes in the form of voltage spikes. Again, we operate independently from the NStar grid, so we won't be affected."

"We also take precautions and have backups," said Susan. "Everything is fully operational today for you guys to review. Tomorrow, Donald and I will disconnect everything and store the electronics in Faraday cages on the eighth floor below us. This will include all electronics and their backup components, like modules, circuit boards and batteries."

"What good will the televisions or computers be if we get nuked?" asked Brad. "The news networks won't be functioning."

"That's true, but you may have international alternatives," said Donald. "Also stored downstairs in Faraday cages is a complete HughesNet Gen 5 satellite Internet system and a DirecTV satellite television package. After we determine the threat to be over, we can quickly replace the fried units on the roof with the shielded backups. We'll have full access to the web and media in just an hour."

"Communications also," added Susan. "We have provided you BaoFeng portable radios and satellite telephones in the Faraday cages at your homes, with corresponding backups here. We also have a base unit stored here. You have to keep that equipment in the cages. After a collapse event, as you military guys know, comms will be critical."

"What we have on this floor is unique to civilians and probably similar to the hardened facilities within the government," said Sarge. "Kudos to Donald and Susan for working tirelessly to put this part of the plan into effect. We have also thought of something else, which in a way led Julia to win a Marconi Award. Julia, would you like to fill in the blanks?"

"We have all discussed at length the scenarios and threats," said Julia. "Our advanced preparations also include the possibility we may have to help rebuild our country. After the initial chaos passes, people will be starved for information. In addition, during a rebuilding process, whether localized or on a national level, there must be a way to disseminate information. Before you can create a connection with people, you must have a mechanism to share and exchange ideas. To rebuild our nation, you would have to be able to identify compatible qualities and find common ground with people throughout the country. I believe our country would not have been founded had it not been for the printing press. What we have here is the ability to gather facts and then distribute the information throughout the world by Internet, ham radio and even paper.

Everything we need is secured in this building. I call it the Digital Carrier Pigeon."

"This is incredible Julia," interjected Abbie. "Very impressive."

"Someone likes to read," said Katie, noting the bookshelves that lined the hallways and nearly every available inch of wall space.

"I hate to be cliché," said Sarge. "But it is appropriate here—knowledge is power. Ironically, in today's wired world, life without electrical power would be life without knowledge. Think about it. Do you know anyone who owns an encyclopedia set? How about a dictionary? When was the last time you read a book—a *real* book?"

"That's old school, Sarge, just like you." Steven laughed.

"Yeah, I know, I'm a throwback," said Sarge. "What you see around you is knowledge. We have gathered the most recent encyclopedia, common reference books and most importantly—manuals. DIY electrical, plumbing, carpentry and repair books complete with photographs are on these shelves. Survival and preparedness guides covering a vast array of topics are here. Important works of fiction are here, and old volumes are in my study."

"I have accumulated the best medical journals and illustrative guides available for our use in case of an emergency," said J.J. "I hope nothing happens to me. If it does, you will have reference materials at your disposal. You will know how to conduct field triage, administer basic first aid and how to set broken bones. Sadly, there are tutorials for dealing with dead bodies. The dead create significant health hazards."

"You have all cooperated and provided me your used iPads and tablets," said Donald. "I have downloaded hundreds of pdf files from the Internet, including checklists, military manuals on civil disturbances, survival guides and specific information on various government facilities. Every imaginable reference book has been included in the downloaded files. These are all safely secured in Faraday cages for our use in a grid down scenario."

Abbie and Brad made their way to a set of double doors to the right of the fireplace.

"What's in here?" asked Brad.

"Don't be shy, Brad, every good soldier appreciates a well-stocked mess hall," said Susan. "This is the prepper pantry."

She walked over and opened the doors to a six-hundred-square-foot storage room. With the double doors opened, everyone could see steel shelves lined with foods, spices and condiments. Donald was proud of the time and effort Susan put into the planning of their food storage. He decided to let her take over.

"The most important aspect of our food storage plan is to provide a balanced, high-caloric daily menu," said Susan. "This shelf is dedicated to vitamins, minerals and supplements. After the event, America may be sent back a couple of hundred years with respect to every aspect of daily life."

"During a collapse event, food will become scarce or nonexistent," added J.J. "Malnutrition will become an issue. Poor sanitation and lack of clean water can lead to dysentery. We have stored enough vitamins and tubs of protein powder to last all of us two years, with more downstairs."

"The remaining shelves contain boxed and canned foods with long shelf lives," Susan continued. "We have placed a particular emphasis on whole grains like rice and oatmeal, more bean varieties than you knew existed, and canned vegetables with a high nutrient content. Because we are such a large group, we used fifty-pound bags for the dry goods and number ten cans for the vegetables."

"We have developed a spreadsheet, which we review every Monday," said Donald. "If something goes out of date, then we donate it to a local homeless shelter and purchase a replacement."

"Where's the chocolate?" asked Katie. "Sometimes a girl needs comfort foods."

She and Abbie locked arms in solidarity.

"We've got you covered, ladies," said Susan. "I had Penny and Rebecca in mind as well. Snacks include peanut butter, crackers, nuts, hard candies, chocolate pudding, Jell-O and Jiffy Pop popcorn—you know the kind that puffs up the aluminum foil."

"Coffee?" asked Steven. "I can't function without it."

"No problem," said Donald. "We have canned coffee and a ceramic campfire pot to brew it in. We also have a big variety of hot and cold tea. These are a great source of antioxidants."

Everyone laughed at the last reference. Sarge picked up on the irony of insuring their survival by stockpiling tea bags full of antioxidants. J.J. did as well.

"Here's the thing," said J.J. "Depending upon the collapse scenario, life will be very dangerous. It would be a shame to survive bullets flying around our heads only to die from being malnourished."

"Yeah, let's talk about bullets," said Steven. "When do we get to the *toys*?"

"I prefer to call them tools," said Donald. "Let's go down to the eighth floor."

Sarge watched as everyone talked among themselves. They seemed impressed with the preparations so far. The eighth floor was a shadow of its former self, as was the entire building. Morgan first approached Sarge in 2009 about the concept of preparedness when Morgan was considering the purchase of 100 Beacon Street. The building was in need of renovation, but one of the conditions of the Board of Zoning Appeals was that it be architecturally restored in a manner consistent with its original construction—dating back nearly one hundred years. Morgan retained ownership of the top three floors, with the intent to create an inner-city safe house during times of societal unrest. He wanted Sarge to oversee the renovations on his behalf, and occupy the top floor Penthouse. Morgan had a vision, and the group was seeing the result—in many ways.

Everyone gathered at the bottom of the stairs. The eighth floor resembled a large commercial warehouse broken up into many smaller rooms. Each space had a distinct purpose and was separated by sound-insulated walls.

"Steven, they're all yours," said Donald. Sarge stood to the side to allow Steven access to the gun vault.

"Here's where we keep the goodies," said Steven.

He placed his hand on the biometric scanner and then punched in an additional four-digit code. The door popped open and he pulled the handle.

"We'll make sure that everyone's prints get scanned and give you the four-digit code. The dual system prevents someone from entering the vault if the code gets compromised—or if your hand does." Steven paused for effect.

"I'm just kidding, you guys, relax." Steven laughed.

Sarge knew he wasn't kidding.

"Come on," said Steven.

Brad and Katie entered first.

"Holy crap!" exclaimed Brad. "My armory isn't this impressive. The BATF would drop a load in their pants over this, buddy."

As Brad circled the room, he ran his fingers along the myriad of weapons. Sarge was pleased with Brad's reaction.

"Here's the bottom line," said Steven. "If you can't defend it, it isn't yours. These weapons are the tools we need to defend ourselves. After a collapse event, we won't be able to run down to Boston Firearms and pick up a gun and some ammo. We have to arm ourselves, and possibly recruits, for battle. I have focused on weapons suitable to urban tactics. But I have also planned for other scenarios—such as abandoning the city."

"Just like our food stores and other supplies," added Donald, "our weapons cache needs to be thorough."

"Correct," said Steven. "Each of you, with the exceptions of Abbie and Brad, has versions of these weapons at home already. In case of a bug-out scenario requiring you to get here on short notice without returning home, we have one of each weapon, plus a backup, in this vault. Additionally, we have six of each type of weapon for any additional group members we take on board. Altogether, there are a minimum of twenty-four of each type of weapon, along with a humidity-controlled ammunition vault." *Nearly two hundred guns.*

"All of this brings to light a certain reality," said Donald. "One of us might get shot or seriously injured. We're lucky to have J.J. on board with his experience as a field trauma surgeon. You've seen it all, haven't you, Doc?"

"Follow me," said J.J., who turned and started down the hallway.

"After TEOTWAWKI, medical supplies will be scarce, and functioning hospitals even scarcer. Medications we take for granted will be gone. I'm a good doctor, but I'm only as good as my equipment."

"J.J. and I have joked that the first place to get looted after the collapse will be the drug store," said Susan. "The addicts will be looking for painkillers, and the preppers will be looking for antibiotics."

"Very true, which is why we keep this place a well-kept secret," said J.J. "With Donald's assistance, I have created a fully functional field trauma facility. We have equipment for resuscitation and life support, including a ventilator, a cardiac monitor combined with a defibrillator, and IV administration devices. We even have a portable ultrasound machine. Your father has supported us all the way, Abbie."

"He has a lot of respect for you, J.J., and your family," said Abbie.

Sarge knew Abbie was making a point. J.J. was estranged from his father. His mother had passed away years ago, and the elder Dr. Warren never forgave J.J. for joining the military. The Warrens were the founders of Harvard Medical, descendants of field surgeons at the battle of Bunker Hill. J.J.'s father was one of the Boston Brahmin, but the two didn't speak. Sarge was certain John Morgan wanted to remedy the situation at some point.

"Thanks, Abbie," said J.J.

"Are those for us?" asked Katie, pointing to a rack of olive drab medical packs.

"Yes, each of you will have an extensive first aid kit to supplement what I have provided you already. I suggest you stow this with your other gear, but be prepared to grab it on a moment's notice. Brad and Abbie, as we know, have access to medical facilities unavailable to the rest of us after a collapse event. While Katie is in D.C., post-collapse medical treatment is undetermined, so I have prepared a bag for her," said JJ.

"All of your get-home bags are current based upon our last

meeting," said Donald. "This medical kit will supplement what you already have in them. Also, before I forget, Sarge and I agree we should conceal-carry anytime we leave the house—no exceptions. After recent incidents, we need to protect ourselves at all times. Please do not leave home without a concealed weapon."

"Hey, I want one of those Mont Blanc fountain pens, Sarge," said Brad. "Steven told me you broke the tip off in the guy's neck. That's how the police apprehended him at the hospital."

"Yeah, Boston CSI had fun matching up the nib to what was left of the pen's barrel," said Sarge. "I tell you what, Brad, I'll buy you a pen if you'll trade me some of your artillery."

"Deal," replied Brad.

Donald led them out of J.J.'s infirmary.

"This entire side of the building is storage," said Donald. "We have long-term food storage for up to five years. There are duplicate supplies related to medical, safety and sanitation."

"Yeah, we have tons of toilet paper," said Steven.

Sarge kicked him in the ass.

"One room has several thousand gallons of stored bottled water," said Susan. "Sarge also had a rain catchment cistern installed on the roof. We will have to purify the water for drinking or cooking. We've tried to think of everything."

"As you guys know, along with the girls, prepping is my life," said Donald. "Abbie's dad has charged me—*us*, with a great responsibility. We will have quite a few lives in our hands should we experience a significant collapse event. Every morning when I wake up I ask myself—*if the world fell apart while I was asleep, what prep do I wish I had*—and then I go get it."

"What did you wish for this morning, buddy?" asked J.J.

"I hoped we would never have to put all of this stuff to use. After today, my hope is fading further."

CHAPTER 58

April 18, 2016
100 Beacon, Rooftop Terrace
Boston, Massachusetts

Sarge topped off his champagne glass. This evening was not originally planned to last this long, but widespread reports of rioting and runaway fires throughout Boston caused his guests to reconsider his offer to stay another night. Abbie convinced her security detail she was safer at 100 Beacon than any place they might want to take her. The group was as relaxed as they could be given the circumstances. Sipping champagne felt awkward, but they had every reason to rejoice in their success. They were committed to protecting each other and their extended families—the Boston Brahmin. In times of unrest, history must be preserved, and like the Boston Brahmin, most of them were the direct descendants of the Founding Fathers. They had a vested interest in preserving the work of their forefathers, and the right to celebrate their initial accomplishment.

"The news reports of unrest are not exaggerated this time," said Susan. "It appears most of the southern part of the city is ablaze."

The group observed at least a dozen large blazes in the southern areas of Boston, likely enveloping Roxbury, Dorchester and Mattapan. Boston lay in the prevailing westerlies, so smoke could be seen blowing across South Boston towards the Atlantic. The sounds of sirens filled the air as first responders from all over the city rushed to assist. According to news reports, there were currently six 9-alarm fires on the south side.

"These events are becoming all too common across the nation," said Abbie. "When I talk to my colleagues in the Senate, from all political persuasions, they agree there is a feeling of malaise and hopelessness spreading across their home states. The polls provided to me the other day reveal the nation's low morale. What we're beginning to witness is a nation that has lost hope. This has turned to anger for many."

"Whether by design or by chance, the American people have turned to their government, looking for answers," said Julia. "Reliance on government support has overwhelmed the system. People in despair don't realize the government is doomed to fail them. Our system of government was not designed to be the cradle-to-grave provider its citizens have come to expect. They will demand more of the government, and with all due respect, Abbie, politicians will try to provide for their constituents. How long will it be before taxes will have to be significantly raised and the taxpayers pitch a fit?"

"Exactly," said Katie. "It's just a matter of time before class warfare becomes the headline of the day—the makers versus the takers."

"History can repeat itself, right, Donald?" asked Sarge.

"It's ironic that the nine of us are having this conversation on one of the most important dates in American history," said Donald. "On this night in 1775, Paul Revere and William Dawes left on horseback to warn their patriot comrades about the British advance on Concord and Lexington. Revere left from the Old North Church."

Donald directed everyone's attention up the Charles River toward the north side of Boston.

"Historically, Dawes was lesser known, though he was equally important as a patriot," said Donald. "Dawes was directed by Dr. Warren, J.J.'s ancestor, to travel a southerly route through Roxbury and Brookline. He crossed the river near the site of the Cambridge Bridge."

Donald drew the circuitous route in the air and walked to the edge of the roof, where he pointed towards Harvard.

"Both of the men evaded detection and capture until their mission was nearly complete," said Donald. "Revere was captured by a British patrol, and Dawes lost his horse, walking the rest of the way to Lexington. A third rider, young Samuel Prescott, rode on to Concord with Revere's message.

"On the morning of April nineteenth, tomorrow, seven hundred British troops arrived at Lexington," continued Donald. "Captain John Parker and his seventy-seven-man militia were waiting on Lexington's common. They were greatly outnumbered. Without warning, an unknown musket fired the *shot heard around the world.* Eight of Captain Parker's men died to only one British soldier. Arguably, the patriots lost the Battle of Lexington. But the American Revolution, our fight for freedom, had begun—and we won against all odds."

Everyone stood in silence, taking in the moment.

"The nine of us are a family," said Sarge. "Our ideals and goals are no different than the patriots who banded together in the 1760s against an oppressive, tyrannical government that did not consider the best interests of its citizens. I believe our nation has become what our forefathers fought so bravely to resist. Tyranny and anarchy are never far apart. Thomas Jefferson recognized this when he said *even under the best forms of government those entrusted with power have perverted it into tyranny.*

"We will protect each other until our dying day. I think we all know that in our hearts. We also have roots dating back to the founding of our nation. Like you, I love this country and I hate seeing what is happening to it. I believe it is destined for collapse. I don't believe the nine of us alone have the power to save it, but we're no different than the nine patriots that stood up for freedom nearly two hundred and fifty years ago. Like those nine Bostonians, we will face challenges, and like our Founding Fathers, when faced with the choice between compromising our principles or choosing freedom—we will choose freedom."

"I have something to give everyone," interjected Brad. "We wear uniforms in the military to honor traditions and mark our branch of service. The nine of us may not wear a uniform as we fight this battle—in whatever form it takes—but we should have a symbol of our loyalty to each other and the noble purpose to which we've devoted our lives."

Brad handed out embroidered patches of a flag featuring five red and four white alternating stripes.

"This is the rebellious stripes flag," said Brad. "This became a symbol of freedom to the patriots who founded our nation. When Bostonians gathered at the Liberty Tree near Boston Common in 1765 to protest burdensome taxation, a clear message was sent to the British government. In 1767, a flagpole was erected next to the Liberty Tree, and the Rebellious Flag was raised. The Rebellious Flag and the Liberty Tree witnessed historic meetings, fiery speeches and celebrations for the early patriots who became known as the Sons of Liberty. This is our past. This is also our future."

"We are a modern-day Knights Templar," said Sarge. "Our mission should be to protect America and its republic from those who would inflict tyranny upon her. This group of nine Americans is loyal to our country and each other. I suggest a tribute to the original nine members of the Sons of Liberty, who had the vision and strength to persevere against all odds to give us the freedoms we enjoy. I propose a toast to us—the Loyal Nine."

The Loyal Nine!

"Like our forefathers before us, the Loyal Nine grew from a few voices into a legion of patriots throughout America. There will be many who join us in the challenge to preserve freedom. To all of those who will join us in the fight against tyranny and for the preservation of our freedoms, I propose a toast they be included with us as—the Mechanics."

The Mechanics!

"Finally," said Sarge, "when faced with the tough choices necessary to preserve our nation's ideals, I say we choose freedom!"

The group toasted together. *Choose Freedom!*

THANK YOU FOR READING THE LOYAL NINE!

If you enjoyed it, I'd be grateful if you'd take a moment to write a short review (just a few words are needed) and post it on Amazon. Amazon uses complicated algorithms to determine what books are recommended to readers. Sales are, of course, a factor, but so are the quantities of reviews my books get. By taking a few seconds to leave a review, you help me out, and also help new readers learn about my work.

And before you go…

SIGN UP for Bobby Akart's mailing list to receive special offers, bonus content, and you'll be the first to receive news about new releases in the Doomsday series:

eepurl.com/bYqq3L

VISIT Amazon.com/BobbyAkart for more information on his next project, as well as his completed words: the Doomsday series, the Yellowstone series, the Lone Star series, the Pandemic series, the Blackout series, the Boston Brahmin series and the Prepping for Tomorrow series totaling nearly forty novels, including over thirty Amazon #1 Bestsellers in forty-plus fiction and nonfiction genres.

Visit Bobby Akart's website for informative blog entries on preparedness, writing, and a behind-the-scenes look into his novels.

BobbyAkart.com

READ ON FOR A BONUS EXCERPT from

CYBER ATTACK

Book Two in The Boston Brahmin Series.

Best Selling Author of *The Pandemic Series*

BOBBY AKART

CYBER ATTACK

The Boston Brahmin Series . Book Two

Excerpt from *Cyber Attack*

CHAPTER 1

May 8, 2016
3:07 p.m.
American Airlines Flight 129
33,000 Feet
Near St. Louis, Missouri

"Good afternoon from the flight deck. This is Captain Randy Gray, and it is my honor to pilot our American Airlines Boeing 757 into Washington Dulles this afternoon. We have reached our cruising altitude of thirty-three thousand feet, after averting the initial turbulence caused by the area of weather north of the Dallas–Fort Worth metro area. With a little help from a tailwind, we should arrive on time at Washington Dulles International by two o'clock local time," said Gray. "I will be turning off the Fasten Seat Belt signs to allow you free access to our newly enhanced cabin. Our flight attendants will begin cabin service shortly. As always, we thank you for flying American Airlines."

Gray began his career as a pilot in 1989 with Command Airways, a small regional carrier based in upstate New York. Initially checked out on the ATR 42, a Czech-made plane, Gray continued his training and became a highly respected pilot within the American Airlines ranks. The flight to Washington Dulles was routine. He shared the cockpit with First Officer William Applegate and his longtime friend Stacy Bird, a Frontier Air captain deadheading to D.C. after a hunting trip in West Texas.

"Bill, Stacy and I would like to say hello to a friend in first class. Would you mind taking over for a bit?" asked Gray.

Applegate had flown right seat with Gray in the past and had earned Gray's confidence.

"Absolutely, fellows, go ahead. She's flyin' herself anyway," said Applegate.

Gray and Bird unbuckled their harnesses and took a quick glance at the controls to confirm everything was in order. He and Bird slipped into the galley through the secured cockpit door, which automatically locked behind them.

"Hi, guys," said Karen Mosely, the chief flight attendant. "May I get you boys anything?"

"I don't think so, Karen, but thanks," said Gray. "We're gonna holler at 3B for a minute before we descend into Dulles."

Captains Gray and Bird strolled down the aisle behind her to greet a former Air Force buddy—when the aircraft took a sudden lurch upward. He grabbed the headrests of the seats on both sides of the aisle and ducked to look out the windows—clear blue skies. The plane quickly corrected, steadying for a moment before nosing downward into a steep descent. Gasps and screams erupted throughout the cabin.

"Is your FO okay?" asked Bird.

Gray knew what he meant by this question. Since the mysterious disappearance of Malaysia Flight 370 and the deliberate crash of Germanwings Flight 9525, every pilot looked at the members of their crew with a different set of eyes. He locked eyes with Bird, both of them sharing the same thought. If they'd hit turbulence, why didn't Applegate activate the Fasten Seat Belt signs?

"Back to the cockpit," he said, edging by Captain Bird.

Gray reached the intercom console next to the cockpit access door and pressed the pound key, praying for Applegate to respond.

CHAPTER 2

May 8, 2016
3:07 p.m.
The Hack House
Binney Street
East Cambridge, Massachusetts

Andrew Lau stared intently at the iMac monitor array as Leonid Malvalaha deftly navigated the mouse. Malvalaha and Lau's other longtime graduate assistant, Anna Fakhri, had continued in their new endeavor, despite the risk of criminal prosecution.

Through the process of pen testing, Lau identified zero-day vulnerabilities in a computer network and took advantage of the security holes before the network's IT department could find a solution. Once the vulnerability window was identified, the zero-day attack inserted malware into the system. The *Game*, as Lau called it, required the attacked entity to pay a ransom in exchange for a patch to their security. Prior to today, their hacks didn't directly risk lives, though their activities on behalf of the Las Vegas union had no doubt resulted in deaths. They had been more selective after Las Vegas, until now.

"Malvalaha, run us through the hack," said Lau.

Lau's core group consisted of Malvalaha, Fakhri and newcomer Herm Walthaus, who had proven himself by creating a cascading blackout of the Las Vegas power grid—no small feat.

"We're monitoring American Airlines Flight 129, which departed Dallas around forty-five minutes ago," stated Malvalaha.

His desk resembled the cockpit of a sophisticated aircraft, with six flat-panel monitors at his disposal. He pointed to the screen that displayed FlightAware, an online tool providing up-to-the-second statistics on any airline flight.

"Flight 129 is currently over St. Louis and has adjusted its flight path directly to Washington Dulles airport. The aircraft is a Boeing 757-200, flying at approximately four hundred eighty knots, or five hundred and fifty miles per hour. Altitude thirty-three thousand feet."

"Tell us what your research has shown," said Lau.

Fakhri addressed her former professor, now hacking partner. "Since 9/11, there have been conspiracy theories surrounding the commandeering of the four aircraft by the terrorists," said Fakhri. "One such theory is the aircraft was part of a false-flag attack initiated by the government. As the theory goes, based upon 2001 technology, NORAD—the North American Aerospace Defense Command—took control of the planes and purposefully crashed them into the World Trade Center and the Pentagon. The most prevalent reason cited for the false-flag operation is that the government wanted to justify initiating a war in the Middle East."

"For our purposes, we're not interested in the false-flag theories," said Malvalaha. "We focused on the concept of the remote takeover of a commercial aircraft. The technology exists, and it has, in fact, been used by the military in the past. Today, we will hack the aircraft via the flight management system, *and* make ourselves known."

"My father is a pilot for the 757-200 airframe," said Walthaus. "We always had sophisticated flight simulators in our home growing up, and naturally they provided more entertainment for me than a PlayStation. I've never physically flown an aircraft, but I am an expert on the flight sim."

"I thought the FAA disproved the theories surrounding remote access of the onboard computers," said Lau.

"True to an extent," said Fakhri. "A security consultant from Germany claimed to have hacked an aircraft using an Android telephone application. Later, one of his peers accessed the aircraft's network by connecting through the in-flight entertainment system. He then used a modified version of Vortex software to compromise the cockpit's system."

"When pressed for a response, the FAA was selective in its choice of words," said Malvalaha. "They equivocated using the phrases *described technique* and *using the technology the consultant has claimed*."

Lau laughed after this statement.

"The government has a lot of experience with misdirection," said Lau. "Our most sophisticated operations were panned as impossible by the experts and their friends in the media—even after we successfully accomplished them!"

"When researching this online, we discovered that American Airlines and Boeing launched a *Bug Bounty* program, offering a million free air-miles to the good guys—the *white-hat hackers*," said Walthaus. "These *ethical and conscientious* hackers shared their findings online. We took their findings as a starting point, and found the vulnerability window we were looking for."

"Continue," said Lau.

If Lau could publish his work, he would surely win the Carnegie Foundation award as Professor of the Year. Then again, he might be teaching second grade math to his fellow inmates.

"We're going to use the government's safeguard technology against them in two steps," said Malvalaha.

Lau turned his Red Sox cap backward—an unconscious signal that it was time to go to work.

"First, we access the Boeing Uninterruptible Autopilot system," said Fakhri. "The patent for the system was granted to Boeing in 2006, as a method of taking control of a commercial aircraft away from the pilot or flight crew in the event of a hijacking. The uninterruptible autopilot can be initiated by the pilots via onboard sensors or remotely through government satellite links."

"As far as the public knows, no Boeing aircraft has been retrofitted to include this technology, although rumors abound to the contrary," said Walthaus. "After the disappearance of Malaysia Flight 370, the Prime Minister of Malaysia claimed Boeing or *certain government agencies* utilized the uninterruptible autopilot to down the aircraft. I'm sure he alluded to the CIA."

"An online search supported his theory," said Fakhri. "We researched the rules issued by the FAA on the Federal Register website and found a Special Condition granted to Boeing for the Model 777 aircraft, allowing the installation of the uninterruptible autopilot software."

"But we're tracking a 757," said Lau.

"Yes, we are," said Walthaus. "The FAA, in its action, authorized Boeing to conduct tests of the new system in six of its 757 aircraft, plus the system was initially designed for the 757. We researched all of the top contractors who work under Boeing's Defense division. Typically, new technology ends up in the hands of our Defense Department."

"We found the company hired to install the system—Alion Science and Technology," said Fakhri. "Their technology solutions sector manager, Robert Hurt, gave a presentation at a Raytheon trade show last year, which was published online. After some digging, we have the details on the six 757 aircraft participating in the program."

"American Airlines Flight 129 is one of them," said Malvahala.

CHAPTER 3

May 8, 2016
3:12 p.m.
American Airlines Flight 129
33,000 Feet
Near Evansville, Indiana

Gray exhaled deeply when the green light on the keypad illuminated. He and Bird quickly entered the cockpit and slammed the door shut.

"What the hell is going on, Bill!" exclaimed Gray as he climbed into his seat and strapped in. Bird positioned himself in the jump seat. Gray quickly examined the onboard computer monitor and activated the Fasten Seat Belt sign.

"Talk to me, Billy!"

"The controls are unresponsive," muttered Applegate. "We are in a rapid descent, and the controls will not respond to any of my commands."

"You have to call a Mayday, Randy," said Bird.

Gray looked at the altitude control indicator. They were in a descent, but not an insurmountable one—yet. The altimeter read twenty-four thousand feet.

"Billy, are you with me?" asked Gray.

Applegate barely muttered a response.

"Billy, why don't you trade seats with Captain Bird," said Gray. "You need a break, and Stacy is an experienced captain. Come on now, let Stacy swap with you."

Applegate slowly removed his seat harness and traded seats with Bird, who immediately leaned across the center console.

"Should I escort him off the flight deck?" asked Bird.

"He's just shook up," said Gray. "Call in the Mayday, and let me figure this out."

Bird's attempt to access the onboard computer proved fruitless. The keyboard was unresponsive.

"We're one hundred miles east of St. Louis," said Gray. "Try SDF."

"Mayday, Mayday, Mayday, Louisville Tower. American Airlines one-two-niner heavy declaring an emergency," said Bird. "I say again. Mayday, Mayday, Mayday, Louisville, Kentucky Radar. American Airlines one-two-niner heavy declaring an emergency."

"American one-two-niner, this is Louisville Tower. We copy your Mayday," came the response from the Louisville Air Traffic Control. "What is the nature of your emergency?"

"Louisville Tower, onboard controls are unresponsive. We are under power and in a steady descent now passing twenty-two thousand feet," said Bird. "All other flight deck functions appear normal."

"Roger, American one-two-niner," said Louisville ATC. "All stations. All stations. Louisville Tower. Mayday situation in progress. Stop transmitting. Repeat. Mayday situation in progress. Stop all transmissions."

Gray sat back in the pilot's seat and looked around the Orbiter flight deck, searching for clues—and answers. Nothing made sense. The entire console appeared normal. The monitors functioned properly, displaying their current flight parameters; however, the keyboard for the onboard computer continued to be unresponsive.

"We're leveling off," said Bird, pointing at the altitude control indicator. "Son of a gun, we're holding steady at twenty K. I've never seen anything like this."

Neither had Gray.

"American one-two-niner, this is Louisville Tower. Boeing technical team is en route, and Homeland Security has been notified," said Louisville ATC.

"Roger, Louisville Tower," said Bird. "Be advised, altitude has leveled off at twenty thousand feet. Steady on original course."

“American one-two-niner. Louisville Tower. Roger.”

“Homeland Security?” asked Bird.

Gray understood the gravity of their situation.. If he couldn’t demonstrate positive control of the aircraft, it would not be allowed to reach Washington.

CHAPTER 4

May 8, 2016
3:13 p.m.
The Hack House
Binney Street
East Cambridge, Massachusetts

"Now that we've entered the plane's Wi-Fi system, it's necessary to hack through the firewall of the aircraft communications addressing and reporting system, or ACARS," said Malvalaha. "This will give us access to the plane's onboard computer system and the uploaded flight management system data."

Lau watched intently as his protégé navigated through the plane's servers.

"You're in!" exclaimed Walthaus. "My turn, Leo."

Malvahala relinquished his chair to Walthaus, whose only experience with an airplane was playing on his father's computer as a teen.

"The aircraft is flying on autopilot," said Fakhri. "That's good. Right about now, the pilots are relaxed and completely unaware of our presence."

"First, I will initiate the uninterruptible autopilot system, which will prevent the flight crew from interfering with us," said Walthaus. "These controls are considered *fly-by-wire,* which have replaced the conventional manual controls of the aircraft with an electronic interface. The yokes that control the aircraft may provide certain inputs into a flight-control system, but with the uninterruptible autopilot system initiated, the crew can flail around all they want, and their actions will not be recognized.

"First, we'll adjust the altitude to twenty-six thousand feet—just to let them know we're flying their plane," he continued. "Watch here."

Walthaus pointed to FlightAware, and Lau turned his attention to the screen. When Walthaus refreshed the screen, the airspeed had declined, along with the aircraft's altitude.

"Whoa!" exclaimed Walthaus. "Sorry about that! It's hard to adjust the controls using a mouse and its cursor. I just took the plane into a dive and probably scared the crap out of everybody on board. Let me level this off at twenty thousand feet."

"Is that too low?" asked Lau.

"No, eighteen thousand feet is considered the upper end of air traffic's transitional level, where the most activity takes place," said Walthaus. "We'll maintain this altitude and course for a few minutes, to give everyone on board an opportunity to catch their breath. Then we'll climb back to thirty-three thousand feet."

Ordinarily, the Zero Day Gamers had a profit motive. The *hijack by hacking* of the American Airlines flight was a test. Today, they would determine whether the hack could be achieved, in addition to gauging the government's response.

"At this point, the pilots have probably reported a *Mayday* to the nearest air traffic control tower—either St. Louis or Louisville," said Malvahala. "Their flight training would dictate a simple procedure of turning off the autopilot and resuming control of the aircraft manually. Unfortunately for them, the Boeing Uninterruptible Autopilot system has built-in safeguards that prevent the pilots from overriding our controls."

"What prevents NORAD or the FAA from taking over the operation of the plane via its satellite controls?" asked Lau.

"We've installed a version of the TeslaCrypt Ransomware onto the plane's servers," said Malvahala. "This malware blocks access to the aircraft's onboard computers by everybody until released by us. In the future, we'll provide them a message with a monetary demand. Today, we're just sending a message."

CHAPTER 5

May 8, 2016
3:17 p.m.
NORAD—Air Defense Operations Center
Cheyenne Mountain Air Force Station, Colorado

"Sir, Wright Patterson has been notified of the situation," said the technical sergeant manning the console tracking American Airlines Flight 129. "I have Lieutenant Colonel Darren Reynolds on the line, sir."

Colonel Arnold pressed the remote transmit button for his headset. "Colonel Reynolds, this is Colonel James Arnold. Please stay on the line as we assess the situation."

"Colonel Arnold, we have scrambled two F-16s. Time is running out. Once ADOC was notified, we ceased communications with Louisville ATC and turned comms over to you."

"Thank you, Colonel," said Arnold. "Sergeant, contact the aircraft."

"American Airlines one-two-niner, United States Air Force Air Defense Operations Center. Over," said the airman.

After a moment, the response came through the overhead speakers.

"Air Defense, this is Captain Randy Gray."

"Captain Gray, this is Colonel Arnold. What steps have you taken to gain control of your aircraft?" asked Colonel Arnold.

"The most logical step is to turn off the plane's autopilot," said Gray. "But the autopilot is unresponsive. In fact, all of our controls are unresponsive. We've had no flight control for nearly seventeen minutes now."

“Stand by, Captain Gray,” said Colonel Arnold.

He pointed to the sergeant to mute the conversation, waiting several seconds before addressing his team.

“If this aircraft is outfitted with Boeing’s new autopilot system, why haven’t we simply taken control of the aircraft?”

“Malware has been inserted into the aircraft’s onboard server network, preventing any type of outside access,” said another airman. “Boeing technical support is working on a solution, but so far they have been unsuccessful.”

“Colonel Reynolds, what is the ETA on your F16s?” asked Colonel Arnold.

Arnold took a deep breath during the pause and studied the global positioning of Flight 129. The aircraft would be over a desolate area of Eastern Kentucky in roughly ten minutes. He had to escalate this to USNorthCom. He was not going to sentence 237 passengers and crew to their death without further orders.

CHAPTER 6

May 8, 2016
3:23 p.m.
F-16 "Fighting Falcons"
180th Fighter Wing
24,000 Feet
Near Lexington, Kentucky

"Roger, Giant Killer, awaiting orders," said Smash Seven, the lead F-16 pilot dispatched to intercept Flight 129. "We will maintain two four thousand at the four o'clock and eight o'clock positions."

"Copy, Smash Seven," said Smash Eleven, maintaining his position above the left rear of the 757 aircraft. "Smash Seven, switch to alternate frequency Charlie. Repeat, switch to alternate frequency Charlie."

"Go ahead, Smash Eleven."

"Are we going to shoot down a commercial airliner?" asked Smash Eleven.

"Certainly not what I had in mind when I woke up this morning," said Smash Seven. "It must be hijacked."

"Look, they're climbing. Return to primary frequency."

"Switching," said Smash Eleven.

"Giant Killer, Smash Seven. Aircraft appears to be in ascent. Repeat, aircraft is ascending. Now climbing to two four thousand," said Smash Seven. "Now, two eight thousand. Please advise."

"Roger that, Smash Seven," said Giant Killer. "Maintain present heading and adjust altitude to three six thousand."

The F-16s rose in altitude to maintain a height advantage over the 757.

"Aircraft has leveled off at three three thousand. Heading has not changed," said Smash Seven. "We have bull's-eye on one-two-nine at three six thousand now. We are a half mile in trail."

CHAPTER 7

May 8, 2016
3:23 p.m.
American Airlines Flight 129
20,000 Feet
Near Lexington, Kentucky

"Those are F-16s," said Bird. "They've remained just behind us since they checked us out a few minutes ago."

Gray was aware the military would not hesitate to shoot them down if the plane was hijacked. Although their altitude had leveled, no one knew whether the plane would fly directly into the Atlantic or nose-dive into Washington. The government would not take that chance. He suddenly felt the urge to call his wife.

"I'm going to call Betty," said Gray.

At a lower altitude, he might reach a cell tower. A second after pressing send on his phone, the plane began to climb. He initiated communications with Louisville Air Traffic Control.

"Louisville, Kentucky Tower. American Airlines Flight one-two-niner. Aircraft has begun uncontrolled ascent," said Gray.

Bird called out the altimeter readings. "Twenty-three thousand. Twenty-six thousand. Thirty thousand."

"American Airlines one-two-niner, roger that," said Louisville Air Traffic Control. "Are you able to gain control of your aircraft?"

"Negative, Louisville," said Gray.

They were running out of time.

"Where are the F-16s, Stacy?"

"I don't have a visual. My guess is they're a thousand feet above and behind us," replied Bird.

"Captain Gray," interrupted the voice of the Air Force colonel, "I'm not going to sugarcoat this. You have about two minutes to gain control of your aircraft before you enter populated areas and D.C. airspace. Homeland Security has established certain protocols in this type of situation."

Gray and Bird exchanged glances. *How could this be happening? I really want to talk to my wife.*

"Colonel, I assure you that we have nothing to do with this," pleaded Gray. "There has to be a solution. This airplane is acting normally, except for the controls. It must be a malfunction. You can't shoot us down!"

"Randy, look!" exclaimed Bird, tapping the monitors for the onboard computer.

Gray immediately grabbed the controls, remembering that the autopilot was activated. He flipped the switch, and the plane responded to his touch of the controls. Flight 129 was his again!

"All stations, this is American Airlines one-two-niner. We have positive control of the flight. I say again, we have positive control of the aircraft!" said Gray.

As he and Captain Bird exchanged relieved looks, the monitor display changed:

Thank you for flying with Zero Day Gamers Airways

THANK YOU FOR READING THIS EXCERPT OF Cyber Attack, book two of The Boston Brahmin Series. You may purchase CYBER ATTACK on Amazon or by visiting www.BobbyAkart.com.

SIGN UP FOR EMAIL UPDATES and receive free advance reading copies, updates on new releases, special offers, and bonus content.

You can contact Bobby directly by email (BobbyAkart@gmail.com) or through his website:

www.BobbyAkart.com

HISTORY OF THE MECHANICS AND THE LOYAL NINE

Those who cannot remember the past are condemned to repeat it.
~ George Santayana, philosopher and novelist

America has a penchant for rebellion. While the dates associated with the War for Independence are well known, the battle for freedom began many years before with the early colonists and continued into the nineteenth century.

Author Bobby Akart explores the trials and tribulations of a fledgling nation with a careful examination of the attitudes of the early colonists and their taste for freedom as they built America.

Seeds of Liberty, an Amazon #1 bestseller in the modern history, sociology, politics and social sciences genres, takes the reader on a historical journey beginning with the settlement of Roanoke Island in 1585 through the British attempts to clamp down on the colonists via the Stamp Act in 1764—the impetus for the creation of *The Loyal Nine.*

Revolutions tend to be brutal affairs, and America's fight for independence was no different.

How did the American Revolution yield a constitutional republic, with greater freedom on a large scale than the world had ever seen? Successful revolutions never begin overnight. The American Revolution was two centuries in the making. Starting with the early attempts at English colonization on Roanoke Island in 1585, and throughout the first settling of the New World, important stones were laid for the foundation of American freedom and independence.

The American colonies had known violent rebellion long before the Revolutionary War. Each of the original thirteen colonies had experienced violent uprisings. Americans had shown themselves more than willing to take up arms to defend a cause held dear. This tradition of rebellion characterized the American spirit throughout its early history.

Seeds of Liberty chronicles certain critical events such as Bacon's Rebellion, Culpepper's Rebellion and King Philip's War. Over these formative years, the seeds of revolutionary thinking took root, and the stage was set for Americans to assert their independence from their British brothers and sisters. Many events transpired between the one-hundred-year period of 1676 and 1776 that served as precursors to the American Revolution. In many ways, the American Revolution had been completed before any of the actual fighting began. The roots had already grown.

The Loyal Nine

Boston, Massachusetts, became the epicenter of the colonist opposition to British rule. In 1765, a group of Bostonians formed a "social club"—attempting to avoid the scrutiny a political organization might provoke. Their purpose, however, was more than social. This group of nine Bostonians, formed and operating in secrecy, plotted a response to the Stamp Act.

They called themselves the Loyal Nine. Although they were respectable merchants and tradesmen, they were not necessarily the most prominent Bostonians. They were private and unassuming, avoided undue publicity, and were diligent in their secretiveness. The names of the Loyal Nine aren't prominent in American history books. But these nine men sowed the seeds of the American Revolution. They were average, hardworking Americans—fighting against tyrannical rule.

Very little is known about the Loyal Nine as they operated in complete secrecy. Since they were a close-knit group made up of nine men, the organization functioned informally and left very little in terms of a paper trail. The membership of the Loyal Nine consisted of club secretary John Avery, a distiller by trade, Henry Bass, a cousin of Samuel Adams, Thomas Chase, a distiller, Stephen Cleverly, a brazier, Thomas Crafts, a painter, Benjamin Edes, printer of the Boston Gazette, Joseph Field, a ship captain, John Smith, a brazier, and George Trott, a jeweler. All nine men would go on to become active members of the Sons of Liberty, and four of the nine men are documented to have participated in the Boston Tea Party.

For ten years following the formation of the Loyal Nine, tensions between the British government and the colonists grew. As pressures built in America, chapters of the Sons of Liberty were formed all over the Thirteen Colonies, especially throughout New England, Virginia, and the Carolinas.

As the independence movement grew, so did the colonists desire to adopt some form of heraldry. Heraldry was used throughout history as a means to express a group's pride and loyalty. In 1767, the Loyal Nine adopted a five red and four white vertical-striped flag as the group's formal standard. It became known as the Rebellious Flag, and the nine stripes paid tribute to the Loyal Nine. With the Rebellious Flag, and the groundswell of support for independence, came the Sons of Liberty.

The Mechanics

In America, the first intelligence network on record was a covert group in Boston known as *The Mechanics.* Beginning with the rise of The Loyal Nine, The Mechanics' activities in the 10 years before the outbreak of the Revolution in April 1775 included some of the earliest uses in America of warning, surveillance, and intelligence collection. Probably the most famous of The Mechanics was Boston silversmith Paul Revere.

The Mechanics grew out of the Sons of Liberty as their insurgent arm. The colonists successfully opposed the burdensome Stamp Act, passed by Britain's Parliament as a revenue generating measure on March 22, 1765. Although the Stamp Act was repealed following Colonial protests in 1766, some of The Mechanics, mainly skilled laborers and artisans, continued to organize resistance to governmental authority and gather intelligence on British activities and movements.

In the words of Paul Revere,

"In the fall of 1774 and winter of 1775, I was one of upwards of thirty,

chiefly mechanics, who formed ourselves into a committee for the purpose of watching British soldiers and gaining every intelligence on the movements of the Tories. We frequently took turns, two and two, to watch the (British) soldiers by patrolling the streets all night."

In addition to their surveillance activities, The Mechanics, who were frequently referred to as the Liberty Boys, sabotaged and stole British military equipment in the Boston area.

They would never have succeeded as seasoned members of modern intelligence networks. They met regularly in the same place—the Green Dragon Tavern on Marshall Street in downtown Boston, and one of their leaders—Dr. Benjamin Church, was an undercover British agent.

Nonetheless, they had resources of their own, and intuitively saw through the cover story the British had devised to mask the march of seven hundred Redcoats on Concord to seize Patriot stores of munitions and arms.

The Midnight Ride of Paul Revere

On April 19, 1775, Dr. Joseph Warren, chairman of the Boston Committee of Safety, charged Revere with the task of warning Patriot leaders Samuel Adams and John Hancock (who was staying at Lexington) that they were also the targets of the British operation.

Revere arranged for warning lanterns to be hung in the Old North Church, to alert Patriot forces across the river at Charleston, as to the means and route of the British advance. One lantern to indicate that British troops were advancing by land, two to indicate that the choice of route was across the Charles River.

After two lanterns were hung in the church steeple, Paul Revere set off on his famous ride. He notified Adams and Hancock, joined Dr. Samuel Prescott and William Dawes, and rode on toward Concord, only to be apprehended by a British patrol en route. Dawes got away, and Dr. Prescott managed to escape soon afterward to alert the Patriots at Concord, 21 miles west of Boston. Revere was questioned and soon released, after which he returned to Lexington to keep Hancock and Adams apprised of the proximity of British forces.

The Shot Heard 'Round the World

Following a skirmish with seventy American minutemen at Lexington, the British column proceeded to Concord, where they burned some gun carriages, entrenching tools, flour, and a liberty pole. The caches of munitions and arms the British expected to find had long since been removed by the alerted Patriots. With the countryside aroused, the British force soon came under sustained attack on its way back to Boston, suffering over seventy dead and nearly two hundred wounded. Four thousand colonists engaged the British at one point on that fateful day at Lexington and Concord, or along the route back to Boston.

One of the minutemen had fired the significant *shot heard 'round the world*, as celebrated decades later in Henry Wadsworth Longfellow's poem. That shot might never have been heard if not for good intelligence work of the Mechanics and the timely warning of Paul Revere and his companions.

The leaders of the revolt, the Sons of Liberty, were faced with a chance to fundamentally change the course of America. They faced a choice—continue to live under tyranny or choose freedom. They chose freedom. By 1775, their opportunity became reality, and the war for independence began. But the seeds of freedom were planted by nine brave Bostonians who had a vision and the courage to stand by their convictions—**the Loyal Nine.**

www.ingramcontent.com/pod-product-compliance
Lightning Source LLC
Chambersburg PA
CBHW020935310726
48980CB00007B/782/J

* 9 7 8 0 5 7 8 4 8 4 3 0 3 *